"Breathless opening chapters . . . Anna's brushes with violent death here extend this series' meditation on the presence of evil in even the most glorious of settings."
—*The Washington Post*

"A riveting series of gut-wrenching events heads the book . . . [Barr's] extraordinary ability to create electrifying drama in the natural world is unequivocal, as is her compelling portrait of Anna—real enough to touch as she struggles to regain her confidence, her enthusiasm, and her sense of self."
—*Booklist*

"Deftly folding in the political subplot . . . Barr manages to weave together musings on life and the afterlife, the hubris of man before nature, current debates on border security in America, and an action-packed plot that all blend quite nicely."
—*The Denver Post*

"Bestseller Barr skillfully blends sticky border issues, marital strife, and politics in her exciting fifteenth novel to feature National Park Service ranger Anna Pigeon."
—*Publishers Weekly*

"Dynamite with Old Testament overtones."
—*The Times-Picayune*

"Riveting . . . What starts out as an enjoyable excursion develops more twists and turns than the Rio Grande and promises to take the reader along for a spine-tingling ride."
—*Southern Living*

"Fierce action . . . Leave it to Anna to tackle both racism and sexism in her usual, indefatigable way."
—*Library Journal*

W9-BUP-386

continued . . .

"The blizzards, the dangerous ice, and the manhunts through the frozen woods are described with crisp, hard-edged beauty. And the wolves, those maligned 'ogres of childhood,' are magnificent." —*The New York Times Book Review*

"Barr's sharp descriptions of the wilderness add a special kick." —*The Seattle Times*

"Barr deftly weaves a grand lattice of suspense as both humans and wolves act out of character . . . riveting . . . The tale is plausible, suspenseful and, in the end, unexpected. The eminently likable Pigeon is a sassy, smart woman who will pilot you through a satisfying adventure."

—*Minneapolis Star Tribune*

"You may want to switch off the air conditioner as you turn the pages of local author Nevada Barr's fourteenth Anna Pigeon adventure. It's that chilling . . . a harsh beauty reveals itself in this action-packed adventure offering chills of every kind." —*The Times-Picayune*

"Barr loves writing about challenges presented by water and weather, and she can make the most benign landscape seem fraught with danger. In *Winter Study*, you can almost feel the deep cold . . . Anna fights her way out of more predicaments in this book than ever before, including a heart-stopping entrapment on dangerous ice and a long sequence involving a snowmobile when, for the first time, I wondered if Anna was going to make it. *Winter Study* is fast-paced, intricately plotted, and filled with foreboding."

—*St. Paul Pioneer Press*

continued . . .

"Barr's intense closed-room drama integrates winter's forces—blizzards and ice—with the psychological play of ghosts and legends . . . tremendously satisfying . . . Barr tackles human depravity head-on while introducing readers to this area's natural beauty."   —*Library Journal*

"Chilling . . . Barr's visceral descriptions of the winter cold nicely complement the paranoia that follows the appearance of the mythic monsters at play."   —*Publishers Weekly*

"The environmental quotient in Barr's novels is always high; the facts about wolves are fascinating, as are descriptions of frigid landscape, alternately beautiful and horrifying. There's plenty of drama, too, as Anna finds herself alone and in danger more than once, but what many readers return to this series for is Anna herself, strong, funny, perceptive, and well aware that she is a small part of a dynamic, ever-changing natural world."   —*Booklist*

"A new Anna Pigeon mystery is a treat for fans of the series who expect the best from Nevada Barr and get it with this strong 'closed door' whodunit in a wintry outdoors setting. As Anna digs into the lives of the scientists and their aides, she uncovers dark secrets and blackmail, hidden agendas and ties to a cold (pun intended) case. Readers will enjoy armchair trekking with Anna as she seeks the truth allegedly of a killer wolf stalking humans."
—*Midwest Book Review*

BORDERLINE

NEVADA BARR

BERKLEY BOOKS, NEW YORK

THE BERKLEY PUBLISHING GROUP
Published by the Penguin Group
Penguin Group (USA) Inc.
375 Hudson Street, New York, New York 10014, USA
Penguin Group (Canada), 90 Eglinton Avenue East, Suite 700, Toronto, Ontario M4P 2Y3, Canada
(a division of Pearson Penguin Canada Inc.)
Penguin Books Ltd., 80 Strand, London WC2R 0RL, England
Penguin Group Ireland, 25 St. Stephen's Green, Dublin 2, Ireland
(a division of Penguin Books Ltd.)
Penguin Group (Australia), 250 Camberwell Road, Camberwell, Victoria 3124, Australia
(a division of Pearson Australia Group Pty. Ltd.)
Penguin Books India Pvt. Ltd., 11 Community Centre, Panchsheel Park, New Delhi—110 017, India
Penguin Group (NZ), 67 Apollo Drive, Rosedale, North Shore 0632, New Zealand
(a division of Pearson New Zealand Ltd.)
Penguin Books (South Africa) (Pty.) Ltd., 24 Sturdee Avenue, Rosebank, Johannesburg 2196,
South Africa

Penguin Books Ltd., Registered Offices: 80 Strand, London WC2R 0RL, England

This is a work of fiction. Names, characters, places, and incidents either are the product of the author's imagination or are used fictitiously, and any resemblance to actual persons, living or dead, business establishments, events, or locales is entirely coincidental. The publisher does not have any control over and does not assume any responsibility for author or third-party websites or their content.

BORDERLINE

A Berkley Book / published by arrangement with the author

PRINTING HISTORY
G. P. Putnam's Sons hardcover edition / April 2009
Berkley premium edition / April 2010

Copyright © 2009 by Nevada Barr.
Interior map by Jackie Aher.

ISBN: 978-0-425-23378-8

BERKLEY®
Berkley Books are published by The Berkley Publishing Group,
a division of Penguin Group (USA) Inc.,
375 Hudson Street, New York, New York 10014.
BERKLEY® is a registered trademark of Penguin Group (USA) Inc.
The "B" design is a trademark of Penguin Group (USA) Inc.

PRINTED IN THE UNITED STATES OF AMERICA

10   9   8   7   6   5   4   3   2   1

For Kendall, who gave us a magical dog

CONFESSION

For purposes of mine own I have done many terrible things. I have moved thousands of tons of rocks from Mexico to America at the rock slide in Santa Elena Canyon. I have rerouted roads and allowed horses to be ridden where they are banned by park regulation. I have changed park protocols and, in some dire cases, rewritten a rule or two. In my defense, I have given the park a shiny new helicopter and updated a few other sundry pieces of machinery. Now that the book is finished, I promise to return Big Bend to the pristine and well-run park that I found it.

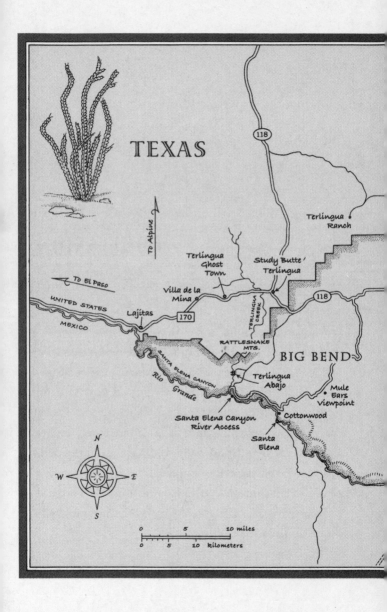

TEXAS

To Alpine

To El Paso

UNITED STATES

MEXICO

Terlingua
Ghost
Town

Study Butte/
Terlingua

Terlingua
Ranch

118

118

Villa de la
Mina

Lajitas

170

TERLINGUA CREEK

RATTLESNAKE
MTS.

BIG BEND

SANTA ELENA CANYON

Rio Grande

Terlingua
Abajo

Mule
Ears
Viewpoint

Santa Elena Canyon
River Access

Cottonwood

Santa
Elena

N

W   E

S

0   5   10 miles

0   5   10 kilometers

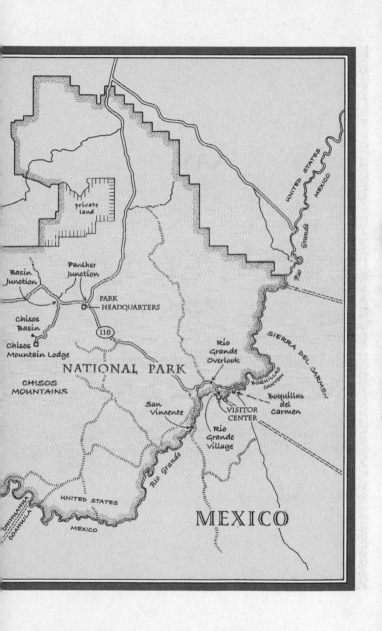

PROLOGUE

Wailing cut through the perfect darkness. Like a machete, it slashed away the tangle of sleeping dreams holding Gabriela hostage, neither unconscious nor conscious. The baby did that to her. Before the baby she'd slept deep and warm and silent, curled next to Marcos. But now there was the baby and Marcos had become a Diablo, a devil, a man who didn't burn up in the fires of hell.

Thin shrieking cut through the walls of her belly and the baby woke kicking, its little heels thumping into the soft flesh beneath her rib cage. "You are a devil like your papa," she murmured, and reached out and turned on the bedside lamp.

"Marcos." Gabriela tugged gently on her husband's earlobe. Asleep he was beautiful, with his round face and straight black eyebrows, his hair falling long on his shoulders like an Apache's. "Wake up," she said. "It's the sirens." She tugged again, harder this time. Marcos caught her hand without waking and kissed her palm. Then his eyes flew open, wide and scared, and he sat bolt upright.

"It's time?" he demanded. "Gabby, I'll—"

Gabriela never found out what he'd do. He was wrapped in the sheet and when he tried to leap out of bed he fell to the floor in a muffle of bedding and curses. She started to laugh but decided against it. The baby liked to sit on her bladder and she had to pee most of the time.

Again the sirens sounded.

Looking sheepish, Marcos got up from the floor. "Oh," he said. "My ride is here."

The sun was going to be up soon and gray light behind the Chisos Mountains made them black like the cutouts children made from construction paper. The street bisecting the village was scuffling with people and horses and dogs and little kids who didn't want to miss the show. Men rode bareback. They had saddles, vaqueros took pride in the tooled leather of their tack, but nobody bothered with saddles now. Diablos also prided themselves on being fast. Men pulled their wives up behind them. Some had sons old enough to be useful and they ran ahead or rode behind.

Gabriela was so fat she could no longer sit behind Marcos. "I got to get a horse with a bigger rump," he joked as he pulled her awkwardly up in front of him.

"Why don't you stay in bed and let one of these worthless boys bring Tildy back?"

"No, I like to see cowboys turn into Devils," Gabriela said. "It's like magic."

Marcos wrapped his arms around her and the baby she carried and drummed his heels on Tildy's sides. Before she got so big they'd race down to the Rio Bravo del Norte, Gabriela holding him tightly around the waist, him bending over the horse's neck. Today they'd be one of the last to arrive at the river and she knew Marcos didn't like that, but he was such a good husband he never said anything or told her she was too big to come.

The Estada de Coahuila in Mexico had let go of their water earlier in the spring. Now, at the bend where the river turned north again, it was shallow enough to walk a horse through without the rider getting his feet wet. Light was leaking around the few clouds on the eastern horizon and the giant reeds on the banks were turning from black to green. The greedy desert gave up little ground to the intrusion of water-hungry plants. Gray stony soil crabbed with the claws of sotol and ocotillo and horse-crippler cactus pushed nearly to the water's edge.

The first of the mounted Diablos rode into the water and a shout went up as the others followed, horses' hooves churning the water, women clutching their men and their skirts to keep them from trailing in the water, children running out to shout across to rangers waiting by a truck with the lights and siren on. Rangers waving and shouting back. On American soil in Big Bend National Park where the Rio del Norte was called the Rio Grande, the vaqueros slid from their horses and caught yellow shirts and helmets from a ranger tossing them from the rear of a truck.

This was Gabriela's favorite part and, though she'd watched it a dozen or more times, she steadied Tildy and stared transfixed as Mexican vaqueros turned into American firefighters, the Diablos, one of the most respected fire crews in the southwest.

"*Adiós*," Marcos called, and waved his yellow helmet in an arc as the truck backed up the slope from the river, the crew in the back.

Tildy twitched her ears and neighed softly but she was as steady as a rock. She acted as if she knew Gabriela was carrying a child and didn't sport around the way she did when it was just Marcos on her back. "*Adiós, mi querido*," Gabriela whispered, and waved until the truck was over the low hill between the road and the river.

The women and boys were riding the horses back across the river to Boquillas to open up their shops. Business was good. Not as good as two weeks before when American colleges were on spring break and kids came to Big Bend to raft the river. Big Bend was proud of the villages that shared the river. Together they showed how countries should live as friends. The rangers came across to visit and to eat in Mexico, visitors were sent to share a Mexican beer. Boys made money ferrying them across in little skiffs for a dollar or two, and the littler kids laughed and joked as they helped them to get astride the tough little burros, and then, for a quarter, they led the burros into the village where the women had crafts and food for sale. Older boys and men lucky enough to own pickup trucks would take the more adventurous tourists into the wild Coahuila Mountains to camp or hike or just breathe the cleanest air in the world.

THREE DAYS LATER, at two-fifteen in the morning, Gabriela's contractions came. Her little sister, Lucia, had been assigned to look after her while Marcos was working fire crew. Lucia, just turned seven and so serious and responsible Gabriela wondered where she had come from, ran to tell their mother.

Alicia and Gabriela's mother-in-law, Guadalupe, packed her into a borrowed donkey cart for the short trip to the river. Boquillas had no doctor, no hospital and no medicines. That was reason enough to have her baby in America but Guadalupe had delivered more babies than a lot of doctors and bragged that she never lost one. Guadalupe had refused to deliver her first grandchild. She scolded Gabriela for asking and told her the best gift a mother could give her child was to be born in the United States, over the river. The baby would then be a citizen of both the U.S. and Mexico and would have work and an education if he wanted it. Guadalupe had no doubt that her first grandchild would be a he.

"I can walk," Gabriela protested until it was clear

they were set on giving her the ride in the cart they had gone to so much trouble to get for her. Guadalupe led the donkey and Gabriela's mother walked beside the cart to hold Gabriela's hand. The jolting down the dirt track made Gabriela groan.

"Shhh," Alicia hissed, then leaned in toward her daughter, the silver in her hair catching the faint light of the moon and running like lightning through the long black hair. "Not much longer," she whispered. "Let the mother-in-law be right. One day you might want money for a house."

Gabriela and her mother laughed and Gabby did her best to stifle any more ungrateful sounds.

The river was up half a foot from rains in the mountains. It wasn't more than thigh-deep, but too deep for the donkey and cart. "You're going to have an early baptism for that baby," Guadalupe joked as she and Alicia helped Gabby to climb out.

"This is my best dress," Gabby complained. "My best fat dress. I guess tomorrow I won't have to wear it anymore."

"No new dresses for you," Alicia said. "Once you have children you get no more treats. They all go to the kid. You'll have to take that dress in and wear it till the baby is in high school." Guadalupe laughed. Gabriela wished Marcos was there. He could drink beer and wait and make up lies with his buddies and, when the baby was born, he could come to the river and carry her and the baby home on Tildy's back.

"God I hate this mud," Gabriela said as her shoe sank

into the cool slime then came free with a sucking sound and a slurp that nearly pulled her sneaker off her foot.

"Don't blaspheme," her mother said automatically. "We've got you. We'll go slow."

"Pick up my skirt," Gabby begged. "I don't want to go knocking on doors looking like my water just broke. Lift it out of the water."

"It's too deep," her mother said flatly. "Your underpants will show."

"I'm not wearing any underpants," Gabby said, and felt a small stab of satisfaction as Alicia began muttering her rosary under her breath.

"You better not let Marcos hear you saying things like that," Guadalupe warned her. "He has a temper like his dad."

Gabriela was glad it was dark so her mother-in-law wouldn't see the smile that came to her lips when she thought of what Marcos would do if she told him she didn't have any panties on.

With her mother holding her right arm and her mother-in-law her left, the three of them waded into the river. The night was kind, seventy degrees with a whisper of a breeze coming down from the Chisos, smelling of pine and heat and dust laid by the rain. The water was cool and felt good on Gabby's legs and groin. The baby in her belly seemed to float on the water, taking the weight off the small of her back for a change.

"Women should give birth in the river," Gabby said. "Women should be pregnant in the river. You can pee anytime you want."

"Don't you dare pee," Alicia said. "I'm down-stream."

"You are going to have that baby in the water if you two don't stop making jokes and move faster."

"Remember your house," Alicia murmured in Gabriela's ear and Gabby laughed loudly.

"Now you did make me pee, Mama."

Before Alicia could make a retort a braying came out of the darkness on the American side of the Rio Grande. A man with a machine amplifying his voice was shouting at them in Spanish:

"Se ha carredo la frontera. The border is closed. Go back. This border is closed by order of the United States government."

"No it isn't," Alicia yelled back.. "Not between the park and Boquillas." There was no answering bray, and Gabby's mother urged her forward. "Some fool ranger not old enough to go to the bathroom by himself gets those talking horns and thinks he's John Wayne at the Alamo," Alicia grumbled.

The Alamo was Alicia's favorite movie. Gabby had had to watch it at least three times. The only thing that kept it from boring her completely out of her mind was that her mother always rooted for John Wayne and saw nothing funny in that at all. "It's only a movie," she'd tell Gabby and her brother. "Nobody's real. I can like who I like."

They'd reached midstream when the voice came again and, with it, painfully bright lights. "The border is closed," the man announced again. "Go back."

"My daughter is having a baby. She's having a baby right now!" Alicia shouted.

The disembodied voice came back over the water. "Crossings are permitted only at authorized border stations. Go back. You cannot enter the United States except at authorized border stations."

The women stopped, dark water curling around their hips, skirts dragging at their legs. "This man is crazy," Guadalupe said, and shaded her eyes against the lights trying to see what sort of man waited on the riverbank to accost pregnant women and their mothers.

"Maybe we should go back," Gabby said. The water, so cool and life-affirming at first, was beginning to chill her. The blackness of it, and the scraps of litter the rising levels had washed from the shores upriver flashing through the beam of the man's light seemed sinister, dirty somehow. She didn't like it between her legs. She didn't want it to touch her baby.

Guadalupe surged forward, Gabby's arm held tightly in her fist. Gabriela tried to turn back and her belly pushed into Alicia. Alicia lost her footing and fell, dragging Gabby down with her.

Gabriela's arm tore free of her mother-in-law's grip and her sneakered feet slipped from the rocky bottom. Her belly was taken up by the current, rolling her onto her back, helpless as a beetle tortured by wicked boys. River water washed over her face and she fought to right herself. She wasn't scared. She grew up on the river. Like most of the village children, she had been in and out of it all of her life. Right up to the mouth of Boquillas Canyon the water was smooth.

From the dark she could hear shouting: her mother and Guadalupe, a man's voice, without the megaphone now, shouting in English and unintelligible Spanish, the phrases "the border is closed" and "go back" probably the only Spanish he had fully mastered.

Gabby floundered until her stomach was under her and her feet were scrabbling to find purchase on the slippery rock of the riverbed when a partially submerged log struck her in the side. She cried out, not because of the pain, but in fear for the life of the child she carried. The log knocked her off her tenuous footing and its branches snatched up her skirts and swung her around, smashing the weight of the sodden wood into her skull.

There was no sense of doom. Only doom itself.

It was May 2002. Eight months after the terrorist attacks. By order of Homeland Security, the border between Big Bend and the villages that had shared the life of the park had been closed.

ONE

"So, how do you feel?"

Anna stared at the doctor. He wasn't a real doctor; he was a psychologist with a Ph.D. out of Boulder, Colorado, who liked very much to be called *Doctor* James. Vincent James was not so-affectionately called Vinny-the-shrink by the rangers at Rocky Mountain National Park. Whenever the brass decided rangers needed to be counseled they were sent down the hill to his shiny little office on the mall. Vinny had decorated his lair in Early Intimidation. The walls were slate gray, the furniture black leather and chrome. An arrangement of dried and very dead grasses in russet and umber was his nod to the real world, the non-Vinny world.

"I feel good," Anna said, attempting to look comfortable in a sling of shiny patent leather. She drummed her fingertips on the silvery armrests, hoping they'd leave prints. She didn't doubt that he leapt up to polish them clean before the door closed on departing clients' butts. Or maybe he carefully lifted the prints with tape and kept them on file.

Vinny smiled slightly and waited. Anna smiled back and waited. Anna liked to wait. If one waited long enough and quietly enough, all manner of woodland creatures might creep out of the underbrush. In Dr. James's case, perhaps they crept out from under rocks.

The psychologist sighed audibly and smiled a bigger smile this time, the one mothers reserve for tiresome children who insist on playing games with their betters.

"How do you feel about the incident at Isle Royale?" he asked.

Feeling like the tiresome child, Anna purposely misunderstood him. "Not bad. The ankle twinges when I step on it wrong and is stiff in the mornings. My shoulder is as good as new, though. Got to find the silver lining."

He sighed again, less ostentatiously this time but still audibly. A shrink should know better than to exhibit obvious manipulation.

"That's a bad habit," Anna said. "That sighing thing."

Anger was pressing up under her sternum, a boil of heat she'd carried since returning from Windigo Harbor on Isle Royale in Lake Superior that February. The balance had gone out of her life, the yin and yang of good and evil, light and dark, peace and pain. What she needed was clean air and warmth and Paul, quiet so deep birdsong could only enhance it, miles free of the millings and mewlings of humanity. She didn't need a shrink with a sighing problem and ergonomically hostile furniture.

"You seem to be carrying a lot of anger," Vinny said in a rare moment of insight.

"Bingo," she said.

Again he waited.

She didn't elaborate.

Vinny might have been an idiot, but he wasn't stupid. He didn't play the waiting game long this time. "You killed a man," he said. "Up close and personal; killed him with your bare hands."

"No," Anna said. "I wore gloves."

The psychologist's chest swelled with another sigh but he caught himself and let it out soundlessly through his nose. Leaning back in his chair, a comfortable chair, Anna noted, he took off his wire-rimmed glasses and pinched the bridge of his nose. He must have seen the gesture in old movies back when psychiatry was new and the public believed in hypnotism and Freud and the dangers of early potty training.

The boil of heat beneath her breastbone was growing. If it burst—if she let it burst—she would spill her guts to this man and she didn't want to go down that road with anyone but Paul. Since Isle Royale she found herself unable to trust anyone but Paul, and that included herself. Most of all herself. Anna wasn't sure if she was a good person. Worse, she wasn't sure if she cared.

"I'll talk about it with my priest," she said.

Dr. James rocked forward in his lovely padded office chair and shifted the papers on his desk. He used the tip of his forefinger, as if merely touching the written dirt of others' lives could soil his soul. "Your husband," he said. "Paul Davidson, the sheriff of Jefferson County, *Mississippi*." The way he said Mississippi annoyed her. He said it like it didn't count, like being a sheriff there was tantamount to being a racist or a campus kiddy cop. "He's also an Episcopal priest?"

"The gun and The Word," Anna said.

The psychologist didn't smile.

"I see you didn't change your name when you got married. You kept Pigeon. Why is that?"

Anna took a deep breath, trying to ease the pressure in her chest. She felt like Mount St. Helens the day before. Steam pouring from her vents, molten lava pressing against a dome of rock, fires so deep and burning so hot nothing could contain them. She had a sudden mental image of her small middle-aged self on a city street, women and children fleeing in every direction, men yelling, "Look out, she's going to blow!" The picture startled her and she laughed.

"You find the question funny?" Vincent James asked.

"I find the question irrelevant and intrusive," she said. It was happening. The crown of rock that was her sternum was bowing under the push of the fire and she couldn't stop it. "I find the question none of your damn business. Yes, I killed a man. With my gloves on because it was so cold your fingers would freeze off without them but, yes, up close and personal. You want to know what that was like? What kind of person could kill like that? Me. That's what kind. The son of a bitch deserved to die. The world is better off without guys like that. There are a whole hell of a lot of people in this world who should be ushered into the next, if there is a next, which I sincerely doubt. If I had it to do over again I would have killed him in his sleep the first night on the island."

Blowing off steam wasn't helping. If she didn't shut up she was going to cry. The inherent knowledge that Vinny would take her tears as a personal victory was the only thing that kept them at bay. They dried in the heat of her anger but there were plenty more where those had come from and Anna had to clamp her mind shut to keep them from pouring out, to keep her face from melting in a flood of saltwater and snot.

Vinny put his elbows on the papers he'd fingered and steepled his hands. He'd never bothered to replace his glasses and Anna wondered if they were merely a prop, the lenses plain glass, or if he decided she was too hard to look at when her edges were clear.

"Would you?" he asked.

She had no idea what he was talking about. The repression of the volcano was making it hard to concentrate on anything else.

"Would you have killed him in his sleep? Killed him in cold blood?"

Anna didn't want to think about that. She didn't want to think about anything but she couldn't stop her mind from pawing through the images of her weeks on Isle Royale. Nights she'd wake up so cold she couldn't clamp her teeth against their chattering, her heart pounding. Days she walked in a fog, blind to the beauty of the Rockies and the needs of the visitors and fellow rangers. April didn't bring an end to winter at that elevation. Snow capped the mountains and the glaciers. Wind blew ragged and vicious down the canyons. She could not get warm and she couldn't think clearly and the man she'd killed stalked her.

"I'm not sorry it happened, if that's what you're getting at," she snapped. The use of *it* and *happened* shuddered with weakness. Anna was tired of the hard words so she made herself say them: "I'm not sorry I killed him. I'm sorry I *had* to kill him."

"Earlier you said"—Vincent poked at his papers again as if every word she'd spoken had been magically and instantaneously written into the report on his desk—"that there were a lot of people who needed to be 'ushered into the next world.' Do you feel you have to kill the bad guys, that you have a calling to do this so-called ushering?"

Anna could tell Vinny-the-shrink thought he was on to something big, that he'd found the key to what ailed her. Anna didn't feel she had a calling to kill or to do anything else. Once she'd thought she had a calling to protect the wild places, but she wasn't even feeling that anymore. What she felt mostly was an inner darkness lit by strange fires from below and haunted by scraps of thoughts and fragments of conversations. The only time she felt good or safe or halfway normal was when she curled under the blankets and buried her face in a purring cat. The purring and the silky warmth of the fur tethered her to the land of the living.

She didn't know what ailed her, and she doubted Vinny knew.

"No," she said firmly. "No calling to kill." To have said anything else would have brought the men in the white coats bearing straitjackets. If they still used straitjackets on crazy people. "Sufficient stopping force if the assailant is a danger to law enforcement or others." She paraphrased one of the rules from the levels of force continuum drummed into the heads of the students at the Federal Law Enforcement Training Center in Georgia, where she and countless others had received their education.

"Stopping force, is that how you think of what you did? That you 'stopped' him?"

Vincent's voice didn't sound combative. If anything, it might have gentled somewhat since she'd first arrived. Anna wished she could read his face but to do that she'd have to see it, and her vision was growing odd. Unshed tears made it hard to focus her eyes; unshed thoughts made it hard to focus her mind.

"Yes." She found the word somewhere in her vocabulary and offered it up on her tongue. It tasted alien and sounded far away. "Killing will do that to some people. For guys like him, killing is all that would do it. I stopped him: stopped him from preying on women, stopped him from killing me, stopped him from taking up space and breathing good air." The anger eating her from the inside out seared the words and she knew she sounded even more heartless than she was.

"This wasn't the first person you've . . . stopped . . . in your career as a law enforcement ranger, is it?"

"Yes. No. I don't know." In that moment Anna couldn't remember if she had ever killed anyone else or not. She remembered parks and jobs and broken bones and wounds slashed into her body with fish gaffs and pine branches. She remembered animals slain and people bloody and covered in flies. She remembered hurting and hurting others. But, as she stared into the face of Vinny-the-shrink, she couldn't remember whether or not she had taken the life of another human being.

Shaking her head, she struggled up from the hammock of leather, pushing against the cold chrome of the chair's arms. "You'd think a girl would remember something like that, wouldn't you?" she said, and laughed. "It's not like I have to count the notches on my gun to know how many. You can't notch a Sig-Sauer— they're all metal." She turned as if to leave, and fixated on the desiccated grasses in their square silver vase. "I suppose you could mark the kills with scratches," she said absently. The grasses were supposed to be beautiful, the pale rust-colored stalks and the tawny feathered tops. "Dead," Anna said. "The grass is dead. Can't anything live in this room? The chairs made of the hides of dead cows, the walls of dead trees." She turned back to the psychologist. He was standing now, as well, his glasses back on his nose. "What's the desk made of?

Plastic? Dead dinosaurs? I can't remember if I killed anyone else."

Her eyes gushed with tears, her nostrils poured mucus; Anna could feel the sides of her mouth pulling down in the wild howl of a child. She was imploding, exploding, her body and mind were turning their blackened insides out and she felt dams breaking and bones melting, steel bands tightening, bowing her spine, puppet strings of piano wire forcing her hands to flap feebly.

"I want to go home," she screamed at the shrink.

Dr. James was around the desk, a hand outstretched toward her. On his face was a look of deep and genuine concern. In his eyes she could read pain for her suffering. She had misjudged him, been unfair, unfeeling and cruel. The knowledge should have made her kinder, but rage would not let it. More than anything she wanted a fight, a hard fight with knuckle bones and edged weapons, an excuse to strike out, to let the pressure smash into a deserving target. James was closing in on her, both hands out now as if he was going to fold her into an embrace.

Time chose this moment to do its petty pace thing and all but stopped. In the grip of this psychic stasis the tears in her eyes acted as lenses that didn't distort but magnified. She could see the wear under Dr. James's eyes, the fine lines growing into folds from too much worry and too little sleep. Patches of stubble smudged beneath his right ear and along the jawline because he had shaved in a hurry or been distracted by thoughts of other than his own vanity. The fingernails on the outstretched hands were clean but short and the hands themselves calloused from hard labor.

Dr. Vincent James was a human being. Barricaded behind her brittle carapace of anger, Anna had neglected to note that.

The need to strike out, the fury of the volcano, the wild lash of rage stopped flowing outward and, with a suddenness that brought her to her knees, turned on her. The burning place beneath her sternum was extinguished by the blast and, where the fire had been, only a great empty hole remained.

Anna felt herself tumbling into it.

TWO

Darden White caught himself doing it again. His hands were folded loosely in front of his crotch. Years in the Secret Service had ingrained the classic pose into his bones. Left to its own devices his skeleton settled into watchful cop stance. The Secret Service was misnamed, he thought. They wanted to be seen and identified to let those with sinister intent know the subject was being protected by the best. A visual presence didn't deter serious criminals, but it helped keep amateurs with big dreams at bay.

Darden no longer needed to be that obvious. Not to mention the addition of his gut didn't lend itself to the pose with any grace or dignity. Since he'd retired he'd put on a pound a year, give or take. Wanting a hobby— and trying to get his mom to eat something other than

Pepperidge Farm white chocolate chunk cookies and peanuts—he'd taken up cooking and gotten too good at it.

Darden sniffed. At sixty-three, a man should be able to have a gut if he wanted. Along with graying hair worn just long enough to make it look like he needed to see a barber, the extra pounds lent him an avuncular look that he found useful.

As a bonus, his doctor told him the added weight, carried out front under his heart, could take years off his life. Darden's mother had changed the way he looked at death and longevity. At eighty-five, as fit and strong as ever, she only had enough mind left to know she hated being locked up.

Poor old bird, he thought, as he did whenever his mother came to mind.

Darden had lived most of his life ready to take a bullet for somebody else—often somebody he didn't much like—and death didn't frighten him overmuch. Alzheimer's did. Idly he considered taking up smoking again to help the gut along, but decided that would be overkill.

Letting his hands fall to his sides, he continued watching the waiters setting up the Chisos Mountain Lodge's dining room for the event. The view couldn't be beat. The lodge was nestled in a ring of ragged peaks. On the southwest side of the tiny valley where the lodge's rooms and cabins were built a mountain was missing, like a tooth pulled from a line of molars. Through the gap one could see the desert below roll out into a misty distance stopped by the mountains of northern Mexico.

When it came to security, the lodge wasn't what Darden would have chosen. Judith had her own reasons, and they were politically savvy, but she left herself open too often. Politicians he'd guarded fell into two categories. Either they were so paranoid there was an assassin slavering after their worthless little lives that he had to check every space big enough to hide a cat before they'd enter a building, or they were like Judith, believing themselves immortal and beloved. Most were like Judith. The good ones anyway.

An elderly couple came and stood at the entrance looking confused as the dining room they'd been using was being rearranged. A young whip of a man, working summers in the parks while going to college, Darden knew—he'd interviewed all the employees working the cocktail party—stopped them from entering. Darden watched the kid's face move plastically through the permutations of a young man who had grown good at telling people they can't have what they want without endangering his tip.

The couple, in their seventies or maybe early eighties, was holding hands. They leaned in toward each other as if they'd grown together until their limbs became indistinguishable, one from the other, like two ancient trees. Darden smiled at them and nodded at the waiter. Judith could afford to feed a few strangers. Fundraising came naturally to her. Looking relieved, the young man led the couple to a table by the window.

Darden had never married. His job didn't lend itself to family life. Sometimes he wished he was gay. Another man would be a better fit for the home life of an agent: sex and companionship, somebody to grow old with and no worries about who'd call the plumber or shovel the walks or scare away the burglars when you were away on assignment.

In the service gay would not have been a plus. A lot of the guys he worked with were flat-out homophobic. It was a moot point. Darden was not gay. Whoever said it was a choice had never considered making it. Men were born wired for a socket or a plug. At least that was how it was for Darden.

Judith Pierson walked in. She was small, five-foot-five, with a boyish figure. In baggy khakis and Converse high-tops she should have looked about as imposing as any mall rat, but the straightness of her spine and the military bearing of her shoulders made her seem bigger, a person to be reckoned with.

Another woman would have been sequestered in her room worrying about her makeup or her dress. Maybe Judith worried and maybe she didn't, but she wasn't one to trust the details to other people. It was why she was going to make it. She was going to be Texas's next Ann Richards, but without the liberal trappings.

"Hey, Darden. Everything okay for the meet-and-greet?"

"I don't think we're going to have any trouble. Big Bend is too far from anywhere for the uglies to bother making the trip. I'm just making sure the tees are dotted and the eyes are crossed." He winked at her.

The hard facial lines of the polished politician softened and he glimpsed his little girl. Judith was forty-three. Darden had known her forty of those years. When she was little her mom used to drop her off at his mother's house to be looked after while she was working, and she was always working. It was from her mom Judith inherited her ambition. Darden was living at home then, going to night school, and he babysat her as much as his mom did. Half the time he'd wake up around ten and there'd be Judith, lying on her stomach, her bare feet in the air, legs crossed at the ankles, pointed chin in her hands, watching him as if his snoring and drooling was more entertaining than anything she could have seen on the television.

She looked around at the preparations like a general assessing his troops and nodded slightly. Darden had learned to watch for the small movement, her delicate chin jerking down infinitesimally. It meant all was as she would have it. When he didn't see that chin go down he knew the fur was about to fly and he'd have to spend a good half hour smoothing somebody's feathers to get them to go back to doing their job.

"Thanks, Darden. Keep your boys to the shadows. This is just an informal party so the good people of Texas can see what a down-to-earth, caring, witty woman I am. Tonight I'm winning hearts. Day after tomorrow we go for the jugular."

"Kev and Gordon will be as ghosts," he said.

"Right," Judith said, and laughed. "You'd have better luck making ghosts of a couple Brahman bulls."

"Don't worry. I'll keep them in the paddock."

"You don't need me," she said. "I guess I'd better go start making myself look gubernatorial."

"And lovable."

"Goes without saying." She gave him a mock salute and walked away, her back straight, her head balanced high on her neck. After a few steps she stopped and turned back. He was shifting his weight from one foot to the other. He'd never had terrific feet and the job demanded so much standing around it never mattered how much money he spent on shoes or fancy insoles, because they still hurt most of the time.

"You can sit down, you know," she said with a wry smile.

"I'll stand."

Laughing, she shook her head. "Of course you will. Suit yourself."

Head of security for the mayor of Houston, Texas, wasn't the same as running alongside limousines in parades. There was no code insisting management couldn't sit. The one time he'd been tempted he'd not even gotten his tush on the seat before he felt like a damn fool and a goldbrick and stood up again.

Security stood and they watched and if their feet hurt that was just too damn bad.

Later in the week Judith was going to announce her candidacy for governor of Texas. She'd chosen to do it at Big Bend National Park. It was a good time to put on the cloak of environmental concern, and the sobriquet "friend of the parks" impressed conservationists. Judith was already known in Houston for her work with environmental concerns, but Big Bend would give her visibility in West Texas.

But it was border control that was going to launch her into the big time. Chisos Lodge housed a lot of seminars every year. Because of the park's renown—and because it was a vacation destination—they were well attended. The seminar Judith was using as her springboard was on the environmental and social effects of the Mexican drug wars on people living in communities along the border. Drug wars scared the good citizens. Ditto immigrants. America no longer wanted anybody to give her their tired, their poor, and their huddled masses made people's blood run cold.

Judith planned not only to announce her candidacy at a dinner in a couple days but to start her campaign. She was gutsy; the audience wasn't handpicked to cheer the way it was usually done at these things. Every heavyweight with a bone to pick or a cross to burn was at the convention. Belief systems ran from open arms to our Mexican brothers and sisters and amnesty for all to building a great wall with sentry towers and drones flying the canyons to keep out the southern hordes and their drug overlords.

Judith decided to open her campaign with fireworks instead of bunting. Reporters from Houston and Dallas, Fort Worth, Alpine, Beaumont, El Paso, Midland, Austin and San Antonio had made the trek across the desert to capture the event. Judith was sure enough of herself that she invited them personally. It was risky, but if she pulled it off, the big boys would have to take a long hard look at her when it came to national party politics.

Darden glanced out the window to the patio where the gentlemen of the press milled around smoking cigarettes. Smoking cigarettes and salivating, he thought uncharitably. There were two women in the bunch: a skinny bleach-blonde from Austin, and Gerry Schneider. Gerry was an old warhorse in her late fifties. She'd covered the last year of the Vietnam War from Saigon, one of the few women they let get close to the front lines. He'd met her in D.C. when Hinckley had taken a potshot at Ronald Reagan. Darden liked Gerry. She was tough. With a woman like her a man wouldn't have to check every darn thing that went bump in the night. From what Darden had heard, a while back, she'd gotten out of the fast track and moved back to Houston to get a job at the *Herald*.

Gordon and Kevin arrived looking as stiff and out of place in their suits as Darden did. Parks were rumpled, quick-dry, bandanna sorts of places. Darden's agents had made a case for going native, but Darden hadn't bought it. A man in a suit was like a cop on a horse; he got respect whether he deserved it or not.

Force of habit made him look at his watch, but they were on time. He'd had a lot of good men working for him during the years he'd been on Judith's staff. Maybe because the marshal service inducted a bunch to put on airlines and the job was so boring they quit as fast as they could hire new ones. A lot of men and women trained to handle weapons were wandering around with shiny new guns and nobody to shoot.

Gordon was good but Darden had hired him because he looked like an agent: big with a square head, square shoulders and short neck. Judith looked great with Gordon hulking behind her, the brawn behind the brains. Kevin was a different kind of hire altogether and one Darden had never been comfortable with, though he'd worked with good men acquired this way. Kevin had been the client's choice—Judith knew the guy from somewhere and she'd wanted him on the team. He was twenty-seven and looked like a younger, beefier, studlier, more dangerous version of Judith's husband. That might have been why she'd wanted him. The two could be thick as thieves when the spirit moved them.

Darden wouldn't have been surprised if Judith was having an affair with the kid. If she was, it was discreet. He'd never seen anything to suggest it. It wouldn't have mattered to him one way or another. Power did that to some people. Or maybe it was the other way around. Maybe power didn't give them greater appetites for sex, maybe greater appetites in general gave them a hunger for power. Kevin wasn't going to be around long enough for anything to get out of hand. He hungered for the big show, the cloak-and-dagger, like agents had in the movies. Darden had news for him: agents only had what they had in the movies in the movies.

He'd chosen both Gordon and Kevin for this detail

because they did what they were told without questions. "Get something to eat," he told them. "That or wait till the festivities are over. I'm going to clean up a little. I'll be back here at nineteen-forty-five. Either of you seen Charles?"

"No, sir," Gordon said.

"I haven't seen him," said Kevin, his eyes following a waitress. Annoyance tweaked Darden till he realized Kevin wasn't gazing lasciviously at her bottom but at the pot of freshly brewed coffee she was carrying.

"Call me when he shows," Darden said. Then: "Dog-gone it. The nearest cell tower is behind a pile of rock and lizards two hundred miles from here. Remind me to get satellite phones in the budget when we get back to civilization." Rustic charm and, probably, profit margins dictated that the rooms in the Chisos Lodge have no phones, televisions or radios. "Gordon, you come and get me. Got it?"

"Yes, sir."

Charles Pierson was Judith's second husband. Darden had never liked the guy, not even when he was doing a better job of pretending he loved his wife. Judith's first husband had been better but she'd dumped him when Charles came along with his literary allusions and su-perb table manners. Darden saw it as a kind of Scarlett/Ashley thing. Charles had the gentleness and charm Judith thought she wanted, and she had the strength Charles thought he needed.

After thirteen years of marriage, Judith was still be-sotted. Charles had grown tired of being Mr. Judith and of the expense of endless campaigning. Darden couldn't blame him, but there was no way Judith could let him have a divorce. One divorce on a candidate's record was pretty standard these days, but two? Maybe Giuliani could pull it off but he was male and Italian and not running in Texas.

Charles had given up on Judith but he hadn't given up on women in general. Darden had had to pay off one and scare off one. An errant husband was another thing a female candidate couldn't afford. It made her appear weak and pathetic to the voting public. Ten years after President Clinton got caught with a female aide and his trousers down around his knees, people still talked about what Hillary should have done. What they had forgiven the president for doing, and thus ending his career, they couldn't forgive his wife for overlooking in the interests of pursuing her own.

It would be easier for Judith. She'd not yet said anything about the White House but Darden had known her a long time. Even when she was a tiny little thing she never wanted to play at being princess. She always played at being queen.

Darden had come down the steps from the patio where the reporters congregated to the small sitting area near the parking lot without seeing anything. Lost in his thoughts. For a man who'd spent his life watching for trouble, this was alarming. This evening, this minute, there was nothing more threatening than three of Big Bend's midget deer. They were hardly bigger than Great Danes. Cute, Darden thought. Maybe he should

get a dog. Maybe he should retire before he got somebody killed. Old men given to wool-gathering weren't
exactly prime bodyguards. Management didn't have to
see the sniper in the trees, he reminded himself. Or the
elephant in the room, for that matter.

He smiled drily at that thought but wasn't much comforted. His SUV was in the first space. When he pointed
and clicked at it there was the dull thud of the locks
opening but the vehicle didn't bleep and its lights didn't
flash. One of the first things he did to a new vehicle was
the removal of audio and visual signals. In the old days,
unscrewing the bulb in the overhead did the trick. With
new computer-run models, getting the things to lay still
and pipe down was a major undertaking.

The evening was perfect: cool and dry and scented
with pine. The sun had gone behind the mountains but
the window to the desert below was tawny gold with
the last rays of light. He rolled down the windows and
enjoyed the short drive to the historic stone cabins built
by the Civilian Conservation Corps during the Depression. Where he was staying wasn't a single cabin but
three rooms, each opening onto a shared veranda with
a view of the valley. His room was on the north end.
Gordon and Kevin shared the southernmost room.
Judith was in the center. As he walked past her window
there was a crack of wood hitting wood, then her screen
door flew open with such suddenness and force it nearly
took his nose off. The gut saved him yet again; protruding farther than his proboscis, its hard fat took the
blow.

Even with the added weight, Darden was quick on his feet; he leapt back to where stone was between him and the inside of the room and snatched his Glock from the holster beneath his left arm. Another reason to wear a suit.

White-faced and ragged-looking, Judith pulsed from the darkened doorway.

"Get in here," she hissed. "I want to kill Charles."

Well, well, Darden thought. Things are looking up.

THREE

A leave of absence, "medical leave," the park was calling it. Anna wasn't sure what she called it. Maybe
the end of her career. More than not knowing what to
call it, she didn't know how she felt about it. Ambivalent was a good word.

"I'm ambivalent," she said to Paul.

Paul Davidson was her husband of less than a year
and most of that spent apart. "Ambivalent is a good
word," he said, echoing her thought. For a moment
Anna just looked at him. He was the most beautiful man
she had ever seen. White hair fell thick and straight
across his broad forehead. There had been more
blond in it when she first met him. Perhaps being married to her aged a man quickly. The white suited him
and the hard bright sun of a Texas spring burnished it

to a fine gloss. Paul was fifty-seven, eight years older than she. He wasn't much taller, five-feet-eight in his socks, precisely the right height to hold and be held, to kiss and be kissed.

"Are you ready to do this? It's all adventure and parky," he said softly. The rest of the rafting group was in the middle of preparations peppered with laughter and chat as they loaded the raft with gear. "We could still do something else. Go to Italy. Hike the Great Pyrenees. Spend a week getting wrapped in seaweed and glopped in mud at a fancy spa."

"It's warm here and I'm not the boss," Anna said.

Paul kissed her gently. He was the best kisser of any man she had ever met. Most men thought they were good kissers, just like they all thought they were good drivers. Most were wrong on both counts.

"Stop kissing! You're setting a bad example for the children!" a girl shouted at them.

Though Anna could have finessed a trip down the river with other rangers, she and Paul had chosen to go with a commercial outfit out of Terlingua. Anna had wanted nothing to do with the green and gray, and it was one of those rare occasions she didn't want to be alone in the wilderness: she needed the distraction other people provided. This group of college kids—three girls and one boy, a boyfriend of somebody, Anna assumed—promised to be more distracting than bucolic. The girl who had shouted at them was a lanky nineteen-year-old who was so thin her bones were held together only by the spandex she wore. Her dark hair was slicked back into a ponytail that stuck through the back of her ball cap. Cyril something. Anna liked her. She had a wide smile full of big teeth, and eyes so black the pupils were nearly lost, giving her the perpetual look of a night-seeing cat.

Paul released Anna but held her hand as they walked over the stones to the raft. This trip was a luxury outing. Camp chairs and sleeping pads, coolers full of food and beer, folding tables, a portable fire pit made from the bottom of a metal barrel, a grill for cooking steaks, pots, pans and tents had been stowed in the raft's midsection. Life jackets had been provided but no one bothered to put them on. Not yet. The guide, Carmen, a small woman of muscle and attitude, told them they'd need them later but here, where the water was flat and amiable, they could use them as seat cushions.

Carmen directing, the seven of them pushed the raft into the water of the Rio Grande River. They were putting in at Lajitas on the western border of the park and would float downriver through Santa Elena Canyon. In all her years in the Park Service, including time in northern Texas at Guadalupe Mountains National Park, Anna had never visited Big Bend. She had always meant to.

"What's with all the black SUVs?" one of the three girls asked. Her name was Lori, Anna recalled. She was quietest of the group and looked to be the strongest, which wasn't saying a great deal. These were urban children, raised on electronics and junk food. Their minds were sharp but their bodies could have used a lot more dodgeball and tree-climbing in their early years.

"Mayor of Houston is in the park. She's going to announce a run for governor."

"You'd think they'd show up in Priuses or Smart Cars or something," Cyril said. "Bc all green in a park."

"Texas does oil," Carmen said succinctly. The raft was in knee-deep water and was twitching as if anxious to go with the flow.

"You hop in," Paul said, and waited to see that Anna slithered over the side without incident before he climbed aboard himself. Anna had never needed anyone to take care of her, or never admitted she did, but she wasn't minding it. She was liking it and that surprised her. The surprise was followed by a twinge of guilt. Raised by hardworking parents who had been just starting out after World War II, the virtue of carrying one's own weight and incurring no debts had been drummed into her and her sister. Anna didn't buy things she couldn't afford and that included things that had to be paid off over time. Since Zach, her first husband, had died she'd more or less run her emotional life the same way: no debts incurred, no promises made for an always unsure future.

Paul, a classic with his gun and his Bible, had found a way to give and love in such a way that it actually seemed he did it because he liked to, because it enriched him, that virtue was, indeed, its own reward.

Anna caught his eye, hazel and full of life under the

brim of a canvas hat. He winked at her and she was startled to think it didn't just seem, for Paul it was.

"This is the right trip," she said, and put her back into her paddling until Carmen hollered that they weren't in a race.

The thundering emptiness that had taken her to the psychologist's office in Boulder, and the broken shards of thoughts and conversations that had come in its wake, began to lose ground to the great state of Texas and the wonders of the Chihuahuan desert. The water in the Rio Grande was high, but where the banks were low and the river could spread out, it didn't require much thought to navigate. Besides, thinking was Carmen's job. Anna didn't want any part of it. Fantasies, when the empty dark and the fragmented thoughts allowed her to have them, had run to quiet gardens in countries where no one spoke English, of severed phone lines and silence and no responsibility greater than pushing her hair out of her eyes and making coffee every morning.

The chatter of happy people little more than children and the wet, friendly lapping of the brown water against the sides of the raft soothed Anna. The sky was huge and deep, on the horizon towers of cumulonimbus clouds rose in great columns exploring every shade of white. Cane grass, growing out from the bank, fought a soundless battle for territory with the exotic giant reeds. The reeds had been brought from the Orient to serve as cattle fodder and had taken over. They had the lush and hungry look of countries Anna had only seen in movies drenched in blood: *Apocalypse Now* and *Full Metal Jacket*. Larger and darker of leaf than the indigenous cane, they reached out far over the water, their stems so thick and interwoven that only the smallest of creatures could travel through them to the river.

They were voraciously beautiful, and for once, Anna chose not to care what was indigenous and what was exotic, what was healing for the park and what harmed it. Later, if she felt truly wild and crazy, ultimately devil-may-care and irresponsible, she might try littering simply to see if she could do it.

"Why's the land all torn up on the left bank?" Cyril asked.

"They're putting in a golf course," Carmen answered. Her voice was carefully neutral; so much so that it left the listener in no doubt that she loathed the idea of the development.

A water-sucking, pesticide-drenched whore of a golf course smacked down in the middle of the desert. Anna snorted. Only Tiger Woods in perfectly pleated trousers could make a golf course attractive anywhere. Even he might fail on the sere banks of the Rio Grande. *Not my problem*, Anna told herself firmly, and put it from her mind with a deep breath. The air was so clean and dry she scarcely felt the need for inhaling and exhaling. Pure as it was, it felt as if it might permeate the flesh without bothering to trouble the lungs.

"It's not in the park?" Cyril asked.

"Nope."

"There wasn't a sign or anything," Cyril said. "You

know, like 'Give Up All Hope, Ye Who Enter Here.' Or 'Now You're on Parkland, Stop Having Fun.'"

"There used to be a sign but the river rangers talked the NPS into taking it down. There's no need for a sign. It makes no difference to the river whose land it flows through. Technically all the land on the right is Mexico and all the land on the left is the United States. Since the border was closed eight or nine years ago, according to the law, if we drift over the center of the river and into Mexico then drift back into U.S. waters—we've broken the law."

Anna recalled a dustup over that issue years before. One of the river rangers was so incensed over the sudden closure, he called the Border Patrol to come and arrest a bunch of lily-white college kids down from New York State to go rafting. He was trying to make the point that if it was illegal for anybody to do it, then the law should be enforced against Americans as well as Mexicans. What he succeeded in doing was pulling off a magnificent career-limiting gesture.

Anna put the border issues with the golf course. Not her problem.

Letting the talk of the others meld again with the chuckle of the water, she watched red-eared box turtles slide off their perches on stones and logs, hiding themselves beneath the dark water. Red-eared turtles were as much an invasive species as the giant reeds, but today Anna wasn't going to hold it against them. Everybody had to come from somewhere and she appreciated that they allowed her to share their space with them.

"We'll be in the park after we round that bend."

Anna glanced back to see Carmen pointing down-river, where the land began to wrinkle then reared up in sudden bluffs, high and sheer and burnt-gold in the strong light. Leading up to—or falling away from—this crown of shale were ash-gray hills pocked with cacti. Here and there a splash of luminescent yellow-green or shocking pink sparked from a blooming plant.

"Cool," Anna heard the boy say. He had a nice voice. Mucho basso profundo and coming out of a rib cage that a big man could probably fit his hands around. The kid was nowhere near the size of the noise he made, at least not in breadth. He was paddling opposite Anna and she watched him for a moment, her paddle idle across her knees. Out of self-defense she bet he'd learned every skinny joke there was, from turning sideways and sticking out his tongue to look like a zipper to having to run around in circles in the shower to get wet. He was at least six feet tall and weighed a hundred and twenty to a hundred and twenty-five at a guess.

"Are you and Cyril related?" Anna asked, seeing it for the first time.

"Twins," Cyril called from behind her. "I'm the pretty one. It's important that you remember that. I'm real sensitive on that issue."

"I'll remember," Anna said.

"Steve." The boy introduced himself in his marvel-ous voice.

"You should go into radio," Anna said before she

realized it would be taken as an insult. He groaned. Evidently he'd heard that one before as well.

Being rude was shoved back to keep company with the golf course and the border issues and the evil intruding grasses.

Not my problem, Anna reassured herself. Much of her life, when she'd chosen to think about it, which was not all that often, she'd assumed being lazy and irresponsible and self-centered was the easy way. Practicing it was turning out to be a lot harder than she'd thought. There was so much in the world to not care about, so much to blow off, brush off or otherwise put out of her mind. Clearly she wasn't going to become proficient in it at the rapid pace she had expected. Littering would be out of the question for at least a year or two. Maybe gum, she thought. In a few months she could begin training by spitting her gum out on the ground instead of carefully folding it in the slip of paper the stick came in and carrying it in her pocket until she remembered to put it in the trash or laundered it with the cigarette butts and pop-tops and other bits of refuse she was constantly picking out of the world.

"*Hola*," Carmen called. Anna pulled out of her mind to see a group of vaqueros on the left bank, three men on horseback and a half-dozen scrawny cows. The rafters stopped paddling and the men on the bank waved. One of the girls, Christine, who, despite being considerably overweight, wore the low-cut spandex shorts and high-cut spandex top that Cyril showed off to such advantage, waved back. A pale fold of fat rounded over the tight band, and Anna hoped the girl had had sense enough to slather her soft white underbelly with sunscreen before exposing it to the elements.

Christine took a camera from her dry-bag and began clicking pictures of the cowboys. A tall Mexican in a wide-brimmed hat that looked as if it had herded many cows over the years smiled widely then pulled a disposable camera from his belt and took a picture of the raft. The other vaqueros laughed, touched the brims of their hats respectfully, and kicked their horses into a walk as the raft drifted downstream of them.

"Wow," Christine said. "Mexicans. All we ever get are Puerto Ricans."

"Chrissie doesn't get out much," Cyril said. "She is from a small desert isle in the Atlantic Ocean."

"Staten Island," Chrissie defended herself. "And I do too get out."

"No," Steve corrected her. "Sometimes they *let* you out. It's a whole different thing."

"They're on the left bank. I thought the Mexicans couldn't cross the river and be in America because of the drug thing," Chrissie said. The raft took them from the last view of the vaqueros as they started pushing their small herd into the water to cross back to the Mexican side of the river.

"Nobody told the cows," Carmen said. "Technically they aren't supposed to come over to get them but the park kind of turns a blind eye. Once in a while the rangers will round them up and take them up to El Paso where they get auctioned off or slaughtered. Mostly they just let the vaqueros retrieve them. It's a whole lot cheaper than trucking them the length of Texas."

Silence didn't fall, but Anna tuned the talk out and put herself back into the natural world. Or tried to. The pit that had opened inside her altered the landscape. She could see it when she looked inward, a great black hole, wide and deep and without light, yawning like the mouth of an underground cavern. Around it the desert hills rolled away, the river wound by, the sky rose into the ether. She could see herself, small and fragile, on her hands and knees at the rim of the crater trying not to be sucked into the darkness.

"Weird," she said aloud, and shook her head to free herself of the image.

"Are you okay?" Paul asked quietly.

Anna wasn't sure how to answer that, at least not if she answered honestly. "Fine," she told him.

"It will be," he promised.

Since she had known him, Paul had never broken a promise to her. Anna contented herself with that and so she forced the pathetic image to crawl slowly away from the abyss on its hands and knees.

FOUR

At the entrance to Santa Elena Canyon, the river grew wide and a rocky beach formed on the American side where runoff had laid down a sandy wadi, as gold as a trail of mica in the afternoon sun. Willows softened the stone views on the east side and on the west huge rocks, tumbled like the blocks from a child's toy box, lay helter-skelter. "This is home for tonight," Carmen said. "Put in at that little point. You'll still get your feet muddy but the rocks will keep the worst of it down."

Anna was tired. An easy day of paddling and she was as tired as if she'd done something. Bone and muscle had not been taxed but the hole inside had been pulling, dragging her from the beauty of the desert, the howling from the depths drowning out the talk of the kids she'd depended on for distraction. As the day wore on the first euphoria of hot sun and river creatures was weighed down by the darkness within.

Thoughts she could not quite catch flitted bat-black through her mind. *I'm wasting the world*, she thought as she helped carry camping gear from the raft to the sandy expanse fifty feet from the water's edge. *I am wasting Texas and Paul.*

By herself and talking with Paul, Anna had tried to think herself free of the miasma. The man she killed was not a nice individual. He was a monster. She killed him in self-defense, though, if justice mattered, she should have been able to shoot him in cold blood and been given a medal for doing so. There were no thoughts that she had robbed a wife of a loving husband or children of a father. No sense that she had taken a fine mind that, left to work on, would have added anything of merit to society. Anna was not sorry he was dead; she wasn't sorry it had been she who dispatched him. Those necessary evils could have been cured by logic. The hole that had opened within her was deeper in scope and significance, her own idiosyncratic Pandora's box. The endless twilight and cold of the north had melded with the endless cruelty of humankind. Her mind turned on war and plague and pestilence, famine and genocide and the rape of the women in the Sudan. The six o'clock news lodged in her brain and played visions of the brutality of her race in an endless tape loop.

She had tried meditating on love and courage, bright

satin sashes and whiskers on kittens, but they seemed such tiny points of light in the ink of her internal sky.

Shaking herself like a dog fresh from its bath, she cleared her mind long enough to help Carmen screw the table legs onto the sectioned tops that unrolled into work surfaces and spread plastic cloths over them. The tablecloths were mismatched, one white with blue figures of windmills and Dutch children in wooden shoes, the other pink-and-yellow plaid. Images from childhood stirred and Anna remembered sitting at a table with a cloth very like these, removing the fingernail polish from nails bitten down to the quick and badly painted in hot pink. She wasn't more than six or seven. Her elbow had knocked over the bottle of acetone and, as she'd wiped it up, the pictures on the cloth had come up with it, leaving a whitish smear where figures had once been. Anna had covered her sin with the toaster and never told anyone. Now, more than forty years later, she wondered what her mother had thought when she'd noticed—as she had to have done—the odd blank patch. Even this thought saddened her. Her mother was gone, wiped away as the little people of ink and plastic had been, nothing left but a blank spot colored with the vague guilt of a child.

"And the groover. Ta-da!" Carmen's voice cut through the fog of the past. She held up an army ammo can, metal with a hinged top, about eighteen-by-six-by-fourteen inches.

"I'll set it up," Anna volunteered.

"No, you're on vacation," Carmen protested.

"What is it?" Chrissie asked.

"This is our commode," Carmen told her.

Chrissie's round face blanked and she looked all of twelve years old. "What do you do with it?"

"You sit on it," Carmen said. "That's why it's named 'the groover.' The can leaves parallel grooves in the posterior of the sitter."

"Gross."

"Not as gross as getting cactus spines in your butt," Cyril said.

Carmen pulled a plastic toilet seat from one of the dry-bags the gear was stowed in. "We are a class act. We have a seat. No groovy butts for us."

The sight of the toilet seat slammed Anna back into the bunkhouse on Isle Royale, the brightly painted Winter Study toilet seat leaning against the wall behind the woodstove, the seat kept warm to be toted through the snow to the outhouse as needed. Post-traumatic stress, Anna told herself. Sudden flashbacks, mood swings, sleep interruption. The diagnosis struck her as pat, trendy, overused and surely not one that could be applied to an individual who had killed one lousy person. Masses maybe, women and children and babies blown apart. She did not deserve to water down the ailment with her single paltry corpse.

"I'll do it. I'll put it up," Anna repeated.

Carmen looked at her too long then, perhaps seeing a shadow of Anna's grim landscape, handed her the can and seat and a mesh bag with toilet paper and hand sanitizer. "There's a great spot up the creek bed. You'll know it when you get there," she said.

"Let me," Paul said.

"No."

"Want me to go with you?"

"No."

Anna sounded ungrateful and weird and she knew it and could do nothing about it. As she walked away she heard the raucous silence of the group and was relieved when Steve's booming voice shattered it with words that made the others laugh.

Setting up wilderness privies was not Anna's favorite thing—though it was much more pleasant than taking them down and infinitely more pleasant than cleaning the cans back at the wilderness cache. She wanted to be away from people for a few minutes. Solitude, not for the joy of it as had formerly been the case, but to hide raw edges beginning to unravel. To be mad was bad enough. To be seen as mad was embarrassing. To see the worry in Paul's eyes was intolerable.

The dry creek bed cut straight as a razor up toward the sheer rise of the entrance to Santa Elena Canyon. Horse manure littered the sand where the animals had wandered over from Mexico to munch on American grass. A bit of housekeeping would be called for before they pitched their tents, but the boulders strewn on the sand made for lovely private sites. In a way, this was Anna's honeymoon. That thought gusted beneath her depression in a zephyr of air scented with the washed cotton and sun smell of Paul Davidson. The momentary joy was damped by the thought that, given her bizarre state of mind, she would not be the wife that he deserved.

"Damn," she said aloud, and again shook herself. Maybe a slight coup contra-coup injury of the brain would have the effect of electrodes pulsing shocks into her frontal lobe.

A feathery willow and a boulder as big as an Airstream trailer marked the entrance to the bathroom. Carmen had been right. She knew it when she saw it. The sandy creek bed angled away into the hills and Anna stood on a gentle shoulder of land. Rocks and trees formed a high wall on one side. On the other was the river, bending wide and smooth into a towering rift in the rock. A room with a view.

The sun was low in the west. The last of its light struck gold from the shale wall and turned the subdued greens of the desert a brighter shade. Above the cliffs the sky was a turmoil of clouds, round and fierce, their bellies sagging close to the mesa. Sunset fired their edges and cast deep purples into their ephemeral canyons.

Don't waste this, Anna told herself. *People are not all there is to the world.*

THE NIGHT CONSPIRED to help Anna hold on to her fragile resolve. There was a moon, not quite full, but bright enough through the clear air to cast shadows. Though she cooked on a two-ring propane stove, Carmen had built a fire in the fire pan and there was the comfort of sitting around a blaze sipping wine from plastic cups and listening to the murmur of the Rio Grande. Coyotes sang briefly and bats came out, swooping low over the creek in search of insects. The towering clouds that had followed them all day surrounded the moon as the last of the chocolate Oreo cake was consumed and a wind smelling richly of rain blew from the northwest.

"Everybody put their flies up?" Carmen asked. Cyril, Lori, Chrissie and Steve scrambled up and disappeared behind the willows and rocks sheltering the kitchen area. "Looks like we might get wet tomorrow," Carmen said. "Did you notice the river's come up since this morning? It's been raining in the Coahuilas. Most of our water comes from there."

"I didn't notice," Anna said, but as she spoke she remembered the sticks and leaf litter and occasional plastic water bottles floating past the raft. When rivers rose they washed the banks clean, pushing whatever floated downstream.

"We should have a good run tomorrow. In a way, it's easier when the water is higher. There's more between the raft and the rocks."

A woman screamed.

Paul and Anna were on their feet before it had time to echo from the cliffs. Steve's voice melted through the willows. "Lori is harassing the wildlife," he called to one of the others. "She's freaking out a national park spider."

"It was about to bite me," Lori hurled back.

"Correction," Steve called to an audience lost in the

rocks and trees. "She was harassing *and* feeding the wildlife. I think there are big fines with that."

The sheriff and the priest and the ranger sat again in the folding chairs.

"What do you guys do when you're at home?" Carmen asked. "Red lights and sirens?"

Paul laughed. "It shows?"

"You two jumped like hunting dogs hearing the whistle."

Before the fire burned itself out, and long before Carmen and the others went to bed, Paul and Anna walked hand in hand to their tent. While she had been setting up the groover, Paul had cleared an area of horse apples, nestled their tent between three boulders, and arranged the dry-bags with their personal gear on a rock the right height for a bureau.

"You'll sleep better if you bathe," he said as they unzipped the tent's fly.

Anna looked back toward the river, not anxious to walk over the muddy banks to bathe in the muddy water.

"Sponge bath," Paul said.

"Do I stink?" Anna laughed.

"No," Paul said seriously. "I just wanted an excuse to touch you, but you will sleep better."

Anna knew that. She took off her clothes, stood obediently on a flat stone and let Paul wipe the day from her skin. In the moonlight, intermittent now that the clouds were on the move, she watched his square strong hands as the cloth drew cool water down her arms and across her breasts, then turned that he might wash her back. They zipped their sleeping bags together but did not make love that night; they let it flow around them. Anna fell asleep with her head on his shoulder and her hand on his heart as the wind teased music from the tent's fly.

FIVE

They woke to gray skies but no rain and, to the east, blue began to peek through the overcast. In the mountains and canyons of the Chihuahuan desert it was hard to predict the weather. Not only did each elevation, each mountain, make its own, but with rock and hill and cliff and distance it was impossible to see what was coming. Big Bend was immense and in its canyons people saw the land and sky with the truncated view of ants in high grass.

Without the sun the temperature was hanging in the low sixties. Anna wrapped her head in an old shawl she'd carried at least a thousand miles and used for everything from a pot holder to a snake catcher and went down to breakfast. She could hear Cyril's laugh and Chrissie's high-pitched shriek that served duty as an indicator of levity, horror, great fun and, on the few occasions Steve bothered to flirt, a willingness to mate.

Carmen's voice filtered through the hilarity: "What do you call a female boatman who does her job and does it well?"

"Lazy."

Anna smiled and tucked her shawl into the front of her down vest. She'd not given much thought to the lives of the outfitters, especially the women in what was traditionally a testosterone-heavy field. From things Carmen had mentioned, Anna knew that boatmen came from all over the country during the season—December through the middle of March when the river was high— but a stalwart few stayed year-round, most living in the town of Terlingua and getting by as best they could.

"What do you call a boatman without a girlfriend?" Carmen was saying as Anna joined the party around the breakfast preparations.

"Homeless." Carmen delivered her punch line while flipping a pancake, as polished as any showman.

"What's the difference between a boatman and a large pizza?"

"The pizza can feed a family of four."

"We are all here," Carmen said as she served Anna two pancakes from her griddle and pointed her toward the butter and syrup.

When they'd settled, the guide said: "This morning's float starts out pretty easy. The first couple miles are flat water. Then we get to the rockslide."

A ragged cheer went up from the narrow twins. The

rockslide—and there were rapids of that same name in most rivers Anna had run—was rated at anywhere from a class II to a class IV, depending on the water levels in the canyon.

"I heard from one of the other guides before we set out that the slide was at about a level three when he went through it," Carmen went on. "But that was two days ago. I'm guessing it will be nearing a four if it hasn't gotten there already. The river's up from last night even. Not much, maybe two inches, but when the canyon starts squeezing the water it can go up fast. Before we hit the slide there's a good place to pull over and beach. We can talk more about it then and I can show you how we plan our run, depending on what the water is doing."

They breakfasted sumptuously—float and bloat, Carmen joked—broke camp and again took to the water, this time wearing life vests. The scrap of blue that had struggled so mightily against the clouds lost the fight and the sky was marbled with silver-gray and black. Anna felt the boil of the thunderstorms in the air and reveled in it. Ozone levels were high and she enjoyed the tingling in her blood.

The raft rounded a bend in the river and floated into the view they had enjoyed from the groover. Anna found her breath being stolen by the sheer height of the cliffs they were heading into. They rose a thousand feet into the sky on either side of the turgid brown water, straight and true as if a cosmic force had cleaved them with one mighty blow of an ax.

"Wow," Anna heard someone breathe and realized it was her.

"Awesome," Lori said.

Anna had heard her use that word in reference to the chicken sandwiches and guacamole they had had for lunch, Brad Pitt and Carmen's straw hat. This time the word was apt, describing that which induces a sense of awe into the beholder, a sense that there is a greater force at work than human minds can conceive. There'd been a time Anna believed in a god or gods of some sort. Meeting Paul had reintroduced this illusive and intoxicating possibility into her soul. Recently, though, she had retreated to the loneliness of the ungodly, the lights on, lights off logic of the atheist. When a light was turned off it didn't go elsewhere to light the rooms of others in worlds to come, it just ran out of fuel and was no more. Much as she wanted to believe it was otherwise for people, she could not. Less could she believe, if other places on other planes existed and were policed by supreme beings, that they would by choice let the rabble of the earth invade. Should there be a heaven it would probably have a border patrol that put Homeland Security to shame.

They slipped into Santa Elena Canyon and the subtle sounds of birdsong and wind in the reeds faded. Even the water lapping against the sides of the raft seemed hushed. Deep and channeled through a narrow gorge of stone, the river boiled beneath them, but its surface showed only the bulge and twist of enormous muscles under a glassy-smooth skin that gleamed where it powered around submerged rock and slipped sharp as knives undercutting the shale cliffs. Anna felt its tremendous strength beneath her and for a moment had a terrifying sense of riding the back of a mythical serpent, a sentient creature who knew parasites sat on its skin, took of its forces without asking.

The momentary fear brought with it a sudden desire to make an offering to the river gods. A libation of wine would be closer to tradition, but Anna hadn't the courage to ask for the stuff. Instead she uncapped her water bottle and poured half a cup over the side. Like to like. Surely a Tex-Mex river beast would appreciate bottled water from New Jersey.

"Are you okay?"

It was Paul. He turned just as she was dumping part of her drinking water into the Rio Grande.

"Just appeasing the nymphs," she said.

He smiled and returned to his paddling. Paul was good that way; he understood sacred duties.

Cameras were pulled from personal dry-bags and the canyon was reduced to digital images to be viewed once, if ever, then never again. Anna seldom carried a camera and only took pictures of dead bodies or other predations. Images of incredible beauty she lodged firmly in her brain, recorded only by her eyes. That way she knew she would revisit them more often.

A mile into Santa Elena, and deep into the internal silence with which the canyon graced her, Anna heard the broken cry of the desolate. A thin creeping moan that penetrated the bones beneath the ear, too low to vibrate the drum or move the air. She stopped paddling, resting the oar across her knees, the cool river water running from the blade down the shaft to insinuate itself beneath her hand. Steve was telling a story about Cyril and a stray cat, destined for the pound and the needle, who barricaded themselves in the family bathroom for three days. Chrissie was taking pictures, the camera held in front of her as if its two-by-three-inch screen was all she could take in of the canyon. Lori was telling Carmen about a river in New York that was "awesome," and Paul was watching Anna.

None of them had heard it.

Anna smiled at her husband and he blew her a kiss that hit warm and thrilling in various parts of her anatomy. Turning her face once more downriver she opened her senses, a prying apart of the gray walls that had risen up around her mind to stave off thoughts of what lay in the pit.

Nothing.

Hallucinations weren't alien to Anna, particularly aural hallucinations. A creative brain frolics in unreal playgrounds, sometimes the devil's, sometimes those of the angels. She returned to paddling, more a dipping of her blade to seem like a working member of the group than actually moving the raft along.

After several minutes it came again, a sound so sorrowful and hopeless it cut to the heart.

"Shhh," she hushed the others.

"What—" Cyril began.

"Shhh!"

They fell silent. Lori and Chrissie looked strangely afraid, like children out after dark, frightened by what might be waiting.

"There," Anna said. "Did you hear it?"

The cry had been louder as the raft floated nearer where desolation began.

"Easter," Carmen said. "She's just past where the canyon wall juts out. We'll be able to see her in a minute."

They rested their paddles and stared at the canyon walls ahead as the river carried them past the bulging shale formation to their left. The push of stone caught and slowed the waters of the Rio Grande, letting the sediment drop and forming a small beach. Bermuda grass, long and green and looking soft as gargantuan moss, laid claim to the high ground. Two Mexican tobacco plants, as big as small trees, lifted their broad leaves toward the sky.

"I don't see anything," Chrissie complained.

"Look up. There." Carmen pointed to a place high on the cliff.

"It's a cow!" Cyril exclaimed. "There's a cow in the middle of the cliff!"

Anna saw it then. Three hundred feet or more from the riverbed a cow, so starved its bones could be seen even at this distance, stood on a ledge, bleating forlornly.

"It's a bull," Steve said. "Look at its horns."

"Mexican cows have horns," Carmen told him. "She's been up there a couple months."

"How did she get there?" Lori demanded. "This is nowhere and you can't get here from anywhere."

"We had a lot of high water in February and she must have fallen in the river and gotten carried into the canyon. We find cows in here once in a while," Carmen said.

"The water couldn't have been that high," Anna said, staring at the poor creature marooned halfway between heaven and earth.

"See the ledge? She keeps going up farther and farther to get food," Carmen said. "Every time I come through she's worked her way up a little more."

"Why doesn't it thirst to death?" Steve asked.

"She eats the cholla. There's enough water in the cactus to keep her alive."

"Why doesn't she just walk back down?" Chrissie asked, sounding slightly annoyed at the cow for making such a fuss of its predicament.

"No incentive, I guess," Carmen replied. "The food behind her has already been eaten."

"That and the fact she has cow brains for brains," Steve said.

"Pull in," Anna demanded suddenly. "Beach the raft." She began to paddle hard. The trip was a leisurely one, the outfitters making a three-day adventure out of a twenty-mile trip that a canoeist could easily do in a day, and Carmen was in no hurry. She helped steer the raft onto the rocky shore. Anna and Steve were out first, pulling it from the water.

Anna had no idea what she was doing, only that they couldn't float by, snapping pictures at the tormented soul on the cliff face. She couldn't stop the man she had killed from stalking her in nightmares. She could not stem the tide of evils flooding from man's cruelty. She couldn't save the women in the Sudan. Some days she despaired of saving herself from a darkness that seemed to be encroaching from all sides. But surely, God dammit, she could save one poor pathetic cow.

If she couldn't save it, she wouldn't pass it by, leave the poor thing to be pointed out to more tourists as it crept ever higher, grew ever thinner, cried ever more weakly until, finally, death came as a blessing and the guides in passing canoes and rafts pointed out the vultures gathering on the high ledge where Easter was served as an alfresco luncheon.

"We have to get the cow down." Anna was not asking for permission or discussion. She was issuing an order.

"Yes!" Cyril said, pumping the air with her fist in an overused gesture, the origin of which was mostly forgotten.

"We become vaqueros, *mis amigas*," Steve said. "To the rescue. What a trip!"

"How?" Chrissie nearly whined.

Lori said nothing.

Paul looked alarmed and Anna knew it was not for the cow or for himself. He hated it when she put herself in danger. He was old school. When they walked together in the street, he walked on the outside so marauding automobiles would have to go through him before they could lay a bumper on his wife.

"It's been done," Carmen said speculatively. "I don't know about getting cows off cliffs, but I know a few have been rafted out of the canyon. The river district ranger, Fred Martinez, took one out last spring."

"How much line have we got?" Anna asked the guide.

Paul groaned. "Oh Lord, there's two of you. You and Anna. You two are going to scale a cliff to rescue two hundred pounds of hamburger, aren't you?" He put both hands over his face.

"You can stay here," Anna offered.

He looked at her in exasperation. "Right. Like I would do that while you bull wrestle on a cliff ledge."

"Three or four hundred feet," Carmen said. "We carry extra."

"For cows?" Lori asked, sounding both amazed and appalled.

"For whatever," Carmen said.

"Anna, did I not hear you say once that free climbing was a fool's sport?" Paul asked.

"We don't have to climb," Anna said. "We can walk up the way Easter walked up." For the first time in what seemed like forever, but was only since the previous winter, Anna knew what had to be done and how to do it. The rescue of the cow unfolded in her mind with complete clarity. The others, even Paul, were relegated to the status of tools, valuable, useful tools like the lines-become-ropes and the lettuce in the cooler designated to be salad for their supper.

"Paul, you and Steve will come with Carmen and me. You three stay down here and rearrange the gear so there's a level place to load Easter when we get her down."

"I'm going with you," Cyril said.

Momentarily nonplussed by the mutiny, Anna stopped unlashing the cooler from which she intended to commandeer green, cow-tempting foodstuffs. She blinked twice, clearing her mind's eye of its single-minded pursuit. Fleetingly, she was aware that she was not General Petraeus and this was not the 10th Airborne Division. "Sure," she said. "Change your shoes. Everybody, change your shoes except Lori and Chrissie, you can keep your Tevas on."

Having liberated the lettuce and a bunch of celery, Anna dug her sneakers out of her dry-bag and swapped her river shoes for them. Carmen put the celery back in the cooler.

"Okay, right," Anna said. "One head of lettuce should do it."

"I take it you have a plan," Paul said.

"Yes. It should work if Easter is as weak as she looks. The ledge isn't all that narrow; it can't be or she'd never have gotten that far up."

"You'd be surprised," Carmen said.

Anna ignored her. "We go up the way Easter did. We turn her around with the lettuce lure and hobble her if we can so she won't bolt. She follows us and the lettuce down. Once we get her on the beach, we get her on her side and immobilize her. Carmen will tell us where best to lash her to the raft."

"Wow. Me, the guide, the paid leader of the expedition, will actually get to make a decision," Carmen said.

Sarcasm tinged the boatman's words, but only very faintly. Carmen was nearly as keen as Anna to get the cow down. What her motives for this altruism were, Anna didn't know and didn't care.

"Yes," Anna replied seriously, too focused for humor or working and playing well with others not of like mind. She would have shouldered the coils of rope but Paul had already picked them up. Anna took the lettuce and broke the head in two, giving half to Carmen. "This will keep her from getting it all in one bite and losing interest in us."

Anna trotted across the beach and began scrambling up rocks to where the ledge started about ten feet above water level. "Stop!" Paul called as she found the ledge and stood.

"What?"

"Wait there." His voice was harder than Anna had heard it before and penetrated the thickness of her determination. She waited.

When he got to the ledge, he stepped ahead of her, between her and the distant cow above. "I'm going first."

She opened her mouth to protest.

"Don't even try," he said. "I grew up on a dairy farm,

remember? Cows are decent beasts but they are not that bright. If she bolts toward us instead of farther up the cliff, there might not be room for everybody. If the choice comes up, she's going over, not you."

Anna didn't like it. Didn't like being slowed down. Didn't like being protected. Rebelliousness fired up in her belly and sparked in her eyes. Paul stared it down.

"Right," she said. "Let's go."

A breath of air wheezed softly from behind her left shoulder where Carmen had crowded onto the ledge. A veteran guide, she'd seen enough of marital discord to feel relief when the storms were averted.

The ledge was several feet wide at the bottom and had a floor of polished stone. Sediment was deposited in the holes and cracks from high water and blown dirt, and opportunistic desert plants took root in the shallow planters. The cholla cacti were grazed down to nubs and what little Bermuda grass had made it up to the ledge was eaten down to white roots.

Paul started up, Anna following. Behind her she heard Cyril and Steve clamber onto the ledge to trail behind Carmen. Five was too many, Anna thought. At Easter's elevation the ledge might not be wide enough for that many people and one cow. This quixotic quest could end in tragedy if the rescue went sour. Anna did not want that on her conscience, but doubted they'd go back if she told them to, so she shoved the thought into the back of her mind. Already crowded with the things she would not think about, the dim recesses of her skull must look like an overstuffed closet. Should the door fail, the flotsam and jetsam of her id would come tumbling out. That thought, too, she shoved in with the rest.

Distracted from her misery by the strange phenomenon of human beings creeping up her path, Easter quit crying and lowed soft questions at them.

"She sounds like she knows we're coming to save her," Cyril said.

"She sounds like she knows we're coming to feed her," her brother retorted.

"I wonder if animals hope," Cyril mused. "Can you hope if you live in the moment?"

"They live in the moment you open the cat food can," Steve said.

The climb was growing steeper and Anna could hear their breath coming harder between their words. She would remember not to count on them for brute force. Paul was powerful and Carmen was a rock. Along with her, they could do the heavy lifting if there was any to be done. The twins would be ideal for holding the offerings of lettuce, she decided.

"Poor old Easter will end up in a beef fajita," Paul said.

"No she won't!" Cyril declared.

"Are you going to lock it in a bathroom with you till the president of Mexico grants it amnesty?" her brother asked.

"I might."

Anna laughed. She hadn't laughed much in a while and it felt wonderful. She reminded herself to take it up again.

Paul laughed then and Anna knew he was happy because she was, and felt the rush she always did when she realized how much he loved her.

SIX

The ledge they followed was rapidly narrowing and the river had grown ribbon-thin far below them. Lori and Chrissie and the raft looked small as toys in the bottom of the canyon and the cliff-dwelling swallows flew by them at eye level. Cyril, Anna noticed, was hugging the wall, and Steve was trying not to. The ascending path they followed was a couple of feet wide, three or four feet in places, but with a drop of several hundred feet and no guardrails, it was not a place for the acrophobic. Anna hoped nobody froze and had to be carried out. Panic struck some people that way, rendering them temporarily catatonic. If it did, they'd have to wait their turn. Easter had priority.

"Let's stop and catch our breath for a minute," Paul said, and stopped. He wasn't breathing hard. Neither was Anna, but it was a nice wide patch on the ledge and the footing was even, a safe place to pause and firm up the rescue plan.

Easter was about sixty feet away, ahead and slightly above them on the ledge. Seen this closely, it was clear the poor cow was on her last legs. She held her head so low her jaw was scarcely an inch from the stone. Bones poked her skin into tents at shoulders and hips and her ribs could be counted at a glance. More than a living, breathing cow, she looked like one of the desiccated corpses of cows Anna had seen at various times in the deserts of Texas and Mesa Verde, the hide shrunk around a skeleton, guts and blood and muscle long gone.

"I don't know if she'll make it down," Carmen said. "Look at the way she's swaying. We may be looking at a dead cow."

"No," Anna said. "Easter has hidden reservoirs of strength."

"Secret powers?" Steve asked.

"Pity the nonbeliever," his sister said. "If you squint you can see her cape."

"What do you want to do, Anna?" Paul asked.

"Let's get a rope around her horns with you behind her on one end and Carmen in front on the other. That way, if she gets the energy up to try and bolt you can control her to some extent. I'll take the lettuce and see if I can induce her to walk down."

"What should we do?" Cyril asked.

"Stay out of the way."

There was a protest but Anna heard it only as murmuring, no more troubling to her than the sigh of the
wind across the canyon rim or the purr of the river below.
She, Paul and Carmen uncoiled the rope then recoiled
it, half to Carmen and half to Paul. In the center, Anna
fashioned a simple loop.

"You can hold the lettuce," Carmen said kindly.

"Keepers of the Kale of the Sacred Kine," Steve said.

"Give us some slack," Anna told Carmen and, Paul
leading, the loop in her hand and Carmen feeding out
line from her half of the rope, they walked toward Easter. Horns that had looked stubby and sweet from a
hundred yards were sharp and intimidating up close and
on a narrow ledge with a three-hundred-foot drop to
one side.

"Don't even think about getting gored," she said to
her husband's back.

"I am thinking about it. I am thinking about avoiding it at all costs. Don't you even think about getting
near the cow till I've got her head," Paul said.

Anna said nothing.

"You're thinking about it," he said. "I can feel you
thinking like cats running up and down my spine. Let
me get her head."

"Stay on the cliff side," Anna said unnecessarily. Paul
was a prudent man, not given to rash decisions. He ap-
proached Easter the way he did drunks and poachers
and frat boys bent on killing each other, firmly and
kindly and, above all, carefully.

This time the worry wasn't warranted. The cow barely had the strength to roll her eyes in his direction as he sidled in between her and the cliff and grabbed hold of her horns. As Anna slipped the loop over them so Paul and Carmen would have a degree of control over the animal, Paul was not keeping the poor starved thing still so much as holding her head up for her.

The rope in place, Paul moved several yards upslope and gripped his end so, if needed, he could stop or slow the animal if it surged forward. Carmen closed the gap to ten or fifteen feet downhill from Anna and the cow so she could control it if it bucked back toward Paul.

Easter stood shaking, head hanging to her hooves, making no move to help or hinder their efforts. But for the occasional eye roll or weary twitch of her hide it seemed she hardly knew they were there.

"Okay," Anna called to the twins. "I've got a job for you. Bring me the lure."

"Lettuce sherpas," Steve said. "For this our parents are paying full tuition at Princeton."

Both of them came forward and they crowded a bit close for Anna's liking but she said nothing. The danger from the cow seemed slight. "You want to lure her?" she asked Cyril.

"Could I?" Cyril sounded so young and so delighted that Anna laughed for the second time in less than an hour. Laughter was definitely medicinal.

"Just don't let your guard down," Anna said. "Be ready to get out of the way if you have to."

"In case she unleashes her super cow powers," her brother kidded her.

Anna and Steve put their backs against the cliff so, if the cow did decide to pursue the lettuce with more vigor than was safe, they'd be out of the way and in a position to snatch Cyril back from the edge.

Approaching slowly, Cyril held out the half-head and spoke in the sweet voice animal lovers are given in lieu of the greater gift with which fiction blessed Dr. Dolittle.

"Here she comes, what a good cow, coming to get the lettuce, there's a good girl, you're hungry, aren't you, here she comes."

Easter wasn't coming. She wasn't moving. Finally Cyril closed in and put the lettuce on her nose, nudged it into her lips. Still no response.

"Damn," Anna said.

"Time for Plan B?" Steve asked.

"Let me try." Anna took the lettuce and tried to make the prospect of following it attractive, but had no better luck than Cyril.

"The carrot isn't working," Anna said. "Time for the stick."

Paul moved up behind Easter and Carmen pulled on the downhill rope. Easter collapsed, knees folded beneath her, chin on the rocks.

"Plan C?" Steve said hopefully.

There was no Plan C. Paul pushed and Carmen pulled and Cyril lured and Anna walked on the cliff side of the cow, prodding her and encouraging her. Steve made sounds that he insisted were irresistible to female bovines and they began the descent with Easter staggering, collapsing, being hauled to her feet, mooing plaintively and stumbling a few more feet before she again went to her knees.

The ledge had been fairly smooth going, a gentle slope leading upward in two zigzags following a natural sheer pattern in the rock face. They'd descended to a place where the ledge broke into ragged steps for five or six yards before the trail smoothed out again for the last turn and down to the river's edge. Where the broken steps began the ledge was wide and only fifty or so feet above the river, forty above the sand hill capped with Bermuda grass. The cow took one look at the steps, dug all four hooves into the rock and leaned back. When Anna pulled hard on the rope Easter fell and no amount of encouragement or harassment could induce her to rise again.

Anna knelt by the stricken bovine and stared into one great brown eye. "Move or die, old girl," she said. "Up and at 'em."

Easter was unmoved in every way.

Anna stood again. "Let's see if we can lift her up. Maybe it will inspire her to help us."

Coiling the rope as he came, Paul joined her on the other end of the cow. "I don't think it'll do any good. I should have thought of that on the way up but my cattle-wrangling days were a while back. Cows will go up, but they won't come down. They'll come down slopes but not stairs. I guess stairs have the same effect on them as cattle guards; they look like horrible traps for some reason."

"What if we pulled her and you pushed her?" Anna suggested.

"We could try, but if I remember right, cows are serious about their phobias."

Anna looked at the cow, then down the shattered rock slope, then down toward where Chrissie and Lori waited with the raft. On the way up, she remembered the drop being breathtaking, the height precipitous. After ninety minutes cattle rustling two hundred feet higher than that, it looked as if they could almost jump down it.

Carmen sat down, her back against the cliff, her feet against the cow's ribs. "I wouldn't mind a little rain about now," she said. "You guys didn't pay me to work this hard."

Anna sat down next to her. She, too, was drenched in sweat and reeked of cow manure where she'd repeatedly stepped in it on her backward progress down the ledge. Paul stood, hands on hips, breathing hard, staring out across the canyon, his eyes shaded by the brim of his hat, his white hair plastered to the back of his neck.

Cyril and Steve were positively peppy. The difference between twenty and forty, Anna thought without rancor. At twenty hard work eventually made one stronger. After forty it eventually made one tired.

"What now?" Cyril asked, squatting in front of the

cow and cradling her nose between her hands. "Do we carry Easter the rest of the way?"

"She may be small and starved but she still weighs a good four or five hundred pounds," Paul said.

"We could just roll her off," Steve suggested. "Have steak for supper. The bouncing would probably tenderize her."

None of the women dignified that with a response but Paul looked interested. He loved animals and was kindness itself to Taco and Piedmont and Anna's little tuxedo cat. But having been raised on a dairy farm, wringing the necks of fryers, butchering hogs and the occasional cow, he tended to be pragmatic about food animals.

Idly, Anna coiled the rope they'd been using to pull Easter with. It was light, a tough plastic line, but a hundred and fifty feet of it was still bulky.

"Hey," Anna said, a thought striking her. She stood, shouting, "Hey!" down at Lori and Chrissie, who'd unloaded the camp chairs and sat on the shore reading. "Will one of you bring up an oar? The longest one you can find."

"What are you thinking?" Paul asked, sounding alarmed. "We can't carry her. We don't have the manpower."

"Woman power!" Cyril said, but didn't look as if she believed there was enough of that to manhandle a cow down to the river either.

"We don't carry," Anna said. "We lower. Tie her feet

up, thread the paddle through, tie a line to either end of the paddle so she swings beneath it the way the great white hunter did in those old cannibal cartoons and lower her to the grassy knoll."

"Grassy knoll," Steve said. "Where have I heard that before? And did things come out well in the end? Could this be a sign?"

"Why do you want a paddle?" Chrissie hollered back up. She'd not yet risen from her camp chair.

"Just bring it, please," Anna called back. "Takes too long to explain," she added nicely. She was beginning to take against the young woman and, on the first day of a three-day camping trip with lots of close encounters on the docket, she didn't dare let even a hint of it show. Backcountry groups most often bonded; it was one of the reasons people loved them, but a group could go sour faster than an arts department at a university. Not only did it ruin it for everyone but it could prove dangerous in situations where working together for the good of the team was paramount.

Chrissie took her time gathering all the paddles together then holding them one against the other in front of Lori, choosing the longest. Anna sat back down and schooled herself in patience. Cyril did not have to. After five minutes of watching this meticulous process, hands on hips, she shouted: "Just pick one already."

Peer pressure did what usurped authority dared not and Chrissie selected a paddle and headed toward the little hill where the ledge began.

"How do you get up?" she called.

Cyril's shoulders slumped and her head fell dramatically to her chest. "Dear sweet brother, wombmate of mine, I will let you be the pretty one for two whole hours if you will go down and help Chrissie find her rear end. I believe she already has both hands and a flashlight but she needs your intellect to guide her."

Steve didn't move. "Three hours," he said.

"Two and a half."

"Done."

He rose gracefully from where he'd squatted on his heels and walked down the sloping ledge. Anna expected a catty remark from Cyril about Chrissie or at least an apology for the other girl by way of distancing herself but it didn't come and Anna was pleased. The vile hordes of humanity raping and squandering the earth would have to take out Cyril Kessler and her brother before they could claim total dominion. Anna hadn't cheered up enough that she could muster any faith that the hordes wouldn't win out in the end, but it was nice to pretend for a bit.

Odds were Anna was wrong about Chrissie, anyway, that she was a fine young woman with outstanding talents and capabilities and simply rubbed her the wrong way. There'd been enough surprises, both pleasant and un-, in Anna's past that she'd come to accept the fact she was not a great judge of character and her first impressions of people weren't to be counted on for much.

Sitting three in a row like monkeys without evil,

Anna and Carmen and Cyril watched placidly as Chrissie handed the paddle to Steve. He extended it back down to help pull her up the short rock scramble between the hill and the ledge then started back toward where they rested, spines to the wall, feet to the cow.

Paul did not join them. He squatted near the cliff's edge, looking down. If Anna was very quiet she could almost hear the gears turning in his mind as he worked through the logistics, risks and practicalities of lowering a cow down.

Anna planned to wrap the lines around solid outcrops, shove her gently over the side, and see what happened.

Steve arrived carrying the oar, Chrissie puffing and panting behind him.

"Carmen, we'll need a couple of shorter lengths to tie her ankles. Can we cut this line?" Now that Anna could almost smell Easter's salvation, her mind had opened sufficiently to encompass civility.

"In for a penny . . ." Carmen said. "Anybody got a knife?"

Paul dug a well-worn black-handled jackknife from the pocket of his shorts. Anna measured a rough twelve feet of rope. He cut it. She folded it in half and he cut it again so they would have two six-foot pieces to tie Easter's ankles together.

As he made the second cut, the rumble of thunder rolled down the canyon, crashing against the walls like a great ball bowling down ninepins. Drops of rain, spaced far apart but cold and large, were hurled down from a sky that touched the canyon rim.

"Things are about to get slippery," Anna said. "Paul, take the back legs." She handed him one of the short pieces they'd cut. When Easter had decided enough was enough and collapsed she had done it like a lady. Her legs were folded neatly beneath her and her scraggy tail curved around her bony shank.

"We're going to roll her so her spine is toward the cliff and her legs are sticking out toward the river," Anna said. "Carmen, you and me and Paul are going to do it. You guys"—she nodded at the three students hovering too near the edge, too near the cow and too close to her—"step back, give us space. Cyril, be ready with the oar. As soon as we get the legs tied together you'll thread it through. Steve, were you a Boy Scout?"

"For a while," he said.

"He dropped out in protest when they got all nasty about gay scout leaders."

"It was the holidays," Steve said. "I was working on my gay apparel badge."

"Knots," Anna said.

"I did knots."

"That's all I need to know. Tie one end of the rest of the rope to the blade end of the paddle. A knot that will hold a cow. Got that?"

"Do you want me to tie the other end on the other end?"

"Not yet." She started to put herself between the cow and the drop, heard Paul's sudden intake of breath and thought better of it. "Let's get hold of the horns. Paul will roll her rump. Ready?" Carmen was on the cliff side of her, her hands partially overlapping Anna's where they held one of Easter's horns in each hand. Carmen wore fingerless leather gloves to keep days and months of paddling from tearing her hands apart and Anna envied them. Between the rope and the sweat, hers burned. Paul had Easter's tail in one hand; his other was on her drop-side hip bone. "On three," Anna said.

Easter hadn't the strength to fight them and they turned her onto her side without much effort. She more or less fell over when Anna hit "three."

The rain was sporadic and the thunder surrounded them, cracking down from upriver, rolling overhead, drumming up from Lajitas. "I'm getting wet," Chrissie said peevishly. "I'm going back." Either it was an idle promise or she realized it would be no drier where she'd come from than where she was. She didn't move.

Anna looped her rope around Easter's leg above her hock so the jutting bone would help keep it from slipping off. Rain made the adventure more dangerous but Anna resisted the impulse to rush. The mental image of the cow's feet slipping through the ropes, the beast dangling by her hind legs while the half-tethered oar beat at her, then slipping from the other knot and falling to her death, was too grim to allow for hurried work.

"I want to help," Chrissie said suddenly.

Anna ignored her.

"Stay out of the way, Chrissie," Steve said, not unkindly.

"You stay out of the way."

Anna tuned them out and looped the rope around Easter's other leg. As she slipped her hand beneath the hoof to lift it, a bolt of lightning struck so close Anna ducked and covered her head as if that could ward off a zillion volts of electricity.

"Holy moly," Steve gasped.

Chrissie shrieked.

"We need to get down," Paul said. "This is getting unsafe."

"We're almost done," Anna said. "Another minute."

"Anna."

She knew if she looked up, he'd never leave off until he'd gotten all of them to a safer place than a stone aerie in a lightning storm. "Done," she said. "You got that rope tied around the blade end?" she asked Steve.

"Done," he said.

"Cyril, bring the oar, handle-first."

"Let me," Chrissie said.

"This isn't the time for improvising, Chris," Steve said.

"You just want to have all the fun. Don't be such a bore."

"Somebody bring me the damned oar," Anna said firmly.

"Thank you," she heard Chrissie sniff. Lightning cracked again. Chrissie screamed and the oar handle slammed against the side of Anna's face. It bounced off, struck Easter between her wildly rolling eyes and the cow began to fight with the last reserves of her strength, flailing with hooves and horns, trying to get to her feet.

Anna leapt backward to avoid the horns. Her right foot landed on wet rock. Her left hit nothing but air and she felt herself falling.

SEVEN

The dinner had gone well, Darden thought. Judith never ceased to amaze him. Given her husband's latest stunt, her insides had to be boiling like a nest of fire ants somebody stepped on. No one would have known it to look at her. Every hair was in place, not a sign of the streaked makeup and reddened eyes with which he'd been met. Cool: that was the word for Judith. Cool and fiery, a terrific combination for a politician. The dullest constituent felt her passion but the sharpest never felt that she was not in control.

For reasons Darden could never fathom, people tended to think her passion was their passion, that she was eager to fight for their cause. She was their Joan of Arc, ready to lead their army to victory. Unlike Saint

Joan, Judith was entirely sane. She would burn on the cross for nobody.

The SUV jolted over a deep rut, throwing Darden so hard against his seat belt that he grunted and swore. Big Bend was made of dust. He'd eaten dust over its unpaved roads for so many hours that even in the air-conditioned cab with the windows tightly closed he could feel it settling in the lines around his eyes and crusting in his nose.

"Psychosomatic," he told himself. He hated dirt. Wearing the same shirt two days in a row made his skin crawl. He couldn't see how men tolerated facial hair. One of the agents he'd worked with when he was in D.C. sported a handlebar mustache, a "soup strainer," it was called. During training Darden had to sit beside him in the cafeteria because if he sat across from the guy and had to look at the food hanging up on the hairs under his nose he'd throw up.

Another jolt hammered up from the road and he slowed the vehicle to alleviate the beating he was taking.

He didn't like to think he'd always been so fastidious.

In college he hadn't gone the hippie route but he'd had long hair and didn't remember being too particular about where he slept or with whom, or what he picked up off the floor to wear the next day. His mother used to nag him about cleaning his room and he remembered Judith wrinkling her little snub nose and saying "pee-euww" when he took off his running shoes after track practice.

As a kid Judith was so honest, it was a wonder somebody didn't wring her neck. She didn't grasp the fact that just because it was true didn't mean you could announce it to the world.

"She must weigh a *ton*," she'd stage-whisper, or "Momma lost her diaphragm," or "Why do you pick your nose? I don't see any boogers in it."

She never deluded herself either. Even as a little girl she knew her strengths and weaknesses and spoke of them openly. A warped world saw that as boasting or having a poor self-image. Judith saw it as inventory. She couldn't understand why other people hated honesty. Once she had crawled into his lap when he was watching a football game on television, crying because she'd been chewed out by the woman across the street who didn't enjoy discussing the fact that her hair was thinning so much her scalp shined through like a pink baby's bottom. Judith turned her face into his shoulder, getting kid snot all over his T-shirt, and wailed: "If nobody tells them, how can they *fix* it? I want to *fix* everything stupid about me."

By first grade she'd figured it out. She still took her own and everyone else's measure, but she kept it to herself. It was one of the things that made her such a formidable opponent. Judith believed all criticism was constructive. She pored over reviews and blogs that ranted against her. If the criticism was incorrect, she'd figure out what she could do to be clearer in her intentions. If it was correct, she'd figure out how to shore up her defenses so the flaw, should she choose to keep it for business or personal reasons, would go unnoticed. And if it was spurious, she said it told her a lot about the mental workings of the critic. Nothing was wasted. Praise, on the other hand, she thought was worthless to receive but good as gold to give—and a whole lot cheaper.

"People will wag themselves to death for a little pat on the head," she'd say.

Thinking of the snotty-nosed little girl burrowing into his shoulder, Darden guessed he couldn't have been a clean freak back then. That was comforting. He hated to think he'd become Felix Unger before he was old enough to vote. It was bad enough now—maybe it was worse now: he cooked for a hobby, lived with his mother, and got the willies if he got mayonnaise on his shirt cuff.

Maybe he'd done so much dirty work in his career he had to root it out of his personal life to feel clean.

When he'd taken over security for Judith, she was deputy mayor of Houston, not exactly the number one target of the uglies. As mayor the stakes went up a little, but not much. Assassins were too expensive to use for taking out local politicians. But Judith was a shooting star. She hadn't quite pulled an Obama and catapulted onto the national stage with a single speech, but she'd gone from Junior League team leader to mayor of one of the biggest, richest cities in America in eleven years. Eleven more and she would be on the national stage,

Darden didn't doubt that. Security for a rising politico wasn't so much about keeping them alive as it was about keeping their political life alive.

The dirty work came in tidying up messes they left behind or sweeping the manure out of their path ahead.

"Hallelujah," Darden said. Paved road. Relieved of the bumping and dusting, he loosened his seat belt and lowered the side window a couple of inches. The day was cool and overcast and he could smell that it was raining nearby. The olfactory sense was an unsung hero as far as Darden was concerned. People put so much energy into what they could see and hear and taste, they missed out on a whole universe waiting to be sniffed.

Darden smelled a rat in this last turn with Charles. It was too perfectly timed to have been an accident. Not for the first time, Darden thought about surgically removing Charles from Judith's life. Judith would make a beautiful widow. Voters would love the strong, grieving woman in subdued colors continuing to serve the public. Once widowed, those still pretending divorce was shocking would forget about her first husband. Nobody dared admit to disliking widows or orphans.

Charles would be easy to kill—everybody was easy to kill—but attacking a high-profile public figure's spouse never went as well as the doers thought it would. The husband of a powerful woman dies, a lot of people figure she did it no matter what the facts said. Especially if the husband had been a philanderer. Careful as Charles'd been and as much of Judith's money as he'd spent, Darden didn't kid himself that an enterprising investigative reporter couldn't dig up evidence of Mr. Charles Pierson's dalliances.

If the press didn't point the finger at the widow, it would still backfire. People wanted to bring a woman who lost her husband to violence a casserole and pat her on the back saying, "There, there." They didn't want to vote for her.

His cell phone vibrated and he plucked it out of his shirt pocket. Down on the desert floor, free of the Chisos Mountains that ringed the lodge, there was service. The call was from the home where his mother stayed when he was out of town. Maybe the poor old bird had fallen and was on her deathbed. He wasn't sure if he'd be heartbroken or relieved.

He flipped open the phone. "Darden White speaking." The woman on duty told him his mom was agitated and wanted to speak with him. "Put her on," he said.

Calls from his mom entailed a dark tunnel down which long conversations trickled as the caregiver reminded Ellen she wanted to speak with her son and helped her to figure out how the phone worked and where to put it against her head. When he figured the receiver was in the vicinity of his mother's ear, he said: "Hey, Mama, what's happening?"

"Oh, Darden! How nice of you to call."

"Just wondering how you were doing, is all." Darden no longer corrected his mother when she forgot. He didn't explain how life worked either. That was a rabbit hole he'd gone down a few times when she'd first started losing it. "You doing okay, Mama?"

"No," she said. Murmuring at the far end of the tunnel ensued as confusion erupted and caregivers gave care.

The sign for Panther Junction, where the park had its headquarters, slid by on his left. The clock on the dash read 4:45. Judith wanted him on hand for the big announcement at a cocktail party she was hosting in the dining room that evening. He should be back in the Chisos Basin in plenty of time. He never exceeded the speed limit in parks. Rangers were a funny bunch. They didn't care for the brotherhood in blue. They wouldn't let him off with a wink and a nod. In fact, they might take a special pleasure in writing a ticket to another cop. After all, law enforcement should set a good example.

Quaint, but charming.

The rain had caught up with him and was beading up on the windshield and making muddy pocks in the dust on the hood. Black was a lousy color for a car in the desert. It was like wearing black knit around yellow cats.

"Darden?"

She was back.

"I'm here, Mama."

"I can't take being locked in this . . . this . . . *hell-hole*."

Being held prisoner was the worst part of it for his mom. On bad days she banged doors and pounded. What amazed him was that she stopped there. A year ago, before she'd stepped off that cliff, she would have picked up a chair and smashed a window, then hailed a cab.

"I'm sorry, Mama."

"It sucks," she said flatly.

Darden laughed. "Watch out, Mama, they'll wash your mouth out with soap. I worry when I'm not home. Could you stick it out a day or two? I'd sure appreciate it."

"A day or two." Either she hung up or walked away from the phone or he'd gone out of range.

His mom didn't think she was going insane, she thought the world was. Normal activities were unutterably confusing, people strange and arbitrary.

In the wild and woolly sixties, Darden had done drugs. He'd done them exactly one time. For no good reason he'd taken a hit of LSD at a party. His mental shit hit the fan. It had taken him months to screw his head back on the right way. One of his roommates took the stuff every weekend and seemed no worse off for it, but it hit in Darden's skull like a grenade.

For a year or so afterward he had nightmares that he'd gone over the edge and he was being locked up in a nuthouse. Watching his mom was bringing that nightmare back.

"Poor old bird," he said, and turned the radio on loud.

Charles was waiting for him when he reached his cabin, sitting on the veranda in one of the plastic chairs. The rain was coming down, not hard but steady, and damp had been added to the gritty feel of his skin.

Gritty and sticky and Charles.

Before Judith had married Charles, Darden had abused his position with the Service to find out all there was to know about him.

Charles Pierson was forty-nine years old. He'd graduated from Georgetown University and gone on to graduate school in Oxford—"England, not Mississippi," as he was fond of saying. Six months into his first year Charles fell in love with a professor eleven years his senior. From the first photographs Darden had seen of Charles's inamorata, she wasn't the usual sort to drive boys wild.

But then morgue shots didn't show people in their best light.

"Mr. Pierson," he said evenly. "Ready for the big announcement?"

EIGHT

Anna tried to change her trajectory but couldn't. She flung out her arms in an attempt to regain balance that had ceased to exist. A strong hand caught her wrist and yanked her back onto the ledge.

"That was scary," Anna said to Carmen. The guide still had her wrist in a grip of iron. Anna didn't mind.

"Scary," Carmen echoed.

A gust of a sigh cut through the sound of falling rain and whispering river. Anna's eyes cleared of the broken bloody death she'd glimpsed at the bottom of the cliff and she looked over at her husband. Paul was spread-eagled on the now quiescent cow. Both looked at her with wide, frightened eyes. The fear in Paul's cleared, wiped away by a glaze of anguish, and Anna knew he had seen the death as well. Before she'd registered the thought, it, too, was gone.

"I think that was Easter's last gasp," Paul said. "Either we lower her now or leave her. She's so worn down from starvation I doubt she'd make it past the first coyote even if we did get her out safely. Let her go to her greener pastures here, is my vote."

The rain was settling into a steady beat. Carmen looked at the cow, then the river. "Leave her," she said. "She's low enough now she might get down on her own." That wasn't true and they all knew it, but it was a nice lie on which to abandon the cow.

Anna needed to save something, prove there was a hope of avoiding at least one miserable death, but not at the risk of endangering seven others. If the rain was not localized, if it was raining this heavily in the mountains of Mexico, the river was going to get more exciting than they'd bargained for.

"I'm afraid you're on your own, Easter," she said, and knelt to take the tethers off the cow's ankles where they'd been left when Easter put up her final fight.

"No. We're almost there. It won't take any longer to lower her than it will to untie her," Cyril said.

"It will," Carmen replied. "And getting her settled on the raft will take longer than that."

"I can't leave her," Cyril said. There wasn't any anger or disrespect in Cyril's tone. She wasn't making a play for power or voicing a threat. She sounded as if she was stating a frightening, inexplicable fact of life.

Anna looked to her brother, Steven, who shrugged. "Three days," he said. "And that was for a cat."

"Paul?" Anna turned to her husband. After nearly widowing him two minutes before, she was acutely aware of his feelings.

"Chrissie, why don't you go down and start packing up the chairs," Paul said. He was getting rid of her and she knew it. For a moment she stared at him mutinously. He looked back, his face relaxed and kind and hopeful. Nothing to mutiny against. Chrissie gave up and started slowly back down the ledge.

"Are you okay with this?" he asked Carmen.

"Do we have a choice?" The three of them looked at the twins.

"I'm sorry," Cyril said sincerely.

"Like the Chinese say, if you save a life, you are then responsible for that life. Cyril, go down and get ready to receive your cow," Paul said. "Let's get the feet tied. Above the hocks and tight. Carmen, would you hold her head? We don't want a repeat of the last lightning strike."

Easter had no more fight in her. She lay quietly as they tied her hocks together and threaded the oar through. Having wrapped the ends of the lines around two boulders that looked as if they would stand till the millennium, Carmen and Anna on one line and Paul on the other, they braced themselves as Steve shoved the cow over the edge of the cliff. The belay went easily, the rain-induced slipperiness working in their favor, and Easter was gently lowered to the bottom of the escarpment.

"She's down," they heard Cyril shout.

Cyril untied the ropes from the cow's legs and they wound them back up for the descent. By the time they reached the bottom, Cyril had Easter up on her feet and was leading her toward the river, one hand on the cow's horn.

The picture of the lovely young woman leading the wretched old cow was such that Anna couldn't help being moved, and any trace of annoyance at Cyril for balking authority evaporated.

"Hey!" Carmen shouted, and began to run.

Lori and Chrissie had wandered up to the bottom of the cliff to watch the bovine events and left their posts at the raft. The river had risen and lifted it from the rocky shore. The stern wagged in the current like the tail of a living thing trying to break free of its moorings.

"Damn," Anna whispered, and she and Paul ran after the guide. They caught it just as the river was taking it for itself and hauled the raft up onto the shore. Lori and Chrissie had not bothered to tie the raft before they'd abandoned their posts. Nor had they packed up the chairs they'd taken out to lounge in.

Anna curbed her anger because Carmen had none. Maintaining safety and equipment was the charge of the guide, and Anna could tell she was mad only at herself for forgetting her primary responsibility in the adventure of saving the cow.

Food boxes rearranged, Easter was toppled over onto

the stern of the raft and lashed in place, her horns wrapped and duct-taped in towels to keep them from goring the rubber. The entire process took forty-two minutes. The river had risen half a foot in that time.

"Put on your life jackets," Carmen said, all traces of humor gone from her. "We're in for a wild ride. Once we're past the rockslide it will get easier."

Debris washed from the riverbanks upstream floated by at an alarming speed and the vacation/adventure cheers that had met the guide's first announcement of the rigors of the rapids were not repeated.

On the water, Anna felt a degree of relief. The rain, the cow and the rising Rio Grande had her nerves strung out. Moving made her feel as if they were making progress. The power of the river was a palpable thing, not only in the pull of the oar but in the muscular feel of the water as it swelled against the cliffs on either side, mounding against the rock, pushing over submerged stones with the oily grace of a giant serpent. Entering Santa Elena Canyon Anna had been struck with the force of the Rio Grande. That had been but a paltry thing; the river fed by rains pouring down the mountain streams from the Coahuilas was that slumbering beast roused to action, the sword that cut through solid rock and rolled house-sized boulders as if they were children's toys.

"We're going to beach the raft just around that big rock," Carmen said after they'd been on the water a quarter of an hour. "There's a good place there to scout out the rockslide."

Carmen shouted directions as they rounded the rock and even Lori and Chrissie followed them as best they could, their silliness ameliorated by fear. "Lighten up!" Anna called to them. "This is going to be fun." Cyril laughed but the other two girls looked as if their definition of fun did not include rain and rocks and rapids. Anna had seen too many tourists in the same state to hold it against them. The realization that, in the backcountry, an indifferent god is in control of one's life came as a shock to most people.

The strand of beach that Carmen used to scout the rapids was reduced to a ribbon under the coming water. They eased the raft to the back of this natural breakwater and beached it. Carmen led the six of them to the last bit of exposed land. From there they could see the beginning of the rockslide.

Enormous blocks of stone had tumbled from the cliffs above and scattered into the river, forming chutes and divides in the water as it found its way through. "A few things," Carmen said. "We want to stay in the center going in here. If we don't we can wrap the raft around a rock. The water can wrap one of these things around a boulder like you'd wrap Saran Wrap around an onion. Once the raft fills with water there's hardly any force on earth that can peel it back off the rock. If we get caught by the rock, it's not the end of the world. We lean into the rock to keep the upstream edge of the raft from getting flooded and we ease ourselves off. The rock is our friend. Hug it."

As she laid out the route they would take, Anna

watched her traveling companions. Paul looked high: alert and keen, a half smile on his lips. Cyril and her brother were nervous but excited. Lori had the look of a terrified sheep. Lori was an abdicator, Anna guessed. The type that, under stress, abdicates responsibility for themselves and becomes childlike, expecting others to take care of them.

Chrissie was a study in personal misery, the drowned cat, the clown with the pie in his face, Carrie at the prom, her dress drenched in pig's blood. Anna didn't doubt that, had Chrissie suddenly been granted Carrie's power, there would be hell to pay.

Easter merely looked resigned. Her horns wrapped up in towels, her legs tied, she lay quietly on the stern of the raft and watched them with what Anna hoped was trust and not terror in her great brown eyes.

"Everybody ready?" Carmen asked.

Nobody said they weren't.

"Okay, time to have fun," the guide said.

This was not white water as Anna knew it. Going into the maze of boulders in Santa Elena Canyon, the water did not froth and break, it bulged with sinewy strength, forming muscular ridges around the stones. The Rio Grande was a male river, testosterone fueled, mover of mountains. The farming out of the waters of the Colorado River up north had robbed it of some of the fierceness it once had and it lazed when the water was low but one could still feel the underlying aggression.

Today the river was flexing and stretching in an exhilarating rush to the sea, people and stones and trees be damned.

Carmen was in the stern with Easter piled around her like a dusty brown bolster. Steve, then Anna, then Lori rowed on the American side of the raft, Cyril, Chrissie and Paul on the Mexican side. "We want to be in the middle," Carmen reminded them, "then, past that boulder, pull hard to the right."

"Aye, aye, skipper," Steve said.

The raft was heavy with the addition of the cow but not overloaded and they slipped neatly into midstream. "Oars on the right," Carmen called. Paul and Cyril and even Chrissie rowed, turning the bow neatly into the current. The Rio Grande lifted them and in a rush they surged toward the great slab of shale that divided the waters. "Hard right, hard right," Carmen shouted, reinforcing the plan she'd made on shore.

Paul and Cyril pulled hard on their oars. Chrissie, transfixed as a mouse eye-to-eye with a snake, did nothing. The oncoming boulder had paralyzed her. The stern was swinging to the right and Anna couldn't see the reason for it. Chrissie's failure to row would not make or break a turn. Running rapids was a sport as much of the mind as of the body. Between them Paul and Cyril had enough strength to control the raft.

"Row left," Carmen shouted. Anna had already dug her paddle deep, pushing a wide arc, trying to force the bow to point downstream. Steve had never learned to steer a canoe or raft and paddled straight ahead. Lori sat unmoving, her paddle thrust in the river nearly to her knuckles. Lori was serving as an unofficial rudder, the raft pivoting on her blade.

"Lori," Anna said sharply. "Row."

The young woman woke as if from a dream, looked back at Anna, her oar slipping from her hand and racing downstream ahead of them. The paddle crashed into the first rock and eddied away to the left. With the freakish suddenness that can turn an adventure into a disaster, the raft was against the rock, with Paul's, Cyril's and Chrissie's oars trapped between rubber and stone.

"We're okay," Carmen was shouting over the lowing of the cow and Chrissie's shrieks. "Lean into the rock, don't let the upstream side take on water, into the rock."

The raft steadied. The river held them fast but they were upright. "We're okay," Carmen said. Then the equation shifted. A dark shape bore down the river on a collision course with the raft pinned against the rock.

"It's going to hit us," Chrissie screamed.

"It's a garbage bag," Carmen screamed back. "We're okay."

Chrissie could not hear her and she scrambled to get out of the raft. The upstream gunwale dipped and the river poured in. Lori was gone in a second, taken from sight into the rapids. Cyril held on long enough to grab Anna's life jacket and yell: "Easter!" before the current snatched her away.

"Go, go," Paul was yelling at her. "Forget the damn cow." Easter was panicked, tossing her head back and forth weakly and bleating. The towel had torn free of one horn and was unwinding from the other in a sodden flag that slapped her and scared her more with each toss.

She couldn't leave it to die a slow death from waterboarding, or, if it was lucky, the raft would flip and it would drown faster.

"I got the head," Carmen said, and began pulling the slipknots they'd used to anchor an unresisting Easter in place. Anna's body was out of the raft and the current wanted her bad. She hooked one arm over the fat gunwale and pulled at the line holding Easter's back legs with the other.

"Cow!" Carmen shouted as the rope came free and several hundred pounds of beef struck Anna, pushing her beneath the brown water. She'd seen Easter coming in time to take a good breath. Rolling herself up like a hedgehog, she hugged her knees with one arm and her head with the other. A hoof or hip or shoulder bone clipped her, sending her spinning. Then she was just with the river. Her life jacket popped her to the surface and she came out of her protective ball and pointed her feet downstream so she could fend off solid objects.

Things had happened so quickly that by the time she had the luxury of thought it was too late. The current was too great to swim back to see if Paul and Steve and Carmen had cleared the wreckage safely and too swift to make her way to the bank until it let her.

As she rounded the boulder the raft was crucified against, a lump almost the same brown as the river rose from the depths. Anna stopped floating and swam after the cow. The beast was trussed and so weak she didn't worry about intentional harm, though she did worry about accidentally getting gored. Four good strokes and she was next to Easter. She grabbed the cow's horns, letting the rest of the animal lead their way downstream, Anna's legs trailing behind, the cow's nostrils barely above water.

The rockslide was less than a hundred yards in length and within a minute had spewed Anna and the cow out onto relatively flat water. Steering the cow like a sled, Anna kicked to shore. Farther downstream, she saw Lori then Cyril, one on either side of the river, emerging from the water. Lori stumbled as if she were blind, and let Carmen, who had her by the upper arm, lead her.

Steve was okay, Anna was sure. He'd waved as he floated past her and the cow. There was no sign of Chrissie or Paul. At this point, Anna didn't care a whole hell of a lot about Miss Chrissie. Had it been a choice between rescuing her or Easter, Anna would have had a tough decision to make.

Paul had to be upstream; Anna would have seen him if he'd passed her coming down. A horrifying image of the raft turning turtle, sucked down and pinned by the river, Paul trapped beneath, loosened her bowels.

"Have you seen Chrissie?" Carmen called as Anna pulled enough of Easter from the water that the cow could breathe and would probably not get washed away.

"No. I'm heading back." Pushing the wet hair from

her face, Anna trotted up the bank toward the jumble of boulders that shouldered both sides of the river where the slide provided such fine entertainment for the tourists.

A scream stopped her.

"Chrissie's alive," Anna said sourly.

Before she had to leave a child screaming for help to check on her husband, Paul floated into sight and crawled gasping from the river.

"Raft's gone," he said. "Easter got a horn in it. It and all the gear are gone."

Anna met him at the water's edge and started helping him off with his life vest. Guilt ate at her that she hadn't stayed to help, hadn't somehow made it back, that she'd floated cheerily downstream steering a cow while Paul hung back trying to save their gear.

The scream came again. In the instant Anna had laid eyes on Paul all thought of Chrissie had flown.

"Chrissie," Anna said before Paul could ask.

Chucking the vest, he began to run down the shoreline toward the noise, Anna and Carmen on his heels. "Stay here," she shouted at Cyril, Steven and Lori as they passed them. Cyril nodded. She was in the process of untying the cow's legs. Apparently, she valued the life of Easter slightly more than she did Chrissie's. Lori stood next to her, so close she was in the way, doing and saying nothing.

"I'll go with you," Steve said, and none of them argued. He loped out to join them, his long thin legs showing the ungainly grace of a colt's.

A smaller slide of boulders marked the end of their

beach. Anna and Carmen, more agile than the men, were up and over them first. Chrissie was on the other side. Apparently unhurt, she stood near the water by a strainer woven of tree branches and reeds. When she saw them she pointed at the strainer and screamed again.

"Chrissie's always had a way with the English language," Steve said as he slid down the rock and landed lightly beside Anna. Paul landed with a thump and a grunt.

Anna was tired and, seeing no blood gushing from Chrissie's mouth, she walked the last ten yards to where the girl stood, gawping like a landed trout.

"What you got?" Anna asked easily, expecting a snake or drowned nutria.

"There." Chrissie managed a word with her point.

"God dammit!" Anna breathed. A woman's body was tangled in the branches, her face only inches above the water, her dress washed up, exposing her legs and her very pregnant belly.

NINE

The strainer had formed between two rocks, one on the shore and one fifteen feet out into the water. An uprooted tree had been caught between the boulders and served as the net that caught smaller debris until a dangerous tangle of limbs and twigs and reeds and garbage was created.

The cause of Chrissie's screaming was nearly dead center, the current holding her fast to the strainer. Her hair was long and black and so intertwined with the nest of debris that had seined her from the Rio Grande that she seemed part of it, the human face of a nature god with the swollen belly of rebirth mocked by death. One arm floated free, the other was threaded up through the tangle as if she was trying to hold her face above the water.

Anna started to wade in.

"Don't!" Carmen ordered. "Let me."

Anna knew what she was thinking. "Law enforcement ranger, EMT," she said, then pointed at Paul. "Sheriff."

Carmen nodded and Anna thought she saw a flicker of relief in her eyes. Guides were better equipped to deal with the emergencies of the living than the dead. "Wait till we get a line on you," Carmen said. "The undertow on a strainer can be something. Sucks you right in with the rest."

Anna suffered a vision of a thorny cavern filled with corpses and was about to send Steve back to the raft for the line when she remembered.

"No line," she said succinctly. "No raft."

"Jeez," Carmen said. She had forgotten as well. The guide should have looked silly: fingerless gloves, black silk long johns worn under her shorts to protect her legs from the sun, Mexican-made hat, brim sagging with water. She didn't; she looked in her element, at home with the rain and the river. "Human line then. I'll anchor. Cyril, Steve, Paul, then you." Chrissie wasn't included in the roster but, this time, there were no complaints.

Steve loped back upriver to collect his sister from where she'd been left with Lori and the sacred cow.

Anna waded a ways into the river, Paul at her side.

"To get her out we're going to have to cut the hair off," Paul said.

"That should be fun." Anna's Swiss army knife had

scissors but the blades were scarcely an inch long. "Did you lose your pocketknife?"

Paul patted the many pockets of his cargo shorts. "No."

Paul kept his blade sharper than Anna kept hers.

"She's either been dead awhile or died recently," Anna said, realizing she sounded like Maxwell Smart playing at Sherlock Holmes. "I mean rigor has either not set in or it has passed off." She pointed to where the woman's free arm waved easily in the current, the hand and fingers undulating as if they'd already abandoned human form and become part of the river.

"We should leave her where she is," Anna said. "I doubt she is a rafter nobody bothered to mention went overboard. Crime scene and all that."

"She's probably from Mexico," Carmen said. "And got washed down the river trying to cross to have her baby in the U.S. In the villages there isn't a doctor or hospital, pharmacy, nothing like that. If they have the baby here, they get some medical attention and the baby is an American citizen. Pretty nice birthday present."

"A wetback," Chrissie said, and Anna wanted to slap her till she realized the girl wasn't insulting the dead, she understood for the first time where the slur had originated. Swimming the Rio Grande.

"If we leave her, the next raft down will have a nice surprise," Paul said.

Anna hadn't thought of that.

Steve clambered over the rocks upstream, Cyril with

him and, drifting in their wake like a sorry little ghost, Lori.

Carmen stood on the bank and held Cyril's wrist in both her hands. Cyril and Steve locked hands on each other's wrists, beginning the links in the human chain. Paul didn't take Steve's proffered arm but began unbuckling his belt. As he buckled it around Anna's waist, she said, "You're going to lose your pants."

"Better my pants than my wife," he answered.

Gripping the leather in one hand, he took Steve's in the other and Anna waded in.

The water where the woman had been caught in the strainer nearly reached Anna's sternum. She could feel the hungry strainer trying to swallow her, drag her feet-first beneath its ragged teeth, and was glad of the sturdy leather belt around her and the feel of Paul's knuckles against the small of her back.

"Pieta," Paul murmured behind her.

Up close, the woman's youth and loveliness shone through the graying mask. Eyes closed, features relaxed, her face was a perfect oval, the eyes dark-lashed and wide set, her mouth full but with a softness that was more maternal than sensual. Either her belly was bloated or she was very long into her pregnancy. Anna had seen more than her share of dead bodies and she'd never held motherhood to be particularly sacred. She'd never been one to coo over infants; but this woman touched her deeply and she felt a sting of tears.

The drowned woman's legs bumped against Anna's rib cage and the pregnant stomach seemed to be doing its best to keep her from getting in a position to cut the body loose. Gently, she pushed the body aside and insinuated herself between the floating hand and the torso. The dead might sadden her, but they didn't frighten her. One of the perks of not believing in life after death, in ghosts and vampires, zombies and animated mummies. Still she wasn't overly fond of snuggling into the embrace of corpses.

Close in, the pull of the water from beneath the strainer was stronger and she took a minute to set her feet as best she could.

"I've got you," Paul said reassuringly.

"And I've got you, babe," Anna said, and heard him laugh.

With difficulty she fished her little knife from her shorts pocket and opened the wee scissors. "This may take a while."

"No need to style it," Paul said. "Hack away."

Thick wet hair and one-inch blades began to do battle. Where she could, Anna pulled the hair free. Her fingers were growing numb from working the minuscule blades and the spring in the scissors was slipping. The rain had dwindled to a drizzle. One blessing to count, that and the fact that none of the rafting party had joined the unfortunate in the strainer.

"How are you doing?" Carmen called.

"Not too much longer," Anna said. The dead hand brushed at her thigh and she jumped.

"What?" Paul demanded.

"Brush with death," Anna said, and went back to her snipping.

Invisible beneath the mud-colored water, the hand brushed her again, a creepy snaking of flesh against flesh. This time Anna didn't flinch externally but her insides were shrinking from the touch. Perhaps she had not completely evolved from the belief in the creatures of the night.

Anna's scissors broke.

She borrowed Paul's knife.

The last hank of hair came free and she sawed it off and fed it to the strainer. The submerged hand touched her thigh again. This time the fingers tried to close. Anna squawked. The instant's belief in the netherworld blinked out.

"She's not dead," she said. Anna should have felt for a pulse, she should have done a lot of things but the body was cold to the touch, the temperature of the river, and Anna had done a bit of abdicating herself when she'd been cut loose on administrative leave.

"Hallelujah," Paul breathed.

What had been a body recovery where the luxury of time and necessary roughness were a given became a rescue. Quickly, but with care, Anna loosed the woman's hand from the sticks. Her fingers were clamped around a limb so tightly Anna had to pry them open one at a time. That done, the woman came free and Anna gathered her into her arms, her back against Anna's chest, her head falling on Anna's shoulder.

"Take us out," she said, and the human chain began pulling her and her charge back to shore. The woman's dress, cheap rayon with a flowered print, probably from Wal-Mart or Target, molded itself to the woman's stomach. As Anna was led backward she had a mother's-eye view of it. Lumps moved beneath the sodden fabric like kittens under a sheet.

"The baby's alive as well," Anna said. Paul did not repeat his short psalm of praise but she knew he was thinking it. As was she. New life was what the world needed at the moment, a life that hadn't been mucked up by people. She didn't believe in babies as blank slates. Genetics wrote in indelible ink. But they were another chance to get things right.

Paul walked upriver. Their gear was stowed in drybags, small ones for the daily use items, larger for the rest. He'd cut two loose before the raft had deflated and the smaller personal bags weren't tied in. If they were lucky, one or more would have hung up somewhere and could be salvaged.

With Carmen and Steve's help, Anna carried the woman up the bank to an overhang where the river had carved out the shale. As a shelter it wasn't much but it did keep the drizzle off. Anna knelt next to her and took her vitals as best she could. Her heart rate was slow, her skin cold, her eyes slightly dilated. There was a lump on her skull the size of a golf ball and cuts and abrasions on her arms and legs. All injuries that could be attributed to the river. Near as Anna could tell, none of her bones

were broken and she wasn't bleeding but for a slight
ooze from the scratches.

"We need to warm her up," Anna said. "Her body
temp isn't much above that of the river."

"Nothing's dry," Steve said sadly.

"Lay down," Anna told him. "Take off your shirt.
You and Cyril, one on each side, put your arms around
her and share your body heat." At another time she
would have asked them to strip to their underwear but
they weren't wearing enough clothes to bother.

Somewhat to her surprise they complied without
question or complaint. "We learned this in Scouts,"
Steve said. "It was a drag till we got to Explorers where
there were girls to save, then they wouldn't let us save
them."

"I remember how desperate you were to save Silvia
Lieberman," Cyril said.

"Yes. If ever a woman was built to be saved, it was
the lovely Silvia."

The twins lay on either side of the woman and pressed
close. Chrissie and Lori had followed them to the shelter
of the cliff and stood together as far from the action as
they could without stepping back into the drizzle.

"What next?" Cyril asked.

Anna had absolutely no idea what was next. The
usual arsenal of hot drinks, dry blankets and fire were
floating down the river or lodged under a boulder.

"Elevate her feet," Anna said. It wasn't much, but it
would keep some of the blood near the vital organs.

"You carry a satellite phone, don't you?" Anna said to Carmen.

"It's in my dry-bag. In the raft."

"Right."

Anna thought for a moment. "What are the chances another rafting party will be by anytime soon?"

"It's late in the season. Usually the water is low and people don't book. We've got nothing till the weekend. There might be a canoe or two. There's always somebody on the river, though. Could be an hour, could be ten."

The woman caught in the long arms and legs of the twins as surely as she'd been caught in the limbs of the river was not going to last another ten hours of exposure. If she had any internal injuries, she might not last another ten minutes.

"Can you get out of the canyon anywhere?" Anna asked.

"There's a rough trail up out of the slide on this side of the river. Very rough. More of a climb, but I wouldn't be anywhere when I got there. The best bet is for me to float out the mouth of the canyon. There's a road there. It's paved and well used. Eventually I'd find somebody with a cell phone."

"How long would it take you to float out?"

Carmen mused for a moment and stared at the river. "It's eight miles out. A few hours, maybe." Carmen would be floating out on her back the way Anna had come down through the rockslide. The river water wasn't particularly cold, and with the cessation of the rain the temperature had risen into the seventies. Even if the sun came out and the air temperatures went into the eighties or nineties, hypothermia could still be an issue, given the woman's long immersion in the river. Anna didn't know enough about rivers to make an informed decision, but it didn't strike her as a sound plan.

"I could make it," Carmen said. Anna heard an echo of herself in the guide's words and it was not reassuring.

"Rafters will be along soon," Anna said, because it was as true as it was untrue and it was always good to look on the bright side.

"Unless you need me here, I'll go beachcombing with Paul."

"Anything we get is bound to be a plus," Anna said.

"Keep a sharp eye out for the groover," Steve said from his position as bed warmer. "Good hygiene is important in times of stress."

The Kessler twins almost made up for Lori and Chris sie. Anna didn't see the four of them as fast enough friends to plan another river trip together.

The unconscious woman wore a single white sneaker, brown now with the silt—the Rio Grande had taken the other one. Anna unlaced it and took it off. Her feet were narrow and swollen. Too much baby for her fragile bones. The soles were soft and the toenails filed and painted.

"Chrissie, I've got a job for you," Anna called. The two girls were still hovering at the edge of the overhang, hating to stay but too scared to go.

Chrissie didn't move.

"A good job," Anna said.

With a sigh that could have been heard in the back row from the stage at Madison Square Garden, Chrissie trudged over. "Kneel here and rub her feet, try and warm them up with your hands."

"Her *feet*?" Chrissie complained.

"Jesus did feet. Doing feet was very fashionable then," Steve volunteered.

"You're Jewish, what do you know about Christ," Chrissie grumbled, but she knelt in the space Anna had vacated and took the feet into her lap.

"He was a Jew," Steve said.

"Don't be stupid." Chrissie set her lips in a thin line and began rubbing the woman's feet with a gentleness that, given the source, startled Anna. Perhaps the old saw was right; perhaps there was some good in everyone.

Anna put Lori at the woman's head to serve as pillow. If there was any spinal injury the poor thing had been bashed around and manhandled so much, elevating her head a few inches wasn't going to make matters any worse. It might make breathing a bit easier and a lap would be warmer than the ground, but mostly Anna did it for Lori. She was uninjured, but too quiet and docile; shock could be induced by fear as well as cold and pain. Giving her something constructive and distracting to do would help.

From upstream a shout of victory melted through the river sounds. Moments later Carmen came back at a jog, waving a cell phone over her head. "Dry and charged," she said triumphantly.

"What are the odds?" Anna asked, and let relief wash

over her. "Dial nine-one-one. I never thought it would feel so good to say that."

"Does this mean the human hot-water bottles may get up?" Cyril asked. "Easter might be ready to eat a little."

"Not yet," Anna said. "Unless Easter wants to take your place. Ever read Steinbeck's *The Red Pony*?" Cyril hadn't and, feeling magnanimous because of the satellite phone miracle, Anna didn't describe the cutting open of the horse and crawling inside to keep from freezing.

"Damn. I've got a signal but no connection. Sat phones are amazing but not infallible. There are places they can't get out, and deep in narrow canyons are them. I think if I climb up a ways I'll be able to get a call out."

"What do those things cost?" Steve asked, his head held up at an awkward angle so he could look at Carmen without peeling any part of his physical and warm self from his patient.

"Twelve bucks a month," Carmen said, and not without a touch of smugness.

"No!" Steve yelped. "Nooooo." In a day of shocking happenings, clearly this was the most disturbing to the Princeton student.

"The federal government picks up the tab," Carmen said. "The poor folks in Terlingua were designated among the lucky few who required sat phones for life, liberty and the pursuit of happiness. Every rusting trailer and tumbledown shack has a satellite phone."

Steve groaned and let his head fall back to the ground.

The clouds had gone, at least from the narrow strip

visible above the canyon rims but, even with the blue, there was little light left in the day. "Can you get up and back before dark?" Anna asked. Boulder hopping without good light was a dangerous proposition.

"Maybe," Carmen said. "I'll stop before the point of no return."

She left, again at a jog. Anna loved her strength and energy. Carmen lived below the poverty level—the subsidized sat phone proved that. From what she'd heard, she lived without running water in an abandoned miner's shack. A goal of Carmen's was to get entirely "off the grid," whatever that meant. Her work was hard physical labor overlaid with the skills needed to keep rich tourists happy and safe. Still, there was a lot to be said for a life lived outdoors and close to the bone. At forty Carmen was vital and strong. She wasn't worried about how much she weighed; a slice of cake wasn't an evil adversary. She smoked when she wanted to and drank bourbon when her day was done and slept on the ground without nightmares.

A flicker of the wildness that had drawn her to the wilderness, the parks and law enforcement sparked in Anna. It died when she turned back to the five people on the ground under the lowering brow of the cliff face.

"Her eyes are open," Lori said in a wisp of a voice.

Anna squatted at the woman's head. "Hey," she said. "Nice to have you back among the living."

Paul returned, dragging a dry-bag. Things were looking up.

"My baby, take my baby," the woman whispered. Her

eyes didn't close but the life went from them. Anna had seen life wink out before. There was no great exhalation of air, there were no celestial choirs, her head did not flop dramatically to one side. Just in one instant there was a person behind the eyes. Then there wasn't.

She laid two fingers on the woman's carotid. No pulse beat there. She tried the wrist, listened at the nostrils and watched the chest.

"She's dead," Anna said. "You guys can get up if you want." Chrissie dropped the feet and crabbed backward as if the meat left behind when the soul had fled was contaminated. Cyril and Steve climbed slowly and stiffly to their feet. Only Lori stayed, cradling the woman's head in her lap with something akin to compassion.

"Is the baby dead too?" she asked softly.

"Not yet," Anna said. "But it will be."

Lori began to cry silently.

"Shit," Steve said.

"Do something," Cyril begged.

"Paul, did I give you back your pocketknife?" Anna asked.

TEN

Paul handed Anna the jackknife. She knelt beside the drowned woman and began cutting away her clothing.

"What are you doing?" Chrissie gasped. She hadn't bothered to stand from her crabbing position and sat in the sand where her rump had first touched down.

"C-section," Anna said. She had never done anything of this sort before. The closest she'd come was watching an old Jane Fonda movie where the heroine saves a victim by giving him an emergency tracheotomy with a pair of scissors or a Bic pen or something.

"You'll kill her!" Chrissie almost screamed.

"She's already dead. His mother isn't breathing for him anymore," Paul explained gently. "Anna's going to try and save the baby. If she doesn't get it out of the womb quickly, the little guy will suffocate."

"Jiminy Cricket," Steve said, sounding all of six years old.

Anna peeled back the wet rayon to reveal the woman's belly, smooth and brown and swollen. She laid her hand on it and the skin was warm. The woman's arms and legs and face were cold but nature had sent what heat there was to the fetus. Life must go on. Nothing moved beneath her palm. The baby was still and Anna wondered if a fetus could die of shock.

"Here goes," she said, sounding as unprofessional as she felt at the moment.

"Shouldn't you sterilize yourself or something?" Cyril asked.

Anna had been acutely aware of how germ-laden she and her surgical instrument must be, but there was nothing for it; no soap, alcohol or fire.

Resisting the compulsion to wipe the blade on her shorts, she said nothing. Cyril didn't ask again.

Anna ran her hands down the woman's abdomen, trying to feel where the little person inside began and ended, visions of thrusting the blade of Paul's jackknife into a tiny eye or through a soft skull dancing like poison plums in her head. A handspan above the pubic bone the uterus softened. If any bit of the baby inhabited that part of the womb it was a hand or a foot. Nothing too vital. Except that a filthy knife amputating a miniature finger couldn't but give a kid a rotten start on life. If it were still alive.

Anna walked her fingers down till they were on solid bone. "Paul, could you rifle through the dry-bag you rescued and see if there is anything to wrap this baby in?" She didn't add, "if I don't kill it first," but she was thinking it.

"Right," Paul said. Like the others, he'd been standing transfixed by the prospect of horror, gore, salvation, death and rebirth. That, and the prospect of a pocketknife slicing into the turgid belly of a dead person. He sounded relieved to have been released from the trance.

"You might not want to watch this," Anna said to Lori, who still had the woman's head in her lap.

"I'm okay," Lori said softly and lifted a wet strand of hair from the woman's face as if it could still bother her.

"Suit yourself," Anna said.

Cyril, Steve and Chrissie had pressed close, none of them making a sound. "Back off," Anna said. "You're in my light."

They circled around so they were on the cliff side of the overhang. Anna could feel them hovering above her shoulders like sentient storm clouds.

"If anybody passes out or throws up on me, they are next to go under the knife," she warned.

Then she forgot about them, her attention narrowed to the tip of the knife. Pressing firmly, she pushed the blade through the cooling flesh till it hit bone. Though the mother was dead, Anna winced as if the cut could still cause her pain. Sawing a little to work the small blade through flesh and muscle, Anna made a cut about four inches long up from the pubic bone toward the sternum. Blood oozed around the knife but, without a heart to push it, it was minimal. Gifts from the dead.

When the incision was long enough, she put her left hand into it, her fingers feeling their way carefully. The blood was still warm. Her fingers traced the bone then slipped off into the uncharted territory of the abdomen.

From behind her she heard the thump of something hitting the sand and turned her head briefly. Paul had fainted. He lay in a heap beside the opened dry-bag, his arms full of sleeping bag.

Anna turned back to her work. Turning her hand palm up, she made a tent of the skin and began to cut with her right hand, her left between the knife's tip and the fetus. As the blade dragged its trail of dark blood upward, Anna felt a nudge against the back of her left hand. The fetus was protesting this unceremonious rescue.

"The baby's alive," Anna said, and was surprised to hear the exultation in her voice.

"Hurrah," was whispered by one of the twins. It passed like a zephyr near Anna's ear and she knew they had pushed closer than before. She didn't tell them to back off again. She needed the company.

Rustling and grumbling let her know Paul had regained consciousness. Anna risked a glance at Lori to make sure the girl wasn't sliding into a shocky oblivion. Lori looked more focused than she had since the raft had overturned; there was nothing in her face but compassion.

Resisting the urge to hurry, Anna continued the incision till the knife scraped against the sternum. In the wake of the blade the belly spread the cut open. Paul's voice penetrated Anna's concentration.

"Oh Lord. Look at that." It was a prayer, given in wonder and awe.

Anna pulled her hand free of the drowned woman's viscera and looked back where she'd made the opening. A tiny hand, fat as a starfish and scarcely bigger than a half-dollar, was reaching out of the incision. "Holy smoke," she said.

"It's *alive*!" Steve said in the voice of horror movie starlets and Cyril laughed.

"It's covered in blood," Chrissie complained.

Paul knelt on the other side of the corpse.

"Are you going to pass out again?" Anna asked. She sounded harsh but she didn't want a hundred and sixty pounds of sainted sheriff crashing down on her baby.

"No."

Anna handed Paul the bloody knife, then slowly insinuated both hands into the abdominal cavity. She cradled the baby's head in one hand and its buttocks in the other and lifted it delicately from its mother's womb.

Cyril had brought over the sleeping bag. "The dry-bag didn't keep things all that dry," she apologized, "but I found a bit that the river missed."

She knelt beside Paul and made a cradle of her arms, the sleeping bag a hammock between them.

The fetus—a person now with rights and privileges, an American citizen—lay quietly in Anna's hands. The face was perfect, smooth and relaxed, all the tiny fingers and toes in place. Anna had not sliced off a single one.

"It's a girl," Anna said.

"Wish we had some cigars," Steve murmured from behind her.

"You're supposed to hold it by its feet and whack it," Chrissie said knowledgeably.

The girl wasn't breathing. Anna bent over the child, put her mouth over its mouth and nose and sucked gently. Warm salty liquid came into her mouth. She spat it to one side. The baby looked at her, made a wet gurgling sound and, breathing, closed its eyes again without having uttered a single cry.

"What a trouper," Paul said.

Anna laid the little girl in the down nest Cyril had made for it. Cyril folded a bit of the bag over the baby, the rest trailing sodden and enormous from her to the dry-bag it had been liberated from.

"You have to wash it and cut its cord off," Chrissie said.

"Do you think it could get any milk from its mom?" Anna was asking Paul. The issue of whether dead women lactate for a moment after death wasn't one she'd ever had the need to consider.

"I don't think so. The milk isn't there right away. It has to come in. I think the baby's nursing is what triggers it."

"Too bad. I need a couple strips of cloth to tie the cord." Anna turned back to what she could do rather than what she could not.

Paul cut and tore two strips of fabric from the sleeping bag piled between him and Cyril and handed them to Anna. She tied them on the cord a couple of inches apart then cut between the ties. As she severed the umbilical cord it occurred to her that the second tie wasn't necessary. The mother was beyond any danger of bleeding to death.

For what seemed like a very long time, none of them moved or spoke. They simply watched the baby, held cuddled now in Cyril's arms, nothing but her face showing from the nest of down.

"She needs a name," Steve said at last.

"Maybe she has one. Her father may still be living."

"If he is, why was the mother swimming about in a raging river all by herself two minutes before she was about to give birth? Her father is a dink," Cyril said sharply.

"An aunt, then. Or a grandmother," Anna said.

"She needs a river name," Steve insisted. "It will do irreparable psychological harm to the infant if, during its early developmental stage, it is referred to as *it*."

"They name them at the orphanage," Chrissie said.

"Oliver Twist," Steve suggested. "Call her Ollie for short? Does anybody still go to orphanages?"

"How about 'Anna,'" Lori said. "Anna saved her."

"No," Anna said. She shook her head and repeated: "No." The prospect filled her with dread. In a moment of pure pagan superstition she believed if the child were named Anna she would be burdened with a lifetime of memories of violence and death.

"I found her," Chrissie declared. "How about Christine if we're going that route."

"Helena," Paul said. "Santa Elena is a bastardization of Saint Helena. The name Helena means 'light' or 'torch.' She's the patron saint of empresses."

"Perfecto," Steve said.

"Helena Christina," Chrissie said.

"Get off of it, Chrissie," Cyril said mildly. "Ugh, I got to get up before I can't." Reaching across the butchered corpse of the mother, she held the baby out to Anna.

"I like babies well enough," Cyril said as Anna awkwardly gathered the little creature into her embrace. "But, hey, I got the cow."

"Fair is fair," remarked her brother.

"I didn't get anything," Chrissie complained.

"That is because you were not a good little girl this year," Steve said reasonably. "Come on, Lori. I think the dry-bag Paul found is yours. Help us rifle through your worldly goods in search of loot."

The students left.

Anna, Paul, Helena and the corpse were left under the shale shelf.

"Bring Easter over and we'd have a nativity scene," Paul said.

"A pretty gruesome one," Anna said. "Poor old Mother Mary kicked the bucket."

"You didn't kill her, you know that."

Anna did and felt no guilt on that score. Even if she had killed the baby with her amateur surgery she would have felt no remorse, sadness perhaps and a sense of failure, but not guilt. Both would have died had they not met up with her.

"Somebody did," Anna said.

"Carmen seems to think it was an accident."

"Maybe," Anna said. "But look at her crotch."

"No."

"Oh. Okay. When I was pulling down her panties to make the first cut I saw that she had a Brazilian bikini wax. Her hands and feet are soft and her nails manicured. I don't add those together and get a desperate Mexican mother-to-be wading the river in search of medical assistance."

Paul said nothing for a while. The sun had returned and Anna welcomed the heat. Life was easier to deal with when one's feet weren't wet. She was getting comfortable holding Helena. The feeling that she would either drop her or crush her trying not to had passed. She was dimly aware of the positive sounds of the rest of the group as they began to get warm and dry.

"Somebody put her in the river," Paul said, trying out the idea.

"Somebody dressed her in a cheap dress and put her in the river. The pedicure, manicure and wax would pay for ten dresses like the one she was wearing."

"She was about to give birth to a child and was . . . what? Hit on the head, maybe. Chloroformed, maybe. Something nonlethal but that incapacitated her in such a way, should there be an autopsy, it would indicate she had drowned." Paul tried that thought on for size.

"It seems a bit draconian and complex," he said after

a bit. "The murderers I deal with are more hapless individuals with poor impulse control and major anger issues."

"Help me up?" Anna asked.

Paul stood and steadied her as she rose from her knees, the baby in her arms. It would have been easier if she'd handed him the child then scrambled up in the usual way, but Anna wanted to hang on to Helena for a while. Though, in truth, the baby would probably be safer with Paul—he knew babies, he could baptize them, marry them, bury them and arrest them as necessary in between—Anna couldn't shake the sense that Helena was only truly safe as long as she held her.

"I guess you're supposed to feed tiny citizens," Anna said when they'd left the shade for the warmth and cheer of the sunlight.

"She'll last till the cavalry comes."

Anna had completely forgotten about Carmen, climbing up the rockslide in search of a passing satellite to bounce her cell phone call off of. She and Paul walked toward the river, where they could look back at the slide where it tumbled down from the canyon's rim.

"I don't see her," Anna said. "Maybe she's all the way out by now."

"No, there she is." Paul stepped behind her and pointed so she could follow the line of his finger with her eyes.

"Nearly to the top," Anna said.

The kids stopped strewing the contents of Lori's drybag in the sun and looked where Paul was pointing. A hundred or so feet from the top of the canyon wall, Carmen was crawling to the top of a giant's stair-step of rock.

Steve cupped his hands around his mouth. "Hey," he called. "We've got a baby."

Carmen got to her feet and, hands on hips, looked down at them. "What?" she yelled back.

"A girl. A baby girl," Steve hollered. He scooped the baby from Anna's arms and held it to the sky, the sleeping bag dragging on the ground.

Carmen hooted a gleeful sound and waved both hands over her head.

There was a sharp cracking sound like that of a paddle smacking the side of a metal canoe and the guide pitched forward. Her body left a red smudge where it hit the next ledge twenty feet below, then bounced and was gone from sight in the boulder field.

ELEVEN

Charles Pierson was looking every inch the tortured Ashley Wilkes. His stylishly cut blond hair, usually blow-dried to perfection, fell across his wide brow as if he'd been running his hands through it, and lines of tension pulled the skin tight beneath his pale blue eyes. With his innate sense of what was right for any occasion, he'd dressed in light gray linen trousers and a dark shirt, not quite a suit but classy, a good mix of casual wilderness and sharp big city. The expensive pleated trousers were creased where he'd crossed and uncrossed his legs and the black shirt had blond hairs on the shoulders.

Charles had chosen to wait for his wife on the veranda—that or Judith had thrown him out. At home, they slept in separate bedrooms and, for the most part, lived separate lives. When he traveled with Judith she insisted they share a room, if not a bed. It would not look right to constituents to be seen as suffering marital discord or, worse, exhibiting the habits of old money.

"How's our girl?" Darden asked.

"What?" Charles looked at him as if seeing him for the first time. "Oh," he said. "Judith. She's Judith." He looked past Darden as if waiting for someone more interesting to come up the flagstone steps from the parking lot.

For the briefest of moments Darden wondered if he had an inkling of what Judith had planned for him, and a feeling that, when he was younger would have been guilt, flickered and went out in Darden's breast. There'd been too many bodies under the bridge for Darden to suffer true remorse for one more, but some jobs were more odious than others.

"I'd better get cleaned up." Darden excused himself and went into his cabin.

In the tiny old bathroom with tile nearly as old as he was, Darden stood under the shower and let the hot water rinse the dust from his hair and skin and tried to foresee the future. For all his civility, Charles was a loose cannon. He'd proven that back in his college days at Oxford. The woman he'd fallen for, the woman Darden knew from her morgue picture, had been one of his professors. English teacher, if Darden remembered right, *Beowulf.* And not the type that usually drove men mad with desire: a little overweight, nice enough looking in a domestic intellectual kind of way—nice but smart, too preoccupied to waste time on hair and makeup.

According to what Darden had been able to glean from the sparse information on this era of Charles's life, Pierson went nuts for his little English woman. Head over heels, bonkers, followed her around in a way that was tantamount to stalking.

At least that was how her husband described it shortly before he threw Darden out of his rooms. Phillip Amblin, too, was a professor at Oxford and somewhere in the neighborhood of three decades older than his nice little wife. Like the handful of others who knew the ins and outs of the affair, the professor would not talk about it.

Public records told Darden Mrs. Amblin had died in a car wreck. A student, Mr. Charles Pierson of America, had been first on the scene. The scene was a foggy night on a seldom traveled country lane in Somerset. The official report deemed it an accident due to speeding and poor visibility.

After the incident Charles disappeared for three years. Darden hadn't been able to find out where he'd spent his time, whether his family had whisked him off to some small country house or he'd gone vagabond or into a lunatic asylum. After the three years passed he emerged back on the Houston social scene and would only smile enigmatically when asked where he'd been all that time.

Judith met him at a fundraiser for the library association and pursued him until he married her, more out of exhaustion than love, Darden had thought more than once. He'd had a couple of previous dalliances but Darden sensed no real passion in them, more desultory boredom on the part of both parties.

Darden doubted Judith had any idea of what Charles was capable of when roused to a passion. She'd never seen it. Maybe that was part of the draw; she sensed a passion there but had never been able to tap into it herself. It kept her always trying and always hurt and always angry. Anger went two ways in Darden's experience, out or in. Out it became violence in its myriad forms—spite, backbiting, shooting, undermining, stabbing, belittling, battering—in and it became depression. Judith was not the depressive sort. Considering what she had in mind for her husband, Darden couldn't but think she was acting the fool.

When Darden emerged from his room dust-free and dressed in a suit and tie, Charles was pacing the veranda. "Would you tell Judith I've gone down to the lodge?" Darden asked as Charles turned at the far end beyond Gordon and Kevin's room and started back, one hand thrust in his pocket, ruining the line of his trousers, the other raking through his hair.

Charles showed no indication that he'd heard, though they were nearly close enough to shake hands. Darden gave up and knocked softly on Judith's door.

"I heard," she called from inside. "Go."

Darden smiled. Judith was in full politician mode, every fiber of her being focused on what she could say that would catapult her to the next level. Walking down the flagstone steps he heard the *skritch* of flint on steel and looked back over his shoulder. Charles was lighting a cigarette. Cigarettes in public were a no-no.

Anger in its myriad forms.

Gordon was already in place at the lodge dining room, crisp and professional-looking in his dark suit. Tonight was for the big guns; tonight Darden didn't want to blend in. The public needed to see that Judith was important and powerful. Nothing spoke of power like the suggestion that there were those who so feared or hated one that bodyguards were a necessity. Darden had known more than one wannabe politico unworthy of anybody's bullets who spent a fortune on protection just so it would look as if he were important enough to kill.

"Keep an eye on Charles," Darden said. "If anybody is going to do Judith in tonight it's going to be him. He's strung out and feeling reckless. I saw him lighting up outside Judith's room."

"Whoa," Gordon said. Though he didn't smoke, Kevin did, and they knew there'd be hell to pay when Judith caught a member of her entourage in the act. She figured if she could see it, the public could see it.

"We might have another snag, boss," Gordon said. He didn't look at Darden as he spoke, and Darden didn't look at him. Standing shoulder to shoulder as if they were on inspection, both of them watched the room rather than each other. It was a habit Darden had trouble picking up for work and setting down for his leisure time.

His mother and the few women friends he saw on a regular basis complained about it. They said it looked like he was just killing time talking to them while he looked around for something better to do.

"Such as?" Darden asked.

"Martinez. He was around this morning looking like a rain cloud. I wouldn't put it past him to try something."

"That's all we need. Doesn't he have a canoe to paddle or something? Drat."

Frederick Martinez was the river district ranger. Darden had been warned about him by the head of the convention when he was setting up Judith's visit. Martinez was an American, but just barely. Darden didn't have anything against immigrants. Every American was an immigrant; the only difference was what time their boat landed. Even the Indians were said to have walked across from Russia or somewhere. What Darden didn't like were immigrants who wanted to be Americans to get the goodies but wanted to be known as whatever they were before: Iranian, French, Mexican, African. Wanted to open the borders so their pals could thunder to the trough but wanted to keep their native "culture." Whatever the heck that meant. What it meant to Darden was that they didn't want to be Americans. They wanted to use Americans.

That was how he had Martinez pegged at first. The guy had been born in Texas but only because his mama had the guts to make it happen. She and his dad were Mexican nationals who hadn't a pot to piss in back in old

Mexico. After discreetly investigating the guy, Darden had to admit he was more than that. He was a fanatic. According to Martinez, the greatest crime ever committed in Big Bend National Park wasn't murder or rape or drug running or stealing lizards, snakes or cacti, it was closing the border. He'd been fighting to get it reopened for over eight years. He'd made a racket but accomplished nothing. Border closings were done in rooms the likes of Martinez would never see. Ninety-nine-point-nine percent of citizens would never see. When edicts came down from on high, the veil of "national security" cloaking them, they were harder to protest if the hoi polloi didn't know who to protest to, which office to march in front of with their adorable little signs and bulk-mail logo-ed T-shirts.

Darden didn't doubt that Ranger Martinez was positively panting to use Judith's party as a soapbox for his cause. If he'd found out Judith was running on a build-the-wall-and-man-the-watch-towers border control platform he might do more than that. If he could get past Darden first.

"Speak of the devil," Gordon said, and gestured out the picture windows with a twitch of his square chin.

"You keep an eye out for Ranger River Rat," Darden said. "I'll see if I can't keep the press happy." Again they had gathered on the patio. Smoking in public didn't damage a journalist's image.

As Darden shook hands, slapped backs and made jokes—what Judith referred to as his warm-up act—he saw Charles walking alone down the slope from the cabins. Head down, cell phone pressed hard to his ear, Charles was walking fast. His shirt had come untucked in the back and his hair had graduated from mussed to standing on end over his ears where he'd been raking at it. The plan was for him to arrive hand in hand with his wife just after the party started so the conventioneers would see a charming picture of good grooming and marital bliss set against the magnificent backdrop of the Chisos Mountains.

Christ on a crutch, Darden thought uneasily. The man was unraveling and Judith was about to pull out the last thread unless Darden intervened.

Darden moved around to the side of the patio away from Charles, dragging the eyes of avid newshounds with him. A political spouse looking like something the cat dragged in would draw journalists like dog droppings drew flies. He scanned the faces of the reporters to see if any one of them had caught sight of Charles in his dishabille. Nobody had, but when he got to Gerry Schneider she was studying him as intensely as he was studying the fourth estate. She smiled and tipped the brim of an imaginary hat at him. Maybe Gerry hadn't seen Pierson, but she'd read in Darden's face that something was afoot. What Darden the man liked in Gerry— hard work, hard knocks, hard edges and lots of laughs—Darden the security guy didn't.

She'd be sniffing like a pig after truffles till she rooted it out.

Careful not to glance in Charles's direction again, he continued briefing the newspaper reporters. The drill was so familiar he didn't need to put a lot of thought into what he was saying, and his mind churned on possible solutions to the whole Charles thing. He didn't like working behind Judith's back, but it was beginning to look like that would be better than the alternative.

TWELVE

A second shot followed close on the first and Paul began shouting: "Get down! Get down!"

"Where is he?" Anna asked no one in particular. At a guess the shooter was on the canyon rim and either shot Carmen in the back, pitching her forward, or he was on the opposite side and the bullet had caught her low enough that her center of gravity and the pull of the earth had pitched her forward. From the rim, the six of them—seven if one counted Helena—were fish in the proverbial barrel.

"Get down!" Paul was shouting at her this time. Steve still held Helena. Anna grabbed his wrist and began running toward where the boulders nested at the bottom of the slide, the only place there was cover from a sniper above. The alcove would work if the shooter was on the American cliff. If the shots came from Mexico, running to the alcove would only serve to make the barrel a little smaller and the fishes easier targets.

Her sense of self-preservation as keen as everything else relating to her self, Chrissie sprinted for the rocks. Lori was huddled on the beach trying to squeeze herself beneath a rock not quite big enough to shelter a Labrador retriever. Anna couldn't see Cyril; she'd retired to the other side of the line of boulders to commune with her cow. A third shot rang out. The stinging sound of a ricochet cut past Anna's ear and she felt herself lifted off her feet and flung forward. For a sick moment she thought she'd been hit but it was Paul catapulting her, Steve and the baby into a narrow space between two square slabs of shale, new enough to the canyon that the cliff they'd fallen from still had matching holes where they'd once been.

Between the stones, Anna took the baby from Steve and he folded like a jackknife, pulling his long legs up under his chin, trying to get as much of his long form into as little a space as possible. Anna crouched as low as she could and still keep her upper body over the newborn. Warmth and weight squashed her down farther and she realized Paul was curled over her much as she curled over Helena.

Anna appreciated the sentiment but she didn't like being held captive and, awkward with the baby in her arms, wriggled out of her husband's protective embrace. Like as not both her gesture to shield the infant and Paul's to shield her were pointless in the face of modern weaponry. Mattel was probably making BB guns whose pellets could pass through a target as soft and squishy as a human body. The knowledge allowed her to move away from Paul. Oddly, it didn't allow her to stop shielding the baby. She was surprised the instinct to protect the young survived so strongly in her.

Paul must have realized his bone and muscle, impressive though his wife found it, was not sufficient to stop speeding bullets. He joined her and Steve where they sat, backs to the shale, feet pulled in close to their buttocks.

"I'm guessing the canyon rim above the slide on the American side," Paul said. "The way she fell forward when she was hit."

"Could be," Anna said noncommittally.

"Carmen told us this happened a few years back," Steve said. His voice was as rich and fat as ever. If he was scared it did not reach unto his vocal cords. "A couple rafters died. Mexican boys were shooting at the raft just to scare them. Just for the fun of it. One guy limped out of the river and they figured they'd hit him so they shot him and the other guy—killed them—because they got scared they'd get in trouble for the leg shot. Turned out the guy had a limp from something else altogether."

"Sheesh," Paul said in a whoosh of sadness for all mankind.

"If it's Mexican boys they've gotten awfully good," Anna said. "Carmen went down with the first shot."

"Practice makes perfect," Steve said. Then: "I've got to go." He started to unfold.

Anna was too shocked by the sudden announcement of departure to do much more than gape. Paul grabbed what he could reach of the younger man and dragged him back down on the sand.

"Don't be stupid," Anna said.

"Go where?" Paul asked.

"Sis and her cow are somewhere. Maybe our shooter is a cattle rustler. Cyril would probably go *mano a mano* with el Diablo for one of her critters."

Steve seemed concerned, but not overly so. Anna wondered if he felt his sister the way twins are said to sense each other, and knew she was okay.

"I'll go," Anna said. Paul started to protest. Smaller than Paul and shorter than Steve, she could hide better. She shoved the baby into her husband's arms, a ruse used to make women ineffective for thousands of years. It worked just as well on men.

As she crawled down the tiny canyon they'd taken refuge in she could hear him murmuring orders to Steve, hoping they could get Lori to a safer place without endangering her or themselves.

In Anna's mind was a sketchy map of the scattered rocks between the alcove and the cow. If she stayed low and headed toward the cliffs she should be able to get over with a minimum of exposure. The last shot had been close, the shooter aiming to kill or frighten her or Paul or Steve. To what end she couldn't imagine, but there was sufficient universal malice floating around, killers no longer needed motive, just opportunity. Like the Mexican boys Steve told them about, some didn't even have their own reasons, just blind boredom. The sense of consequences, or of good and evil, or even of tomorrows was missing from their psyches; a quirk of evolution, people becoming like the overcrowded rats in an experiment and turning to murder to keep the species at a sustainable number.

Or the fundamentalists had it right; God and Satan warred for the earth using hapless human saps to man the front lines.

Anna had made her share of enemies over the years but she doubted any of them were dedicated enough to her demise to travel all the way to Texas, find her on the river and take her out. There were many more practical places and easier ways to commit murder. It was hard to imagine anyone not loving Paul Davidson, but those whom he had sent to Parchman Farm for an extended stay probably didn't feel as warm and fuzzy about him as she did. Most of them were poor; most had never been out of the state of Mississippi; most never expected life to deal them a better hand. Traveling across the great state of Texas to shoot the local sheriff didn't make any more sense than her old nemeses doing her the same courtesy. As a rule, criminals were a lazy bunch, not given to seeing tasks through. Otherwise they'd have gone into a field that paid better and had health benefits. Had there not been a woman caught dying in a strainer, Anna would have opted for the chance shooter. The two things taken together were a bit thick for the universal-malice theory.

She had crept closer to the cliffs and was going belly-down to squeeze through the opening left beneath two boulders that had crashed together. Water seeped through her clothing. If she remembered right this area had been dry an hour earlier. The river was still rising. Rain in the Coahuilas. The beach they'd washed up on was narrow and level. If the water continued to rise it would be inundated in fairly short order, forcing the seven of them up out of the sanctuary of the stones.

She chose not to think about that. Suffering pangs of claustrophobia, she squirmed beneath the shale, propelling herself with elbows and toes.

Given the odds the shooter and the dead woman were somehow connected, it was possible a Mexican national—maybe Helena's father—had reason to hate. It could be he was on the canyon's rim searching the river looking for his wife. It could be he thought they had killed her. If he'd seen Anna opening her up with Paul's pocketknife, that would be a logical conclusion.

Another possibility was that Carmen had been the target. Anna doubted she had money or power or secrets worthy of such notice but she did live in a limited society, a desert Peyton Place, where gossip was rife and sexual tension ran high. A scorned lover could do a lot of damage. She worked with people who knew the river, knew the rockslide and knew, even without the loss of the raft, that the bottom of the slide would be a good place to take a shot. They would probably have the equipment to get to the rim—four-wheel drives or ATVs. The additional shots might have been for fun or an attempt to take out the witnesses. That the witnesses had witnessed nothing but their guide taking a nosedive off a cliff might not matter to the mentally disturbed.

Anna reached the main spine of the litter of shale separating the two areas of the beach. To get to Cyril and her cow Anna had to scramble up a boulder slightly higher than her head and down the far side. For those moments she would be exposed to the shooter regardless of which side of the river he shot from. During her slithering, crawling travels she had tried to be as uninteresting and unseen as possible in hopes the rifleman, if he was still there and hadn't hightailed it after the first spatter of gunfire, would not know she'd moved, that his attention would be elsewhere and by the time he caught her movement and took aim, she'd be down the other side. If he'd followed her progress and had a bead on her, she was a dead woman the moment she was fully exposed on the rock.

Overdramatizing, Anna chided herself. Most shots missed their mark. This guy had hit Carmen but he'd missed with his other two bullets, presuming he was going for a couple more murders and not just having scary fun. One of the Park Service's most famous shootouts was between a ranger and a small airplane pilot bent on taking off on a beach with a load of contraband. It was back when NPS law enforcement rangers carried six-shooters. The ranger and the smuggler were no more than fifty feet from each other. Both fired six shots, reloaded and fired six more. Nobody was hurt. Rifles were more accurate than handguns but whoever was pulling the trigger from the cliffs was at least three hundred yards from his targets.

Anna was not a dead woman the moment she showed herself. Still and all, she wished she'd not put on a raspberry-colored shirt that morning. Taking a deep breath to get up her nerve, she gathered her legs under her to make the first jump to where she could get a foothold.

The sound of yelling stopped her. No words, just raucous sounds and the noise of rocks being pounded together. Paul. He'd been counting off the minutes till he figured she was in place. He was creating a diversion.

Good man, Anna thought, and sprang up the rock. In a bump and a tumble she was down the other side on her hands and knees in river water four inches deep. Still rising. When the heavens thundered retribution and lightning struck sparks from the canyon walls, the rising of the waters seemed appropriate. With sunlight and birdsong it didn't. It felt personal and hostile and unnatural.

No gunshots answered Paul's racket. No bullets pinged off the rocks where Anna had recently been. She scuttled backward under the nearest—and merest—overhang anyway. The tiny beach was empty: no Cyril, no Easter. There wasn't anyplace to hide and Anna got a sick feeling that they'd run for the water, been shot and floated downstream unnoticed while the rest of the party were distracted with saving their own skins.

Anna remembered only three shots—the first that hit Carmen, the second and a third that ricocheted off a chunk of shale near her. That would only leave one for both girl and cow. A tricky shot at best. She knew from experience witnesses are unreliable when it comes to the number of shots fired. Fear made the number seem greater or fear deafened the hearer and made the number fewer. Simply because she was an erstwhile law enforcement ranger didn't immunize her from the phenomenon. Cyril and Easter could have been killed by bullets fired while she was focused on Helena and Paul and safety and she'd never heard them.

The far end of the divided beach was walled off by the huge stones forming the rapids. Water piled up between the rocks, its foam a dirty brown, its force enough to pull trees up by the roots and roll stones the size of trucks. Since Anna had floated through steering the cow, the river had risen at least a foot. Either it would drop soon or they would have to head for higher ground. Slow-rising water was a pain. Flash flood was deadly and, a thousand feet down in a crack, she had no idea what was coming.

Like her brother, Cyril could probably hide in a mail slot. But as far as Anna could see, the boulders between the water and cliff were too close together to provide sanctuary for the cow. Quiet, unmoving, she tried to see around corners and through solid obstacles.

Movement caught her eye and she looked up nearer the cliff where the sand piled up and the Bermuda grass was rich and thick. Cyril and Easter were not hiding anywhere. Basking in sunlight and bucolic splendor, the cow was grazing unconcernedly while the young woman sat cross-legged on the grass talking to her.

Cyril hadn't seen Carmen fall. She'd undoubtedly heard the shots and written the sound off to some non-lethal source. The tranquil scene, unsullied by the knowledge of violent death by gunshot, of fear for life and limb, was in such juxtaposition to the mad race for cover Anna had just left that it was hard to believe she hadn't made the whole thing up, or dreamed it. It remained real enough, however, that she wasn't anxious to dash out from under her rock and join the lovely targets on the green. Staying as close as she could to her big friendly rocks, she worked her way toward the cliff till she was nearer Cyril.

"Cyril," Anna whispered.

Cyril's dark head turned and she shaded her eyes with her hand, her ball cap lost to the river. Anna didn't want to shout. If the rifleman was still around and still feeling hateful, she wasn't going to draw his attention down on them.

"Over here," Anna said softly.

Cyril finally found where this tiny pest of a noise that was Anna was coming from and pivoted around to face her. They were twenty feet apart; she in the sun, Anna tucked in the shadows.

"Is that you, Anna?" Cyril squinted into the glare.

"Yeah."

Cyril waited for Anna to explain why she was cowering in crevasses. Anna didn't know where to begin. "Are you okay?" she asked.

"Easter and me are fine."

"Easter and I," Anna corrected her automatically, and

wondered why the shade of her first and beloved mother-in-law had chosen that moment to visit her mind.

"Why?" Cyril asked.

"Could you come over to me? Walk slowly, okay?"

"What's going on?" Cyril asked as she stood and began to walk casually toward where Anna was hidden. Alarm had crept into her voice. Cyril and Steve were smart kids, smarter than most people, Anna guessed. It hadn't taken her long to figure out that something was very wrong and that her best bet was to do as Anna suggested.

The next leap of logic was easy for the young woman: "Were those gunshots?" she asked as she snuggled into the small alcove where Anna was.

"They were."

"What's with that? Why would anybody be shooting? Hunters . . . Are you guys okay?" she asked, and Anna knew she'd grasped the seriousness of the situation.

"Nobody was hurt but Carmen," Anna said, trying to put the good news before the bad. "She was nearly to the rim of the canyon when the first shot hit her and she fell."

"Dead?" Cyril asked. The younger woman wasn't cold or uncaring; Anna didn't get that sense at all. Cyril was a realist: a shot and a fall from the height Carmen was would probably be fatal.

"I don't know," Anna said. "We can't assume she is. I've seen people survive worse falls than she took, and we don't know where the bullet hit her—or even if it did; it could have been a shard of rock from the impact—

only that there was blood left on the rock where she bounced on her way down."

"We have to check," Cyril said.

"We do," Anna agreed. The prospect of leaving a wounded woman to die alone in a heap of rocks in the desert was too miserable to contemplate. That vision, added to Anna's existing nightmares, and even Paul's arms couldn't shut out the horrors waiting behind closed lids.

"We also have to get ourselves out of here," Anna said.

"Another raft will be along," Cyril returned. "Why not wait? They can take the baby with them and call somebody for us when they get out."

"Look at the river," Anna said.

In the time it had taken Anna to get Cyril's attention and explain what had happened it had come up the beach a yard or more. The ribbon of land they occupied had been reduced from a generous forty feet of sand to less than half that.

"It has quit raining, won't it go down?"

"Not if it's still raining in the mountains."

"I can't leave Easter," Cyril said with that sad and determined edge Anna had heard before.

"If you don't leave the cow I will personally slit its throat," Anna said.

Cyril looked hard into her face. She could see Anna would do exactly what she said she would, whether she wanted to or not.

"Okay," Cyril said, and stood. "We should get back with the others."

Anna had not been chatting in the shade while rivers rose and bodies rotted because she was a lazy beast. She'd been hoping the passage of time would enlighten them in some way, shape or form as to what the shooter was up to. That or give him time to get over his killing rage and leave the premises. "Let me go first," she said. "See if our buddy on the rim is still mad at us."

As she rose and walked back to where they could get over the spit of rocks most easily, she wondered if she was doing Cyril any favors by going first. Maybe she'd bring the shooter's attention to them, and when Cyril showed, he'd be all ready and aimed. The thought didn't take root; she knew that there were too many variables and too much was given to chance to win every hand.

Walking quickly, she hugged the rocks where she could but she couldn't shake the feeling of a bull's-eye on her chest and was aware that she was checking her person for the red laser dot that preceded death on occasion. When nothing untoward occurred she turned around and motioned for Cyril to follow.

No shots. Maybe he was gone. Maybe he was a she. That was a thought that usually came late to law enforcement. Anna was no exception. Violent crime wasn't solely a man's profession, but it tended to stick to the old traditional gender roles: men committed violence in the home and at work, to loved ones and strangers, for profit and sexual entertainment; women committed violence in the home and to family members for the most part. Women tended to outshoot the men in training for some reason, but it seldom translated to shooting animals for the fun of it, or hunting down people.

For now, Anna would think of the shooter as *he*.

She and Cyril scaled the rock, slid down the other side and made their way back to where Paul and Steve waited. Lori was with them now, and Chrissie, having no intention of leaving the really terrific shelter she'd dived into, was carrying on a campaign of questions in an attempt to ascertain precisely whose fault all this was and what they were going to do about it.

"Chrissie is the daughter of Mother's best friend from high school," Cyril said, distancing herself from the complainer.

"Ah," Anna returned.

They squished themselves into the crevice, Cyril tight against her brother, Anna pressing into the comfort of Paul's right arm. Without her knowing how it happened, she was also holding Helena. The baby was so still and quiet Anna wondered if she'd died, and a searing pain rose up from her chest into her throat. Desperately she pressed an ear to the tiny chest and was reassured by a steady pulse of heartbeat.

Coma was her next thought but she resisted the impulse to wake the baby up. If she was sleeping, that was a good thing. If she was comatose, there was nothing that could be done about it.

"Helena's going to get dehydrated," Anna said. "We can drink river water if we have to but I'd hate to give her anything that could induce diarrhea or vomiting. Little as she is, she has no reserves."

"There's some bottled water in the dry-bag we fished out of the river," Paul said.

"That's my water." Chrissie's voice came from the crack next door.

Nobody responded.

"I take it there was nothing in the bag that she could eat," Anna said.

"Not unless she'll eat chocolate-covered cherries."

"Those are mine," Chrissie's disembodied voice said.

"They're melted," Steve called back.

He was answered by a pathetic groan, then: "They're still mine." Steve rolled his eyes.

"Can I hold her?" It was the first time Anna heard Lori speak. It was easy to forget she was there. For no good reason, Anna didn't want to give her Helena, but she did. Lori was more centered, more present when she was caring for someone. Not a bad trait.

"We wait here for the next raft?" Paul was asking Anna.

"Maybe we can't," Anna said.

"The water's way up," Cyril added. "You can really see how far it's risen on the other side."

"Nobody shot at you two. Maybe whoever it was has gone," Steve said hopefully. "We can climb partway up and wait it out. These river things don't last all that long, do they?"

"Depends," Anna said. "But usually, no."

"Good thing we have all those chocolate-covered cherries to live on," Steve said.

"Those are mine," came predictably from the ether. Steve and Cyril joined in on the "mine" to keep Chrissie company.

For a time nobody said anything. Helena's breathing, soft and tiny and regular, comforted Anna in an odd way. The baby was a cradle of life and Anna had, by lucky timing and an old jackknife, been able to preserve that life. It didn't make up for the rest of the mess the world was in but she treasured it anyway.

The silence went from active and listening for dangers from above to empty as thought drained out of brains and it became clear to the Kesslers, to Lori, maybe even to the quiescent Chrissie in her private condo that their leader was dead or dying and that Anna and Paul had no miracles to produce on their behalf.

Unable to remain torpid for long, Anna was the first to rouse. "I've got to find Carmen. She may not be dead."

"Correction," Paul said. "*We've* got to find Carmen."

"We've got to find Carmen," Anna amended. Using the inclusive form of the verb was still new to her.

"I'm getting wet all over again," Chrissie wailed. She was a few feet closer to the river than the rest of them. Steve, closest to the exit of their miniature fortress, leaned out.

"River's at the doorstep," he said.

"We could float down feetfirst, like you showed us with Easter," Cyril said.

"Baby," Anna replied.

"Where did we leave our life jackets?" Paul asked. It

was a rhetorical question. Glad to be on solid ground, they'd all doffed their vests and dumped them by the water's edge. They'd be long gone by now.

The day had worn on; the sun was no longer in the canyon. In the not too distant future it would no longer be in Texas. Darkness might protect them from the rifleman, assuming he was still on the rim, but it would not protect them from the river, and climbing in the dark was not an option.

"We all go," she said. "Paul and I will go first, see if we attract any undue attention from our hateful buddy, and get as close to where we saw Carmen go down as we can. Lori, you take care of Helena for the time being." Anna did not intend to let the plumpish, distracted young woman go boulder hopping with her baby if she could help it. "The four of you come behind us as far as there's cover of some kind. Everybody got that?"

"Easter . . ." Cyril made one last try.

Anna drew her finger across her throat from ear to ear and the younger woman desisted.

Chrissie hurtled into their crevasse, sprawling onto her knees and nearly knocking Cyril over. "It's way wet back there," she said as she bulldozed a place for herself between the twins.

Anna suppressed the urge to deal with Chrissie the way she'd threatened to deal with the cow. "How does that sound to you, Paul?" She wasn't asking her husband to be polite. She—they—needed all the help they could get.

"We need to get the bottled water for the baby," he said. It meant a trip into the open.

"I'll do it," Steve said.

"We should wait here," Chrissie said. "Somebody will come get us. No way I'm going to climb up there and get shot to death."

"I'm afraid of heights," Lori confessed in a rush.

"I've heard drowning is one of the nicest ways to die," Steve said. "Be sure and come back from the Other Side and let me know if it's true."

For once Chrissie had nothing to say.

The faces of the college kids looked pale and drawn. The four of them were tired and scared, hungry and thirsty and in a situation they had never been trained to deal with. The twins were resilient but Lori and Chrissie had not been taught to face adversity. They were products of the Barney generation where everybody always wins, trophies are given all around regardless of which team wins and playground insults are dealt with by the courts. They had been trained to passivity and entitlement, skills that were useless in the present situation. Had they also been trained to obedience it would have helped, but in Barney's world everyone was a leader, regardless of ability.

Anna didn't have any trophies to hand out for not being drowned or shot yet, but she could offer them comfort. She hoped it would be enough to motivate them to climb.

"With luck, when we find Carmen, we'll find her sat phone," Anna said. "Then, when we get to the top, we'll just call park headquarters and they'll send a helicopter for us." Anna doubted Big Bend had a helicopter on tap to rescue people but she thought it would sound spiffier than a three-hour wait while the rangers hiked in or came on horseback. There were backcountry roads in Big Bend but Anna couldn't remember one that ran along the edge of Santa Elena.

That lightened the mood somewhat, and Anna decided to move before the mini-cheer winked out. "Paul, shall we?"

"Let's." He stood, and they chicken-walked over the knees and ankles of the four college kids to the mouth of their personal canyon. Paul was ahead of Anna and stepped out first. He stopped for a moment and she knew he was purposely trapping her in safety behind him in case there was more gunfire.

She poked him in the ribs. "Enough of that, Father Davidson," she said with a laugh.

"Can't blame a man for trying," he said. There was no gunfire, only the sound of rushing water and the deepening of the shadows as the sun traveled farther west. Staying close to the rabble of rocks, Paul walked quickly the few yards to where the ascent began. Anna looked back at the Rio Grande. It had devoured most of the land.

"Steve, Cyril, come ahead," Anna said. "You're inches from getting your butts wet if you stay where you are."

Steve emerged first. He didn't stop and block the way Paul had. Gender equality must have been inculcated in the womb. Cyril emerged from behind him and, as if

Easter knew her savior was about to abandon her, she lowed plaintively. The water would have reached her Bermuda grass dining room, Anna guessed. Cyril's lips thinned but she said nothing and she stopped short of giving Anna a dirty look, for which Anna was grateful. Lori, with Helena in her arms, was next.

The baby was so good, Anna thought. Or so weak. Anna chose good because there was nothing she could do about the other. Chrissie was last. No surprise there. She'd be first to the dinner table, first to line up for dessert, but leave the honor to others when lining up to possibly take a bullet. Clever girl.

Seeing the way she tried to shrink into herself, to surreptitiously shield herself behind the others, Anna almost felt sorry for her. Almost. It was good she'd never gone into teaching or motherhood. She most definitely had her favorites and very little compunction about showing it.

Paul had worked his way up the slide, climbing between boulders on the route Carmen had taken. It could not be called a trail, but was doable with effort. The waters were not going to allow Anna her plan of leaving her rafting mates on the beach while she and Paul reconnoitered. The river was rising steadily and more quickly than before. Maybe it would continue this civilized inundation. Maybe it was heralding a flash flood, the buildup of too much rain in too little time at higher elevations.

They would have to go together.

"I'll take the tail," Anna called to Paul, invisible between the huge rocks. "I'll also take Helena," she said to Lori as she filed past to follow the others into the ascending maze. Lori stopped and with a sigh the size of what a three-week-old kitten might heave, she handed the bundle down to Anna.

There was a crack as if the cliff was breaking in two and Lori fell forward. Blood came out of her throat in a gush. There would be no stopping it. The soft flesh of her throat was blown away, flesh and bone and cartilage splattering the pale gold of the shale, the crumpled body nearly beheaded by the blast.

THIRTEEN

The bullet that killed Lori smashed into the shale by Anna's shoulder and splinters of stone pierced her back. Blood blinded her, dripped down her forehead and into her eyes, ran warm and dead over the backs of her hands. Chunks of Lori's flesh adhered to Helena's makeshift swaddling cloth. Clutching the baby tight to her breast, Anna spun around the corpse and into the rock pile. This shot had come from the American side. Lori had fallen into Anna; the exit wound was in the front of the throat, not the back. Paul and the others were climbing into a death trap. She didn't shout for them to come back. In a minute more there would be no back to come to, only the river, and it seemed as vicious as the man with the gun.

Retching pulled Anna back into the moment. Chrissie,

her face gray beneath her tan, eyes so wide the whites showed around the pupils, was vomiting, the bile running down her front because there was no room to bend over.

"It's okay, it's okay," Anna was saying.

"You've got blood all over you," Chrissie screamed, as if it was Anna's fault, as if she was doing it to scare and harass her. "And . . . and . . ." She puked again.

"I'll buy you a new one," Anna promised the baby as she used the brief respite to try to wipe her face clean with a corner of the down bag Helena was wrapped in.

When Lori's throat exploded out, Anna and the baby had been hosed down with the final pump of her carotid. The human body contained about six quarts of blood. It felt as if half of that had been poured over her face and hair.

Eyes cleared, Anna saw Chrissie again staring at her, trembling, her mouth starting to go soft and stupid.

"Snap out of it," Anna said. "Now. Lori is dead. If you don't get past that you're going to be dead too. You got that, Chrissie? Do I have to slap some sense into you?"

Chrissie's sense of self overcame her horror. "Bitch," she hissed at Anna, and turned abruptly to begin the climb.

"Keep your head down," Anna called after her.

Chrissie didn't look back, just raised one hand and flipped Anna the bird.

Anna wished everyone was as easy to manipulate as Christine Atwater. Life would be a lot less pleasant but a good deal easier.

"She's not dead," she heard Chrissie saying. "She's a bitch."

Given the choice between the two, Anna delighted with bitch.

"Anna?" Paul was in front of Chrissie, too little room to get around her; he held her shoulders between his hands and looked past her. "My God," he said when he got a clear look at her face.

"None of the blood is mine or Helena's," Anna said quickly. "Lori's dead."

The twins had come back with Paul. Cyril perched like a praying mantis one boulder up from Paul, her head below the line of sight from the canyon rim. Steve stood in front of her, his hand resting on one of her sandaled feet.

"I thought he was done," Cyril said. "Why didn't he shoot at us when we were strolling along after you made me leave Easter?"

"He could have shot me when we came out of our cubby," Steve said. "Easier even when I went and retrieved the baby's water."

"Why now? Why Lori?" Cyril finished her and her brother's common thought.

"Why don't you quit yakking and do something about it?" Chrissie demanded.

"I'm sorry," Anna said. "I don't know why Lori or why now or why at all. What I do know is he's not going to kill anybody else. We know where he is and what he is capable of. Don't worry. We're going to be just fine."

"Fine," Paul echoed in his light, warm voice and he

smiled his slow, safe smile. Anna knew he didn't have any better idea of what to do than she did, knew he was as aware of the gravity of their situation as she was. Still the smile and the word settled her nerves as it settled the nerves of the others.

Water coiled cold and dirty around Anna's ankles. "It's coming fast," she told Paul. "Let's see how far up the slide we can get before we've got to show ourselves. Maybe we'll find a spot high enough we can wait this out."

Paul and the Kesslers began a careful ascent up between the boulders. Chrissie didn't move. Anna didn't know if fear or spite or hatred or fatigue glued her feet to the ground. "Maybe we'll find Carmen's sat phone," Anna said. "You could call home on it."

The offer of electronics and contact with civilization did what flood and gore failed to. With a huff that sounded so much like the word *harrumph* Anna had seen in books over the years that she almost smiled, Chrissie began hauling herself up after the others.

Before following, Anna set Helena down on a flat ledge. The little girl opened her eyes the merest slit. "Hello, little girl," Anna said, and believed she saw intelligence and trust in the infant's eyes. Whether or not it was true or only a trick of the light, she couldn't know. It would be a cruel twist if, after all the baby had gone through, fate chose to snuff out that wee spark.

Anna ripped her long shirttail from hem to armpits and fashioned a rude sling. Immodesty was the least of her worries at the moment and, should a flash of breast offend anyone, they would have to avert their eyes. She needed both hands free. Baby and the scrap of down sleeping bag were stuffed into the makeshift Snugli, then Anna began the scramble up the rock face, leaving water that had risen to her knees.

Shadows had claimed the low places and the maze of rock and scree was dusky in the blue light. Good for the fishes, Anna thought. The closer they hugged the American bank and the deeper they were in shadow, the more difficult they would be to kill. No shots followed the one that killed Lori. Before, Anna had read the shooter's lack of action as his losing interest or being frightened by the carnage and running away. This time she read it as stark professionalism. The guy wasn't going to waste bullets on targets he could not hit.

Whoever it was had shot Carmen, then tried for Anna or Paul or Steve. They'd been so closely grouped there was no way to tell who the bullet was meant for. Then he'd stopped. Anna had been exposed, Cyril, too, and he'd not shot at them. Steve had been an excellent target when he made the short run to get Helena's water before they began the ascent. The rifleman had not fired. Then he'd killed Lori, the most harmless and least interesting of individuals.

It was possible the bullet that killed Lori was meant for Anna, but she'd been a far better target when she and Cyril were returning from the cow side of the beach. If the shooter had a method to his madness, Anna could not see it. She could only see the madness.

As she climbed, she wondered if Easter was drowned, if the cow was struggling to keep horns above water as the flood washed her farther downstream, if she had once again taken to a ledge and was working her way up as she had the first time she'd found herself in this predicament and future rafters would snap pictures of a Mexican cow trapped hundreds of feet above the water and marvel at how she got there. A darker thought intruded and in her mind Anna could hear future generations of river guides pointing out the slide above the rapids and recounting the awful slaughter that had taken place there for the ghoulish delight of their patrons.

It wasn't long before she caught up with Chrissie and had to slow her ascent and suffer the view of the young woman's backside. Chrissie was gasping for breath and emitting little grunts each time she had to pull herself up a step more than a foot high. Scratches marked her arms and one elbow was oozing blood where the shale had scraped off the skin. Anna was proud of her for keeping on. Chrissie might be a selfish little twit, but she wasn't abdicating. Once the choice between climbing or drowning had been given to her, she hadn't crumpled but instead fueled herself with anger at Anna and at the unfairness of the situation and climbed.

Abdicators became as dead weight. Like Lori. Dead weight.

Without any conscious thought on Anna's part the girl's death replayed itself in her mind, the image so real the rocky escarpment before her vanished, replaced by the gout of blood and the woman falling. Anna's foot slipped and she toppled sideways. Sudden movement and fear for Helena brought her back from that black hole where horrors lived on as real and horrific as the moment they had transpired.

"Watch it!" Chrissie snapped, Anna's thud startling her. Maybe under the surliness was a thread of concern. Maybe it was even for somebody besides herself.

"Wow," Anna said as she righted herself, one arm clamped around Helena.

"What now?" Chrissie demanded between gasps.

"Nothing," Anna said.

The baby began to whimper. The pathetic little cries made Anna feel more helpless than the raging Rio Grande and a gunman on the rim of the canyon. "It's okay," she murmured. Helena knew otherwise. Okay was milk and Mom.

The ascent was no more than that of a small building in New York, twenty or thirty flights of stairs at most, had they been able to simply go up. With the twists and turns, dead ends and stops where Paul had to boost and pull people up, the baby passed up like a watermelon from hand to hand, Chrissie heaved up by Anna's shoulder under her butt, and the twins, both tiring and neither with any upper-body strength in their long thin arms, drawn up like bony bits of rope, it was nearly dark by the time they neared the place fifty yards from the top where Carmen had turned and waved and died.

Paul stopped on a wide flat boulder top, adjacent to the slope where Carmen had left blood as she hit the shale. Desert evenings were long and sweet and there was enough light to see the darker smear on the light-colored rock. Cyril and Steve sat, backs to a rock, knees drawn up, taking the opportunity to rest, as Paul strong-armed Chrissie up the last climb to where they waited. Helena was passed up and Anna followed. They tucked themselves tight to the rock with Steve and Cyril, too close in for the killer to get a bead on them.

"I think we should stop here," Paul said. "It's getting hard to see and one of us is going to break a leg if we keep going." He didn't bother to whisper. The racket they made on the climb would have kept their whereabouts broadcast to any listener.

Anna nodded. "I think so too. How much water do we have?"

Chrissie's half-liter water bottle was clothed in a lovely pink nylon carrying case with a Velcro closure for securing it to one's belt. Steve had strapped it to his when he'd retrieved it. Twice during the climb it had been passed around and they all drank sparingly. After Lori was shot, there'd been no recurrence of the "It's mine" theme. On both occasions, Anna had tried to get Helena to take water but she screwed her face up and refused to do more than suck a drop or two from Anna's little finger. In the last half hour she had ceased crying and Anna missed it. Though it had stricken her to the bone, it signified the mite had strength to protest her situation. Now she lay so quiet Anna found herself resting her forefinger on the tiny wrist to see if she could feel a pulse.

Steve shook the water bottle. "Maybe a cup or so," he said. "Want to see if the baby will drink some?"

This ordinary statement was anything but ordinary.

Anna was so thirsty she had to wiggle her tongue around to keep it from sticking to various places in her mouth. Steve had to be as thirsty or more. To offer the gift of water in the desert as if merely passing the salt at the dinner table was a form of grace that Anna couldn't help but admire. She'd never wanted children but, if she could have ordered a pair like the Kessler twins to be delivered fully baked, she might have given it another thought.

"You try and see if she will drink," she said, untangling Helena from the mess of down and ripped linen that had been her home for the past few hours. "We need to find Carmen while there's still a little light."

Steve took the baby with such confidence Anna guessed there were smaller Kesslers in the world.

Anna didn't bother to get to her feet but rolled onto hands and knees and crept to the edge of their platform to peer into the darkening cracks between the boulders under the bloodstain. "Carmen!" she called.

There was no answer and she'd expected none. Fortunately, there were not many places the body could have landed. A couple of yards beneath the ledge they inhabited and beneath the stain on the shale were three enormous blocks of shale, each the size of a mobile home standing on end. They'd sheared from the cliff along fault lines, straight as a die, leaving them as square and neat as if a mason had cut them. They leaned against one another, forming V-shaped crevices twenty or thirty feet deep. Carmen could only be in one or the other of them.

Anna stretched out flat on her belly and stared into the inky bottoms of the two natural shafts. A change of what little light remained in the day made her look back. Paul was standing astraddle her, between her and where the shooter was presumed to be.

"Hey," he said when she looked at him. "This way we go together. For better or worse," he said, and smiled.

Anna had nothing to say to that and turned her eyes back to the dark below.

Carmen had dark hair and wore a dark long-sleeved shirt and black silk long johns; not a great ensemble for being discovered at the bottom of wells or rock falls. Anna crabbed across the ledge to where she could see into the second of the crevices.

"Could that be an arm?" she asked Paul. He knelt beside her. Like a lot of men, Paul was strong but not supple; he couldn't coil up and snake around the way Anna and Cyril could.

He stared into the crack. Then he went and looked down into the crack Anna had first studied. "I think it's our best bet. Too bad we didn't save any rope. That's a ways down and those rocks don't promise anything in the way of foot- or handholds."

"I can do it," Anna said.

"Somehow I knew you'd say that," Paul said. In the thickening dusk Anna couldn't tell if he was smiling or not.

No matter, she had a plan.

"Let's jury-rig whatever we've got for line. Even a few feet might help."

Steve gave up a belt. After some modest twisting and contortion, Cyril offered up a spandex sports bra, and together with Paul's belt and the linen Anna had torn for Helena's hammock, they cobbled together a line close to seven feet long and fairly sturdy.

There wasn't enough that it could be tied off or wrapped around something to create a decent belay, and Paul was the only one with the strength to hold it or use it to pull anyone up. He made no argument as Anna made preparations for the climb down.

Anna was relieved. The arguments had already been made in her head and, evidently, that of her husband. On the slim chance Carmen was alive, a wait till morning could well kill her. Should the shooter be waiting to make another kill, waiting till morning would give him light to aim by. Without water Chrissie and possibly the twins would be too weak to finish the ascent in the morning. Weighed against those, the dangers of Anna making a low light climb seemed paltry.

Paul held the makeshift line and Anna scraped, belly down, feetfirst over the edge of the ledge. With the line to hold on to, the seven feet was an easy descent. Steve handed the baby to Chrissie and he and Cyril took the line to hold it so Paul could follow but Chrissie huffed to life.

"Take this baby," she said as she thrust Helena into Cyril's arms. "I'm going to do it with Steve. I weigh more than you."

Cyril was either too tired or too shocked to protest. Anna watched as the girls changed places and Chrissie and Steve knelt and braced themselves to take Paul's weight. In the end, he didn't use the line. Afraid, probably, that the two college students couldn't hold it. He got most of himself off the ledge, hung on for a moment, then dropped with a thud and an *oof!* to the platform where Anna waited.

"You sure you can do this?" he asked, hands on hips, staring down the crack Anna had chosen to descend.

Close up, it looked wider and deeper.

"It is Carmen," Anna said. Crouching, she could see the pale outline of an arm and part of the guide's face, mere smudges of paleness in the gloom but definitely human in shape. "Carmen!" she called, hoping for a twitch or a moan signifying life.

"I'm pretty sure I can," she answered Paul's question.

"The drop doesn't look as far from here," he said.

Easy to say when he wasn't the one about to go down it.

"No time like the present," Anna said.

She took one end of the line and put it between her teeth. It wasn't long enough to do any good but it served the purpose of Dumbo's white feather: it gave her courage to begin. The top of one of the boulders had been sheared off, forming a steep ramp that funneled down into the space between the two leaning rectangles of rock. More blood was smeared where Carmen had hit, then slid down and fallen after being shot. Anna sat at the top of the slide. Paul lay on his stomach on the flat. She took one of his hands then turned over on her stomach as well, facing him.

Panic gripped her as she felt the pull of the black hole she was being funneled into, a pit like the pit in her soul.

"You don't have to do this," Paul said softly.

"Yes I do," Anna mumbled around the spandex bra strap clamped between her teeth. The phrase *blind panic* was not a metaphor, it was a description. She could see almost nothing. Black tunneled her vision till only Paul's hands remained. Gripping them so tightly she would have broken finger bones had he been one of the twins, Anna loosed the grip her feet had on the funnel's side and let herself slip down the length of her and Paul's extended arms. When she could slide no farther, she forced herself to let go of Paul's left hand, took the line from her teeth and held on to it. Paul closed his fingers around the line.

"Got you," he said.

With a feeling she was letting go of life and sanity, Anna let go of his right hand and gripped the line tightly in her fists. The added couple of yards brought her easily to where the funnel ended and the rocks met. The space between them was no more than a yard wide for the most part, no wider than the average doorway.

Holding tightly to the bra and belts, Anna knelt on the slope and looked down. It was not as far as gloom and fear had suggested. No more than fifteen feet. Carmen, now the merest outline in the growing dark, lay at the bottom.

"It's doable," she said to Paul.

"Be careful."

There wasn't any more line but Anna didn't think she would need it. Lowering her legs into the crack, she pushed hands and feet out to the sides and, braced between the rocks, began to spider-walk down. She made it nearly halfway before she lost purchase on the smooth shale and fell. The chute she was shinnying down flared out near the bottom, and she struck the slanting base of the rock and rolled down.

Her squawk and the forthcoming thump brought Paul's voice down, high and frightened, the warmth gone. "Are you okay?" he shouted.

"Okay," Anna managed, her voice sounding hollow and strange in this dry well. She hadn't fallen and rolled more than a few yards and she had landed on something soft. Carmen. A woman Anna had killed in a similar fashion years before and beneath the surface of the earth in Lechuguilla Cave in New Mexico rushed out of the past and the pit and Anna felt again her knee crushing the throat, felt the weight of a mile of limestone on her neck and chest and she could not breathe.

Rolling off Carmen as gently as she could, Anna found herself crying, great fat tears creeping down her dusty cheeks.

"Wasting water," she whispered. Carmen's eyes were open, catching the last dull gleam of evening from the opening above them. Anna didn't bother with a field exam. The exit wound in the middle of the guide's chest was as big as her fist and the blood around it dry. "Sorry I landed on you, Carmen," Anna said, still crying. "I am glad it wasn't me who killed you, though.

"We need your sat phone. Tell me you didn't fling it from you when the bastard shot you." Anna's tears were stopping. Carmen was a southpaw. Anna felt her way down Carmen's left arm to her hand. The phone wasn't clamped in her fist. "Butterfingers," Anna said, and began sweeping her hand over the ground around the corpse.

"Anna?" Paul called.

"Carmen's dead," Anna answered, and was relieved there was no sign of her recent weeping in her voice. "I'm trying to find her sat phone."

Anna could see her hands moving like pale spiders over the dirt and gravel. She could feel the muck of blood and dirt commingled and nearly dry. She hoped she would not feel an angry scaly creature or wake up a scorpion or tarantula. It was dark enough she'd never see them till they were getting to know each other far better than either party desired. Finally her hand landed on what she'd been looking for, the smooth small rectangle of plastic that could send signals to objects rotating the earth.

"Got it," she called to Paul.

"Hallelujah!" filtered back down the crevasse. "Does it work?"

Anna opened the face of the sat phone. It lit up and displayed the usual options. She chose not to shout the answer to Paul. Knowledge they had a satellite phone might inspire the killer to be more aggressive in his quest. Or it could scare him away. Undecided, Anna slipped it into her pocket.

For reasons rooted in ancient ritual but as necessary now as they'd been then, Anna knelt by Carmen. She straightened the guide's legs, folded her arms on her chest and closed her eyes. That done, she smoothed the hair off her temples and into the braids she wore. This was unquestionably a crime scene and she was messing it up. Since she'd begun the process by dropping eight feet onto the corpse then fondling it and running her hands and scrabbling her feet over every inch of the place, Anna didn't feel any compunction about paying last respects.

"Good-bye, Carmen. The Rio Grande is rising to take you but I doubt even he can climb this high. We'll be back for you.

"I'm coming up," she shouted to Paul. Checking to make sure the sat phone was secure, she crawled up the slanted cut at the bottom of the westernmost rock. The crack narrowed there and she was able to get hands and feet on opposite sides of the chimney without any trouble. Unable to fall up, the ascent was longer and harder than the descent had been. Halfway her arms and legs began the quiver of nearly exhausted muscles.

Another five feet and she knew she was not going to make it.

FOURTEEN

As children Anna and her sister, Molly, had often "chimneyed up" door frames, their small hands and feet leaving dirty prints all the way up. It wasn't a skill Anna had been called upon to use all that much in her adult life: once in Texas and once in Lechuguilla Cave in New Mexico. The idiosyncratic activity relied on muscles seldom called upon. Or so Anna told herself. The possibility that it was age and the more sedentary life of a district ranger, that perhaps the leaping tall buildings in a single bound had been left behind in her salad days, didn't appeal to her at the moment. Caught as she was, hands and feet crabbed out to the walls of the stones in crushed cruciform, there was little she could do if her strength gave out but fall. She'd been lucky she'd done herself no more damage than a few bruises and scrapes when she dropped the last few yards into Carmen's sarcophagus. Now she was a good fifteen or twenty feet from the bottom of the cut. Enough to break a leg or back or neck.

Trying to ease the tension in her muscles while keeping the tension against the rock, she debated whether to try to climb again, try to wedge herself into a position where she could ease and rest for a moment, or holler for help.

"Paul!" she shouted after an exceedingly short deliberation. "I'm stuck."

"Wedged?" he called back.

Getting wedged was funny in the comics. In caves or climbing it wasn't. People wedged between the proverbial rock and hard place often died there.

"No," she reassured him quickly. "I ran out of steam. I don't think I've got the strength to get myself out."

"How far up are you?"

"Too far."

"How far down are you?"

She knew he was thinking of their paltry lifeline of bra and belts.

"Too far."

"Hang on," he said, then began talking rapidly in tones too low for Anna to catch the drift of the conversation.

She thought about trying to throw the sat phone out so they would be able to make a call—if they could get high enough to get a signal without getting their heads blown off—but knew if she moved a hand from the wall to her pocket she'd likely as not lose her tenuous position and join Carmen in more than just physical proximity. It didn't matter in the grand scheme of things. If she could get at it, she couldn't throw it; if she could throw it, it would slide back down into the crack.

The palms of her hands were growing numb where they were splayed against the shale and the quadriceps muscle in her left thigh shuddered from quivering to cramping. Looking up, she noticed a narrow band of gray light, no more than six feet above her head, vaguely crescent-shaped. Rather like a sinister half smile on an evil mouth viewed from the vantage point of the glottis. Don't swallow, Anna prayed to the Rock God.

"Paul?" She tried not to sound too desperate. Paul would be doing everything he could, even if it included stripping everybody naked and twisting rope from their clothes. A good plan, but not timely. By the time the rope was done Anna would also be done.

"Hang on," Paul said again. "A minute, no more. You hang on." He wasn't trying not to sound desperate. "We're coming."

The pit yawned.

Anna did not wish to die today. She had one more son of a bitch to kill before she went gently into anybody's good night. Perhaps Dr. James was right and she did have a calling. Certainly the bastard who shot Carmen and Lori had forfeited his right to a long and happy life.

By force of will she kept the cramp from metastasizing into the rest of the thigh and the calf. "I'll be here," she called back, and was startled to hear the fierceness in her voice.

"You better be. Okay. Ready, Steve?"

Anna's right foot slipped an inch and she ground her teeth trying to find the lock for the bones to hold when the muscles gave out, wedge herself in the Devil's throat like a sharp stick.

Scraping came from above and pebbles rained down on her.

The silhouette of two birds cut the dying gray of her truncated sky; one of them dropped a snake from its beak. The shift of realities was over in the same instant it hit the back of her eyes. Black birds were hands and the snake was the line.

"Heads up," Steve called, and Cyril's bra hit her in the face. After the initial insult, Anna was not displeased. Her teeth were the only bits of her free to do any serious grabbing. The makeshift line was none too long. Anna bit at the fabric till she caught it between her teeth then kept chomping. When she let go, she didn't want the spandex to tear where her teeth perforated the cloth.

"Got it?" Steve called down.

"Unmph," Anna managed, and clamped hard on the wad of bra in her mouth. Choosing what must be done quickly, she snatched her right hand off the rock wall and grabbed for the line. The palm had gone numb and the fingers pawed weakly at the belt above Cyril's sports bra.

Anna's feet were slipping. She grabbed at the line with

her left hand and was able to close her fingers around the belt, but there was no strength in her grip. She jammed it back against the wall. With a mind-wrenching scrape both feet began to slide. Anna was hanging on by her teeth. The skin of her teeth, she thought absurdly. Through her mind zipped a fragment of material from high school science class: the jaw muscles are the strongest muscles in the body. Anna hoped the lecture hadn't been referring to titmice or voles.

A lucky moment or a kindly god silhouetted the strap of the bra against the last of the daylight and Anna threaded her hand through it and twisted it until it was tight as a tourniquet. Left on long enough and she'd lose the hand. If she lost her grip the hand wouldn't matter, so Anna didn't dwell on it.

"Whoa!" she heard huffed from over her head.

"Don't do anything," came Paul's voice. "Let me do it. You're just rope."

"Rope," Steve said, and Anna's mind flew inexplicably to the Alfred Hitchcock movie of the same name starring Jimmy Stewart.

The bra was pulling tight, stretching as the line drew upward. Anna had managed to stop slipping down by shoving her heel into the wall and almost sitting on it to keep it in place. She wished she could have gotten her hand caught in a belt. As the spandex expanded and grew thinner and thinner, it wasn't looking quite as stalwart as it had when she and Paul first attached it to the rest of their rope.

Finally it could stretch no farther. Still holding the

end in her teeth, she snatched her left hand from the wall and grabbed with what strength remained in the fingers. Without this third point of contact her feet slipped suddenly and completely free of the walls and Anna fell a foot or so but the line held. Then, with painful slowness, it began inching upward. Anna closed her eyes so the infinitesimal progress wouldn't seem so hopeless but, without that dim reality of the darkened stone creeping past, the pit beneath and within her was overwhelming, spinning her brain inside her skull till she was afraid she would pass out.

"Hang on," she heard Paul say once more, and the line, with her dangling on it like a landed fish, jerked her upward a foot, then another, and she watched her knuckles lift into the twilight above her.

"Hurrah!" she heard Cyril and Chrissie shout and knew they had seen her emerging fists. "Hurrah," she murmured against the spandex that was nearly choking her.

The line pulled her wrists to the edge of the boulder and couldn't move them. The line of her body, nearly perpendicular to the slide that heralded the entrance to the crack, acted as a doorstop. The line sawing against the stone was only serving to cut through the spandex and peel the skin from her hands.

"Can you help us, Anna?" Paul's voice sounded so close it gave her heart. It didn't give her strength. Scrabbling with her feet on the slate she tried to find purchase, enough so she could boost arms over the lip of rock. Either she lacked the power to push hard enough or the ascent and descent had sanded off what little tread her river shoes had.

"Mmnh, mmnh," she said through her self-imposed gag.

"Stay right there," Paul said. Scraping and pebbles rattled down the slope above her. Then the light winked out and skinny arms reached down. Steve Kessler's face was inches above her, his head and shoulders over the edge of the fall.

"Don't worry," Steve told her. "Paul said he saw this done once in a cartoon."

Steve's thin arms wrapped around her rib cage and he laced together his long-fingered hands—a poet's hands or a surgeon's, Anna thought—till the knuckles locked and she was pulled tightly to him, her face buried in his shoulder and his in hers.

"Okay," his voice came muffled from the region of her armpit. "You're supposed to climb me."

It took a moment but Anna saw Paul's plan. "Ready?" she heard her husband shout and the tension on the line tightened. With her unfettered left hand Anna grabbed a handful of one of Steve's elbows and began pulling herself up. She had to be stomping and clawing him with every move, but he did no more than grunt occasionally when the pain got too bad. Then she was above the edge of the rock. With Paul holding tightly to his ankles, Steve's long body was laid out on the slope from head to heel for her to scramble up like a ladder.

She wasted no time. She climbed up his body like a rat up a palm tree and kept right on going till she had climbed nearly into her husband's lap. It had been her intent to help Paul reel in her bony and marvelous savior but she found she could barely lift her arms and her legs were cramping so badly she could hardly keep from screaming.

Steve was pulled up to cheers from his sister. Anna was glad the only light left was that of a rising half-moon so Cyril and Chrissie above and a few yards away couldn't see the cuts and scrapes with which she'd marked him on her exodus. Both of his elbows were bleeding freely from abrading against the sandstone, and his shorts were torn from pocket to hem, exposing cobalt blue briefs.

"Thank you," Anna said sincerely.

"A pound of flesh is nothing," Steve replied.

"Can I use the phone?" Chrissie asked.

FIFTEEN

The phone didn't work. The last swallows of water were consumed. The six of them sat in the dark with their backs against the stone. No one spoke, each lost in their own thoughts. Warmth from Paul's shoulder permeated the tired muscles in Anna's right arm. In her left she held the tiny scrap of life she'd cut from the drowned woman's womb. Helena no longer whimpered. She didn't move. Anna knew she lived only by the thready pulse in the miniature wrist she held gently between thumb and forefinger.

Adults were said to be able to live three days without water and considerably longer without food. Newborns were not that sturdy.

"I wonder if Easter made it," Cyril said into the darkness.

"She's tough and resourceful," Steve said. "She probably body-surfed out and is halfway to Rio Grande Village by now."

"That or back up on a ledge for the next boat to rescue," Anna added. It was easier to speculate on the welfare of a cow than to think about the trail of bodies left behind. That vein of conversation mined out, they fell silent again.

"I guess we may as well make ourselves as comfortable as possible," Paul said after a few minutes. "We'll climb out in the morning and holler for help."

"Why can't we climb out now?" Chrissie demanded. "I am not going to sleep on some rock just because everybody got shot."

It reassured Anna to hear the heartlessness in the girl's voice. Lori's death had hit Chrissie hard and she'd used anger to keep going. Now she was using selfishness. Both were transparent. If any of the kids imploded and had to go into therapy over this, Anna's money was on Chrissie.

"Boulder hopping in the dark will get you a room next to Carmen's," Cyril said, saving Anna the trouble.

"A night on a rock with a murderer looking for us wasn't in the trip itinerary," Steve said. "Do you think we'll be charged extra?"

"Right, like by then we won't already be dead," Chrissie said.

"First light," Paul promised.

No one moved. Getting comfortable was a chore too great for any of them to tackle for a while.

"Helena won't live till first light," Anna said quietly. The sorrow in her voice annoyed her. By default, she and Paul had become surrogate parents to the twins and Chrissie. One didn't burden the children with one's own emotions, not when they already had enough misery to deal with.

Death and Anna were old acquaintances. She didn't hate the grim reaper the way most did, nor did she fear him inordinately. Everybody died; it was simply a matter of timing. What she hated was cruelty and wasted lives. Though a lot of people wasted their days watching mindless television or endlessly carping about their lot in life while ignoring sunsets and breezes and strange, wonderful bugs, that was their business. On some level, they were living. Death snatched away the opportunity to bungle life as one saw fit. In the death of a baby the reaper stole too many years of possibilities.

Anna did feel this way, but babies died all the time. Their tens of thousands of little lives were thrown in the pit inside her along with the rapes and murders and religious wars and genocides her species was so fond of. In other circumstances, she would have weighted the lives of the three young people, strong and established among the living, with mothers who were not being flushed from canyons in the desert, fathers who, she presumed, loved them, over the life of a newborn. The good of the many.

This time was different. Helena was different.

The thought rang hollow in the caverns of Anna's mind and she knew it wasn't true. Helena was too new to show any differences to an indifferent world. She was still in the larval stage, more or less; her personality, if not unformed, was as yet unexpressed by word or deed or gesture. The realization that it was she who was different dawned on Anna. Maybe because she had delivered this baby under such traumatic circumstances, maybe because of the way the dying mother had said, "My baby . . ." and looked to Anna to save the little tyke. Whatever the reason, Anna had a fierce need to keep Helena out of the reaper's hands and in her own.

"I'm taking Helena out tonight," Anna said quietly.

Paul said nothing for a moment or two. He was as interested in keeping her alive as Anna was in keeping the baby alive. A climb toward a shooter through a dark rockslide was dangerous and difficult. Doing the same with an infant tied to one's chest nudged it toward the foolhardy.

Paul didn't argue. He knew the baby would not last too much longer without proper food, water and care. "Why don't I take the sat phone and climb out?" he said reasonably. "You stay here and take care of Helena." He didn't add "and the kids" out of respect for the three teenagers' feelings.

"I'm guessing it's going to take half an hour or more to climb up," Anna said. "I don't know how fast the rangers will be able to get to us. I want Helena as close to the EMTs as we can get her."

Steve sacrificed his T-shirt—his sister had little to offer, her bra already gone to make rope—and Anna fashioned a serviceable sling by creative threading of her arms and head through the various apertures. A misshapen moon appeared from behind the mountains to the east and cast enough light through the superclear air that the boulder field shone in black and silver. The light wasn't sufficient to provide anything like depth to the landscape. A shallow scrape an inch deep showed as inky as a crack to the center of the world.

As Anna tucked the limp infant into the soft hammock, she said, "Ready?"

"Ready as I'll ever be," Paul replied.

"You guys keep talking," Anna said to the twins and Chrissie. "If our shooter is still around, I want him to think we are all here and going nowhere till daylight."

"Not a problem," Cyril promised.

"I shall tell them how wonderful I am and how lucky they are to know me," Steve added. "That should take most of the night."

Paul leading, he and Anna and Helena crept into the first black crack wide enough to allow it and angling uphill. Faint light from the moon gave them a hint of an ever-changing horizon. Anna's great fear was not that she would break a leg or get shot or fall backward into a pit between a couple of house-sized boulders. She didn't worry about Helena getting shot either. A bullet that killed the baby would kill Anna as well.

Anna's fear was of falling forward, crushing the baby strapped across her chest and living to tell about it. Living to remember it as she was sucked down into the internal hell she had been unable to escape in the months since Isle Royale. Deaths she had nothing to do with—such as the death of Helena's mother—were sad or tragic or a relief, but she could live with them. Deaths she failed to prevent—Carmen and Lori—were harder but doable. Deaths she caused were the ones that stuck like burrs in the mind.

The death of this baby was unthinkable. Fear slowed her down, made her cautious, footing was tested, and handholds tested twice, grips made sure and hard. Fear was getting them safely up the incline. Had they not gotten within shouting distance of the rim before darkness poured ink over the passages and routes, and had they not spent the bulk of the day studying the slide in all its deadly magnificence, she doubted they would have managed it. As it was, the journey of less than fifty yards as the swallow flies took them an hour and seven minutes. Anna timed it, not because it mattered but because it was a way she could give herself the illusion of being in charge of events.

A couple gigantic rocks short of the rim, they stopped and tucked themselves deep in shadow, as close together as they could get without squashing Helena between them. Paul pulled Carmen's sat phone from his pocket and opened it. "Searching for signal" popped up as it had in the canyon, as it had where Carmen had died. Anna held her breath as the graphic finished its scanning movement. Connection. They'd made it. Paul pushed 911. Anna breathed again.

He pressed the phone to his ear.

Pebbles skittered down from the boulder they had tucked themselves beneath.

The shooter was waiting. Quiet as they had tried to be, climbing in the dark is a noisy business. Paul closed the phone before the operator answered, and he and Anna stared up at the bulge of shale above. Scraping followed the first skitter of gravel as boots walked across stone. Either he knew where they were or knew approximately where they were.

There were three ways out from the shallow niche in which they sheltered: right, left and down. If the shooter remained directly over them, all three directions would end with a bullet in the back. For what seemed hours, no one made another sound, not Paul, not Anna, not the owner of the boots. Not Helena. Not a gurgle or a sigh, nothing. Fear that the child had died took hold of Anna. Fumbling as silently as she could she found a tiny arm and followed it up to where the brachial artery was closest to the surface. Maybe she felt a pulse. Maybe she didn't.

Curling down, she managed to put her ear on the baby's chest. Her own heart was pounding so loudly she couldn't tell if she heard a faint thumping in Helena's breast or not. A feeling akin to panic gripped her and she lifted the newborn from its T-shirt hammock and held the baby's mouth next to her ear to see if she could hear her breathing. She heard nothing but the rustle of her own hair against the baby's skull and the soft susurration of fabrics as she dragged cotton knit over linen. In desperation she pinched Helena's bare toes, toes no bigger than baby peas.

Helena protested the mistreatment and Anna felt the weight of all the rock in Texas lift from her shoulders. Scraping from above, purposeful now, let her and Paul know the shooter had heard the mewling as well. In her concern for the baby, Anna had forgotten a man with a gun was listening for breathing as intently as she'd been but with altogether different reasons.

Paul put his lips so close to Anna's ear that his breath thrilled her despite the unthrilling nature of their situation. "You look after the baby; I'll look after you. Do not argue." As his whisper penetrated one ear, the other could hear the scratch of hard soles on loose gravel; the man was making his way down the rock.

Anna had no intention of arguing. She needed time to put the baby in as safe a place as she could find on short notice, then help Paul to save them both. Probably this was not what her husband had in mind, but Anna said nothing. Even if she stashed Helena where snakes and scorpions and coyotes and mountain lions and javelina congregated for meals, she would probably be safer than anywhere mankind was.

The thud of a man landing from a short leap sounded to the right of their alcove. Anna pressed her lips to Paul's ear and breathed: "He's coming. Give me the phone." While stashing, she might as well be dialing 911. If the shooter didn't kill them, the natural vicissitudes of being born an orphan in the desert with no proper care available was going to take Helena anyway. They were in dire need of rescue and park rangers were particularly good at that kind of thing.

Paul helped Anna find her feet, then pulled himself up using the rock overhang. Sitting after the ardors of the day had left their muscles so stiff that Anna was staggering after the first few steps and would have fallen had there been any room to do it. They had some time—even if the shooter was well versed in the ins and outs of the rocks this near the rim, it would take a few minutes to check under each one.

Moving as quickly as she could she clambered for the lip of Santa Elena Canyon. Paul was close behind, between her and their pursuer, hoping to find higher ground to make a stand. Confrontation was the last of a lawman's choices, or should be. If they could have left the man in place while they called for backup or hidden until he grew bored and left the scene, that was what they would have done. The danger to Helena—not to mention their own mortal coils—was too great to risk by fighting with an armed assailant who, it was safe to assume, was better hydrated and rested than they were.

The ifs, unfortunately, came with a caveat: if it could be done without endangering the lives of others. Whoever the man behind them was, he'd proven he could not be trusted to babysit the three other children while Anna and Paul went for help.

Light crashed into the rock ahead of Anna. After hours of darkness the glare splintered and cut into her eyes with the force of a bullet hurling shards of stone.

Momentarily blinded, she stopped. The shooter had a flashlight.

"Go, go, go," Paul whispered urgently, and strong hands shoved her up the next slurry of rock and sand. The flashlight changed the time factor. With a light the shooter could move much more quickly than could they, find them more quickly. Kill them more quickly. Wrapping a protective arm around Helena the way a quarterback might around a football, Anna speeded up, ignoring the battering of rock outcroppings against elbow, knees and ankles.

The moon was high enough now and the going was easier. In minutes she'd moved ahead of Paul.

Sudden silence made her scrabbling ring loud. Paul had stopped. Above her she could see a wide opening between two boulders, then, straight as a ruler, the false horizon drawn by the floor of the Chihuahuan desert. Moonlight loved the desert, and beyond the rock fall that shattered the cliff from desert to river, the land glowed pale silver and shadows were sharply drawn.

Making as much noise with her feet and hands as she could, Anna pushed on, heading for that gap and the light. Over her own racket she could hear nothing of the men below her and hoped the shooter would mistake her for two and not realize Paul had stopped to lie in wait.

She hoped Paul had armed himself with one damn big rock.

The cut from the fall sliced down from the desert

cleanly and Anna heaved herself up a waist-high step to the flat world she'd nearly forgotten existed. Clutching Helena to her chest, she crawled on hand and knees till she could no longer be seen by anyone below the edge of the canyon. But for the ragged stones tumbling into the chasm, there was no cover for miles, nothing but cacti, horse-crippler, round and low to the earth, creosote bushes and ocotillo with arms so thin and long only a Kessler could hide behind one.

A horse was tied to the branch of a creosote bush. For a moment it stared at her with scared and rolling eyes. Its nostrils flared, then, maybe smelling that she was not in the market for horsemeat, it went back to cropping the meager grasses. A fire smoldered nearby in a battered iron pan. Beside it, right off the set of a hundred westerns Anna had seen as a kid, was a saddle turned top down to provide a headrest. The only modern note was a sleeping bag instead of a bedroll.

Had Lori and Carmen been killed by an outlaw, a psycho living out dreams of Wyatt Earp, Doc Holliday, Jesse James, Billy the Kid and various other serial killers that myth had transformed into heroes?

"Sorry, buddy," Anna whispered as she dragged the blanket off the horse. Out of the ring of firelight, in a swale no more than eight inches deep and protected by cholla cacti with stunningly yellow blossoms, she spread the blanket and laid Helena in the middle of it so crawling things would have to make an effort to get to her and to protect her from accidentally throwing a tender little hand into a spiny plant. That done, she moved far enough away so she would not draw anything near the baby should she become a target and dialed 911.

She didn't know if she reached an operator or a dispatcher and didn't take the time to find out. As briefly and quietly as she could, she told the responder where they were and what they were up against and requested police and medical assistance and a meat wagon for the bodies. Then she pushed the off button and closed the phone. Leaving Helena to be watched over by the creatures of the night, Anna quickly searched the cowboy's camp: no guns, no alcohol, no knives but for one so beat up she doubted it would cut the three apples he'd brought for snacks, and a half-smoked pack of Marlboro Lights. Taking the pathetic knife, she slipped quietly back into the black crevasse leading into the rock fall and the place she had last seen Paul.

Stopping often to listen, Anna crept to the back of the boulder they had sheltered beneath, the one the shooter had paced atop as they cowered below, too afraid to breathe. Without the baby to keep alive from one instant to the next, Anna found she was breathing just fine and the fear, though still with her, had lost its panicked edge. Without Helena in her arms, Anna liked the dark. With the pit black beneath her esophagus, she liked the danger. The danger to Paul was something else, a fear as sharp as that she'd carried for Helena but not as bone deep. Paul Davidson was not a helpless dependent. Paul was her partner. To worry too much about him felt disrespectful, as if he was not a good enough sheriff to stay alive or, should the worst occur, not a good enough priest to get into heaven.

Going to the right of the rock so that with luck she would be behind the killer, Anna slipped back into the black shadows.

SIXTEEN

The hard edge of night was broken by the moon and, this close to the iridescence of the desert floor, a faint glow from above. Anna's eyes had recovered from the blast of light from the shooter's flashlight and she could see well enough to move quietly. Slipping down from rock to rock, placing each foot carefully, she crept to where she and Paul had sheltered with Helena. Still there was no sound from either her husband or the hunter.

The fatigue that adrenaline had been keeping at bay struck from nowhere, and Anna was suddenly dizzy with it. Dehydration, hunger, the climb up and down the crack to Carmen's body, the trudge up the rock-slide, coalesced in her muscles and it was all she could do to remain upright. Hunting a hunter when she was as weak as a newborn kitten, as weak as Helena lying all but lifeless on a horse blanket, Anna felt helpless. She felt like crying and falling in a heap and giving up, abdicating. It was a rotten sensation.

For a moment that rang in her ears like a symphony, she stood still in the shadows and sent her senses out into the maze of dark and light, shadow and stone. Down in the rocks it felt as if hearing, sight, the flight of mind was smashing into shale and the world was no bigger than the crevice she waited in. Then came the faint sound of a footfall. Not the rasp of rubber that Paul's river shoes would produce, but the hollow knock of a boot heel.

The shooter was also waiting, listening. Now he'd heard or seen something and was on the move again. Forcing herself forward, hands on the boulders at either side, eyes and ears wide in the night, the effort of lifting her feet and putting them down taxing what was left of her energy, Anna followed the sound. Her sandaled foot struck a rock and she stopped. The boots stopped. Feeling for what had stubbed her toes, she found a rock roughly the size of a baseball and picked it up. The weight felt good in her hand, the smoothness comfortingly deadly against her palms and fingers.

Where was Paul? A vision of him already dead, his skull smashed in by a six-cell flashlight, burned like a flash fire behind her eyes. The anger that followed it gave her a last gasp of strength and she took it to her like a drowning woman grabbing at the last straw. Rock firm in her grasp, she moved up the narrow incline sandwiched between the boulders quickly, no longer worried about being quiet.

A banshee's scream and the sound of bodies colliding thundered down her tiny canyon. The shooter had found Paul. Or vice versa. Exhilaration flooded her. Paul wasn't dead. Yet. Anna flung herself onto the next rock and, stone in hand, skittered over it like a three-legged lizard. Ahead, where the last lip shadowed the climb to the desert floor, Paul's silvery hair shone as he grappled with the shooter. The flashlight had fallen to the ground and rolled, creating an eerie kaleidoscope of illuminated feet in a shattered dance. In glimpses she could see the shooter wore a pistol on his hip like a gunslinger.

The man who had killed Lori and Carmen was tall and broad with ink-black hair and long arms. His face was dark with blood where Paul had struck him with something. He was bigger, stronger, watered and fed. And he was winning. Locked together, the two men slammed into the lip of the canyon and Anna saw Paul's head snap back, heard it strike stone. He reeled and the tall man drew his arm back to hit him in the face.

Anna stood. "Hey!" she shouted. In the second the shooter's fist hesitated, she threw her rock.

The hurling of spherical objects was not an art girls were trained in. The repetitive task of "playing catch" had never appealed to her any more than had running after shagged balls like a rat terrier after a tennis ball. The rock went wide and cracked into a boulder between her and the fighting men. It served one small purpose.

The shooter was distracted long enough Paul got his arm up and deflected the blow from his face. Anna leapt from her boulder and landed on all fours, scrambling to hands and feet, running like a Navaho skinwalker, more wolf than woman, closing the distance between herself and the fight.

No rocks neatly to hand, she sprang on the shooter's back. Wrapping one arm around his throat, her other hand grabbing at the six-shooter in the holster, she tucked her head tight against his shoulder where he'd have trouble hitting her and squeezed. Knuckles whipped across the side of her face and she felt the blood start. She squeezed harder.

With a grunt the man reeled backward, smashing her against the wall of the ever-present, unforgiving prison of shale she'd been sentenced to. Air gusted from her lungs and she couldn't pull it back in. The panic of suffocation did what metal to her skull had failed to. Losing her grip on the man's throat, she fell. Silhouetted against the curtain of stars and faint moonlight she watched him stoop quickly, then rise. He'd retrieved the flashlight. Crouching, he cocked his arm back and swung at her head.

A black shape crashed into him and the flashlight went flying. The wind that had been knocked out of Anna came back in a rush. Crawling between the kick of boots and the slash of river shoes, she retrieved the flashlight and rolled free of the fracas. Again on her feet she swung the flashlight like a baseball bat at the shooter's head. The fight turned and her blow glanced off his temple and cracked into Paul's hand. Paul cried out in pain. The shooter slumped to the ground.

"Thank you, love," Paul gasped. Both of them were panting heavily.

"Gun," Anna managed.

Paul knelt on the man's shoulders and Anna unsnapped the keeper and pulled the gun from the shooter's holster. Not a six-shooter. A nine-millimeter semiautomatic, the kind she'd carried most of her career. Why hadn't he drawn it? After Lori and Carmen, she doubted he had any feel for the sanctity of life.

"We . . . tie . . . him . . ." she gasped.

"With what?" Paul backed off the shooter's body and he and Anna slumped together against a rock trying to breathe. Wrists braced on knees so she wouldn't drop the thing, Anna held the gun on the man who was now their captive—or their corpse, depending on how hard the flashlight had hit him.

"Good point," she said. Every scrap of anything that could make rope had been sacrificed already. Anna was barely decent in her ripped shirt, and Paul's pants were riding at an inner-city half-mast without his belt.

Anna's and Paul's breath began to even out. The gun stopped shaking in her hand and steadied on the downed man. The shooter had fallen forward and lay on his side, half curled around a beach ball–sized rock, his face in the angle between the proverbial rock and the hard place. One leg was bent over the other like those of the hanged man in the Tarot deck. One arm was cocked behind him, palm toward Anna and Paul. The other was out of sight. All in all it was a good position as far as Anna was concerned. There would be no sudden leapings up from that tangle of bones and flesh.

"Do you think he's dead?" Anna asked. The question was one of indifference to her and that indifference sent a jolt of horror through her that started the edges of the pit in her soul bleeding. She felt herself starting to fall and was only stopped by the sharp rap of the pistol barrel against her scraped shin. The external pain snapped her from the internal. Paul was looking at her with concern, his eyes unreadable in the faint light.

"Hand fell asleep," Anna said as she retrained the weapon on the body at their feet.

Paul looked back at their predator-become-prey. "I sure hope not."

Anna envied his hope. His voice was rich with compassion for the guy who'd stalked and murdered two girls and tried to murder them. Paul would have killed him if he'd had to, to protect himself or others, but he was genuinely happy it might not have been necessary. Anna tried to care and failed. She cared that she failed; maybe that counted for something in the final reckoning.

"Unh," emanated from beneath the stone beach ball.

"Not dead," Anna said.

"Hallelujah."

Anna was heartened at the surge of, if not joy, then relief she felt when life was confirmed.

Paul had switched the flashlight off when they'd collapsed against the rock. He turned it on now and shined it on the groaning man.

The crabbed hand behind his back twitched then began to be pulled under him, reminding Anna weirdly of the witch's feet sliding under the house in Munchkin Land. Keeping the gun trained on the shooter, Anna pushed herself to her feet, grunting as if she, too, were stirring from a death sleep. Paul stood as well. Anna heard the companionable crack of his knees.

She had intended to grow old with this man. She hadn't planned on doing it all in one night.

The hand vanished beneath the torso, seeking the empty holster pinned beneath the hip.

"We've taken your weapon," Paul said quietly. "Do everything carefully and slowly."

Anna relaxed her eyes and flexed her fingers on the butt of the gun. Annie Oakley, she thought absurdly. She shook her head to clear it of witches and sharp-shooters.

"I hear you," returned a voice muffled by rock and earth. "Easy it is. I'm going to sit up, okay? Real slow."

The shooter didn't sound calm, precisely, but he didn't sound psycho or hyper the way Anna had thought he would. His voice was as quiet and rational as Paul's had been. He was trying to calm and reassure them so they wouldn't shoot him the first time he blinked. This guy wanted to stay alive.

"Okay," the man said in the same calming tones. "I've got my hands under me now. I'm going to do sort of a push-up then get myself into a sitting position here. Real slow. That okay with you folks?"

Folks. What kind of cold-blooded killer of young women caught red-handed and coldcocked with his own flashlight called his captors *folks*? Anna and Paul exchanged looks.

"Go ahead," Paul said. He didn't add any warnings or caveats. He seemed as nonplussed as Anna.

The calming, folksy cooperation was making Anna nervous. The guy had done this before, he knew from experience—or instinct how best to put his enemies at ease.

"We are not reassured," Anna said, and her voice was cold and flat. "Do not make the mistake of thinking that."

The man, halfway into his push-up, froze, and Anna wondered if he was changing his plans or if her tone had frightened him as much as it had her. It was not a good thing to channel the grim reaper, especially when one had been avoiding him most of the day.

"I hear you," the man said, easing himself onto one hip and gathering his long legs in front of him so he was sitting, shoulders against his round rock, hands, palms up, one on each thigh like innocence on display.

He looked the cowboy Anna's quick perusal of his camp had suggested. Tall and lean with black hair worn long over his collar and a black mustache Tom Selleck would have been proud of in his *Magnum P.I.* days.

"I'm Freddy Martinez, the river district ranger here

in Big Bend. You folks get caught in the flash flooding?" He didn't sound like a man with a gun trained on him. He sounded like a ranger at an evening program talking about environmental concerns.

Paul blinded him with the flashlight. He didn't raise his empty hands to protect his eyes. Too wary for that. "You're a park ranger," Paul said.

"For twenty-two years, most of it right here," he answered. "I started out as a river guide for a commercial outfit out of Terlingua. I've been on the Rio Grande all my life."

"Do you have any identification?" Paul asked.

"In my saddlebags."

Anna didn't need an ID. He had "ranger" written all over him. Though he wasn't in uniform, he had on an old cordovan uniform belt, only with the buckle changed out; his boots were NPS uniform boots, recycled for casual wear when they got too scruffy for work.

"Where's your rifle?" Anna asked.

"No rifle. Just the Glock," he said. "And you got that."

She hadn't seen a rifle in the camp, but he could have thrown it away. "He has a camp up top," Anna said. "We need his water and I need to check on—" She started to say "the baby," but thought better of it. Hostages in small packages were easier to deal with than older, crankier ones if it came to anything like that.

"You want me to go first?" Freddy said. "If you get up on the rock behind you, you'll be able to keep a bead on me when I get up the lip so whoever comes second won't be in danger from me."

It annoyed Anna that he was being so helpful.

"Good plan," Paul said. "Lead on."

As the ranger stood, he weaved slightly and Anna's finger tightened on the trigger. It wasn't a feint but a hangover from the clout he'd taken on the head. He righted himself and hefted his considerable length up over the lip of the canyon. Anna kept her sights on him until Paul was up, as well, and Freddy had stepped away and sat down without being asked to.

Anna quickly covered the distance and scrambled up, Martinez only out of her sight for a second or two. Still she was levitating on what had to be the very last drops her adrenal glands had in stock when she stood again on the desert floor. Martinez had not moved.

A voice came out of the darkness of the camp and Anna wheeled on it, the gun held rigid at arm's length in both hands. He had no rifle. Maybe someone else did. One horse, one saddle, one sleeping bag. She'd let herself assume there was but one shooter. Sometimes monsters ran in packs.

"Say again," came a different voice and a crackle.

"My radio," Martinez said. "It's in the saddlebag there with the water skin."

Water.

"You first," Paul said, and eased the Glock from her fingers.

"That is true love," Anna said, and trotted over to

where the bleats from the radio had come. The ranger had said "water skin" and that's what she found, the old three-gallon burlap water sacks that she remembered from when she was little. Her parents carried one strapped across the radiator of their old station wagon to refill the radiator when it overheated.

Three gallons, two and a half left. She felt rich and wild and drank deeply before carrying it back to her husband. They traded water for gun and Paul drank.

"You folks lose your water?"

"Yeah," Anna said as she and Paul traded life for death again and she took another long pull on the water skin.

Drinking restored some of Anna's strength and most of her mental acuity. She noticed she was now able to understand actual words coming from the radio. Dispatch was sending rescue. Martinez's eyes followed hers to the radio and for the first time she saw fear in his face. If he was going to try anything it would be now, before the metaphorical cavalry arrived.

Paul still held the Glock. Anna saw the same thought register on his face, the usually gentle planes hardening in the silver light. Giving Martinez a wide berth, Anna returned to where his saddlebag was flung over the bit of log he'd centered his camp around. She dug the radio from the leather bag and keyed the mike.

"This is Anna Pigeon on Ranger Martinez's radio," she said clearly. "I am the person who called in the nine-one-one emergency."

The fear went out of Martinez's face.

Something about the man wasn't right.

SEVENTEEN

Keeping her eyes on the ranger and Paul, Anna talked into the radio, giving details as she walked over to where she had laid Helena on the horse blanket. "Do you want me to give them our exact location?" Martinez called. Anna ignored him. She had no doubt he could describe where they were more precisely but he could also warn them off, say it was a false alarm, send them to the wrong location. She doubted it, but it was possible and, since there was only one huge rock-slide in Santa Elena Canyon, she felt telling the rescuers that she was at the top of it should do the trick.

Helena was where Anna had left her, her round perfect face pale and ashen in the moonlight. She hadn't moved at all, not even to disarrange the T-shirt Anna had tucked around her to keep out the chill. Anna fell

to her knees on the horse blanket, the radio falling forgotten from her hand. "Oh, baby, no," Anna whispered
as she gathered one of the tiny hands between her fingers. The baby's flesh was neither warm nor cold; it felt
like a scrap of velvet that had taken on the ambient temperature of the air.

"No, no, little girl," Anna murmured as she laid
her ear on a rib cage scarcely as big as the palm of her
hand. Nothing. Nothing. Then there it was, the *thump-
thump* of a heartbeat, thready and faint and absolutely
wonderful.

"Hurrah!" Anna shouted before she even realized
she'd opened her mouth to do so.

"What?" Paul called through the darkness.

"She's tough, our little cookie." Anna gently lifted
the baby and said nothing else. She'd heard herself and
realized she was actually cooing. It was more disconcerting than many things had been on this most grimly
disconcerting day.

Anna loved cats because they were beautiful and lazy
and deadly and didn't apologize for any of it. She loved
dogs because one could make them happy. People could
not be made happy. They could only be made miserable.
Human happiness had to come from within. Not so
with dogs. Dogs could be made happy with a kind word.
With a kind word and a pork chop they could be made
ecstatic.

Maybe the same applied to Helena, Anna told herself. Maybe she loved her because Anna seemed able to
keep her alive. Not something she'd managed for a lot

of people. Keeping people alive was difficult. Making them dead was a piece of cake. The radio left behind on the horse blanket, Anna carried the baby back toward the men and the water.

Martinez stared uncomprehending at the bundle in her arms till in a feat of strength and liveliness that made Anna want to crow with delight, Helena managed to shake a cherry-sized fist at the moon.

"You brought a baby on a whitewater rafting trip?" The horror in his voice sounded genuine. Even though he was still being held at gunpoint by Paul, Martinez half rose. "How stupid can you get?" he demanded.

"Sit," Paul said.

There was enough of the southern sheriff in Paul's tone that Martinez sat again immediately. "Just kill me now," the ranger said. "I've seen it all, what's to live for? A baby on a whitewater trip. Jesus." He shook his head and appeared to be fuming at the risk they had taken with this unknown baby's life.

"Appeared to be" was the phrase that caught in Anna's mind. Martinez was smart and had excellent survival skills. Had it been otherwise he would not have lasted so long on the river or risen so high in the Park Service. Even schoolyard bullies knew that the best defense is a good offense.

Anna collected a plastic coffee cup Martinez had left on the log and threw out the last dregs of what smelled like Constant Comment tea, then sat cross-legged near Paul and cradled the baby in the basket made of her bones, the torn down comforter, sans most of its stuffing by now, used as padding. Having rinsed the cup out, Anna put an inch of water in the bottom and began dipping her finger in it then putting her finger to the baby's lips. To her enormous relief Helena took it.

"We need to get water to the kids," Paul said.

"I'll go as soon as Helena's got some in her," Anna said. Helena took another couple of drops and Anna felt triumphant.

"Let me. I didn't do the chimney."

For a moment Anna looked from Paul to Freddy and Paul looked from Freddy to Anna and Freddy looked mystified.

"Will you be okay here with him?" Paul asked.

"With him and a gun," Anna said. She was being flippant. Helena's survival had buoyed her spirits and she felt little threat from Freddy. From Paul's willingness to leave, she expected he didn't sense evil either.

Paul took the flashlight and the water skin and slipped back over the lip of the slide. For a freefalling moment Anna felt utterly helpless. She had the Glock. And she had the baby. It was not an auspicious combination. There would be no feeding and firing simultaneously; it took both hands to drip water into Helena's mouth and, with an infant on one's lap, moving quickly was problematic. Not to mention firing a gun so close to a newborn would probably deafen it for life. No wonder women didn't tend to favor war.

Panic subsided. Freddy's nonthreatening vibes again.

The Glock handy at her right knee, Anna continued

to attempt to lure Helena into sucking water from her little finger.

"Paul's taking water to 'the kids,' plural?" Freddy Martinez asked.

It jarred Anna to hear her husband's name spoken so easily by the man they'd captured, but of course he would have heard her say it.

"Plural," Anna confirmed.

"Let's see if I can figure this out," Martinez said. "You, your husband?"

Anna nodded.

"And … how many kids?"

"Four," Anna said, then remembered Lori had been killed. "Three," she amended.

"An unknown number of kids," Martinez said, "climb up a rockslide to escape the rising river—"

"Among other things."

"And you leave the kids and bring the baby and decide to attack a park ranger to hijack his water. Water, I might add, that I would have given you in any case." He sighed. "Nope. I can't figure this one out."

The sinking feeling that had started when Freddy was so outraged at anyone bringing a baby on a whitewater rafting trip sank another foot or so. It was beginning to look as if she and Paul had pounced on the wrong man, a federal law enforcement officer and fellow ranger, no less. Not that rangers couldn't kill innocent people; it was just that between shooing skunk kits out of campgrounds and telling people where the bathroom was there wasn't a whole lot of energy left for mass murder.

Anna chose not to tell him of the cow, the raft, the woman and the emergency C-section, at least not at the moment. She told him there'd been a shooting, how many there were in the party needing to be rescued, and what kinds of resources the victims might require.

When she'd finished he rose and went to retrieve the radio where she'd dropped it on the saddle blanket. Anna made no move to stop him, she just watched. Martinez pushed down the mike button and repeated what she had told him to dispatch. Dispatch began ordering various people to various places.

Martinez came back and sat where he'd been before.

"Sorry about mistaking you for a venal craven murderer of children and trying to crush your skull," Anna said.

"I won't tell anyone you attacked me if you won't tell anyone you won," Martinez said.

Anna laughed. "Deal."

"Can I have my gun back?"

"No."

"Can I hold the baby?"

"No."

EIGHTEEN

They made the entrance Judith had planned. A lovely couple, easy together, old enough to have power and young enough to keep it. The kind of comets people like to hook their hopes to the tails of. Because he knew what to look for, Darden could see the strain around Charles's well-cut mouth, a pulling down and in of the corners. Stress suited him, Darden thought. The tautness of the muscles helped to diffuse the natural sensuousness of his lips. Judith's knuckles, outshone by a couple of very fine rings, big enough to exude wealth, small enough to look as if a regular person could earn it, were white where she held tightly to her husband, keeping him on a short leash. Charles did have a bit of the rabbit-in-the-headlights look about him, but Darden doubted anybody would notice.

Well, anybody but Gerry, and whatever Charles's other faults might be, running off at the mouth to the press wasn't one of them. Pride, Darden thought not for the first time, a handy thing for people who knew how to use it. Darden didn't know if he had much in the way of pride. He was proud that he could make a sharp heavy barbeque sauce and a light buttery béarnaise sauce with equal skill, but not so much so that he'd push anybody else into a hot stove for doing it better than he did. He was proud his chili won second place at the state fair, but not enough to bribe a judge or pour salt into a competitor's pot when nobody was looking. He was about to mentally pat himself on the back for not housing that particular sin in his breast when he realized he was no better than Charles. He'd do anything—underhanded or otherwise—to keep his pride intact. Tonight he was swelled with the toxic stuff as he watched his beautiful little girl, in her neat powder-blue linen slacks and her white silk blouse, working the crowd like a pro.

The thought made him uncomfortable and he shifted his weight to the balls of his feet. Instantly he was sorry as his big toes smashed against his second toes and started up the whole shooting match of foot pain. Maybe when Judith started speaking he'd take a seat somewhere, he thought, but knew he wouldn't.

Towing Charles—who was going to have to be removed soon by the increasing distraction he was showing—Judith had worked her way through the assembled press, remembering family names of those she knew, asking about basketball games and graduations and birthdays, smiling at the rest like they were going to be just as good friends once they got to know each other, and was heading into a clot of people less likely to respond to glad-handing. The people she was here to ignite, preferably with her own fire.

Darden watched them: those determined to hate her and those determined to keep open minds and those determined to be part of the drama and the spotlight, whatever it turned out to be. Whoever they were, they had to admit she made a nice change from the incumbent, a jowly, overweight liberal who didn't get his nose hairs trimmed as often as somebody who went on camera ought to. In a way the convention at Big Bend was the incumbent's party. Which was why Judith decided to crash it. Governor Bloward—a name even those in his own camp couldn't resist changing to Blow Hard occasionally wanted to reopen the border between Big Bend National Park and Mexico. Mexico had set aside a huge tract of land across the border from Big Bend as a natural area and were doing a good job of husbanding it, given they had about a half a ranger for a zillion acres. Bloward had a dream of making Big Bend an international peace park like Glacier in Montana was with Waterton in Canada, half the park in one country and half in another. Before 9/11, the border closure and the Mexican drug wars, Big Bend had been an international park in all but name. Bloward wanted to turn the clock back "to a time when we had hope," he liked to say. And he'd point out that Homeland Security didn't close the border between Glacier and Waterton.

Of course, Canada wasn't in the middle of a drug war. The White House was lobbying for a one-point-four-billion-dollar aid package to Mexican law enforcement. It seemed like big money, but it was chump change compared to the fifteen-plus billion Americans were pumping into the drug lords' armies to keep their supply of cocaine, heroin, marijuana and methamphetamines pouring in.

Bloward's argument was that the stretch of wilderness border along the southern edge of Big Bend wasn't ever going to be a major smuggling route for the cartels. No roads to speak of and acres of patrolled nowhere to get across before reaching any major markets. To that end he'd had his minions in the academic world plan this "summit meeting" of the brains on either side of the issue.

Not the brains, Darden corrected himself, the intellectuals. Big difference.

His eyes roved the room looking for signs of incipient trouble, a habit so ingrained he found himself doing it even at children's piano recitals. Kevin stood near the entrance to the lodge dining room, natty in a suit.

About time, Darden thought. The young agent was also scanning the room; when his eyes locked on Darden's, he started across the room. Darden shook his head and pointedly looked at his watch. Now was not the time. He needed to focus on Judith. And Charles. His happy-husband façade was starting to crack. Darden noticed his free hand was returning ever more frequently to his front trouser pocket where, he presumed, the satellite phone was kept. Darden wasn't sure who it was Charles was so desperate to be in contact with but he could make an educated guess. Given cell phones were the next best thing to broadcasting live on the air, he'd rather Charles didn't make a show of it tonight.

Kevin didn't acknowledge Darden's mime show. Darden didn't even register on the kid's radar. Kevin hadn't been looking for his boss to explain where in the heck he'd been for the last forty minutes, he'd been searching out Judith, lost in a snarl of tall men on the far side of the dining room. Then again maybe he was looking for the boss, Darden thought. The thought nettled him. Not that he'd ever had any illusions that he and not the client was the boss—even if he had made the client hotcakes in the shape of Mickey Mouse when she was five. It nettled him to be kept out of the loop. It was disrespectful. And it was dangerous.

Judith caught Kevin's eye before he plowed into her act and stopped him with a nod and a smile. Darden started to relax, then Kevin winked at Judith. Before the shock wore off, anger flashed under Darden's breastbone and the well-publicized hug between Monica and Bill replayed behind his eyes. The appetites of the powerful translated into heartburn for everybody else. For an instant Judith's face froze mid-smile, then she broke eye contact and was back in the middle of a conversation with a graying professor Darden recognized from a liberal talking-head show out of Dallas as if she'd never had any interest other than in his dry theories.

Looking smug, Kevin was about to strut back to the sidelines when he saw Darden. Darden crooked a finger once and the smirk evaporated from the young agent's handsome face. He looked around as if salvation might appear in the shape of somebody behind his shoulder that was the real target of Darden's displeasure, but he was alone in a sea of innocent bystanders.

Darden met him halfway and put a fatherly hand on his shoulder to escort him genially out of the dining room.

"Don't tell me you're knocking off before the show's gotten started?" Gerry, with her instinct for news, had appeared out of nowhere.

Darden's fingers tightened on Kevin's shoulder till he could feel the kid wincing under the pressure of his thumb.

"Just getting a little air, Gerry. Too much IQ in here for an old warhorse like me. I've got to get out and think like a rock for a few minutes."

"Hah," Gerry said, and, taking a drink, looked at him over the edge of her wineglass, up through her heavily mascaraed eyelashes. The trick had probably worked like a house afire when she was eighteen, and it was still working. Maybe it was the half-laugh of self-mockery that sparkled in her eyes. Then the reporter winked and Darden knew she'd seen the exchange between Kevin and Judith and knew why he had decided to take Kevin for a short walk outside.

Gerry laughed and, turning away, said, "Don't let the lizards get you."

The gift shop had stayed open to accommodate any shoppers of the party and Darden smiled at the girl behind the cash register as he took his agent out into the parking lot behind the lodge.

Kevin had morphed from smug to scared to sheepish to belligerent in the time it had taken Darden to excise him from the party. Defensiveness had him puffed up like a toad in the clear glow of the desert moon. Darden had no time for theatrics.

"You know, son, every now and then I like a little Bible study," he said kindly. "It's good to know your Bible, don't you think?"

Caught off guard, Kevin deflated some and managed an: "Uh, yeah, I guess so."

"I can't quote you chapter and verse but there's a real important part where it says, 'If thine eye offends me I'll pluck it out.' You remember that part. If you ever forget your Bible studies again, I will pluck it out with a dull Boy Scout knife. You got it?"

Kevin gawped, his lips moving like a fish looking for air or an underling looking for an excuse, but he had the good sense not to let any words escape.

"Good man," Darden said, and slapped him on the back hard enough the agent had to take a step forward or lose his balance.

Darden watched the young agent walking back toward the lodge. Some of the swagger was gone, but not enough. Darden's Bible study classes usually instilled more humility in his underlings. Either he was slipping or Kevin was bedding Judith and it was giving him a sense of invulnerability. Judith could be counted on to tell Darden pretty much everything. Pretty much. Her bedroom and Charles were off limits. Once upon a time that would have been fine. Darden was old school. Unless it was with enemy spies, where politicians slept should be none of the public's business. Now that the public was addicted to tabloid titillation, as happy with the sex life of presidents as they were with starlets, he was going to have to make it his business.

He wasn't looking forward to it. There were definite downsides to clients one had read bedtime stories to.

Once upon a time.

Darden thought about the age-old lead-in to fairy tales, to better times when magic was as common as the west wind and, unless one read the German tales, ogres never prevailed. True love won out every time.

The good old days were a fairy tale. There'd never been a time the world was a safer, kinder, better place. There'd only been a time human beings were young and strong and ignorant.

A slight drizzle had started, so fine it would take a while to get wet, but it woke Darden from his musings and he shook his head like a blind old dog. More and more he was slipping into his own thoughts, mentally, if not physically, abandoning his post. Maunderings of an old man, he chided himself, but a sharp fang of anxiety bit deeper: Alzheimer's. There was a genetic component.

He thought of Lou Bearing, a hit man he'd come to know during his White House years. Maybe he'd call Lou and give him a password, have Lou phone him every day and ask what it was. If he forgot the password three days in a row, Lou could take him out. The black whimsy cheered him and he started back to his duty station. Judith would be starting her speech soon and he didn't want to miss it.

The automatic doors to the lodge slid silently open and rangers began leaking out from the gift shop: the chief ranger, the deputy superintendent—both off duty and out of uniform—and two uniformed rangers whom Darden didn't know. Their radios were out and crackling and worried looks clouded their faces.

"Bernard," Darden addressed the chief ranger, Bernard Davies. Darden didn't have to dig for the name. Memorizing names was the cheapest and easiest form of public relations. "What brought on this exodus?" He smiled to show he wasn't prying, but one in the circle of those who need to know.

"There's been some trouble on the river," Bernard replied. He wasn't much younger than Darden but he was of the tall, long-boned, wiry-muscled type Texas was known for. Darden was of the German peasant type, strong and squat and doomed to go to fat in later years. "The river rose pretty fast and some rafters got caught."

There was more to it than that. Lawmen didn't abandon free food and drink and the promise of a terrific row because a handful of tourists got their bottoms wet. Darden waited for the rest of the story.

"We don't have all the details yet," Bernard said, responding to the open expectant look Darden cultivated with a degree of success. "Apparently a couple of them were killed or badly injured. It shouldn't have any effect on your doings up here."

"If there's anything we can do to help . . ." Darden offered, safe in the knowledge one law outfit would eat their own guns before they would accept help from another law outfit. At least at the outset of an incident.

"We've got it covered," Bernard said curtly. Then added: "But thanks."

The four of them walked out into the drizzle. Darden waited, listening to the radios and the uniformed rangers. Shots had been fired. A paramedic had been called. The report of gunshots surprised Darden. Of the things that could kill a person in a national park, one didn't put bullets at the top of the list. He remembered the shootings by the Mexican kids years back—didn't remember them happening, but remembered Judith talking about it when she was assembling what she called her "emotional factors" for her argument. Stories that would scare the pants off people in a close personal way.

Darden couldn't help hoping this was a repeat. Judith would make hay with it.

His Judith could make hay with anything.

When he turned to go inside to watch the show, Gerry was standing under the eaves of the lodge putting a scarf over her determinedly blond hair. With her un-canny sense of where the story was, she'd followed the green and gray out of the party.

"Give the mayor my regrets," she said. "Bigger fish to fry." And she followed the rangers into the drizzle.

NINETEEN

For a while Anna and Freddy Martinez sat in silence. The lanky ranger continued to be as unthreatening as Smokey the Bear without his shovel, and Anna relaxed enough she could feel what the day had robbed her of, at least physically. Her muscles didn't ache yet but they would, come morning. At the moment they were warm and had lost their elasticity. It was hard to lift her arm to give drops of water to Helena.

"Anna Pigeon," Freddy said.

"That's right,"

"Out of Rocky Mountains?"

"Yes."

"You're the one got tangled up in that mess on Isle Royale this winter?"

"Me all over," Anna said. She wasn't surprised Martinez knew of the incident. The Ranger Report was on the NPS website. Parks entered items they were proud of or thought would be of general interest to other Park Service employees. The "mess on Isle Royale," as Martinez put it, would have been well disseminated and discussed.

Anna didn't want to talk about it.

Freddy Martinez was looking at her differently than he had before two and two had come together in his brain, like she was no longer quite respectable or viable or trustworthy. Or maybe she was projecting what she feared onto his face, which was blank and mostly unreadable in the silvery light.

"Scuttlebutt was there was going to be a big federal investigation. What's happening with that?"

"Nothing," Anna said. She focused her attention on Helena so it wouldn't look like she was avoiding his eyes. "The Park Service is doing the usual." The usual was investigating to see if Anna's killing of another person was justified.

"Homeland Security is doing something, but it's all on their side. Nothing to do with me," she added, sounding evasive if not outright defensive. She didn't feel defensive, she felt belligerent but, if Anna was on her sister Molly's black leather couch in her psychiatrist's office in Manhattan, she'd probably be informed that belligerence was defensiveness in one of its nastiest forms.

She forced herself to look at Martinez. She didn't know what she was expecting to see in his face, maybe fear because she was dangerous, maybe revulsion because she was a killer. What she saw was pity, and all at once she saw herself through his eyes. Freddy Martinez wasn't seeing a bad-ass renegade, he was looking at a sad middle-aged woman with graying hair, small and tired and pathetic and maybe crazy to boot. Not a vision she welcomed in any mirror. In the mirror of another ranger's eyes, it was almost unbearable.

"Want to tell me what happened today?" he asked kindly.

"What time did you get here?" she asked instead of answering him. Time for being defensive had passed. She intended to be as offensive as circumstances permitted. It was Freddy, not she, who had been at the rim of Santa Elena Canyon when shots were fired. This mess, at least, was not hers.

For a second she thought he wasn't going to answer her but he did. "A couple of hours ago, maybe less," he said easily. "Why?"

"Was anyone here when you arrived?"

"Nobody." Again he asked: "Why?"

"Shots were fired," she said. "They weren't from the Mexican side of the river." Instead of looking alarmed or guilty, Martinez looked relieved. Relieved of what? she wondered. Had the shots somehow been fired from the other side and she'd miscalculated? Was he relieved that she hadn't figured that out? Given he was the man they'd found in the shooter's place, she would have thought the opposite answer would be the one he was hoping for.

"Did you hear the gunshots?" she asked him.

"I didn't, but then the river was making a lot of noise throwing rocks and rafts around."

It was a believable answer. The grinding of the immense shale molars as they chewed through another layer of the world had been stunning. Still she looked hard at him to see if he would waver, admit to hearing something like a shot, anything that would mark a man trying to sound believable when he was lying through his nice white teeth.

Freddy didn't embellish.

The last shot, the one that killed Lori, had been fired in the late afternoon while they were still at the bottom of the slide. If the shooter had taken off right after that, he would have been gone before Martinez admitted to coming on the scene.

"Which direction did you ride in from?"

Freddy pointed upriver. "West. The road runs along the rim of the canyon from Lajitas."

Anna had noticed the rugged dirt track when she'd stolen the saddle blanket from the back of Freddy's horse but it hadn't registered on her consciousness. She remembered it now. "Did you pass anybody?"

"Nobody."

"Where does the road go?"

"It cuts back up and joins Highway 170 just outside the park boundary."

Anna hadn't heard the sound of a car or truck engine but then she might not have, given the constant racket of the river tearing up its bed. The shooter could have left that way, unseen by Freddy and unheard by the people struggling up from the killing grounds.

"How long would it take to drive out that way?" she asked.

"Depends. An hour or two. Help will be coming in from the Lajitas side," he said, mistaking—or pretending to mistake—her questions for concern about how long it would be till rescue reached them. "They should be here in a little while. We do have a helicopter but with fires so bad this early in the year, the park detailed it to Big Thicket. A lot of our LE rangers are there too."

Everything he said made sense. He seemed to be precisely what he said he was: a ranger who was patrolling on his day off because the river was raging and who happened to come upon them by chance. Freddy might even have saved their lives if the shooter had seen him coming and stopped the carnage to save his own skin.

"Are you going to tell me what happened here?" Martinez asked.

Anna couldn't think of any reason not to. "Sure," she said. Helena had stopped taking water and was sleeping. At least Anna hoped she was asleep. She fought down the urge to disturb the baby by lifting her and pressing her ear against her chest for the umpteenth time that day.

Filling the time with the tale so she wouldn't humiliate herself by falling asleep while on prisoner watch duty, Anna started at the beginning. In her mind the beginning was Easter, back when they were all still alive and having fun. Martinez was annoyingly unsurprised by their daring rescue of the stranded cow.

"We haul one or two out every season. Leave it to Carmen to lower one down a cliff, though." He laughed, and Anna felt bad that she had to tell him Carmen was dead. She had forgotten how tiny worlds were. Boatmen knew boatmen. Of course Martinez knew Carmen. Anna chose not to blurt it out but to let it come at its natural time in the story. Partly, she was putting off the moment, but mostly she wanted to see Freddy's reaction to events as they unfolded. Maybe he wasn't the shooter—she'd been charmed or lulled or convinced of that for the time being—but it didn't mean he knew nothing about the shooting.

A weird sense of shame came over her as she was approaching the telling of how they'd wrapped the raft around a rock. She spent too much time explaining how Lori and Chrissie and fate had conspired to keep them too long, push them too far toward the American bank, how the girls' panic had turned the situation more serious when they'd leaned into the current and the raft had taken on all the tonnage of water slamming down from upriver, and it came to her that she was afraid, actually frightened, that he would think her a rotten ranger because she hadn't been able to navigate the slide without falling victim to a great hungry rock, that she would rather blame the dead than appear inept in front of her fellows. This was not who she'd once been, not who she was before she'd gone to Isle Royale.

It was not who she wanted to be.

"So, we lost the raft and the gear, saved the cow and ourselves," she summed up quickly, and waited for Martinez to tell her how it should have been done, what mistakes rookies make.

"It's easy to do," he said. "I wrapped a canoe so bad once we spent a half a day rigging zigzag winches to pull it off. Finally we had about ten zigs and nine zags to increase the power of our pull and ended up shifting the rock. The canoe sucked under and is probably buried about forty feet deep by now." He laughed easily.

Rather than feeling relieved he had no need to make her feel small, she felt small for caring, for once again projecting her fears on a stranger. Her mind flashed back to the bitterness with which she had thought of Dr. Vincent James, the psychologist who had tried to help her in Boulder. Little broken people were the ones with the sharp edges, the ones who needed to saw bites out of others to feed themselves. The pit, the nightmares, the administrative leave—she'd let something cut her down to little. She laid her fingers against Helena's cheek as if to comfort the child. In reality she was comforting herself.

"When we got everybody fished out we were missing Chrissie," Anna went on with her story. "We heard her screaming a ways downriver. She'd found a woman caught in a strainer and started shrieking. When you meet Chrissie, this won't seem as farfetched," Anna told Martinez.

Freddy knew there had been shots fired and he knew not everybody had survived, yet the mention of the woman in the strainer brought him up rigid, his back pulled away from the log he'd been leaning against. "Pregnant?" he demanded.

Anna stiffened and felt Helena stir in the crook of her left arm. Pregnant wouldn't be her first assumption when told of a person caught in a strainer. Anna was a bit past the age when Helena would automatically be assumed to be hers, but there was no reason not to assume she belonged to a deceased member of the party.

"Yeah," Anna said warily.

"Did she live?" Martinez's eyes were too wide. Even in the vague light of the moon, Anna could see them spark black against the whites surrounding them. The liquid lines of his muscles were frozen now and he looked a man made of angles and edges.

"No," Anna told him. "She died."

"God dammit!" Martinez cried. "Mexican?" he demanded.

"Mexican."

"God dammit!" and he started to his feet, his fists clenched as if he planned on battering Anna until she changed her story.

"Sit down." Anna had the Glock in her hand and the muzzle pointed unwaveringly at his chest, the biggest target and nearly impossible to miss at this distance.

Martinez stopped cold, his hands still bunched into fists at his sides, the knuckles big and gleaming white in the reflected light from the desert floor.

"Sit down," Anna said again. "You're going to wake the baby."

For a long miserable second Martinez stared down at her and Anna worried that, if she shot him, he would fall on Helena. Finally he sat, folding down with all the grace of a broken chair collapsing. He dropped his head in his hands with more drama than Anna thought the passing of a stranger, pregnant or not, called for.

"Did the baby die too?" he mumbled through his fingers.

It crossed Anna's mind that the guy was psycho, had stolen Martinez's gun, radio and horse and wandered Texas killing people. It wasn't unheard of, not even in Anna's limited experience with murderous psychopaths.

"The baby did not die," she said carefully and without taking the Glock off Martinez. "I delivered her by C-section after the mother died. Helena—this baby—is the child of the dead woman in the strainer."

Martinez lifted his face from his hands, his eyes glowing with a fanatic light—or that of a man pardoned at the eleventh hour. "No kidding?" he said, and the bizarreness was as if it had never happened. He spoke with the joyous clarity of a nice park ranger hearing the most fabulous news.

"This is the baby," he said in a voice close to awe. "Venus, the child from the sea."

"Helena. From the river," Anna said tersely. It annoyed the stuffing out of her that he was messing with the name, as if he had a claim on the baby. She liked him better as a crazed killer. At least she could shoot him in that persona.

"I've got a new baby," he said. "My wife gave birth to Edgar Allan Martinez six weeks and two days ago."

A new father. That could explain the manic-depressive episode but Anna didn't quite buy it. She wasn't sure she bought the bit about his wife having a baby. Edgar Allan? Not an auspicious name, not to mention not exactly a Spanish name.

"Can I hold her?"

"Would you stop with that?" Anna snapped. "No baby. No gun. You sit and stop being weird. I'm too tired and hungry for anything but nice, ordinary, sane people. Or dead people," she added, and was gratified to see that the pity was gone from his face and alarm had taken its place.

They fell silent. The small fire in the metal fire ring had gone out and a cool breeze was coming down from the Chisos. Anna wrapped the rags of T-shirt and sleeping bag closer around Helena. Without the sun the air had an edge to it and Anna wished she'd thought to drag the horse blanket back with her. Cold was seeping into her, mixing with fatigue and beginning to set up like concrete in her joints. Paul should be getting back now, Chrissie and Steve and Cyril with him. Regardless of the hazards of four people ascending the slide with a single flashlight, Anna knew there was no way Paul would be able to keep Chrissie on that rock overnight short of lowering a feather bed and shower down to it.

"Sorry about the outburst," Freddy said finally. "When Homeland Security closed the border they killed a lot of people in one way or another, killed their hope, killed their income, some it just plain killed. Closing the border was a crime of violence. This woman was probably trying to cross so her baby could be born in America, in a hospital with proper medical care. The river came up and she got carried down canyon. Because she wanted the best for her child, we killed her. Jesus."

Anna said nothing. She didn't have a dog in this fight.

Martinez took a deep breath and blew it out noisily, then another exhaled on the noise. "Lisa—my wife—is a big yoga person. Can't hurt." He did it again and seemed calmer.

"Lisa just had the baby?" Anna wanted to see if the story would change at all.

"Edgar."

"Eddie?"

"Never. Edgar. Lisa's thesis was on Poe. She thinks the man was the greatest writer of the nineteenth century."

Anna guessed Martinez was in his mid-forties. Lisa was probably the second wife. Or the third. A twenty-something wanting her own family on the tail end of her husband's, whose children were already grown and gone. It was common enough: Sir Paul McCartney was frolicking with a child who would graduate from college when Papa was an octogenarian. Anna had never much liked the picture, but she suspected it was more because of the iniquities of aging from gender to gender than because it was evil in and of itself. Money was a factor, so the child might lose a father at an early age but there would be a Ferrari in the offing to take the edge off her grief.

Where the heck was Paul? She looked at her watch. It had died at twenty past three. "What time is it?" she demanded.

"No watch. It's my day off."

Anna remembered they were in the twenty-first century and rolled the satellite phone over so she could see its face. Paul had headed back down no more than forty-five minutes ago. It would be an hour before she could begin to expect him. She wished she'd had him leave some of the water. There was an inch left in Helena's cup and the baby was fast asleep. Absurd as it was, Anna could not bring herself to drink it.

"If you'll tell me the rest of the story, I promise I won't do anything as horrific as preferring live babies to dead ones again," Martinez said.

He'd recovered his sense of humor. The least Anna could do was to pretend she'd recovered hers. She proffered a fake laugh. The sound amused her so much she laughed outright. It would be good to have a distraction.

"Sure," she said. "But no asking to hold Helena."

"Holding babies is the best therapy there is," Martinez said.

"You're sure warm and fuzzy for a Texas ranger," Anna grumbled. "Whatever happened to stiff upper lip and smile when you say that, pardner?"

Martinez just smiled. She was beginning to like the smile. No light but that from the moon and the desert, his big white teeth in his dark face put her in mind of the Cheshire cat.

"So after the C-section . . ." Martinez cued her.

Anna told him the rest. Carmen's death, Lori's, Easter's probable demise; he heard it all with solemn dignity, none of it yanking him up by his roots the way the news of the woman in the strainer had. Freddy Martinez was somehow connected to the dead woman, to the baby she held on her lap, a connection that moved him from rage to exultation and back again.

Careful not to disturb Helena, Anna moved the Glock closer to her thigh. Until she knew what that connection was she would keep both it and the baby close.

TWENTY

Shortly after nine o'clock Darden was riding down from the Chisos with a seasonal ranger. The dinner was still in full swing and he hated to leave but it wasn't his choice; it was Judith's. Word that shots had been fired on the border resulting in the injury or death of tourists had become common knowledge almost before Darden had made it back through the gift shop to the dining hall. This common knowledge was not accurate. The few known facts had been passed through imagination, misinformation and self-interest until the final result was as screwy and varied as the end of a children's game of Rumor.

Judith knew this phenomenon better than most. "I don't care what is true," she'd whispered to Darden after giving him his orders. "I care what I can use."

Shots fired on the Rio Grande should come in handy in the next few days while she hammered out her platform on border control. He could have dashed out and tried to corner Bernard Davies, but he doubted that would do anything but get the ranger's hackles up. Staying out of the way until they'd gotten things under control was the better part of valor and, too, he didn't want to miss Judith's announcement speech.

She was stellar: strong and smart and convincing without losing her charm. Unfortunately the press—and it was they who this week in the wilds was primarily aimed at—were distracted by the smell of blood from the direction of the border. Several had disappeared but came wandering back, looking disappointed. Gerry, he didn't see again. She must have gotten in on the excitement one way or another.

The mayor's entourage had no shortage of vehicles but in his experience, car trips bred conversation, so Darden cadged a ride from a boy ranger. The kid had to be twenty-one—he had a gun on his hip—but with his downy cheeks and acne, he looked about fifteen. Clearly it galled him that he was patrolling campgrounds when the most exciting thing that had happened all season was happening without him. A good subject to pump for gossip, Darden thought.

As it turned out, no pumping was necessary. It hadn't taken but one interested look—and that was overkill—to set the kid off. Boy Ranger was anxious to let Darden—whom he mistakenly thought was still Secret Service, a delusion Darden did not disabuse him of—know that, though not chosen to help with the rescue, he was definitely in the know.

"I gotta make one more pass through the campground before I head down," the kid said. "You'd be surprised how much trouble campers can get up to."

Darden would be surprised but he didn't say so. "You figure those people on the river were camping?" The segue was about as awkward as it could get, but it forced the conversation Darden wanted back on track.

"Oh, yeah, for sure," the kid said. "They were with this commercial outfit out of Terlingua. There's been radio traffic about it all night. A couple of people were shot, from what it sounds like, and there was a ranger from Rocky Mountain on the trip with her husband and kids, I guess."

The kid drove like little old ladies are supposed to and seldom do. He gripped the steering wheel at an eleven and one position and leaned forward as if he was afraid the car would try to break away on its own if he let down his guard for an instant. If the kid didn't have neck and back trouble already, he would by the time he was thirty. Which, at the rate they were creeping around the snaky blacktop between tent sites, he'd be by the time they started down to headquarters.

"They didn't know what they were doing and lost the raft at the slide. That's a rapid about a mile or so in," the kid said. "I've been through it half a dozen times. It's a piece of cake if you know how to read the water."

Darden knew he was supposed to be impressed so he

murmured: "Impressive," and all was well; the kid powered on.

"Was the ranger leading the trip?" Darden threw in to keep the kid on subject.

"No, the ranger was this woman named Anna Pigeon. She got mixed up in some funny business on Isle Royale and killed a guy. I guess she flipped out over it and they put her on administrative leave. From what I heard, it was a righteous shooting. Me, I wouldn't bat an eye. So you have to shoot a bad guy? Isn't that what we're hired on for?"

The last bit sounded like a quote and Darden wondered who the lucky ranger was that this boy wanted to be like. He didn't have any desire to meet him.

"Anyway, they didn't make the rapids and lost all their gear."

Finally they were done with the dangerous campground patrol and turning onto the main—the only—road leading down from the Chisos Mountain Lodge to the park headquarters below. Darden heaved a sigh of relief before he could stop himself. He'd wanted the gossip, but the kid was a pain in the patootie, the sort of person who drains the life out of life by trying too hard. It occurred to Darden to overlook it due to the ranger's youth, but he didn't. This kid would be the same at thirty and forty and fifty, mid-level boring at some oversized firm, kissing up and talking down.

Darden took off his seat belt. Not that the kid was so bad it made him suicidal but, with his present physique, there was no way to get comfortable with the belly band cutting one way and the shoulder strap another.

The kid slammed on the brakes and Darden nearly bashed his head on the dashboard.

"You have to wear your seat belt in all government vehicles," he said. "Safety issues." Then, realizing he sounded like the little prig he was, he added: "I don't bother with them when I'm on my own. When your number is up, it's up, right?"

"Riiiight," Darden said sourly, and put the belt back on.

"What was it I heard about shots being fired?" Darden said when they had again reached their snail's pace. The ride with the kid had been a bad idea, but he might as well get out of it what he could.

"I guess somebody was shooting at them or something."

The boy ranger went on after that, but Darden had quit listening. The opening sentence didn't bode well for even a scrap of truth making it into subsequent statements.

HEADQUARTERS WAS HUMMING. The rescue team had returned with the victims, the ambulance was back, half a dozen cars were parked hurriedly in the front lot and all the lights were on. The boy ranger insisted on escorting Darden in, probably in hopes of being included in whatever was going on inside. He wasn't. The chief ranger wasn't particularly thrilled to have Darden show up unannounced, either, but Darden was good at ingratiating himself when the need arose. He poured on humility salted with a need to understand the park's issues and was allowed to join the group in the conference room. He took a chair in a corner, out of the limelight and the line of fire, and proceeded to vanish as best he could by looking older and fatter and sleepier than he actually was, a person of no import, nobody to be reckoned with. Wallpaper, Darden liked to think of it. In moments he was forgotten.

The room was spacious and, during the day, probably had a spectacular view of the mountains. At this hour the big square windows on the southwest side of the conference table showed as black mirrors. On the internal wall were three good photographs of scenic stuff and one in black and white of the park in the early days, but other than that it looked like any of a hundred conference rooms Darden had wallpapered.

Bernard Davies sat at the head of the table in an office chair made to match the oak of the table. He had it tilted back as far as it would go to accommodate his long legs and sat with his right ankle crossed over his left knee, exposing eight inches of white sock. His left hand rested on the ankle, looking too big and too rawboned for a man with an office job. Beside him was a compact man wearing wire-rimmed glasses. He looked to be in his forties, but had already lost most of his hair. What remained was still dark brown and curled over the tops of his ears and collar like fringe on a threadbare carpet. Darden remembered he was the head of the law enforcement wing for the park but couldn't recall his name. Bad PR. He was slipping. Once he got Judith into the governor's mansion he would step down, he promised himself. Judith needed a sharper man than he'd become. A younger man.

The head of law enforcement had his elbows on the table and an open, sympathetic look on his face that Darden bet got him a lot more information in a week than the old hard-line cops got in a lifetime. Across from him was the river district ranger, Freddy Martinez. He was dressed like a cowboy, down to his high-heeled boots, a Mexican cowboy—vaquero, that was what they called themselves. Darden knew a lot about Martinez; he was so outspoken about the evils of closing the border between the park and its companion villages on the other side of the Rio Grande that Judith had figured she might have some trouble with him, or be able to use him as a foil if he wasn't all that bright. Darden was surprised how good-looking he was. Sitting comfortably in one of the swivel chairs, a foam coffee cup in his hand, he didn't give off the aura of a fanatic, but one never knew.

The others—there were six of them if the baby was counted—were at the other end of the table. Had he no clue what was going on, Darden would have known where the power was by the obvious separation between Us and Them. Rangers and tourists or, in this case, victim tourists. A double Them.

The three teenagers, two obviously brother and sister

if not fraternal twins, and the third, looking like she was going to burst into tears at any moment, he spent little time on. They were as lost as sheep and he was pretty sure the boy ranger had been mistaken. He didn't peg any one of them as belonging to the older couple. The woman sitting, holding the baby, had to be the Anna Pigeon Boy Ranger had waxed so derisive about. The fallen ranger from Rocky Mountains, wherever the heck that was. Montana probably. One of the square states in the middle of the country, anyway.

She was small, her hair was a bird's nest, dried blood or catsup or mud speckled her face and arms. The shirt she was sort of wearing was ripped till it would have put a bag lady to shame and she was no spring chicken, forties at a guess. But she didn't look crazy and she didn't look like the sort of person who gave up without a fight. Or gave up with a fight, for that matter. She struck Darden as the kind whose corpse would kick you three days after you shot her.

Davies and the law enforcement ranger—whose name Darden still couldn't recall—didn't see her that way. They were too professional to want to let their condescension show but not good enough actors to do it up thoroughly. In the tone of their voices and the tiredness of their smiles Darden could see that they didn't want to deal with her as a fellow ranger, as another law enforcement professional, as a peer of any kind. It was more comfortable for them to put her in the role of poor little crazy middle-aged victim. A waste, Darden thought, one of their own was front and central to the incident they wanted to investigate and they were ignoring her.

There were reasons: she wasn't in her own jurisdiction—cops, even tree cops, didn't like anybody else stirring in their pot—and she was in bad odor with the central office. Cooties were not merely a malady of elementary school children. Adults were as vulnerable as any third-grader. Nobody wanted to get somebody else's cooties on them. But Darden guessed it was much simpler than that. Anna Pigeon was a woman and women were easier to deal with when they were cast as mommies and wives and victims, roles most of them had never played from a time before many were born.

Underestimating women was the last gasp of male dominance, Darden figured. He used to do it himself. A first lady of the U.S.A. had cured him of that before he was thirty. She was little like this Pigeon woman and ladylike and perfectly groomed and soft-spoken and he'd mistaken that for being weak. It nearly cost him his career. He'd not made the same mistake again with any woman.

Anna Pigeon might look like a waif out of a Dickens novel but she was taking in everything that was said, scanning the table the way he scanned a room, looking for anything amiss. Women noticed different things than men did. Darden hadn't exactly made a study of it, but he'd paid attention. Female agents were better at noticing personal details and interpreting them: unironed shirts, beard growth, body language, vocal tones, sidelong glances, lapses in personal hygiene, cosmetic surgery, hair dye, what clothing cost and where it came from. In the political jungle this paid off more often than watching for the glint of gun barrels in windows or bulges under sport coats.

The man standing behind her chair—Darden assumed he was her husband by the way he was standing guard over her—interested Darden as much as the Pigeon woman. He didn't look any better than she did, white hair, a little too long for corporate work, was matted on one side and sticking out in wires on the other. His face was drawn with fatigue and years, his clothes were filthy and torn. Scratches marked his arms and his legs between the drooping cargo shorts and the battered Tevas. Yet he was utterly dignified. No, dignified wasn't the right word. There wasn't any sense of class consciousness or pride. More that he seemed completely comfortable in his own skin, completely devoid of insecurities. He was still as an oak tree is still on a windless day; the life is there, and the strength, but what one notices is the welcoming shade.

Darden figured he'd like Mr. Pigeon if he ever got the chance to know him. He doubted Judith would have much interest in him. He didn't look like a man who could be used. That's what Darden had been sent here for; things and facts and people Judith could use. Mr. and Mrs. Pigeon didn't look like good bets. He was turning his attention to the three college kids when the door to the conference room opened and a tall woman with tightly permed gray hair slipped noiselessly in. A secretary, nobody but secretaries had so soft a footfall and so firm a determination. They had to be trained in it in secretarial school but Darden could never get one of them to admit it. They'd just laugh and say, "Oh you!" She leaned down to whisper in Bernard's ear.

"Good. Thank you, Darlene." Darlene whispered out and they all sat quietly, watching the open door till she returned with another woman whom they had apparently been expecting.

"Thanks, Lisa, you're a lifesaver," Bernard said as a Hispanic woman in her late thirties stepped into the conference room. She looked ordinary: nice eyes, a little thick around the middle, black hair with a stylish salon cut, Levi's over a broad, alluring bottom and a very generous bosom. Very generous. Anna Pigeon seemed to find her extraordinary. She looked startled when the name Lisa was proffered. Then the set of her mouth changed subtly and she looked pleased or respectful. Darden wasn't sure which. Maybe both.

"Hi, baby," Martinez said, and stood to give his wife his chair.

She didn't sit but walked around to the "Them" end of the table. "Is this the famous river baby?" she asked Anna.

"That's it," Bernard said. "Thanks again, Lisa. You can take it into my office if you'd be more comfortable there."

Lisa ignored him, waiting for Anna to answer her question. "Yes," the ranger said. She didn't offer up the child and there was a fierceness in her manner that Darden didn't understand unless the baby was her grandchild and her daughter was one of the victims of the "shots fired" reports circulating up at Chisos Lodge.

"Do you have a name for her?" Lisa asked, as if she and Anna and the baby were alone in the room.

"Helena," Anna Pigeon said, and she finally held out her arms so Lisa could take the baby.

"Helena and I are going to dinner," Lisa said, smiling down at the woman with the empty arms. "Then I'll bring her back to you."

"Lisa, we haven't decided—" the chief ranger began.

Lisa Martinez shook her head fractionally and he stopped mid-sentence. She smiled again at Anna and took the infant from the room. Before they had all settled back into their chairs there was a gabble of noise from the hallway and the door was opened again by Darlene, who did not look pleased.

"Mayor Pierson," she said flatly.

Smiling, Judith managed to slip by the secretary and still appear to have been ushered in.

Darlene wasn't the only one displeased. This was a bad idea and one Judith had not shared with Darden.

He half rose, hoping that she had come down the mountain in the shank of the evening merely to give her good old Darden a ride back to his cabin. No such luck. She settled into a chair on the Us end of the table with the aplomb of one for whom the meeting has been called and nodded graciously at Bernard Davies, granting him permission to resume his job.

Darden suppressed a groan. Had he not been feeling

so sorry for himself, he would have felt sorry for the chief ranger. Bernard cleared his throat, probably trying to think of a way to throw her out, get his conference room back, and he might have done it, too, had Judith not preempted the decision.

Leaning in a bit, not flirty but conveying sincerity, she looked Davies in the eyes and said: "I sure appreciate what you're doing." Without saying so she made it sound like he'd invited her, that this was her party.

Darden eyed her narrowly. Her linen trousers were still unwrinkled and her silk blouse had not wilted. The short blond bob was neatly in place and her makeup perfect, but she had a feverishness in her eyes. Drugs would have been the first thing that popped into Darden's mind, but Judith didn't do drugs. As far as he knew, she didn't. After the wink from Kevin, he was beginning to think he didn't know as much about Judith as he'd believed.

Sex was his second thought, but if it was a roll in the hay with Kevin or anybody else, it had not left her languorous or satisfied. Judith was avid, greedy, not so the general public would notice, but Darden could see it. He thought she was afraid, as well, and anything that frightened Judith was bound to terrify him.

TWENTY-ONE

"I know you've gone through this all before for Jessie and I know you're tired so I'll try not to make this any longer than I have to." The chief ranger was talking, Bernard Davies. Anna knew him vaguely from a forty-hour refresher they'd attended in Apostle Islands some years before. He'd been a district ranger at Great Sand Dunes, if she remembered correctly. She tried to concentrate on what he was saying but she found herself watching the door through which Lisa had gone with Helena. Anna had been dead wrong about Freddy Martinez's wife. She wasn't number two or three; she was his first love and mother of two children, a nineteen-year-old son and Edgar. Edgar had been, as Martinez had put it on the ride out from the canyon, "a pleasant surprise."

Lisa had volunteered to serve as temporary wet nurse for Helena. For this Anna loved her, but she suspected she would have liked her even if she hadn't proved useful. The baby was a curious thing, Anna thought. She left an empty place in Anna's lap when she was taken to dinner with the generous Lisa Martinez, rather like when a cat jumped off her lap. The fleeting moment of acceptance and comfort was gone, replaced by a sense of freedom to move. Realizing she was holding her arms in an awkward bowl ready to accept baby or kitten, Anna relaxed them and let them lie in her lap. They were heavy, so much so she wondered if she would be able to lift them again when the time came.

"Mrs. Davidson?"

Lost in her thoughts, Anna hadn't been following the conversation around the conference table. A prolonged silence brought her back from her woolgathering expedition. All eyes were upon her.

"Mrs. Davidson?" Bernard Davies said again.

That was her. Anna was Mrs. Davidson. "Yeah. Right," she said, shaking her head to clear it. "Sorry. Tireder than I thought, I guess." Did Bernard recognize her from the Apostle Islands class? For reasons she could not put her finger on, she believed he did. The "Mrs. Davidson," once a title of respect, had become one of dismissal in certain circles. Ranger Pigeon, or Ms. Pigeon, or simply Anna, would have put them on a more equal footing. The chief ranger was putting distance between himself and her, she could feel it as clearly as if he'd straight-armed her, but she hadn't a clue why he would act that way.

He didn't keep her in the dark.

"I understand you're on administrative leave from Rocky," he said. "Down here on vacation?"

Bernard had called her chief ranger. Anna had hoped her lapse into tears in Vincent James's office had been confidential, but she knew the hope was in vain. Nothing was confidential but that which was kept in one's own skull. Records were subpoenaed, people talked or, if they didn't talk, they told by their silences. Every move Bernard made, the inflections in his voice, the way his eyes slid away from her when she tried to meet his gaze, told her he believed her to be a broken vessel. The use of her married name let her know that he preferred it that way. When he'd first laid eyes on her—given that he'd erased Apostle Islands from his mind—she'd been holding a baby. That, too, would count against her. Women with babes in arms were seen as victims. Not that there was malice in it, but they were to be protected, given parking places nearer the supermarket doors, and first, in theory at least, to be handed into the lifeboats when the ship was going down.

Anna didn't know whether to fight it, give in to it or laugh. In the end she did nothing; she answered the chief's question. "Yes. Vacation."

Relief flickered momentarily in Bernard's eyes and she knew he was well aware of what he was doing, that he was intentionally putting her on a shelf—or out to pasture. She flattered herself that it was because he knew she would not let go of this, administrative leave or not, till she had found out who killed the three women and where Helena would go from here. Flattered herself because even as she enjoyed the thought, she was aware it was not true. Bernard just wanted her in a pigeonhole where he would not have to deal with her.

Anna smiled at him. This was one pigeon it was going to be hard to label and forget. The smile bothered him and he looked quickly to Paul. Anna was surprised until she caught sight of herself in the black mirrors night had made of the windows. The smile on her face had a wolfish quality, a tinge of the cold of a Michigan winter hardening the edges.

"Mr. Davidson—"

"Paul." In the mirror of glass Anna saw her husband's smile as he put things on a less formal basis. There was nothing cold in it. Nothing warm either. She suspected he was as aware of Bernard's dismissal of her as she was and it was making him wary.

"Paul," the chief said, more comfortable now. "Why don't you sit down?"

Anna had known but not given any thought to the fact that Paul, as exhausted as he must be, had chosen to stand behind her and Helena rather than relax. Something, maybe just instinct or habit, was keeping him on guard.

He took the chair next to hers, reached over and lifted one of her hands from her lap and folded it into his, both resting on his thigh. The heat and the touch buoyed Anna up and the title Mrs. no longer nettled her. Not for a moment did she doubt it had been meant to belittle but, given her Mr., it never would. She closed her fingers around Paul's and waited to see what Bernard had next on his "to do" list now that he believed she had been summarily disposed of.

"You've been through this with Jessie." He nodded at the head of Law Enforcement, Jessie Wiggins. He'd been with the paramedic and the two rangers who had fetched them off the rim of the canyon. Jessie nodded. As far as Anna knew, Jessie didn't have an agenda and hadn't seemed to react to the news that she was on administrative leave for PTSD or whatever the park had chosen to call it. "I'm going to have to ask you to go through it once more for me. Mayor Pierson of Houston and her head of security, Darden White, are in the park for the border impact convention and asked if they could sit in."

Because Bernard was being a twit, Anna was tempted to allow herself a small curl of the lip to let him know they were all aware that the mayor had railroaded him, but she was too tired to be petty. The mayor was an interesting woman. She was petite and, though she had a gym-toned body, she worked at hiding the fact with soft silk that flowed from her shoulders, lending fullness to small breasts and roundness to what Anna guessed would be sinewy arms. Her hair was incarcerated in what Anna thought of as a Texas bob, very expensively blond and done in stone. Rather like a toned-down, Bumble & Bumble version of Ann Richards's coif.

The eyes were her most captivating aspect. She had schooled herself in dress and makeup, hair, nails, even body type and managed to create a package that was

both attractive and businesslike, physically unremark-
able, neither sexy nor unsexed, the fine line women in
politics had to walk every day on the way to their clos-
ets. To a careful observer, though, her eyes gave her
away, Anna thought. They did tonight, at any rate.
Surely she hadn't been entrusted with running a city
with eyes like that. The Christian right wouldn't allow
it. Not in Texas.

Judith Pierson's eyes burned. If Anna squinted, she
believed she could almost see the conflagration behind
the brownish green irises. The mayor had the eyes of a
hungry vampire or a sainted lunatic in mid-vision.

"Mayor Pierson."

The man Bernard had introduced as Darden White
spoke from his corner. Anna had forgotten he was there
and his voice startled her. Darden had drifted out of her
consciousness as a fat old guy in the mayor's entourage.
When he spoke he was so very much *there*, she was surprised she could have overlooked him.

"Can I get you a coffee or a soda?" White asked his
boss deferentially.

The mayor paused, took a breath, then said: "A soda
if they've got it. Thank you, Darden." When she turned
back to the table the fire in her eyes might not have
been extinguished but it was no longer in sight.

As he left the conference room it occurred to Anna
that he might have intentionally disappeared into the
woodwork, the way she often disappeared in plain sight
along trails, situated where the natural line of sight
would miss her, quiet and unmoving as a rock. People

would hike within feet of her, chattering and laughing, never noticing that they were being watched.

"Paul, could you tell us what happened?" Bernard asked, and sat back as if he didn't wish to have the messiness of their adventure splash on him during the telling.

Paul looked to Anna to see if she needed to say anything before he began. She didn't. Paul started with the rescue of Easter, and then told of losing the raft. The chief ranger rolled his eyes at the mention of the cow but otherwise made no comments.

Anna watched Cyril and Steve and Chrissie. The twins were uncharacteristically quiet and Chrissie slumped in her chair with no more life than a deflated balloon. They were exhausted and, now that the adrenaline had been reabsorbed and they were no longer living from moment to moment trying to stay alive, the full impact of the deaths of Carmen, Lori and Helena's mother would be hitting them.

The deaths were waiting to hit Anna. She could feel them like black shadows drifting between her and the overhead fluorescents, swimming past the corners of her eyes always just out of sight but for a gray wisp or a stealthy movement. Ghosts were not the spirits of the uneasy dead, but the projections of the living, drifts of guilt, fear, failure and mortality too great to be contained in the mind.

Anna didn't know why they had chosen to join the specters that had followed her home from Isle Royale or whether or not they would remain with her. Logically she should have been able to banish them easily. She had neither caused nor contributed to the cause of any of the deaths. She had saved whom she could, doing the best she had with what was at hand. That used to be good enough to get her to sleep at night.

No more.

"Chrissie found the woman caught in the strainer," Paul said, and he leaned over to pat Chrissie's shoulder. He smiled at her with the full force of priest and father figure behind it. Chrissie visibly grew stronger; she sat up straighter and tossed her head. Her hair was so filthy and matted it more or less clunked but the gesture had a smidgeon of the old arrogance and Anna was pleased.

"Do you want to tell this part?" Paul asked. Years as a priest would have taught him the necessity of letting people share their horrors, Anna realized. There was much about her husband she did not know, they'd not been together long enough. Instead of making her uneasy she enjoyed a tickle of excitement at the wonders she had yet to discover in this man she had married.

"Yeah. Okay," Chrissie said as she pulled herself together to be a productive member of the adult world.

"Paul, if you don't mind . . ." Bernard left the sentence unfinished but his meaning was clear. He wanted to hear a real account, not one by a girl in her teens or a middle-aged woman who'd recently fallen apart.

Chrissie began to deflate again. "I wasn't in on a lot of this part," Paul said easily. "Chrissie's the only one who was there start to finish."

Paul leaned back, closed his mouth firmly and smiled encouragingly at the bedraggled teenager.

Chrissie regained the oxygen she'd lost and puffed up a bit. For a moment she scanned the table the way a practiced speaker might assess their audience. Anna's eyes followed hers, interested to see how the mayor would respond to the change of narrators. Mayor Pierson had lit up again. The soda White had brought back—a diet 7UP—was at her elbow, the tab not yet pulled. She was leaning in, her lips slightly parted as if she wanted to lap this part of the story up like rich cream.

"I was down farther than everybody else," Chrissie began. "And I was kind of freaked out, the water was so . . . you know . . . so pushy. I'd gotten turned around and I was walking away from everybody else instead of toward them when I saw this bunch of branches and things caught between two rocks, like a beaver dam or something, just a bunch of sticks and logs and brush."

"The woman was caught there? Washed down by the river?" Judith jumped in, and Anna was glad to see Chrissie had recovered enough spirit to be annoyed by the interruption.

"I'm getting to that," she said with exaggerated patience. "*Anyway*, there was this bunch of branches and things caught between two rocks."

The backtracking was sawing at Judith Pierson's nerves. Her lips were pursed as if her tongue was busy checking the sharpness of each tooth.

Satisfied the woman had been put in her place, Chrissie moved the story along. "I thought pieces of our stuff had got caught up and I went to see if maybe I could get it. When I got close I saw it was this Mexican woman.

The water had tangled all her hair into the sticks and her arm was woven through it so she looked like one of those sculptures of people becoming trees, you know like the Greeks liked to do, people turning into different things?"

It wasn't actually a question; Chrissie was in the habit of ending her sentences on an up note.

"She was dead," Judith said. "My God, how awful for you." She reached a hand across the table but Chrissie was having none of it.

"She was *not* dead," she said repressively. "She was all alive and pregnant."

The mayor reacted as if Chrissie had slapped her, unaccustomed to being rebuffed, probably. "She wasn't dead?" she asked Paul.

"No," Paul said. "She died later but she was alive when Chrissie first found her."

"Did she say anything? Did she talk to you?" the mayor asked Paul.

"She did *not* say anything." Chrissie took back the floor. "She was alive but she wasn't exactly conversational. Jeez Louise, she'd probably drank about half of Colorado or wherever. She didn't say anything."

"Sorry," Judith said, evidently recalling her manners. "Please go on."

"Thank you," Chrissie said, unappeased. "We made a line of us holding to each other and Anna cut her out of the sticks. Then we floated her back to shore and carried her up out of the water to the cliff where there was shade."

"And the poor thing died there," Judith said, shaking her head. "Such a waste."

"Not yet," Chrissie said. "She didn't die right off. She said 'my baby' then she died, okay?"

"God, that is so sad," the mayor said. "I suppose she was trying to cross the river so she could have the baby on American soil. As long as they think they can, they'll try it. It's not fair to anybody."

Martinez put down his foam cup and unfolded his legs.

"We don't need to go into the political ramifications now, Mrs. Pierson," the chief said as he shot his river ranger a hostile glance.

Mrs., not *Mayor*. Bernard definitely used the title as a way to strip a woman of her professional power, should she be so brazen as to have any.

"Did she have any ID on her?" Pierson asked Jessie Wiggins. "Do we know who in Mexico to inform?"

Wiggins shook his head, the bald spot flashing dully under the overhead lights. "Unless somebody comes asking after her, we may never know. If she was crossing to get to relatives here—that's often the case—if they're here illegally, they won't come forward. Even if they did, identifying the body might be out of the question. The river will have taken it. Next time we find it, if we do, the turtles and fish won't have left us much to go on."

"I don't think she was a poor Mexican woman crossing the river to have her baby in the U.S.," Anna said.

Jessie and Bernard and Judith stared at her as if toads had just hopped out of her mouth.

"Mrs. Davidson," Bernard began.

"Anna," Anna said.

Bernard's face settled fractionally and was made older and kinder. "Anna," he said. "This kind of thing happens on the border every day. Not this tragic or dramatic, but people die trying to smuggle themselves in. Truckloads sometimes."

"I read the papers," Anna said. The breach in the chief's charade when he was forced to say her name had been shored up. He was pushing to get her back into her assigned role. "I first thought she was washed away trying to cross so she could give her baby American citizenship. But she wasn't a poor village woman with no resources. At least I don't think she was."

"And why is that, Mrs.— Anna?" The chief caught himself and, not being rude by nature, used the name she'd given him, but Anna could tell she was Mrs. Davidson, tourist/victim again.

"She had a Brazilian bikini wax and a pedicure," Anna said.

Judith smiled, a testament to the art of cosmetic dentistry. "You're not from Texas, are you, Mrs. Davidson?" she asked with a hint of conspiratorial humor in her tone that kept the question from sounding confrontational.

Anna didn't reply. Regardless of twinkles of merriment, the mayor was being confrontational. Anna waited to see why, which direction the attack was going to come from.

"What was the woman wearing?" Judith Pierson asked.

Anna drew a blank.

"She had on a rayon dress with a floral print from Wal-Mart," Chrissie piped up. Anna raised an eyebrow and the girl looked slightly abashed—not because she'd interrupted, Anna guessed, but because she'd admitted to being a Wal-Mart shopper and in the fat section, no less.

"You are a very observant young woman," the mayor commended her, and Chrissie shot Anna a glance of triumph. At some point during the long, long day Anna had evidently become The Enemy. Perhaps the fact that she was wearing Chrissie's friend Lori's blood all over her had something to do with it.

"Mexican girls might not have good medical care or education, but they've all got television sets in their houses. These girls watch their idols and emulate them, giving each other pedicures and manicures and waxes," Judith said. "They are no different from American girls when it comes to fashion."

The comment was a mild reproof aimed at Anna's perceived prejudice. Anna resisted the temptation to ask the mayor if she had a bikini wax.

Dismissing the question of the woman's motives for being caught dead in Santa Elena Canyon, Judith turned her attention to Jessie Wiggins. The chief ranger had lost control of the meeting and, by his look of tired annoyance, Anna figured he didn't know how to get it back.

"Up in Chisos we heard that there had been shots fired," the mayor said. "Is there anything to that or was it just a rumor? I know how these things can take on a life of their own through the grapevine."

Jessie took off his glasses and brushed one hand over his brow, an homage to the hair that had once fallen in his face. "There were shots," he said. "Two people were killed. We can't give out any names until we've notified the families."

Pain carved lines down from his nose to the corners of his mouth. The chief ranger was suffering as well. Good men at heart, Anna thought, they grieved the death of innocents and the blow those deaths would deal their park and parks in general. Parks were not places people expected to die.

To her credit, the mayor was stricken as well. Judith Pierson had made all the right sounds, shown the appropriate facial expressions while listening to the story of the Mexican woman caught in the strainer, but the news of the deaths by shooting penetrated the perfect façade to affect the muscles beneath the makeup. Her eyes widened then narrowed, and knots rippled on her cheeks as her jaws clenched.

"Two people were shot and *killed*?" she asked, heat and horror taking her voice up half an octave.

Stirring behind her caught Anna's ear and she looked to where the mayor's head of security sat. Confusion and concern clouded his wide soft face. From the way his eyes were fixed on his boss, Anna believed it was more for the mayor's reaction than the murder of two women.

White women.

The death of the Mexican woman hadn't brought on such a tsunami of barely suppressed emotion. Uncharitable, Anna thought of herself. There was a difference between a tragic accident and homicide. She hoped that was what had unbalanced the scales of their compassion. And maybe the death of Helena's mother was a tragic accident, precisely what they said it was, a woman who cared enough for her child to want it to be born in a country where it might have a better chance at a good life. Whatever the reasons, the woman had ended up in the river, Helena had been born on American soil. Anna had no intention of letting that fact slip away in the general circus that was forming around this incident.

In the canyon, it had crossed her mind that the shooter might have thought she had murdered the woman and, bent on revenge, shot the party up then panicked and ran. Of course that would mean the avenger had been atop the canyon watching the woman dying down below and done nothing to help her. Or he could have come too late to help, only in time to see the woman die and the baby being brought out.

Anna wasn't so much thinking as falling asleep in her chair.

She bestirred herself to hear the chief ranger speaking her dreams: "Lots of times these girls come across and are met by a relative or boyfriend. Could be the boyfriend was waiting, saw her go under and was following along the rim trying to see where she washed up. When he saw the rafters, he panicked and began shooting."

"That makes a horrible kind of sense," the mayor said. Her firm mouth, the drop in her voice, indicated the end of the discussion, but the fire Anna had seen burning behind her eyes was not extinguished by this line of logic, merely banked. Anna hadn't taken to Mayor Pierson the way she had to Lisa Martinez but, when it came down to it, Anna was a lousy judge of character. It was a weakness she'd had to shore up with observation and patience. For her the days of rushing headlong into relationships of any kind had been sufficiently perilous she learned to wait and watch. It was possible this smoldering politician was a fighter for justice and the rights of the downtrodden, that the fire was burning for a good cause.

Too tired to maintain this optimistic view, Anna let it slide.

"It's after midnight and these folks have had a hard day," Jessie Wiggins said. "This thing isn't going to be figured out in an hour or two. What do you say we finish up in the morning?" He looked at Bernard and the chief ranger nodded.

"Where are you staying?" he asked the table in general.

"Campground," Steve said. "Our stuff is in our car. The gear we used on the river was provided by the outfitter." It was the first time he'd spoken since he'd been introduced to the chief ranger when they first arrived.

The richness of his voice had thinned and he sounded forty years older than he had on the river. His eyes had a hollow look and though Anna knew—or hoped—he would again be the nineteen-year-old boy whose wit and courage had helped them get through, she doubted that the shadows of the deaths he had witnessed would ever truly disappear. Cyril had aged, as well, and Anna got a glimpse of what the twins would look like in their forties: still reedy, still as close to identical as opposite genders could get, but no longer straight-backed and supple, no longer light on their feet.

"Is there someplace we could get a shower before you take us to the campground?" Cyril asked. "We don't want to attract skunks."

The glimmer of humor cheered Anna. Cyril was stronger than she had thought, more resilient. Watching the young woman straighten her shoulders and steady her gaze, Anna made a mental note to find the cow, save it again if it was still alive. The thought was absurd. How would she know one scrawny Mexican cow from another? What difference would it make even if Easter was still alive, which wasn't bloody likely?

Absurd or not, Anna would do it.

At the moment she wanted a shower and she wanted Helena back and she wanted to curl up with her head on Paul's shoulder and sleep until Rip Van Winkle called her to breakfast.

"How about you two?" Bernard asked Paul.

"We have reservations at the lodge," Paul said.

"For tonight? I thought you were supposed to be on the river for the next couple of nights."

"Right," Paul said, and sighed. "No reservations. Surely they'll have one empty room."

"Not with the convention and the mayor here," Bernard said.

Anna stood. She'd been sitting too long. People had been talking too long. The room had too little air. Currents from the rangers and the mayor and the three traumatized kids buffeted her brain and the fluorescent lights burned like acid on the backs of her eyes. "We'll work it out," she said, and began edging around the table toward the door. She wanted a shower and food and all the niceties but more than that she wanted out of there. The desire had blown up from a spark to a conflagration and she felt her skin would begin to curl and peel and fall away if she didn't get into real air, air with space around it to breathe free of the pressure of the suffering souls incarcerated in this room.

Paul stood, as well, the intention to stay by her side clear on his face. The need to settle them safe for the night kept him from following. "We'd appreciate the showers and anything else you can do for us," he said.

Anna grabbed for the doorknob. The misery clogging the air, the walls of dun and the acid light were coming together, the crush of humanity pushing down her throat. Unease was turning to panic, and the fact of the panic scared her even more. She jerked on the door and it opened so quickly the edge caught her in the shoulder, knocking her back and into the still-seated mayor.

In front of her, as startled as she, Lisa stood, Helena in her arms.

Anna reached for her, an unformed vision of taking the child and running into the night ricocheting around in her skull. Lisa let her take the baby but didn't step out of her way. Instead she tucked her arm through Anna's like an old friend on a shopping trip.

"Helena ate like a little pig," she told Anna. "Then she burped all over Bernard's in-box and fell fast asleep. When we get home we'll give her a bath. I got more baby stuff than one little boy could ever use."

The warmth of the baby safe in her grasp, the warmth of Lisa's arm in hers, the warmth of the woman's eyes, poured into Anna and the freakish need to flee was quieted.

"Thanks," Anna said simply.

"Good, you two will stay with us," Freddy said. "That's settled." He wasn't entirely successful at keeping the dismay from his voice but Anna didn't care.

Mayor Pierson stood, making a cramped threesome between the door and the conference table. A confused half smile was on her neatly lipsticked mouth and her head was cocked slightly to one side, as if listening for an explanation that was being given too quietly to be heard by human ears.

"What a lovely baby," the politician said smoothly. "How old is she?"

"Twelve hours, give or take," Anna said. She held

Helena closer. If the mayor went in for kissing babies, she was going to have to wipe the lipstick off before she laid a lip on this one.

The half smile didn't slip. Judith turned back to the men, an audience she was surer of. "Am I missing something?"

"Mrs. Davidson—Anna—was able to save the woman's baby," Bernard said. "It's the one bright spot in this mess."

"But the woman died," Judith said, sounding annoyed at the chief ranger's stupidity.

"Anna performed a C-section soon after and the baby was close enough to term it survived," Bernard explained. He stood, as well, probably hoping the women would begin to clear out of his conference room, preferably as a precursor to clearing out of his park and his life.

Judith didn't move. "This woman is not a doctor, I take it? I find it hard to believe she had any surgical equipment with her."

"She used Paul's pocketknife," Chrissie volunteered.

"She just cut the dead woman open with a jackknife and took the baby? Isn't that illegal?" the mayor demanded. Despite the makeup, her face was losing color under the fluorescent lights and the age the plastic surgeon had excised glowed up from her bones.

Helplessly Bernard shifted his eyes to Jessie. The head of law enforcement shrugged, then said: "Exigent circumstances, ma'am."

"I know it sounds horrible," Paul said gently. "Even ghoulish. But it was the only way Anna could save the baby's life. Without oxygen from its mother's beating heart the baby would have died in the womb."

"Don't be stupid," Judith snapped. "I know that."

The vehemence startled everyone into silence. A slight cough pulled their attention off the unraveling mayor. The head of security, Darden White, the man Anna had forgotten again despite the fact that she suspected it was what he wanted them to do at the moment, was heaving himself up from his chair.

"We sure appreciate you letting us sit in on this, Bernard. The mayor already had a high regard of how Big Bend conducts business, and watching you all at work tonight has done nothing but raise that regard even more." White's interruption gave Judith Pierson time to collect herself, which she did with a speed that impressed Anna. It spoke of a powerful self-discipline that Anna had found herself lacking in recent months.

"Mayor Pierson, would you be so good as to give me a lift back to the lodge?" Darden said.

"Of course. Of course I will." Freed by the request, Judith dutifully thanked her reluctant hosts and left the conference room.

Lisa and Anna followed as far as the hall outside and waited there for their husbands. Darden, following more slowly, stopped to shake Bernard's and Jessie's hands. As he did, Anna heard him murmur, "Lost a baby herself a few years back."

The men murmured back, relieved that Judith's outburst could be written off to hearth and home, women and babies.

Anna wasn't buying it. If Judith had vulnerabilities—and if one was not a sociopath, it came with being human—she wasn't the sort to wear them on her sleeve. She didn't get to where she was by going to pieces every time a baby died.

She struck Anna as more the type to kill and eat them.

TWENTY-TWO

Anna and Paul rode in the cramped backseat of Freddy Martinez's four-by-four truck as they drove through the desert from park headquarters to Terlingua, the little town on the eastern edge of Big Bend where their rental car was parked at the outfitters who'd planned the float trip. Lisa and Freddy lived several miles farther south in Terlingua Ghost Town. Whether this was a real name or a nickname given because it was dead, Anna didn't have the energy to ask; she hardly had the energy to breathe. Leaning against Paul's shoulder, the hum of the tires on pavement, the contented warmth of a baby full of mother's milk sleeping in her lap, Anna drifted in and out of consciousness, falling into a doze then jerking awake as a dream dropped her from a cliff, or shot her in the back, or sent rivers to snatch Paul or Helena from her arms.

But for Carmen the Rio Grande would have taken the dead. The river was licking at Anna's ankles near the canyon wall when Lori was killed. The alcove where Helena's mother died was slightly lower than that. When the river crested it would have scoured out the alcove and caught up the two bodies. Corpses had a nasty habit of turning up, but there was a good chance neither of these two would be found. The giant reeds could swallow up elephant carcasses in their impenetrable tangles and never show so much as a lump or a trunk. The river could bury bodies of people as easily as it could canoes; they could wash up on the Mexican side and never be found, or if they were, the citizens might be afraid to report it. They could get lodged high enough on the canyon walls that rangers and rafters would never suspect they were there.

Snipers were hard to catch. But for the bullets in the bodies, they left no physical evidence at the site of the crime. If it could be ascertained where the shots were fired from there was a chance a bullet casing, tire or foot tracks, cigarette butts remained—depending on how careless the shooter was. It was said the world's best swordsman's worst enemy was the world's worst swordsman because of the unpredictability of the untrained. For law enforcement, perpetrators of random violence were the hardest to catch. They didn't conform to logic.

The truck pulled to a stop and Anna opened her eyes. The Honda Accord they'd rented in Midland was parked in front of the trailer that housed the business end of the rafting trips. The moon was nearly set and the landscape was featureless and shadowless, as stark as T. S. Eliot's nightmares.

The cold teeth of ambient anxiety nibbling at her insides, Anna handed Helena to Lisa to hold while she climbed down from the truck. Her knees buckled and she grabbed on to the door to keep from falling.

"You poor thing," Lisa said. "Do you want me to take Helena the rest of the way?"

"No," Anna said, then, realizing she sounded rude and ungrateful, she forced herself to add: "But thank you for offering." The stilted formality added to the surreality of the night, and the nibbles became bites.

Lisa looked infinitely sad, her round face limned in the faint light from the stars and the waning moon so like the sculpture of Mary holding the crucified Christ that for a breath-stopping instant Anna knew Helena was dead. Before she could cry out or fall to her knees, Lisa was snuggling a live and now thriving infant into her arms and supporting her as they walked toward the Honda.

Paul drove, following the Martinezes' truck. A mile or so south of the rafting concession they turned to the right. The headlights raked across a graveyard, old adobe monuments melting into the dun of the desert floor shocked into the present by the acid-bright reds and yellows and greens of plastic flowers left at the bottom of crosses. Before Anna's teetering brain made sense of the images the car's lights picked a sign out of the night, a child's skeleton wearing red gym shorts and dribbling a basketball.

Dreaming, Anna thought, and eased a hand out from under the baby to rub her face hard. As they wound up a gentle slope houses in varying states of decline were snipped out of the darkness. Some had new additions, ramadas and trailers and bright new adobe rooms tacked onto the ruins.

Another road sign leapt out of the headlights. This one was of a child—again a skeleton—wearing a T-shirt and shorts and riding a skateboard.

A town of dying houses and dead children. Anna couldn't stand being alone in her insanity anymore. "Did you see that?" she asked her husband.

"Interesting, aren't they? They sure catch your attention better than 'Slow, Children at Play,' don't they?"

"They do," Anna said, relieved that her mind had not become as unhinged as she'd feared. In the light of day, without Helena in her arms, Anna would have found them delightful, macabre and funny. Given the day she'd survived, she found them unsettling.

The truck's taillight blinked, indicating a right turn, and Paul followed Freddy off the narrow paved lane onto a dirt track. Here, surely, there would be no skeletons of children frolicking under the stars. A hundred yards farther on, the truck pulled in behind a tidy house made of many things: natural twisting trunks of trees, cacti in painted tire planters, a ramada of sotol and sticks, a house trailer painted with a mural of the Chisos Mountains, rooms of adobe with arched windows and low tile roofs branching out to either side, walkways of crushed white gravel and benches of stone.

The Martinezes' home appeared to have grown from the desert itself, taking on various sheltering elements the way a hermit crab takes on the shells left behind by other organisms. The effect was as charming as the enchanted houses unwary children came upon in fairy tales.

Uncharacteristically, Anna allowed herself to be taken care of. She and Helena and their luggage were unloaded and brought into the Martinezes' home. The inside was as eclectic and perfect as the outside, bright with Mexican rugs and artwork, handmade furniture and colorfully painted tables.

She and Paul were established in what Lisa referred to with a smile as the West Wing, in the room of their son who was away at college in Delaware. Lisa put Anna into a tiny shower, so small that if she fell asleep on her feet she wouldn't have been able to collapse, and took Helena away to bathe and feed her once more.

Much as Anna would have loved to stay in the tiny shower under the beat of hot water until it melted away every ache, if the hot water heater in the house were as cleverly scavenged as the rest of the building components, it was most likely small. The knowledge that her love for Paul was greater than her love for a hot shower after a couple of nights in the wild places cheered her up considerably. Another cheering thought came to her as she dried off. She got to sleep with him tonight. Not even her first husband, Zach, whom she had loved with all the passion a woman in her twenties has to burn, affected her the way Sheriff Paul Davidson did. Seeing him across a room, or covered in dirt and sweat from the backyard, gave her a rush she'd thought one lost the ability to feel after the age of sixteen.

Not only did she get to sleep with him tonight, she could sleep with him every night. All she would have to do was quit her job with the Park Service and move back to Port Gibson, Mississippi.

Once that thought would have made her blood run cold but then she'd fallen in love with Mississippi, with its stunning richness of creatures both two- and four-legged, and then she'd fallen in love with Paul. Should she truly and honestly fall out of love with being a ranger, his solid little two-story house in Port Gibson would be a soft place to land.

"Your turn," she said, stepping out of a bathroom only slightly bigger than the coffin-sized shower stall. "I even left you some hot water."

"You are so good to me," Paul said. He peeled off the filthy rags his boating ensemble had been reduced to and kicked them under the bed. "And you are so beautiful, naked and lovely." He stopped to kiss her lightly before he enclosed himself in the miniature bathroom.

Still toweling her hair, Anna wandered over to the small square mirror screwed to the back of the door leading into the hall. She didn't give much thought to how she looked, one of the perks of wearing the same uniform every day and spending time in places without mirrors.

Because Paul complimented her with every indication of sincerity, she looked hard at herself in the glass. Sun had had its way with her but she didn't regret the wrinkles that had formed around her eyes and across the bridge of her nose. Cancer might be brewing in her cells but she wouldn't trade the pure hedonistic joy of turning her face to the sun for smooth skin. Or even longer life, for that matter. Her hair was long, nearly to her collarbone, mostly because she didn't take the time to get it cut very often. It startled her to see how much white there was in it. A streak that the bride of Frankenstein would have been proud of went from her side part down the left side of her face.

Maybe it had surprised her because it seemed to have formed since she'd returned from Isle Royale, her hair turning white overnight the way it was said to do in old ghost stories. More likely she'd simply grown older when she was doing other things.

Her mind in free fall, she lost interest in her reflection and sat on the edge of the double bed, thinking it small after so many years in queens and kings. Her parents had slept every night of their thirty-seven years of marriage in a double bed. Now they gave them to children because twins were too small. The double bed was the beginning and the end of the room's romance. A boy's room, it was decorated with things boys admire: adventure posters with climbers hanging in midair, photographs of proud kids with dead fish. Freddy and Lisa's son did step out of the mold with two of his decorative choices. A black-and-white poster of Greta Garbo smoldering down at the viewer had pride of place at the foot of the bed, and a collection of kachina dolls were lined up on a shallow shelf above the dresser.

As the shower came on, there was a light tapping on the door.

Before Anna could get her mind around standing up, the door opened a crack and Lisa's voice trickled in. "Are you decent? Can I come in?"

"Please do." Anna stood and wrapped the towel around her lest she offend.

The door was pushed open and Lisa stood in the doorway holding two bundles of humanity. Both babies were wrapped in soft flannel blankets, swaddled from shoulders to toes, both had black hair as wispy as the new feathers of ducklings, both had button noses and eyes squinched shut. To Anna they were nothing alike. Edgar Allan produced her customary sense of awkward indifference and a loss of something nice to say to the proud mama. Helena was a different thing. She would have been able to pick her out of a thousand black-haired, brown-eyed infants. Indifference was not an option; Helena was fascinating, her smooth skin, plump and honey-colored with food and a bath a miracle of beauty and biological engineering. Helena made one believe that evolution was headed toward a greater good rather than random chaos.

Without being aware of asking or reaching, Anna

found Helena in her arms. A release of tension she'd not known she was harboring let her draw deeper breaths, smile with more than just her lips. Sitting on the bed again, with the baby held snugly to her chest, she managed a compliment for Lisa, the woman from whom all good things flowed. Not only the milk of human kindness, but actual real milk.

"That must be Edgar Allan. He's a cute little guy," Anna allowed generously.

"Our next-door neighbor was looking after him for me," Lisa said. She jiggled him and he opened his eyes momentarily. Lisa was so easy with her son, relaxed and comfortable. Anna realized her embrace must feel to Helena like she'd been nailed into an apple crate. Consciously she loosened and rounded her arms around the baby. Helena didn't respond by opening her eyes for so much as a nanosecond.

"Are they supposed to sleep so much?" Anna asked. "Or is Helena—" Sudden superstition that if she named any malady—autism, retardation, dyslexia, hypertension, eczema, diaper rash or tax evasion—Helena would then have it.

Lisa smiled and sat down on the bed beside her. "They sleep all the time. No, they wake up and want to eat and cry and poop when you're asleep. They come with tiny sensors that let them know when you are really, really deeply asleep and then they wake up."

Anna laughed. She remembered having been reintroduced to laughing on the river. Shortly before all hell broke loose. She quit laughing.

"Edgar is happy to share his crib with Helena. He is a perfect gentleman and promises not to steal the covers or any kisses."

Anna waited to hear herself accept the invitation on Helena's behalf. A crib with sides so tiny persons could not roll out, a mattress that undoubtedly had been tested for the perfect firmness to keep them from suffocation, soft blankets and another warm baby to snuggle with, that was ideal and Anna wanted to say yes but she sat there, clutching Helena, wondering what was wrong with her.

"Or would you like me to make up a little impromptu crib for her here? In your room?" Lisa asked softly.

"Yes, here," Anna said. She couldn't say more because she didn't want to cry, particularly since she had no idea what she would be crying over. Embarrassment, she thought sourly, for being such an idiot. Lisa left Edgar on the bed next to Anna and Helena and left the room. Edgar blinked unfocused eyes at Anna and moved his mouth sleepily as if dreaming of dessert.

"Hey, Edgar," Anna said, wanting to be polite.

Within a few minutes Lisa returned with a cardboard box, a sofa cushion and several little blankets, all in yellow. Anna watched as she took the scraps of flannel out of the box.

"I take it you didn't find out whether Edgar was going to be a boy or a girl before the shower," Anna said.

"No. We didn't want to spoil the surprise. We thought everybody would think it was fun. Jeez, you would have thought we were keeping the cure for cancer secret. People got almost mad because we wouldn't find out. My mom even thought we had found out and just weren't telling. I guess she thought we were just trying for an all-yellow layette." As she talked, Lisa set the box near the side of the bed away from the bathroom, wrapped the sofa cushion in a yellow blanket with green shamrocks on it then made a bed of the other two blankets.

"There," she said when she'd finished. "She can't fall out and she'll be plenty warm and you can reach out and touch her anytime you feel like it."

"Sorry I'm being such a pain. You've got to be the most understanding human being I've ever met," Anna said honestly. "Almost psychic."

"Just been there, done that," Lisa said. "Having Edgar so long after his brother was like having a first baby a second time. Would you believe Freddy slept on the floor of the nursery almost under the crib for the first week, afraid of crib death?"

Anna believed it, but she couldn't picture it.

The bed in the box neatly made and turned down, Lisa picked up Edgar and settled him against her shoulder in a practiced motion. "Are you going to be okay?" she asked.

"We'll be all right," Anna said. "Thanks."

For a moment Lisa stayed, her face open and kind in case Anna had a last-minute breakdown. "Good night, then," she said finally. "If you need anything, come and bang on me and Freddy's door. We're right across the living room at the end of the hall. The East Wing." She gave Anna an encouraging smile and left, closing the door softly behind her.

The bathroom door opened a crack.

"Is it safe to come out?" Paul asked.

Anna had forgotten Paul was trapped in the bathroom with nothing but a towel to wear in mixed company. Many men might have made an entrance regardless, but Paul was not one of them.

"It's safe."

Leaving the towel to dry on a hook on the back of the door, he came and sat next to her on the bed, smelling of soap, his hair falling damp on his forehead and neck.

"Whatcha got there?" he said conversationally.

"It seems to be a small toothless, featherless, furless, clawless creature of some kind," Anna said, looking down at Helena asleep in her arms. "I believe it to be a human larva."

Paul took the baby and laid it across his knees. "Do you think we should peel it before we eat it?" he asked as he unfolded the blanket Lisa had wrapped around the little girl like a tortilla around a bit of chicken.

"Too small," Anna said.

"Shall we throw it back?" Helena was dressed in a yellow onesie with a green frog appliqué on the shoulder. Paul lifted her up, his hands the size of her torso and so dark from the sun, her golden skin glowed in contrast. Helena opened her eyes.

"Hello, little citizen," Anna said, awestruck by the rush of gratitude she felt.

"We won't throw you back yet," Paul said. "We'll fatten you up for when things get lean in the winter."

He cradled the baby to his chest as naturally as Lisa had and Anna was dumbstruck by the absolute perfection of man and child. For the first time in months she could believe that good overcame evil, at least on alternate days.

"Time everybody was in bed," Paul said, and laid Helena in the cardboard box on her stomach. Tucking the yellow blankets around the yellow-clad baby, he said, "I suppose Health and Human Services will be by to take her sometime tomorrow."

Reality slammed into Anna with the force of a punch thrown in anger, and the ghosts of the hurt, the murdered, the molested, the raped, the lost children handed from home to home, flapped and screamed inside her skull, harpies chasing her back toward the yawning pit.

No. Not even on alternate days.

TWENTY-THREE

Anna had mentally rolled her eyes when Lisa told her the story of Freddy sleeping under the crib for a week. Now it wasn't so droll. Crib death. Another thing not to think about. There were too many things in Anna's brain that she didn't want to think about, that to think about brought her closer to the edge of the abyss. Not thinking was exhausting her. Trying to sleep with her fingertips resting on Helena's back to make sure she was still breathing was exhausting her. Paul, as always, slept the sleep of the innocent.

Eventually she must have slept because whimpering dragged her from its murky depths. The clock on the bed stand, plastic molded into the shape of a football helmet, said three twenty-seven. For a groggy second she was confused and terrified, then she remembered the formula Lisa had left for Helena. The baby wasn't dying. She was hungry. This is a good thing, Anna told herself, and threw back the covers.

The pajamas she had brought were pink with little yellow ducks on them. Not an outfit she'd ever intended to wear in public. She pulled them on to make herself decent and lifted Helena from her cardboard box.

The baby was so warm and, for the first time since Anna had ripped her from her mother's womb, so alive. She wriggled and waved tiny fists and made angry little sounds. Anna reveled in this show of spirit and strength as she carried Helena from the bedroom to the kitchen. As good as her word, Lisa had prepared the formula. Helena clutched to her shoulder, Anna retrieved the bottle and put it in the warming pan and turned up the heat.

From an ancient race memory or an old movie, Anna remembered women testing the temperature of the baby's milk on the inside of their wrists. With Helena in her arms this wasn't feasible. Anna put the nipple to her lips and squeezed.

"No wonder babies cry," she whispered as she transferred the nipple to Helena's mouth. "This stuff is vile."

Helena evidently thought so as well. She was having none of it. She shook her head to escape the intrusion of plastic and cried. Anna sat in a chair and settled the baby more firmly in the crook of her left arm.

"Got to eat," she told the baby. "Keep your strength up for what's to come."

Helena looked at her, eyes wide, and Anna knew the

baby saw her, understood, and she laughed out loud. When Helena accepted the nipple and began to suck, a marvelous sense of triumph poured into Anna, and for a moment she wasn't tired or sore or scared. Dragged into living in the moment as babies do, there was nothing she didn't have to think about.

When half the bottle was gone, Helena refused to drink any more.

This was the first time Anna had ever fed a baby. Had the survival and continuance of the human race been left up to her, overpopulation would not have been an issue. Helena was looking at her with expectation, or so it seemed to Anna.

"What do you want, little girl?" Anna asked helplessly.

Helena's face was screwing up as her disappointment in Anna grew.

"More milk? A kitten? Two kittens?"

Burping. Babies needed to be burped. Everybody knew that. Relieved at having an action to take, Anna put Helena to her shoulder the way she'd seen it done and patted her back gently. Soon the baby quieted and spewed a warm substance down the collar of Anna's ducky pajamas.

"What a good girl," Anna said, and: "Ish." The baby's face relaxed and then grew beatific. An unpleasant odor let Anna know it wasn't her child-care skills that had brought on the moment of pure joy.

"We've got to teach you to use a litter box," Anna said.

Lisa had said the changing room was down the hall near the master bedroom. Anna had never changed a baby's diaper. As she carried Helena down the hall following the spill of light from the kitchen, she envisioned stabbing the baby with huge safety pins, great squares of inexpertly folded white cloth falling off the child.

Anna switched the light on in the laundry room. Lisa had laid a soft mat over the top of the washer and dryer, creating a changing table. On a shelf above were boxes of disposable diapers. Nobody had folded a cloth diaper in over thirty years, she realized. She should have known this. She'd carried enough soiled disposable diapers out from the shorter loop trails off the roads in the parks where she'd worked. Rotten parents would shove the things under logs or in bushes rather than pack out their child's mess.

"You have been saved by modern technology," Anna whispered as she laid Helena on her back on the de facto changing table and began unsnapping the yellow onesie. "I am untrustworthy with stabbing weapons." To Anna's eye, Helena smiled and she wondered if it was anthropomorphism if human traits were attributed to neo-humans. All needful things had been left ready to hand, for which Anna was grateful. Helena was clean and a new diaper with nifty Velcro closures was laid out and ready when the bubble of her and Helena's nocturnal aloneness was broken by a voice, sharp and close and scorching with intense emotion. "Crucified on broken branches."

Anna gasped. Hands spread, knees bent ready to

fight or grab Helena and run or scream, Anna spun around to face the intruder.

Nobody was there.

It crossed her mind that she had, indeed, gone over the edge, but she didn't dwell on it. Of the many things in her head of late, strange voices were not among them. And this voice wasn't altogether strange. It sounded like Freddy Martinez amped up about a thousand volts. This was the voice of a man who could have stood on a canyon's rim and shot the fish in his own personal barrel and deemed himself justified in doing so. Nice stories about sleeping under cribs and kissing his wife and giving Anna and Paul and Helena shelter suddenly didn't outweigh the fact that it had been Freddy whom she had found in the place of the shooter who had murdered two young women while the rest of them watched.

Barefoot, in pink pajamas, a naked baby behind her, Anna knew the unique sense of helplessness that many women lived with all the days of their lives. She hated it.

A murmur. Lisa.

The laundry room and the master bedroom shared a wall, which obviously hadn't been soundproofed.

"In the dream it was all happening again," Freddy said, his voice less fraught but still clearly audible. "The water taking her, her trying to grab on to anything, and I just stand on the bank and do nothing. Can't do anything. Man," he said so low Anna could barely hear. Then a sob, the kind that men turn into an aborted bark rather than give in to tears.

Anna was eavesdropping on the late-night bedroom conversation of a married couple who had been kind enough to take her and her husband and Helena in out of the cold and she hadn't a shred of guilt or any intention of stopping.

Murmuring again—Lisa—and Anna stepped across the narrow utility room to shamelessly press her ear against the wall. Ranger Martinez might or might not be the shooter who'd killed Carmen and Lori, but he was connected to the woman in the strainer in a way that woke him in the wee hours with nightmares and honed his voice sharp as a razor.

"The hell it wasn't!" was shouted so loudly Anna jumped, her butt hitting the washing machine with a thump.

Silence echoed from beyond the plywood separating her from Freddy and Lisa Martinez. Then came the sound of a drawer opening, followed by the unmistakable metallic swallow of a round being chambered.

Anna flicked out the light of the laundry room, grabbed up a naked Helena and moved soundlessly toward the faint light spilling down the hallway. When she reached the kitchen she turned that light out as well.

The door to the master bedroom opened and stealthy footsteps crept down the hall. Baby in arms, Anna didn't know what to do. If she ran to Paul she would be leading an armed and mentally disturbed man to his bed, yet she couldn't leave him. Backing into a corner formed by two kitchen counters, she put her hand over Helena's mouth and waited. The steps reached the doorway to the kitchen and stopped. In the city there would have been ambient light from streetlights or next-door neighbors. Here, with the moon long since set, there was nothing but perfect night, the stars too faint to penetrate curtains and shading eaves.

Darkness was her friend. Anna sank into a crouch, making herself as small as she could, and hoped Freddy would pass through without seeing them. Moving as quietly as a hunting cat, he was through the kitchen before she'd known he'd left the hall. She could see the dark outline of his shoulders against the big windows in the living room.

She was preparing to breathe again when Helena, displeased with the hand over her mouth, made a small cranky noise.

The light came on with blinding suddenness and Freddy Martinez, wearing nothing but old sweats and unlaced sneakers without socks, was pointing his Glock at her head.

TWENTY-FOUR

"I want him fired. Tonight."

Judith was pacing in a room that was barely four paces wide. Watching her stalking like a beast in a cage was getting to Darden. At three-thirty in the morning thinking was difficult at best. Trying to do it with a wild woman wearing a hole in the carpet was proving impossible.

"Why don't you sit down, Judith?" he said reasonably. "Let me get you a Coke or something. There's a machine at the bottom of the steps outside."

"I don't want a Goddamn Coke," she hissed, but she sat, her narrow behind barely perched on the edge of Darden's bed. He sat in a straight-backed wooden chair, one of two, one more uncomfortable than the other, that flanked a small rectangular table, the kind they used to cram into kitchens before breakfast nooks became the fashion.

"Now tell me why you want Kevin fired," he said.

Judith sprang up again and began the pacing. She hadn't changed since the party and still wore the tailored blue linen trousers and white silk blouse, but they no longer maintained their pristine lines. Matter of fact, Darden thought, it looked like she'd slept in them. Or rolled in the hay in them. Her manicured fingers had run through her manicured hair so many times the latter was standing in blond spikes like sheaves in a wheat field. "Frankly, Darden, it's none of your damn business why I want him fired. It's your business to fire him."

She might as well have slapped him in the face. The sting of her words burned through his tough old hide till he could feel the faint acid burn in his tear ducts where tears had once resided before he'd replaced them with ash. Darden pulled himself straighter in his chair and tried to suck in his gut. Tonight it wasn't his friend; it was a sign of how little respect he or anyone else had for the man who used to be Secret Agent White.

Before he could think of a rational way to fall on his sword, Judith stopped pacing and threw herself to her knees on the carpet in front of him, her narrow hands on his knees, her head in his lap. "I didn't mean that, Darden. I am so sorry. Please don't hate me. God, I doubt I could stand it if you hated me."

He stroked her short hair. When she was little it had been a sweet gentle brown and as soft as a puppy's belly. It probably still was when she didn't fill it with goop and spray and dye and whatever else women did to make themselves look younger and more appealing. At her age he doubted it would be that same soft brown but a nice color, maybe a little gray but not much. Her mother hadn't had a single gray hair at sixty. He knew; he'd seen her in her coffin. Ambition had run her heart out. Ambition and speed and cigarettes.

"Don't ask me why I want you to fire him." Her mouth against the soft folds of his flannel robe, she sounded so young. Darden continued to stroke her hair absently but he didn't answer. Firing problem employees was only a good idea if they were all of the problem. If the boss was half of it—especially the half that the tabloids would love to buy an exclusive story about—the aftermath usually cost more than it would take to turn a bad employee into a good retainer.

"Please?" Judith looked up at him through wet eyelashes.

Darden was surprised. He doubted she'd cried any more recently than he had, but it was a night for realizing she no longer told him all her secrets.

"I don't want to pry into your personal affairs," he said, and heard the stiffness in his own voice. Had he missed it for some reason, her deep sigh would have enlightened him as to its existence. "I really don't, Judy. You're a grown woman and can do what you like. I'm asking because why's going to dictate how. We fire him out of hand right now and he goes running to the press or—if Gerry's around and gets wind of it—the press runs to him and the governor's mansion might as well be on Jupiter for as close as you're going to get to it."

Judith pushed herself to her feet, using his knees for leverage. The old plaid robe fell partly open and Darden could see his leg from knee to beat-up slipper. A white leg with dark hairs, skinny at the shin and heavy at the knee, where muscles had melted away and bones had taken over: it was the leg of an old man. A year ago, a month, even a week ago and he'd known he was in his sixties, he'd known he wasn't in the best physical condition, and he'd used it to play old to put people off their guard. When in the past seventy two hours had playing old slid into being old?

"I can't have him around me, Darden," Judith said. She'd walked over to the bathroom counter and was looking at herself in the mirror. From where he sat he could see her in profile.

"Okay," he said slowly. "Tell me this: Can it wait a day or two or better a week or two? At least till we can get off this godforsaken mountain and back into civilization where I can get a handle on what he's likely to do if we fire him?" Though Judith was besotted with her worthless husband—or maybe because she was— she'd had several affairs over the years. Very discreet, very upscale—Darden had known about them but only because she had wanted him to for security reasons. Out of respect for him—or so he'd once thought, now he wasn't sure, maybe it was because she didn't trust him anymore, not like she did when she was a little girl and he was the biggest, strongest, bravest, handsomest man in her world—she'd not asked him to shuttle lovers in and out of back doors or watch outside hotel rooms. He'd done that kind of work for other politicians and always felt like a bit of a pimp when he did.

Judith's liaisons had always been upper crust; rich, married men with as much or more to lose as she had if the secret were to get out. He'd always believed her too smart and too cold to go the route Clinton or Edwards had and get mixed up with somebody who could use the affair to blackmail her one way or another.

Kevin didn't seem like a likely candidate for her first try at slumming. Except that he looked like Charles had when he was young. A rough and dirty version of Charles; what better way to get even with him.

"We'll get rid of him," Darden promised. "I'll fix it so he won't be able to come back at you and do you any damage."

"It might be too late," Judith said, still staring at her reflection in the mirror. She picked up Darden's hairbrush and began brushing her hair methodically, her hand following the bristles, smoothing the spikes down into a neat gold cap.

When it was all flat and tidy, she dropped the brush and closed her skull between her hands as if it might blow apart if she didn't.

"Where is Charles?" Darden asked gently. He might not care much for his boss's husband but if Judith needed him, Darden would get him for her, if he had to drag him out of bed with a Supreme Court justice to do it.

"I don't know." Judith didn't move, didn't stop holding her brain between her hands.

"Did he get another room?"

"I think so."

"He knows that's verboten on these junkets," Darden fumed.

"I think this time things are different," she said. Dropping her hands to her sides, she turned from the mirror and he could see all of her face. The sadness he'd expected was there, and the fury, but what shone naked and cruel was fear.

Judith was absolutely terrified.

She'd been afraid when she'd come into the chief ranger's conference, he recalled. The fact had gotten lost in the myriad other emotional currents he'd been following. At the time he'd thought it was fear of the unknown, of the rumors that were flying and how they would affect what she was trying to do by spending a week in the Chisos Mountains instead of running the city that had elected her mayor.

There was more to it than that. Judith was scared of Kevin, one of her own security men. By the depth of terror he read in her eyes, Kevin must have threatened her with murder—either of herself or her career, a kind of murder that she couldn't protect herself against with money and connections.

"What has he threatened you with?" Darden asked softly.

Judith shook her head. "Nothing."

"But you want him fired?"

"Yes."

"And you won't tell me why?" Darden sighed in exasperation and stood, folding his bathrobe closer around him. The window was open and the night had grown cold. The smell of pine and sage came in with the cool air. Darden would have preferred the smells of diesel and rain-washed pavement.

"No." Her face grew less rigid and her eyes took on the shine they did when she wanted something. She walked across the room and leaned against his chest, her arms around his waist.

"What is it? What do you want, Judy?" he asked warily.

"This isn't going to go away. Not if we pour money on it or shake our big guns."

For a minute they stood without moving, her head on his chest, his arms loose at his sides. Darden had known what she was asking for from the minute she'd started across the worn carpet toward him.

For once he didn't want to give her what she wanted.

TWENTY-FIVE

O h. It's you," Freddy said.

The Glock was lowered but still held at his side.
Anna had never been on the wrong end of a gun when
it was this close. The bore, not much more than a quarter inch in diameter, if that, had appeared the size of a
fifty-cent piece when it was pointed at her. Witnesses left
alive after being threatened with guns were notoriously
unable to tell law enforcement anything useful and now
Anna knew why. With that terrible black eye of a death
Cyclops staring one in the face, it took in the entire
world for that instant. Everything outside the hole's pe-
rimeter disappeared in a fog of incipient mortality.

Anna pushed herself and Helena to her feet.

"What did you hear?" Freddy asked. His head was
cocked to one side, listening. Anna had written off the

idea of voices in her own head but she wasn't all that sure about the river ranger's.

"Nothing," she said cautiously. "I didn't hear anything. Why?"

"I heard a noise. We've been having trouble around here lately. A bunch of punks—lost teenage nomads with lots of piercings and no hygiene to speak of—have been hanging around Terlingua for a couple weeks, homesteading in an old miner's shack. There've been several break-ins. Wake Paul. I'm going to check around outside."

Freddy left her standing there holding Helena. Once again, baby in arms, Anna had been excused from danger. Once again, baby in arms, Anna let herself be.

Paul woke quickly and, because they were closest, pulled on the ragged, filthy shorts and river shoes that Anna had deemed unsalvageable garbage the night before. Under different circumstances, Anna would have left the baby in Lisa's capable hands and gotten dressed to lend a third pair of eyes to the search. Since it was her butt that had made the offending bump, she knew there was no danger to Freddy or Paul. She returned to the laundry room to finish what she had started.

"Everything okay?"

It was Lisa. Clad in a T-shirt and a pair of Freddy's boxer shorts, she stood in the doorway to the hall.

"I think so," Anna said. Freddy had seemed to be after punks in the night but Anna wasn't convinced. Why he would stoop to such elaborate theatrics when he could have shot her and told everyone he'd mistaken her for a burglar in the dark, she couldn't fathom. "I think he heard Helena and me banging around in the kitchen."

The baby was laid out on the paper diaper and Anna was deftly taping it in place. Disposable diapers made infant care easier by far, if less environmentally friendly.

Lisa drifted over to watch, her hand reaching out and holding on to one little foot, fingers caressing toes no bigger than pencil erasers.

Helena liked the attention and was lying on the changing mat looking up at the huge faces looming between her and the overhead light, her eyes wide in awe as if such amazingly huge creatures who floated in the ether were a new miracle to her.

She was looking at Anna and Anna was looking at her. "Hazel!" Anna blurted out.

"Like the maid in that old sitcom? I like Helena better."

"Her eyes are hazel," Anna said.

Lisa leaned close, blocking Anna's view of the child's face.

"Didn't we learn in biology that brown always wins out genetically?" Lisa asked.

Anna was remembering the same lesson but she couldn't remember precisely what eye color came from what parent or if it mattered.

"Her mother looked Hispanic," Anna said.

"What color were her eyes?"

Casting back to when the woman had opened her eyes, once on the strainer then a second time under the overhang in the alcove, Anna tried to see. "I don't know," she admitted finally. "I thought they were brown but I might have just assumed that. The light was funky and my mind was on other things."

Clattering from the kitchen let them know Freddy and Paul were back from patrol. Lisa helped Anna thread the baby into the yellow onesie then followed the two of them out.

Lisa put four glasses and a carton of orange juice on the table, Paul took Helena and the five of them sat around the kitchen table, no one quite ready to go back to bed.

"Helena's eyes are hazel," Anna said to her husband. "Do you recall what color her mom's eyes were?"

"I don't," he said, and held the baby away so he could look into her face. "They are. Am I to assume this is anything more than just an observation?"

"If her mother was a poor Mexican woman swimming the Rio Grande at the eleventh hour, wouldn't her eyes be brown?"

"Not necessarily," Freddy said after a moment's thought. "This close to the border there's a lot of cross-pollination. Her dad or her mom could have been white."

"She'd still have had brown eyes, wouldn't she?" Anna asked.

"I guess she would at that," Paul put in. "But Helena wouldn't necessarily, not if her father didn't."

"Helena's father was a white man," Anna concluded. "If her mother was married to a white person and most white persons are American in this part of the United

States, why would her mother have to sneak across the border at the height of the river's flooding?"

"Because he never married her," Freddy said flatly.

The four of them digested that unsavory thought for a minute.

Paul kissed a sleeping Helena on top of her feathery head. "Lucky for you Hollywood made being born out of wedlock a badge of honor," he told the baby.

Anna would have liked to sleep in—she would have loved to sleep for a week—but it was not to be. Helena and the National Park Service deemed the Davidson and the Martinez families were to rise early. Anna was still in the changing room, marveling at how much stuff it took to tend to one small scrap of humanity, when Freddy grumbled out of the master bedroom and called Paul to the phone.

Curious, Anna carried the baby back into the kitchen to listen in on the conversation.

"Sure," Paul said. "We can be there in an hour, does that work for you?" He listened and Anna listened and his face grew stonier.

"What?" she whispered.

He ignored her. Into the phone he said: "No. Anna's the only one who saw her. Your best bet is Anna. Do you want to talk to her?"

Anna was reaching for the phone with her free hand but evidently whoever was on the other end of the line did not want to talk to her.

"No," Paul said again and coldly. "I'm afraid I can't be of much help." Again he listened briefly. His face softened up. "Sure, no problem, we'll see you in an hour or so."

"That was Jessie Wiggins," he told Anna before she could ask. "They're doing the body recovery today. They want us to go with them and show them where Carmen fell."

"They want *you* to go show them where Carmen fell," Anna said hollowly. Immediately she was ashamed at her naked emotion. Evil she could deal with, stupid was harder, pathetic curled her insides. Where was her righteous anger? Righteous rage was what she needed right now, a shot of good old-fashioned hate to buck her up. She couldn't find it.

Hollowness wasn't precisely an emotion; it was a lack thereof, a confusion of nothing because, other than the elusive anger, Anna didn't know what to feel. A little insanity, a little maternity and she was cut out of the life she'd known for the past decade or more. Sexism was a word she'd never use out loud, not in front of the boys, certainly. It wasn't near as bad as it had been when she started out and she dared to hope it would be virtually nonexistent to the women coming of age in the twenty-first century. For now it was damped down but it was not gone. Societal pressures had forced old practitioners of the dark art underground, but time had yet to cull them from the collective conscious.

Men around her had occasionally shot somebody. Rangers had burnt out, gone over to the other side, fallen apart, showed up drunk at firearms practice. A few had been fired, one she knew of put in jail, most had quit of their own volition. These guys would have been frozen out to some extent before they found their way out—or were tossed out—of the NPS.

But Anna had done none of that. She'd burst into tears in a shrink's office and she'd carried a seven-pound Homo sapiens in her arms for less than twenty-four hours and yet she was given the pariah treatment as surely as the ranger/felons and ranger/drunks.

No, she realized. She was not being treated as a leper. She was being treated as a helpless, ignorant member of the general public. In other words, as if she didn't count when it came to taking actions or making decisions. The shunning wasn't because Bernard or Jessie or anybody else disliked her or even particularly distrusted her. They didn't want her on the body recovery because she did not want to stay in the box they had put her in.

"There's no reason I should go," she said. "I am on vacation."

"The rockslide is a gigantic maze," Paul said. "I doubt I can find where she fell. Between the two of us we should be able to."

He was lying. They'd left marks all over hell and gone coming up that slide. The ledge where they'd camped out for a while probably still had smudgy muddy butt prints from where the kids had sat, not to mention the smear of blood on the face of the boulder where Carmen had bounced on her way down.

She loved him for the lie but in a flash of insight she

knew she didn't need it. The hollow feeling wasn't because she was rejected or female or petty or suppressing anger; it was because she was feeling nothing. She simply did not give a rat's ass what the guys were doing or thinking. There were things she needed to do and was better doing them alone.

"No," she told her husband. "You go. I want to drive up and check on Cyril and Steve and Chrissie."

"I'd guess they're flying home today after all that's happened," Paul said, eyeing her narrowly, looking for pain she might be trying to hide from him.

"Maybe but I need to go anyhow."

The return to normalcy of her tone reassured him.

"Okay. I'm off to find a corpse."

"Have fun."

"Give me a kiss. Men who kiss their wives good-bye are significantly less likely to have automobile accidents on their way to work. Did you know that?"

"You're not driving," Anna reminded him but kissed him anyway because she could.

Anna was loath to leave Helena, not because she didn't think Lisa would take good care of her—better care than Anna could—but because she was afraid by the time she got back one or more bureaucracies would have conspired to spirit the little girl away into places children were better off avoiding, like foster care. Helena had sufficient birth trauma for a lifetime's neurosis should she choose it. She did not need any more.

Lisa promised she would keep the forces of evil at bay

and that Helena would be safe and sound and there when Anna returned.

"We won't camp in your guest room forever," Anna promised after thanking her. "We've got reservations at the lodge tomorrow night. That was when we were supposed to come in off the river."

"You have to stay here," Lisa said. "This little one has to eat." She was holding Helena, Edgar in a sling snuggled in where arms and breasts and cuckoo babies hadn't usurped his mother's chest.

Anna hadn't thought of that. She could buy formula but there was no place to heat it in the rooms at the lodge. It wouldn't matter in the end. Helena wasn't hers to keep. She needed to go to a loving home where she would be treasured and taken care of. The problem was Anna had no faith in the child-care system as it pertained to unwanted or unidentified children. By the time the decision to allow adoption was ground out by the slow wheels of justice and the process of screening prospective parents had been crawled through, Helena would have been in foster limbo for months and months, maybe years. By then what sparked pure and beautiful in this little river nymph might be dead.

"You're sure keeping Helena today won't interfere with any of your plans?" Anna asked.

"I have no plans and today is Freddy's lieu day. I hope he will stay home but I think he is going to talk himself into unemployment instead."

The comment was sufficiently cryptic Anna might

have pursued the meaning on another day. This morning she was too distracted to bother.

Driving out in the clear light of a desert morning the macabre signs of skeletal children in ball caps enjoying various sports was as charming as Anna had known it should have been the previous night. The ghost town, with its casual and comfortable mix of the dead and the living, decadence and growth, and the idiosyncratic lunacy of people at the end of the line—those who wash up on the shores of Caribbean islands, ski slopes and other destinations most of humanity chooses only to visit. Paradise doesn't work as a steady diet and those who remain there are tough and, as Carmen said, the goods are odd.

Anna loved the intrinsic art in the psychedelically painted trailer-cum-ramada that sold cold beer, the lot where a long-departed entrepreneur had put a life-sized pirate ship in hopes of luring tourist dollars, but mostly she loved leaving Terlingua and heading into the open spaces of the park.

Pushing buttons, Anna lowered all four windows and let the dry, fragrant air blast the confines of the Martinezes' home from her mind, the smell of talcum powder and formula from her nose. Freedom blasted in on the desert wind and she realized it was the first time she'd been free in a long, long time. District rangers were tied to their radios, wives to their husbands, mothers—or caregivers—to their charges, farmers to their fields. Where one loved one was tied. Responsibility for the welfare of others was an anchor and chain.

Once she wanted to sever those ties and walk deep into the backcountry where she owed allegiance to no one. That hadn't been her wish for many years, certainly not since she'd fallen in love with Paul. Still it was good to leave the fetters of the heart behind now and then.

This Eden, like those she'd been contemplating on the drive through Terlingua, wasn't a place she could do more than visit. The closer she came to the Chisos Mountains, a ring of peaks, an entire circular mountain range marooned in a sea of desert, the more heavily thoughts of Cyril and Steve and even Chrissie weighed on her mind.

They'd probably left and were headed for the safety and warmth of their parents' homes by now, but she hoped not. Human nature was geared to escape from pain, run from danger, but she'd noticed over time that those who stayed close enough so they could work through the trauma with others who had survived it with them healed more swiftly and more completely. The bond formed under duress was allowed to hold them together in mutual understanding till they got a little more of their psychic strength back. Scooping up the survivors and shipping them to different destinations isolated them.

Though people would deny it, adventure was a high. If there wasn't anyone who had shared the feeling it was easy to believe the event had turned one into a monster.

Lost in her thoughts, Anna had been driving blind for thirty minutes. The entrance to the campground in Chisos Basin whipping by her passenger side window brought her out of her brown study.

Using the lodge parking lot to turn around, she headed back the short distance to the campsites. Awake now and paying attention, she noticed a black SUV pulling out of a parking space behind her. It stayed in her rearview mirror, following too close for comfort as she drove down the gentle incline from the lot to the turnoff. As she clicked on her turn signal the SUV did the same. Then it started honking its horn and flashing its lights.

"What now?" she muttered, and pulled to the side of the road. Before the SUV had made a full stop behind the Honda, Anna was out of the car.

The SUV, hulking like a great shiny dung beetle on the gray and tan landscape, hummed secretively for a moment, the life behind its tinted windows invisible to those outside. Then the driver's door opened and the heavyset guy who'd been in the conference room, the one who knew how to hide in plain sight and fetched soda pop for the mayor of Houston, climbed out. Moving stiffly he uttered a little "ugh" as his weight shifted from the seat of his pants to the soles of his shoes. Anna couldn't tell if he was as stove up as he was acting or if it was just that, acting.

Leaning back against the car door, she crossed her arms over her chest and her legs at the ankles. The sun on her face felt like a sacrament.

"Anna Pigeon, isn't it?"

"It is. Darden White."

"That would be me."

Anna watched the mayor's security chief shake out

the stiffness and walk toward her. Right off she'd kind of identified with this guy for reasons she hadn't a clue about. White struck a chord that sounded of old and better days. Probably precisely the chord he wanted to strike.

"You saved an old man a trip down the hill."

Now Anna was sure it was an act. "That shtick ever work for you?" she asked pleasantly.

White started a bit but then he smiled. "It does," he said. "It can backfire on you but I've gotten some good use out of it. And lately there've been times I wasn't sure where the act left off and old age began. Won't work for you, though. It's gender-specific."

"Women don't need it," Anna said, answering his smile. "We get underestimated without even half trying."

"Not by me you don't." He sounded almost grim. "The phones being what they are, I was going to drive down to Ranger Martinez's place on the off chance you'd be in. The mayor wants to see you."

It sounded more like an order than an invitation. From what Anna had noted about Mayor Pierson the previous evening, she wasn't a woman who took kindly to those who said no to her. "What does the mayor of Houston want to see little old me about?" Anna asked. Darden White stepped between her and the sun, providing shade for her. He thought he was doing her a favor.

"You'd have to ask the mayor that," Darden said.

Anna liked that he didn't say he didn't know what it

was she wanted. Choosing not to lie to her was respect-ful. She returned the courtesy by not pushing him to tell her what the unexpected summons meant.

"Sure," she said. Judith had rubbed Anna the wrong way. She doubted the two of them would become fast friends. But she found the woman interesting. More to the point, she found the mayor's avid interest in what had happened to the woman in the river interesting.

"I want to check on the rest of our ill-fated rafters, then I'll come on up. The lodge dining room suit her? I haven't had breakfast."

"She was hoping you'd come to her cabin."

"After breakfast," Anna said, and pushed away from the Honda to let White know the chat was at an end.

"Mind if I join you for breakfast? I could do with a bite myself."

"Give me about an hour."

Darden turned smartly and walked smoothly back to the SUV, his spine straight, his shoulders square.

He's showing off, Anna thought.

White stopped before he opened the door to his ve-hicle and threw her a mocking smile to let her know he was showing off and they both knew it.

Anna laughed and waved. Breakfast would be good. Anna wanted to know what in the hell he and his little blond mayor were up to.

TWENTY-SIX

An hour. That would give him time to check on Judith. When she'd sent him down the mountain to invite Anna Pigeon to lunch, her RPMs were getting close to the point her engine was about to start screaming. Or freeze up. He'd never seen her so strung out. He'd been with her through a lot of political battles; the underhanded backstabbing world of politics didn't tax her nerves, it exhilarated her. Domestic traumas were the ones that got to her little girl's heart and she often reacted like a kid, Darden mused. Wild and emotional and not always completely rational.

This was a rotten time for Judith to go to pieces, Darden thought. There were too many plates in the air. Darden felt like the guy on Ed Sullivan who had to run from pole to pole to pole keeping the darn things spinning so the whole mess wouldn't crash to the floor and shatter.

Judith had been upset by the news of the woman found in the strainer. That didn't surprise Darden; he hadn't much liked it either. She was concerned about the baby the Pigeon woman had saved. Darden thought about that for a while.

He didn't know much about babies—didn't know anything about babies, if the truth be told. They were an uninteresting mystery to him but he'd seen enough sane women and a few sane men lose their minds over the little things to know they were powerful magic.

Charles had wanted kids. To carry on the Pierson name, no doubt, Darden thought sourly. To give the guy some credit, he did like kids. His sister had three and he doted on them. Judith had nixed that idea shortly after the wedding. Kids and political ambition didn't mix and she'd known what she wanted. Now that she was in her forties, had her biological clock kicked in? She hadn't said as much to Darden but then that wasn't the sort of thing they talked about. Thank God.

Did she have an idea of using that baby to further her career? That might make sense, in a warped kind of way. He could see her, looking every inch the concerned maternal woman, holding the golden-skinned child up as an example of the evils of a porous border.

He shook his head and smiled as he eased the big SUV around the parking lot and headed up the narrow back road to the cabins. Judith was the one to sell it. The kid snatched from the Rio Grande by the mayor of

Houston would make a fine emotional appeal and soften the hard edges that could turn off women voters and bleeding-heart liberals.

Darden didn't want any part of that scenario but it was better than some he could imagine. At least the little bugger would get a good home. That is, if it was a little Mexican baby and if its mother was trying to cross to the promised land and instead went to the Promised Land.

That speculation was one Darden had been studiously avoiding. He was trained in obedience and loyalty. It suited him to follow; he'd known it since he was a youngster. Men like him were born to be soldiers in somebody's army, to give their lives for somebody's flag. Whose flag was an accident of birth. Born in the U.S.A., Darden had followed the stars and stripes and was loyal to the commander in chief, whoever he was and whatever he believed in. When he retired he'd shifted that allegiance to the mayor of Houston.

Worry about right and wrong wasn't a concept he embraced. Right and wrong were ephemerals; they changed from every angle, from hour to hour, depending on which side of any of a thousand borders a soldier was born.

The armor of blind loyalty that he'd worn so comfortably for so long was beginning to show cracks. The corpse in the river, the baby sliced out with a priest's pocketknife. How biblical was that? Anna should have put the kid in a basket made of those great big reeds that were taking over and floated it to the nearest pharaoh.

That whole mess crawled under Darden's protective skin. The coincidence of it happening now and here and in that way was hard to swallow but if he didn't swallow it he was obliged to check on it. Swallowing the truth that might uncover would be worse; it would be swallowing hemlock as far as he was concerned.

A man loomed into the periphery of his daydream and he cursed himself for a fool. He'd never used to have problems concentrating, observing his surroundings clearly. Maybe a little hemlock was just what the doctor ordered.

The loomer was Gordon. Heavy with the thoughts he'd been entertaining, Darden stopped the SUV and lowered the tinted window. "Hey, Gordon," he said. "I've got a job for you. And take your buddy Kevin with you. He's been getting on the mayor's nerves."

Dispatching his agents made him feel both better and worse but it also allowed him to shelve the speculation for a while. At least until he had hard information.

A SPACE HAD OPENED up nearest the stone stairs to the cabins; he parked the SUV and stepped out. For a moment the peace of the Chisos Basin swept away the turmoil in his mind. Rain had washed the air so clean it nearly sparkled. Each twig and branch of the pines glistened and the intoxicating smell of pine and sage and sunlight eased the wrinkles from his gray matter. It was so close to narcotic he stood and breathed for a minute, the need to hurry and fix, abort, dissuade, dissemble washed from him for that brief time.

Maybe when he retired and his mom died, he would buy a cabin in the mountains, grow his beard out and become a hippie. He'd missed the whole free-love, tune-in, turn-on, drop-out business when he was in college. Revisiting it in his so-called golden years might be entertaining.

Probably not, he thought as he shook off the joy of the day; he'd been born in a city and he would die in a city. The pulse of the life of the human hive was as necessary to him as the pulse of his own heartbeat.

Comfortably shouldering the weight of his world once again, he started up the walk. He heard the hissing when he was still fifteen feet from the shared porch. It evolved into words as he stepped under the overhang.

"Keep your voice down!" A stage whisper carried through the open screened window of Judith and Charles's cabin. "I will not have a scene. I will not."

"My voice is down," Charles said in a conversational tone. He didn't sound angry, just tired. "Don't fight this, Judith. If you do, I promise you I will make a scene that will bring your whole house of cards down around your ears."

"Please wait. You don't have to make a decision now, do you? Please wait awhile." Judith no longer hissed like an angry snake. The change was painful to Darden's ears. She was begging, a lost little girl begging for her life. God but he hated to hear that. When her mother had finally walked away for good, abandoning her seven-year-old daughter to the care of the babysitter, Judy had pleaded in that way, so tiny and afraid. Hearing it from the grown woman brought back the pain and helplessness Darden had felt as a young man trying to soothe a brokenhearted little girl.

Damn Charles.

Usually, when Judith and Charles fought, Darden made himself scarce. What went on in the marital arena was none of his business and he liked it that way. It was when it was out of the arena that he stepped in. Given there was so much at stake and he was the man who was going to have to put Humpty Dumpty back together again after the fall, he sat down quietly in one of the plastic armchairs outside his cabin, no more than five feet from their door, and listened.

"I've waited long enough, Judith. You've got what you wanted. You're a big wheel, the mayor of Houston. I'm sorry if that's not enough for you, but I'm through putting my life on hold while you conquer the world. It's a done deal. I saw to it before we left Houston."

"I'll fight you." The anger was back, the cold anger of a grown woman.

"No you won't, Judith. How would that look? Desperate."

"Do you love her?" The little girl was back and tugging at Darden's heart if not at Charles's.

When Charles spoke again his tired voice held a peculiar mixture of steel and sympathy. "I'm going to marry her, Judith. As soon as the divorce is final."

There was an intake of breath, then, razor-sharp edges cutting out of her throat, Judith said, "Don't tell me you've knocked up your bitch this time. What a cliché you are. She going to walk down the aisle with a big slut's belly?"

"Don't do this," Charles said.

"Why? You can do it but I can't talk about it? You're such a hypocrite!"

"Please, Judith, don't do this. It's over. Let me go quietly. Neither of us needs this at the moment."

Again Judith regressed to that seven-year-old watching her mother drive away for the last time. "Stay, Charles, please, I love you. Just stay for a while. It will be different, you'll see. Wait until the election is over, give me that at least. Give me time. Please."

Darden could hear Charles's sigh from where he sat, an exhalation of the years of bowing down to Judith's wishes, of his family's need to keep the Pierson name free of scandal, of his own inability to shake off the chains shackling him to live his own life. For a moment Darden thought he was going to knuckle under again, give Judith what she wanted, and was about to heave his own sigh, one of relief, but Charles surprised him.

"Sorry, Judith, I can't."

"You won't marry your bitch," Judith nearly snarled. "Never."

Charles opened the screen door.

"Never. You might as well get that through your head, Charles. You aren't going to leave me and marry some little whore. Never."

Charles stepped out onto the porch and gently closed the screen door behind him, holding it until it latched the way a person would who was afraid any small noise would disturb those within.

"Charles, please, I love you," trickled on tears from inside.

Darden half expected Charles to say, "Frankly, my dear, I don't give a damn," but he only turned away.

"You heard?" he asked when he saw Darden sitting on the porch.

"I heard," Darden said.

"I filed for divorce before we left Houston."

"So I gathered."

"Stay out of it, Darden."

"Why don't you go do whatever it is you need to do," Darden said as he pushed himself up out of the plastic chair. "I need to see to Judith."

"Stay out of this, Darden," Charles said again, this time with a hint of threat in his voice.

Darden said nothing, just reached for the door to Judith's room. Charles turned and walked quickly down the shallow stone steps. He was pushing buttons on his satellite phone as he went.

Steeling himself for Judith's pain and anger, Darden knocked gently on the wooden frame of the screen door then opened it, not waiting for an invitation to come in. Judith would be beyond words at this point. All he could do for her was provide a shoulder to cry on. In the past, when Charles strayed there'd been something he could do about it, pay people off, scare people off, force Charles back into the mold for another month or year or ten years. This time he didn't think that would work. Charles had finally grown a spine and was willing to take the punches that would be thrown at him to get what he wanted.

He wouldn't get what he wanted and Darden found himself feeling a little sorry for the guy, *little* being the operative word. Stepping into the room he was rocked back onto his heels as Judith flew at him, eyes streaming, and glued herself to his chest. Burying her face in his shoulder, she let the sobs come. She was a little thing; bones like a bird, Darden thought as he gathered her up and carried her over to the bed. A chair would have been more comfortable for him—after she'd turned eight or nine, he felt she was grown up enough that no man should see her undressed or be in her bedroom—but the straight-backed wooden chairs were too small for the both of them. He settled against the headboard, one foot on the floor and one knee bent under to make a bit of a lap for her and let her cry it out.

"You're okay, you're strong," he murmured as he gazed over the top of her blond head at the rustic wooden dresser against the wall. Judith was strong. Whether he was strong enough for the storm forming around her, he wasn't sure. The situation might have gone too far this time.

"Charles is leaving me," she cried, the words gurgling with tears and misery.

"I know, Judy. It's been coming. You'll be all right. You'll get through this, wait and see."

"I won't!" she wailed, and he patted her back and stroked her hair.

"Shh, shh, you're okay."

"My head is so full of monsters," she cried.

When she was little and had bad dreams or horrible thoughts after her mother left, she'd called them monsters that lived in her head. He'd not heard her use the term in thirty years. Tears came to his eyes and he did what he had done then, when he was a young man and she was a child. He pressed his lips to her forehead and made a loud sucking sound then spit with a noisy *p'tui*.

"Got one out," he said. "A nasty bugger. Black and leathery and spiny."

Again he pressed his lips to her forehead and slurped then pretended to spit.

"Ouch! That bugger had claws!"

Judith looked up at him and smiled, a weak watery smile but he was glad to see it.

"What would I do without you, Darden?" she asked, and had the same look in her eyes that had captured him so many years before.

"Just what you always do, Judy. You'd dry your eyes, suck it up and run back into the fray."

She laughed and got up from his lap. It was a relief. Light as she was, his right leg was going to sleep.

Judith crossed to the small mirror and, taking a hairbrush from the top of the dresser, began putting herself together. Darden escaped the bed and took one of the straight-backed kitchen chairs.

"Charles thinks he's going to marry the bitch," she said without looking at him.

Darden didn't say anything. He knew better than to talk when Judith started speaking in a voice sharp as lemon juice. He didn't like to hear her like that and he didn't like what the sourness did to her face. From where he sat he could see it in the mirror, how her lips became twisted and her eyes narrowed.

When she did it she reminded him of the witch in *Snow White*, the animated version Disney made, a beautiful face in the glass turning dark and sick and ugly. He looked out the window so he wouldn't have to see it anymore.

"He said he loves her and she wants to have a litter of his brats."

A little black-and-brown bird with shining bugle bead eyes hopped up from the fieldstone steps to the concrete slab of the porch. Cocking its head, it fixed one eye on Darden and waited expectantly. Deciding he wasn't going to proffer any crumbs, it hopped away on its spidery feet till it hopped out of sight beneath one of the armchairs. Darden kept his eyes fixed on where it had disappeared, trying not to imagine Judith's face. The sound of the hairbrush was loud, scraping her scalp with each pull. If she kept at it her thick bleached hair was going to stand on end.

"Charles wants to rush the divorce so he and his brood mare can start playing house right away. Not in Houston—he said that like he was doing me a big favor—he's going to move to Virginia to be near the bitch's parents, who are all slavering like dogs over the aspect of having little grandkiddies shrieking underfoot."

"Stop it, Judy," Darden said. The bitterness was beginning to erode the core of him where his love for her was housed.

"He's in for a big surprise," she said with a black brand of satisfaction. "No wife. And if I've got anything to say about it, no brats."

"Judith, that's enough," Darden said sharply. She stopped brushing her hair. He'd been right; it was standing out in a ragged halo around her head.

"Leave it alone for now," he said a bit more gently. He started for the door.

"Where are you going?" she demanded. The hairbrush was held stiffly in her hand, the arm half raised as if it was a weapon and not a tool for personal grooming.

"I'm meeting Anna Pigeon, the woman who saved the baby, for breakfast."

"Don't leave me," she said pitifully.

"I'm not leaving you, honey. I'm just going to get something to eat. I doubt I'll be gone even an hour. I'll be back before you know it."

"Can I come?"

Darden looked at wild hair, the tear-streaked face and eyes that were clouded with pain and fury and God knew what else.

"I don't think that's a good idea, honey. Why don't you take a hot shower and relax. I'll bring Mrs. Pigeon up after we're done."

"Please let me go with you," she begged. "I'll be good."

Darden had never been able to say no to her. He considered doing it now for her own good but the hope and hurt on her face wouldn't let him.

"Do you promise?" he said.

She traced a cross on her chest and said, "Cross my heart, hope to die, stick a million needles in my eye." There was a mocking edge to the smile she gave him and he laughed.

"Fix your face and flatten your hair and come on," he said.

TWENTY-SEVEN

The Houston security guy hadn't shown up yet and Anna was outside the dining room on the patio, sitting backward on a picnic table bench, her elbows on the tabletop, her feet stretched in front of her, the sun on her face. She didn't mind waiting when she could do it in such a magnificent spot. Lazily she watched as a bright summer tanager worked its way through the crooked branches of a pine. One of Texas's little-known delights—little known to everybody but birders—was that it was home or host to a tremendous variety of winged creatures, some quite rare. Anna loved the colorful birds, indigo buntings and hummingbirds and bluebirds and tanagers, but her favorites were common house sparrows. They were so delicate and curious and brave. Often too brave. Piedmont, her big ginger tiger cat, had nailed one on her balcony in Colorado not a month before and Piedmont was getting on in years and not as quick as he once was.

Cyril and Steve and, to Anna's surprise, Chrissie had no plans to fly out before they were scheduled to in five days. The moment their folks were told about the shootings, Anna had thought they would demand their children come home. That would have been the case, Cyril assured her, so she and Steve hadn't told them. Asking whether Lori's mother would have told them was halfway out of her mouth before she remembered that these were college kids. Their parents didn't know one another. They probably had only a hazy idea who their friends were and not a clue from which part of the country they hailed. In college it was nothing to wander off for a weekend or a vacation after giving the parents the sketchiest itinerary.

They were staying because Cyril was determined to find out what happened to Easter. Vaguely, Anna remembered swearing to herself that she would save Easter no matter what it took, but she'd been under a lot of stress at the time. Fed, clean and out of danger, the beast was looking less and less like a symbol of all that was good in mankind and more and more like a skinny old Mexican cow.

Santa Elena Canyon was closed to raft trips but the NPS wouldn't be able to maintain that for long. There was too much economic impact on the outfitters to shut down their livelihood for any length of time. Since they couldn't get another raft or canoe trip down the river, the three kids had other plans. Anna suspected they involved sneaking across the border into Mexico, where the land was flatter leading up to the Rio Grande, and hiking upriver. Probably mooing and strewing bits of hay or grain as they went, she thought with a smile.

Crossing into Mexico, except at officially sanctioned border stations, was illegal, but Anna wasn't worrying about it overmuch. These were three white college kids from New York. Nobody, including the Mexicans, cared whether they crossed the border. It was the other way around that got Border Patrol and Homeland Security's undies in a bundle.

A bit of pure Texas came walking up from the parking lot. Big blond hair, makeup heavy and perfect, clothes from Neiman Marcus or Saks or some store neither Anna's budget nor her inclination had her shopping at anytime soon. This woman did it up right. She pulled it off with such a natural grace that, on her, it looked good.

Anna smiled and nodded politely when their eyes met then was immediately sorry she'd done so. Miss Texas veered off course and walked over to Anna's picnic table.

"Aren't you the woman who saved that baby from the river?" she asked. There was nothing Texas about her speech patterns. Upper Midwest, Anna thought, but she was only guessing; she had none of Henry Higgins's talent.

"There was a bunch of us," Anna said. "Prenatal salvation is kind of a group sport."

The woman laughed and Anna liked it. It sounded well-used and never rehearsed.

"I'm Gerry Schneider," she said, and stuck out her hand. Anna shook it.

"Anna Pigeon." She didn't add that she was a park ranger. For one, she was on vacation. For another, she wasn't sure she still was.

Without waiting for an invitation, Gerry sat down on the bench opposite Anna. "I'm beginning to think this is my lucky day. I've been wanting to talk with somebody other than NPS brass about the incident. They're on the body recovery today but the head of law enforcement—Jessie Wiggins—had no intention of letting me tag along. I suppose I could have rented a jeep and followed, this being, at least nominally, a free country. Even in Texas. But by the way he was clouding up at the mention of my presence I didn't think the antagonism I would earn would be worth the story I got. Body recoveries aren't terribly gripping. Mostly they underline that the event is truly over and the good guys lost."

While she rattled on, Gerry Schneider plopped a shapeless leather bag, scratched and nicked from years of hard use, on the rough planks of the table and removed a tiny tape recorder, a yellow legal pad so rumpled she must have been sleeping with it, and three ballpoint pens, the cheap kind that come in packs, and set these items in a neat row between her and Anna.

"So, tell me what happened?" Gerry said, and turned an open, interested face upon Anna.

Anna sat up straight and put her elbows on the table,

resting her chin in her palms. "And you want me to do this why?" she asked.

Gerry laughed again. "Cart before the horse," she said. "I guess I should be glad I can still get carried away with a story. I'm a newspaper woman. I report for the *Houston Chronicle*."

"Of course it was interesting to me and to the park that a couple people were shot and a baby was brought out of the mess but I'd think a big city paper like the *Chronicle* would have more shootings than they could shake a stick at outside their back door," Anna said. "Why would they send a reporter all the way out here to be Johnny-on-the-spot in less than twelve hours to cover our measly two dead?"

"They wouldn't," Gerry said flatly. "We were all sent here to cover Mayor Pierson's big announcement. Not that it was news but that woman has a way of getting coverage that other politicians can only dream about, so El Paso was here, Middleton, three reporters from the Dallas Ft. Worth area and me."

"Where's the rest of the pack?" Anna was getting a creepy feeling she was going to be pestered to death simply because a passel of newspaper people had a room paid for, per diem and nothing else to do.

"Don't worry," Gerry said. "It's just little old me. The pack left first thing this morning. Some even left last night as soon as the dinner was over."

"Why are you still here?"

"I thought the C-section rescue of the river baby would make a terrific color piece." Gerry Schneider's eyes grew skittery and her voice went up a few notes. As a liar she was hopeless.

Anna raised an eyebrow and waited.

"Don't you want to see your name in print?" Gerry tried.

"Not so much. In high school I did," Anna said. She was enjoying sparring with Ms. Schneider. "I was on the debate team and when we won they'd print our names. Now when it happens it's nothing anybody wants to hang up with a refrigerator magnet.

"What story did you really stay out here to cover? Or should I say, 'dig up'?"

Gerry planted both palms flat on the table and fixed a level gaze on Anna. "I have been in this business for thirty-six years—and before you start thinking I'm as old as Methuselah, I am counting my years on the high school yearbook—and I have never mastered the art of lying. It has been a terrible burden, as you might imagine.

"I haven't packed and gone because there is something going on with our mayor and I don't know what it is. I'm skulking about, sniffing in corners, hoping to turn up something juicy. There, now you know the worst. I will stoop to tabloid scandal if it makes a good story."

Anna appreciated the candor. "Do you know anybody in Health and Human Services in Houston, anybody you could lean on to make sure a baby is taken proper care of?" she asked on impulse.

"I might," Gerry said carefully. "Is this about the baby you rescued?"

"Yes."

"And in return I'd get an up-close-and-personal account of the rescue so my time here won't be totally
wasted?"

"That's the deal."

Gerry's gaze was distracted from Anna, flying over
her shoulder toward the parking lot. "If you want someone with real connections, here she comes."

"Uh-oh," Darden said with joviality that sounded
forced. "Gerry Schneider. Watch out, Anna, she'll be
dragging every skeleton you ever had out of your closet
and have them dancing the samba before you know it."

"Hello, Darden," Gerry said sweetly, and Anna
guessed the two old warhorses had a shared past or
wished to have a shared future.

"Anna, you've met Mayor Pierson," Darden said.

"Call me Judith," the mayor said.

She was standing with her back to the sun so Anna
could not see her face but, in silhouette, it was clear her
shoulders were an inch or so higher than normal and
her hands, though not formed into fists, had fingers that
curled into claws. Tension radiated from her the way
sound will from taut wires when the wind blows.

Before they could settle in, Anna rose from the bench.
"I don't know about anybody else, but I'm hungry."

"Mind if I join you?" Gerry asked, echoing Darden's
words from his roadside stop.

"That would be great," Anna said. "The more the
merrier." She liked Gerry but mostly she was thrilled
with the new addition to their impromptu breakfast

club because Darden and his mayor almost growled out loud when Gerry crashed the party.

Inside the lodge dining hall, at a table for four near the immense glass windows overlooking the basin, Anna got a clearer take on Judith Pierson. In contrast to the perfectly pulled-together politician she'd met the previous night, this Judith was pale and pinched, her hair hastily combed and her makeup slapped on rather than applied. Gerry noticed as well. Anna believed if she squinted she would be able to see the reporter's ears pricking up the way dogs' will when they hear a whistle.

Over eggs and bacon Anna told her story. She'd been so caught up in trying to stay alive and put one foot in front of the other, so tired afterward and so busy with Helena, she'd not thought the events through in an orderly manner, but merely snagged bits and pieces as her brain had a free moment. When she was a young woman, she remembered wondering why stay-at-home moms, known to her generation as housewives, didn't write epic novels, create great paintings or memorize all of Shakespeare. They had nothing to do all day but sit around, play with the baby, tidy up, why not be creative? Having spent part of a day and a night with an infant, Anna knew she owed each and every one she'd internally sneered at an apology. It was mind-boggling how all-absorbing caring for an infant was. Cute little aliens who stole one's brain and rendered their body a slave.

With an interested audience and no interruptions, putting the story chronologically, and attempting to put it logically, information and images that had gotten lost resurfaced. Events that she had accepted at the time showed themselves as unacceptable.

She'd finished describing how the woman had appeared caught in the strainer when Gerry said: "Bernard—the chief ranger—thinks she was probably trying to cross to have her baby on American soil and got swept downstream."

Anna hadn't entirely bought into that idea because of the pedicure and the bikini wax, signs of a woman living an urban and urbane life. Hearing Gerry make the statement in the clear light of day, she realized it was absurd.

"That's a tragedy," Judith was saying. "But—"

Clanking her fork down against her plate, Anna cut her off as the scene tried to play out in her mind and failed. "She couldn't have," she exclaimed. "If she wanted to cross she'd do it where there was a road, easy access to a vehicle, maybe a family member or friend waiting to pick her up and get her to a medical facility. The only place that fits that description is Lajitas." Her three dining companions stared at her blankly. They did not know the park.

"Lajitas is almost on the park's western boundary. There's a crossing there, a little bit of development, a road—that sort of thing. Lajitas is one of the places people used to cross back and forth before the border was closed after nine-eleven. That's where a woman wanting to have her baby in America would cross. On that side of the park, anyway."

"And she must have fallen and been swept downstream," Judith said, stating it as known fact rather than conjecture.

"Lajitas is miles from Santa Elena Canyon, two or three at least. Maybe more. We found this woman a mile into the canyon."

"Couldn't she have washed down there? I mean the cow did and you said rocks and trees were rolling," Gerry said.

"Yes," Anna said. "Easily. But what are the odds she'd still be alive after she did? Three or four miles of wild river bashing a very pregnant woman against everything that floats and everything that doesn't; she'd have drowned before she'd been in the water three hundred yards."

"What are you saying?" Gerry said at the same instant Mayor Pierson said: "If she was a strong swimmer—"

"Either she crossed near the mouth of Santa Elena Canyon and lost her footing, which makes no sense—there's nothing there for a woman in her condition to cross for and no easy access to shelter or medical help or even a phone—or this was no accident. She was put in the river by somebody who wanted her dead and wanted it to look like an illegal border crossing that had tragic results."

Saying the words, Anna knew she should have thought of this before. Once seen it was obvious. The next step in the equation was equally obvious.

"They wanted her and her baby dead," she said. What she didn't add because it was too frightening to speak aloud was maybe they—whoever *they* were—still wanted the baby dead.

Stunned by these conclusions, Anna ate mechanically while the conversation clattered around her. Helena's mother, nine months pregnant, had a bikini wax. That bit of information should have screamed louder than it had. To have that bit of vanity attended to in the late stages of pregnancy didn't suggest poor Mexican girls keeping up with the latest trends. It spoke of pampering and spas and a social stratum where services could be bought at exorbitant prices. According to Chrissie, and she had been confident of her observations, the dress was a cheap rayon number from Wal-Mart.

The woman had been taken, forced to change into cheap clothes, transported to the mouth of the canyon and dumped in the river, possibly after knocking her unconscious for good measure. The water provided a cause of death—drowning—wreaked havoc on trace evidence and, if the perpetrator was lucky, obscured identification of the body. Heavy rains and the river rising had been icing on the cake, stealing the body away before it could be autopsied.

"Homicide," Gerry said, and though Anna suspected she was not a ghoul at heart, she heard the glee in the reporter's voice. This was a story worth hanging around for.

"Looks like it," Anna said.

Gerry started scribbling on her yellow legal pad. Anna paid no attention; she was interested in Darden, sitting across from the reporter. He'd been the one to call this meeting of sorts, and now it was clear he wanted to get away as soon as he could. His physical self was shrinking away from the mayor as if his body was not waiting for his mouth to make the excuses before it removed itself from the premises.

Judith must have sensed the incipient exodus as well. She laid her fine-boned hand on his beefy arm to pin him down. Darden flinched and Anna wondered what sort of relationship the two had. It was more than professional, that much was clear, but the mayor didn't touch him like a woman touched a lover.

"This homicide sounds convenient," Judith said. "The ranger you are staying with, Frederick Martinez, is speaking to the convention today on the evils of the border closing after nine-eleven and continuing to keep it closed today. Handy that such a tragedy happens at the moment he needs to highlight his argument with an emotional appeal none of us can help but identify with."

"Freddy can't speak at the convention—" Anna began but stopped mid-sentence. That was what Lisa's cryptic statements about unemployment referred to. Freddy was a government employee. As an employee, and therefore a representative of the government, he was not free to express his political beliefs. The Park Service cut rangers a lot of slack on this issue, but to fly in the face of the rule in one's own park on topics under debate by local politicians that affected that park would probably get Freddy fired. He could lose his retirement. Anna marveled at the good face his wife had been able to put on what had to be a family disaster.

"Originally he turned the invitation down," Judith said. "I had my secretary keeping tabs on who was to be here and what their arguments were likely to be. It was my guess that he had turned the invitation down because his arguments for opening the border were threadbare. His premise about the death of the little border towns and the vacuum it left to be filled by crooks and drug dealers was old news from before the Mexican drug wars broke out."

Gerry looked up from her pad of paper. "Are you saying this park ranger murdered a pregnant woman and tried to kill her fetus to get the border reopened? Is this guy a fanatic or a lunatic or a psycho or what?"

"All I am saying," the mayor stated quietly, "is that it looks as if Ranger Martinez has decided he now has an argument worth making."

Darden eased his arm out from under Judith's and glanced at his watch. "If you ladies will excuse me," he said as he pushed back his chair. "I've got to meet Gordon and Kevin in a few minutes. Don't worry about the check." He winked at Gerry then smiled to include Anna in the gesture. "I'll have it put on the mayor's tab."

"Darden—" The mayor said his name with a desperation that startled Anna. The fragility that had vanished while she listened to the story of the river incident and discussed Freddy's nifty new argument was back. For the briefest of moments she sounded like a little girl afraid of being left alone in the dark.

"You'll be listening to this Martinez?" Darden asked her.

"I guess." The childlike quality was fading but not yet gone.

"I'll see you there," Darden said with a depth of reassurance that only served to confuse Anna further. Maybe they were family, niece and uncle or cousins. They looked nothing alike and the vibe between them wasn't that of father and daughter, not quite.

In the few seconds the exchange required, Judith Pierson's expression had hardened, matured. "When you see Kevin, tell him I need to see him, will you?"

Darden didn't answer right away and Gerry's eyes took on a predatory gleam. Maybe this was the scandal she'd sensed brewing. "What about the Martinez thing?" Darden avoided the request.

"Tell Kevin to come and get me out," the mayor said, and smiled. She may have thought the smile was seductive or suggestive. To Anna it was snaky, no lips and all fangs.

"Ladies," Darden said by way of excusing himself, and walked away.

"I'm disappointed you didn't bring the baby," Judith said to Anna. "I only got a glimpse of her last night but I would love to see her again. Is she staying with you at the Martinezes' place? Where is that, Terlingua?"

There was no need for the mayor of Houston to ingratiate herself with an out-of-favor ranger from a park not even in her state, so Anna figured the interest was genuine and answered.

"For now," she said. "At some point the child-care people will take over."

"And you don't want that," the mayor said. The woman had more insight than Anna had been prepared to grant her. That or Anna was more transparent than she liked to think she was.

Anna didn't say anything. She stirred her coffee so she'd seem to be doing something and stared out the window. Judith could help Helena; Anna wasn't fool enough to think she couldn't. Had Judith Pierson not been the mayor of a huge and rich city she would have been able to help Helena. Judith was a woman who knew her way around the system, Anna guessed. The woman sounded sympathetic and Anna's first impression of her as a person who might kill and eat the children was undoubtedly off base. Still, she didn't want Judith's help with placing Helena and she didn't know why. Gerry's help she'd solicited, bartered for, and Gerry, well connected as she might be, probably didn't have the clout Judith had to cut through red tape.

"That's an area I'm familiar with," Judith said gently. "Just let me know if you need anything."

"Thanks," Anna said. "I will—and I will need something." She pushed as much gratitude into her tone as she could. Because she had taken against the mayor was not reason enough to turn away anybody who might be in a position to make Helena's life better.

"I do believe it's time," Judith said, and Anna was glad of a change of subject. "Are either of you going to come see what Ranger Martinez will make of this unfortunate circumstance?"

Anna thought three murders rated more than "unfortunate circumstance," but being a woman who could enjoy understatement in better circumstances she mustered a smile. "I think I'll pass," she said. "I expect I've heard most of it before."

Judith left Anna and Gerry sitting at the table nursing their third cups of coffee. Anna had the day to kill before she met Cyril, Steve and Chrissie for dinner at a place in Terlingua they had raved about. The Starlight Theatre on the Terlingua Porch; at least it should be colorful.

After a moment she poked the disreputable leather satchel at Gerry's feet with her toe. "What else have you got in there?"

"The rest of my life," Gerry answered. "What do you need?"

"Do you have a laptop and satellite hookup?"

"Does the Pope like long dresses? Of course I do."

She lifted the shapeless sack and plopped it on the table between the salt and pepper shakers and the crumby toast plates. Having cleared a place in front of her, she set up her laptop and phone. "What are we looking for?"

"Bernard, or maybe it was Jessie, said this had happened before. That a woman trying to cross the Rio Grande to get medical treatment had been carried downriver and drowned. Can you find something on that, if it happened?"

"Nothing easier," Gerry said. From one of the satchel's many zipped pockets she took a pair of reading glasses, the frames a tiger print with sparkles at the temples, and put them on the end of her nose. "Okay."

While Gerry searched new databases for stories that related to what they were after, Anna watched three vultures drying their wings on the top of a mountain, a small mountain from where she sat but big enough if it were to be measured from the ground up. Black and wide-winged, the center bird on a high finger of rock, the two flanking on slightly lower crags, they put Anna in mind of the thieves on either side of Jesus at Golgotha. That put her in mind of Helena's mother crucified on deadwood and garbage. Had she been sacrificed on the altar of Freddy Martinez's belief that the greater good would be opening the border between Big Bend and Mexico, that the new and better life breathed into Boquillas and San Vicente and Santa Helena—villages where the economy had been all but shut down with a single stroke of a pen—would balance out the evil of two murders?

Anna couldn't imagine Freddy in that story. A man with a wife and children, a man with a family he appeared to love, might kill other men or even women, but a pregnant woman? Anna doubted it. Unless she was more to him than a symbol, unless she posed a threat to the life he had or wanted, then this hypothetical dad could do it. Kill for personal reasons and pose the body for political reasons. Was this woman blackmailing Freddy, threatening to tear his family apart, take from him all he had? Was she carrying his child?

That wasn't beyond the realm of possibility but, even with the proposed obliteration of his world, Anna couldn't see Freddy killing the fetus. Racism was a wretched thing, the putting on of individual traits to an entire race of human beings, but in Anna's experience, Mexican men loved kids, venerated mothers-to-be. Not that one didn't get knocked off now and then for the usual reasons, but she felt it would be a harder murder for them than for people raised in certain other cultures.

Had another person killed the woman and Freddy helped dispose of the body in such a way it would look like an accidental death? That didn't work, not unless Freddy and the supposed murderer were such dimwits they hadn't known the woman was alive when they put her in the water. Particularly since it would seem one of the major motivations for putting her into the river while she was still alive was so the corpse, when it was found, would attest to death by drowning.

Regardless of Anna's continuing belief in Freddy's intrinsic humanity, she wasn't as comfortable leaving Helena in the care of his wife as she had been when she left that morning. That was another point in Freddy's favor: if he'd wanted the baby dead, why had he asked his wife to feed it? To get his hands on it before child services whisked it away? To kill Helena before a DNA test could prove she was his daughter?

That was a little draconian, Anna thought. With the mother dead, who would be demanding the DNA test? And, in this day and age, outside of his own family, it wouldn't have much in the way of repercussions if it was Freddy's child. Lisa might forgive Freddy an affair, but she would never forgive him for murdering a baby to hide it from her. At least Anna didn't think she would.

Two anti-Freddy facts were inescapable: Freddy knew something about the drowned woman and Freddy was sitting pat in the shooter's seat when Anna and Paul had climbed out of the canyon.

"Well, that didn't take long," Gerry said.

"What've you got?" Anna hitched her chair around to the end of the table so she and the reporter could both see the computer screen.

"An article written eight months after nine-eleven, about the time when the border was closed between the park and the villages."

They read together and silently. The article was short. Two days after the border was closed a young mother, the wife of one of Big Bend's Mexican firefighters, the Diablos, had been stopped by Border Patrol while trying to cross the river with her mother and mother-in-law. In the confusion of the border patrolman trying to turn the women back and the anxious women, one of whom was in labor, trying to explain their predicament, the pregnant woman had fallen. The river wasn't at flood level, but it was high enough she couldn't regain her footing and drowned.

The surviving women, mother and mother-in-law, had never been told the border had been closed.

After three days of searching, a young river ranger named Freddy Martinez found her body in a strainer. The body was recovered and taken out by way of Rio Grande Village. The ranger who had found the dead woman attacked a border guard and had to be pulled off by his fellow rangers. The Park Service attributed the uncharacteristic behavior to fatigue and stress. Martinez had refused to be taken off the search. Another ranger told the reporter that Martinez had been without sleep for close to seventy-two hours.

The border guard did not press charges.

"Poor Ranger Martinez," Gerry said. "The worst kind of déjà vu all over again."

"That or revenge," Anna said. "Re-create the crime but this time the victim is 'one of theirs'?"

"I thought the woman you found was Mexican?"

"Hispanic," Anna said, and: "Maybe. Her baby has hazel eyes."

Gerry suffered a moment's confusion, her sharp eyes clouding till Biology 101 came to her rescue. "Right," she said. "Dominant gene."

"Nobody in America is all of one thing or all of another anymore," Anna said. "But it's interesting."

"It is interesting," Gerry said. Her eyes were again going out of focus.

Not confusion, Anna guessed. "What are you thinking?" she demanded.

"Nothing."

"No woman is ever thinking nothing," Anna said.

"It has nothing to do with Freddy."

Anna tried to stare her down but it was clear this was the sort of secret Gerry had decades of practice keeping from more persistent and alarming inquisitors than Anna.

Giving up with good grace, Anna leaned back in her chair. The coffee cup tempted her for a moment but one could only drink so much of the stuff before it warped the taste buds. "The article says Freddy stayed up seventy-two hours, then attacked a border guard," Anna said. "You don't hear a lot of reports of ranger brutality. We are a peaceful people for the most part, trained to use our radios rather than our guns, teach bad people to be good conservators of the wilderness and campers to work and play well together. Yet this river ranger with a nice wife and a kid at home drives himself to the edge of his endurance on a body recovery, then punches out the first border patrol agent he sees."

Gerry raised her eyes from the computer screen where she'd already clicked onto another train of thought.

"Freddy knew the woman killed in 2002," Anna said. "Don't you figure? Why else all the dramatics?"

Gerry glanced back at the laptop. Anna didn't know if it was merely a habit that gave her time to think or if she'd continued the research while Anna deliberated the old-fashioned way.

"The article didn't say he did," Gerry replied.

"Freddy hasn't said he did either. He hasn't mentioned the case at all. The two mirroring each other so closely, wouldn't you think he'd have brought it up, told the story of when he stayed up for three days running? Most people would have."

Anna stopped talking and let her gaze wander back out the window. The mountains were compelling, ever-changing as the angle of light changed. For a while now she'd not felt like herself, or like the self she remembered. The pit was new, the fear of spiraling down until she was everybody's albatross and nobody's friend. Or wife.

But the pit wasn't the whole of the difference in her internal landscape. Mindscape. Fog was a part of it. She'd always been good at multitasking. For the past week even mono-tasking had been an effort. Part of it was this was not her park, not her crime to solve, not her evil to root out. Most of her consciousness wanted to pull away, go to the movies—if there were any movies within a day's drive of Big Bend—sit in the desert sun and watch lizards. She would have, too, she told herself, if there was anybody trustworthy to look after Helena, if Cyril's cow was found safe and growing fat on beaver tail cactus, if Freddy would shut up and keep his job.

"Would you?" Gerry's voice brought her back into the dining room.

"Maybe," Anna said. "I'm getting tired of fighting the good fight. If it is a good fight. No. I wouldn't," she said with sudden determination. "Good or bad, this isn't my fight."

As soon as the words were out of her mouth she realized Gerry had not been listening in on her thoughts and then questioning her about them. She was referring to whether Anna would speak of the old case when it was reenacted years later.

"Yes," Anna said. "Sorry. My mind has been wandering of late."

"Ahh," Gerry said knowingly. "The Change." She said the phrase the way Rod Serling used to say "The Twilight Zone."

"Jeez," Anna said. That was all she needed at the moment. "I'm not even fifty."

Gerry looked at her over the top of her leopard-print half-glasses, one eyebrow lifted high. "But I expect you have always been precocious, haven't you?"

TWENTY-EIGHT

The itching under Darden's armor was getting worse. If he could have peeled off the skin of humanity and left it lying in the dirt, he would have. Over breakfast, the way Judith was, the women discussing the corpse in the strainer, the baby, all of it grated against the speculations he'd been avoiding. Judith was different. She'd changed, and recently. Since they'd come to this god-forsaken wasteland of gray rubble the state was so proud of. Even as a girl she'd been a creature of extremes, and she had grown into a woman who seemed capable of molding those extremes into visions, of holding opposites within her whose opposing natures would have destroyed a lesser woman: fragile and unbreakable, wise as a crone and innocent as an eight-year-old child, mean as a snake and capable of great kindness.

Stomping down the uneven natural stone steps that led from the lodge to the parking lot below, Darden startled a herd of deer no bigger than Great Danes and they scattered onto the pavement, their tiny hooves making a faint clipping sound.

Darden never saw them. He was looking for the city SUV his security men were driving. Where in the hell were Kevin and Gordon? Automatically he reached for his cell then stopped, snorting his displeasure like an old and angry bull. Why did anybody live in these primitive places? Cell phones were useless. Nothing to look at but snakes and spiny plants that would kill a man as soon as feed him.

And Judith hissing that Charles would never have kids, that he would never marry his girlfriend. Not saying it the way any woman would but spitting it like a curse or a promise. A line had been crossed and he hadn't been paying attention at the time. Probably lost in one of his furry old-man dreams. Damn it!

His little mayor had that look that said she'd crossed a personal Rubicon and there was no going back for her. Darden had seen the change before a couple of times. Once when an agent he was working with had made the decision to kill his wife and himself because she was running around. They'd been on assignment together, Darden remembered. Out of the country for two weeks while the president made the rounds of the Middle East, for all the good it did. Terry, the guy's name had been Terry, Terrance Clark or Parks, a short name full of barking. They'd been standing around doing what they were paid to do, looking for trouble, and Terry had been out of it, not paying attention, caught up in whatever he was playing in his head. Then his face firmed, a sucking in like skin being shrink-wrapped to bone but subtle, a thousand tiny muscles and sinews tightening up a fraction. Terry had changed himself with the decision, Darden was sure of it. From that minute on he'd been a little different. He said things that didn't make sense until after he committed the murder-suicide, cryptic comments about his wife doing or not doing a thing again, about what he would or wouldn't need in a couple weeks. Little things that nobody commented on. They were just weird. Off.

Judith was weird and off. The fixation on the baby. She'd been upset when he'd told her on the way to breakfast that Anna didn't have the kid with her.

Her and Charles and kids and divorce, that had to be it. The worm turns and Judith falls apart. Darden had never asked her but he knew she never thought Charles would leave her. Never. She was aware on whatever level she allowed herself to be that he had had a couple of affairs. She didn't like it but they hadn't seemed to worry her, not in the sense that she felt she was losing her husband to another woman. For a man like Darden it was hard to see how a woman, especially a woman like Judith, who could have pretty much any man she wanted, could love a man at the same time she believed him to be such an utter coward that he'd never get up the gumption to walk out of a marriage he hated.

Well, now he had. Was that enough to bring the whole house of cards she'd so painstakingly erected down around her ears?

He caught himself fumbling for his cell again. He wanted to make a Goddamn phone call. Was that too much to ask?

Wanting to give Judith time to get herself together, they'd walked down from the cabins to the dining hall, not more than a few hundred yards, but Darden wished they'd driven. Too ornery and set in his ways to listen to the voice of reason, he'd brought his usual shoes, black leather lace-ups with leather soles. He hadn't been standing long enough for his feet to hurt, but the leather clapped against the asphalt with each step. The racket jarred him. A fat squirrel, dun-colored with a white stomach that hadn't gotten so round gathering nuts, sat on a flat-topped rock at the side of the lane. It sat up and pressed a paw to its white chest and chittered at him as he neared it.

"What are you looking at?" he snarled. The creature dropped to all fours, twitched its tail, and vanished off the far side of the stone. No phone, no television and glamour rats mocking the paying guests, Darden thought.

The itching was killing him. Where the hell was Gordon?

A car was coming up behind him too fast. Needing

to have a place to put his anger, Darden swung around to glare at the driver.

"About damn time," Darden muttered, and pointedly looked at his watch. They weren't late; in fact they'd turned the job around in record time. Darden wasn't appeased. He would have liked to have an excuse to ream somebody out.

Gordon let down the window.

"Hey, boss."

"Meet me at my cabin," Darden snapped, leaving his subordinate wondering what he'd done to deserve it.

It crossed his mind to ask for a ride the rest of the way, or pull Gordon out through the side window, Eastwood style, and drive the last forty yards himself, but he did neither. The first was embarrassing, the second was no longer possible, maybe never had been possible, only a trick for stuntmen and actors.

Standing close to attention, Gordon and Kevin were waiting outside his room. Thin cool air and a hot desert sun at high altitude left Darden feeling overheated and chilled. He was also out of breath but he would die before he'd puff and pant in front of these two.

"Kevin, the mayor wants to see you," Darden said.

"Where is she?" Kevin asked.

"How the hell do I know? Find her. There's only about three places she can be in this hellhole." Darden was being unfair but that was the breaks. He didn't want to see Kevin's face for a while. Didn't want to hear his voice or smell his aftershave.

"Come on in," he said more kindly to Gordon. Now that relief was in sight he could afford to slow down and be civil. Sitting in one of the straight-backed wooden chairs, he gestured Gordon to take the other. When the man was settled, Darden said: "Tell me what you found."

"Lajitas Resort is quite a setup. I sure wouldn't mind being shunted off to cool my heels there for a week. All the bells and whistles. It must be setting the mayor back four hundred a night easy. That's if our friend leaves the minibar alone."

Darden knew it was a luxury resort. That's why he'd picked it. That and it was close. He would have preferred to set the woman up in a five-star hotel in Tai Pei or Queensland but she wouldn't budge farther than Lajitas.

Gordon seemed to be enjoying sitting inside with the boss but Darden didn't have the patience to let him come to the news in his own time. As he was about to ask, he realized he was scared; he was afraid the answer would not be the one he wanted.

Ashamed of the weakness, Darden spat it out: "And Miss Emerson, is she doing okay there?"

"I guess," Gordon said. "She hasn't checked out or anything. I went up and knocked on the door to her room but she was out by one of the pools. Kevin was walking the grounds and saw her. He said she acted happy enough, like she was going to stay put for a couple more days. He said she got snippy when he asked if she'd gotten in touch with Charles but other than that she seemed to be going along with the game plan."

Relief hit Darden like two scotches on an empty stomach, he was so giddy with it. Miss Emerson was alive and well and had apparently kept her promise and not called Charles or accepted any calls from him. Otherwise the fool wouldn't be walking around punching numbers on his phone and scowling.

"Great," Darden said, and laughed. "Good work. That's just great."

"Thanks," Gordon said. Puzzlement shivered down one side of his face but he wasn't stupid enough to look a gift horse in the mouth. If the boss wanted to commend him for driving to a fancy resort to see a woman and back again, he would take it and be glad.

That made Darden laugh as well. Giddy.

"Why don't you take the rest of the day off, Gordon? The mayor is . . . occupied. I doubt she'll need you this afternoon." The specter of Judith parading Kevin in front of Charles in an attempt at revenge or to spark jealousy flitted darkly through his mind. Behavior like that anywhere was a huge no-no for female politicians. Doing it anywhere within a ten-mile radius of Gerry Schneider was political suicide.

"If you see Kevin, tell him to take the day off, too, go hiking." Hiking very far away, Darden thought.

"Will do, boss. Thanks."

Gordon rose gracefully from the hard niggardly chair. He'd shown no emotion at the mention of Judith being occupied, though Darden had put it in such a way that he could have read a lot into it, and he hadn't smirked when Darden had suggested he tell Kevin to go take a hike, literally as well as figuratively. Maybe things hadn't gone as far as he'd thought. If Judith was having a fling with her security guard, the other guard was seemingly unaware of it. There was hope for discretion and therefore avoidance of detection.

If they stayed clear of Gerry.

TWENTY-NINE

Anna and Gerry spent a fruitless hour or two trying to track down Martinez's connection—and Anna was positive there was one—with Gabriela, the woman who drowned trying to cross the border eight months after 9/11.

They learned a lot about Freddy Martinez. His continuing agitation to reopen the border between the park and Mexico had landed him in the news several times, cost him promotions and nearly gotten him fired more than once. His mother and father were Mexican, from the village of Boquillas, just over the river from Rio Grande Village in Big Bend. Freddy's mother made the crossing when she was eight months pregnant and stayed with relatives in Alpine, a college town in the mountains that formed the spine of west Texas, so her son would be born on American soil.

Freddy was raised on the border, one foot in each of his countries. Summers were spent in Alpine with the great-aunt who had sheltered his mom during the last month of her pregnancy, winters in Boquillas. By the time he was eight he was ferrying tourists over the river to visit the village. Because he was bilingual he was much in demand. He saved enough to buy an ancient pickup truck, and at fourteen, he was taking tourists who wanted a more pristine wilderness to explore on camping trips in the Coahuilas.

At sixteen he went to live with his great-aunt to finish high school in the States. He went on to college at the university in Alpine and got a BS in forestry. His first job was as a boatman for a rafting outfitter in Terlingua. His second was as a GS-2 seasonal in Big Bend.

Though Martinez never mentioned the drowning incident, at least not in any way the press could get ahold of it, his border activism dated from the body recovery of Gabriela. In 2005 his mother died of a brain aneurism. His father was still living in Boquillas.

Blind to the beauty of the desert, greening with recent rains, flashing past the windows of the car, Anna turned this information over in her mind on the drive back to Terlingua. No great revelations came to her. The trials and tribulations of a river ranger, economically stranded villages and women fording rivers weren't things she wanted to dwell on but, with her own life in disarray, worrying about events that did not lead to the abyss was a bit of a vacation.

The closer she got to Terlingua the more her thoughts turned to Helena. The day away from infant care had been a relief. Returning to the baby was a greater relief. Anna wanted to see and hold her, make sure she was happy and fed, reassure herself that the spark of life she'd wrenched from the dead flesh of the woman in the river still burned brightly. Its tiny light was, in some incomprehensible way, able to penetrate the darkness that had bored the hole in her soul in a way Paul's love, her sister Molly's concern and even the beauty of the Chihuahuan desert could not.

Health and Human Services would take the baby and she would be put into the system. The only way around that was called "kidnapping," and Anna wasn't prepared for that battle. Even adoption would be a drawn-out process during which Helena would be in the hands of the state. Anna couldn't bring herself to think about what could happen if Helena was dropped into the system.

Anna sniffed and turned up the radio, tuned to a Tex-Mex station. It bothered her that she was carrying on with the stunted maternal instinct scenario. It wasn't as if the little creature was a kitten, for God's sake. Helena didn't even have a tail or the good sense to chase a bit of string.

Two cars were parked in front of the Martinezes' idiosyncratic home. One was Lisa's Subaru. The other wasn't Freddy's truck and Anna wondered if he had been fired yet or if he was sitting in the superintendent's office being read the riot act for his political activities on park property. A horrible thought stabbed through the possible destruction of the Martinezes' livelihood; what if the second car belonged to who Anna thought of as the Evil They, who were going to take Helena and drop her into the meat grinder of foster care?

She pulled in crosswise behind the foreign vehicle so it could not be driven out except through the steel bones of the Honda. The trapped car didn't sport government license plates, but it could be a social worker's private car. Most state employees didn't rate government vehicles but charged mileage on their own when on state business. Anna locked the Honda then walked around the offending vehicle, wondering why she was acting paranoid. Wasn't it possible Lisa had friends? Might they not drop by? Family from Alpine? The Avon Lady? The babysitter? As she disparaged herself for borderline behavior, her brain was collecting information: silver Chevy Malibu, current year, Texas plates, probably a rental, on the front seat a map of Texas, in the cup holders two thirty-two-ounce drinks in nondescript cups, the kind sold in gas station food stores with on-tap sodas.

If these were any of the benign visitors she'd mocked herself with, they had arrived from a distance in a rental vehicle.

"Damn," Anna whispered. During the drive from the park she'd been bracing herself for the reality of

Helena's removal by authorities. Now that it was very probably upon her, she wasn't ready for it. In ways the "authorities" could wrap in red tape and choke on, Helena was hers; her mother had given her to Anna to care for with her dying breath. Though the woman had said only, "Take my baby," there was no doubt in Anna's mind that she was giving her unborn daughter into Anna's—and, probably, God's—hands. God might be busy stirring up typhoons or loading clouds with lightning, but Anna was not. Until God got through His "to do" list, Helena was Anna's.

At least this was what she told herself, in thoughts traveling through her brain at such high speeds they did not form into words but shot straight into her blood and cells, bones and muscle as she walked up the short gravel path to the front door of the Martinezes' home.

The door was open and, through the screen, Anna heard voices. Stepping to the side where she would not be seen, she listened.

"Is the child in the house?" a woman asked. She had a slight southern accent and a well-modulated voice in the lower register, still Anna loathed her immediately and found the pleasant sound false and smarmy.

"She is with a friend," Lisa replied.

Good woman, Anna thought. Maybe it was true Helena was elsewhere, but she doubted it. If Lisa was home she would have the babies with her. The Martinezes didn't have the money to throw around for babysitters when Mom could do it.

"Where's this neighbor live?" asked a second voice,

this one a man's, rougher around the edges and not as educated or politic as that of the woman. Anna liked his better; she didn't have to rationalize hating this one. Whether he sounded demanding or threatening or she was projecting her darkness on an innocent man, she didn't know. She didn't care either. Hating him was fun—or at least satisfying.

"Mrs. Martinez, I don't think you are being completely open with us," the woman came in smoothly before her male counterpart could say anything more. "Cooperating with us can only serve the client—"

Client, Anna sneered in her mind. This female was a heartless, bloodless, government whore who cared nothing for small and helpless beings. Hating her was getting much easier and Anna doubted it had anything to do with reality. Again she didn't care. Hate was a wonderful drug until, like every other wonderful drug, the high turned to acid and burned the addict out from the inside.

"From the reports, this infant is even more in need of expert medical intervention than most newborns. The manner of its birth was singularly traumatic."

Kind, rational. Anna hated her.

Infant. It. Anna really hated her.

As strong and good as Anna believed Lisa to be, she had a baby of her own to look after and a husband who could lose his job—if he hadn't taken care of that aspect of things already—if she refused to cooperate with state authorities. That coupled with the wretched bitch from the silver Malibu pretending to be a human being, Lisa might fold if the cavalry didn't come over the hill in the near future.

Making more noise than was absolutely necessary, Anna opened the screen and went in. Having made an entrance akin to that of Marshal Matt Dillon into Dodge City, or Wyatt Earp—some famous gunslinger with questionable ethics and a penchant for violence—Anna felt a bit silly to find three respectable grown-ups sitting around with cups of coffee on their laps.

"Hey," she said, letting the stunning anticlimax settle into her febrile imaginings.

"This is Anna Pigeon, the woman who saved Helena," Lisa said. She sounded relieved and Anna thought the gunslinger attitude might not be such a bad idea after all. It occurred to her that she was spoiling for a fight. Not merely the exchange of heated words and insults but a donnybrook, a brawl, a bar fight John Wayne could be proud of. Since the graphic deaths on Isle Royale she had been running from violence, frightened that she had turned killer because others were frightened that she'd become a were-ranger and, once tasting human blood . . .

When had she gone from fleeing violence to embracing it?

Embracing it *again*?

Anna would think about that ugly possibility later, preferably in Paul's arms where she could believe she was a good person because he believed she was.

The two social workers stood. Both had on casual clothing but were neat and clean and conservative, she in dark blue slacks and a lime blouse with matching flats and earrings, her short dark hair waving around a pleasantly plump face that was between thirty-five and forty years old. He was in khakis, once pressed but now the crease ballooned out at the knees from hours in a car, a short-sleeved white shirt and a dark red tie. Short-sleeved shirts with neckties were as cheesy as pocket protectors and much less practical. He looked as if he had worn pocket protectors well into his twenties. An overgrown nerd who had discovered the gym and thought it would turn his life around. Or so Anna thought until the light from behind her was deflected from the lenses of the dark-rimmed glasses he wore.

He didn't have a cold steely gaze but there was a wariness Anna found too sharp for the job he was presently doing, an edginess that suggested he watched for assailants with deadly weapons more regularly than babies with rattles.

Taking children from their mothers might easily result in the deadly weapons scenario, so perhaps he wasn't so much an oddball as a bodyguard.

An enormous cat Anna had not met the night before, its long white fur weirdly mottled as if a white cat had been standing nearby when a bottle of India ink was shattered, was stretched out nearly the length of the sofa back watching the goings-on through slitted blue-green eyes.

The woman in the lime and navy stuck out her hand and smiled. "I'm Nancy Roland from the child-care di-

vision of Health and Human Services out of Midland."

Perfunctorily Anna shook the proffered hand. Ms.
Roland's grip was firm and her skin pleasantly cool to
the touch. This did not affect Anna's dislike of her one
whit.

"Charmed, I'm sure," Anna said drily.

Nancy cocked her head, her smile glued in place, as
if a fish had flapped its tail in her face, and emotion
flickered behind her irises. Pure meanness, Anna
thought.

"This is Manny Rhoades, he's new to the office and
has come along to observe." Manny didn't offer his hand
and Anna didn't offer hers.

"Observe what?" Anna asked with all the innocence
of a cougar who had eaten Shirley Temple for lunch.

Ms. Roland allowed herself an audible sigh and a
sidelong glance at her compatriot.

"Would you like some coffee, Anna?" Lisa asked.

"That would be great," Anna replied. Once clear of
the living room, Lisa turned down the hall to the back
of the West Wing. Edgar and Helena were probably
napping in the crib off the master bedroom.

"Why don't we sit down?" Anna invited politely to
keep Roland's and Rhoades's attention away from where
Lisa went or how long she stayed there.

The two social workers returned their butts to the
wildly colored Mexican blanket Lisa used to decorate
the couch. The navy polyester stretched over Roland's

ample behind was liberally salted with white fur. Anna nodded at the cat in brief salute. Slowly the cat closed its eyes, acknowledging the tribute.

Anna walked around the coffee table and sat in the chair Lisa had vacated. There were others but she wanted Lisa's absence to go unnoticed to a certain extent. The best way to do that was to fill the physical space she had occupied so the visuals did not change.

"Long commute?" she asked pleasantly.

"Not bad," Nancy said at the same time Manny said: "You can't get here from anywhere." Nancy shot her apprentice babysnatcher a cold look, which glanced off him without leaving a mark. Either he was indifferent to his boss's opinion or she wasn't his boss.

Nancy scooted forward on the sofa, a move designed to suggest the mood was now to be more intimate. Behind her the cat opened its eyes the barest fraction and Anna smiled. White fur would be bunching up in rolls beneath the woman's buttocks. A small thing, really, but enjoyable for her and the cat.

"Anna," Nancy began in a lowered and slightly conspiratorial voice, "I'm hoping you won't mind saving that baby—"

"Helena," Anna said.

Again the flicker. Anna was willing to bet Nancy had one hell of a temper. "Helena? Someone named it already?"

"Her. Yes. Me." In truth it was Paul but, according to the rules of engagement and marriage they were now one, so she took credit for the name without any qualms.

For a moment the woman seemed genuinely confused as she put together the pieces of the English language Anna had given her. In a moment she had it. In another moment she remembered where her train of thought had been when Anna derailed it.

"Nice name," she said. And began again: "I was hoping you would be willing to save Helena a second time." It was one of those questions like "Do you want to save money?" that phone solicitors come up with, questions only answerable with "yes."

Anna scooched forward, joining the intimate circle Nancy was trying to create. Putting her elbows on her knees she leaned in, a thoughtful expression on her face. "No," she said finally. "Not a second time. For one thing, cutting women up with knives, even dead women you don't know all that well, is a drag. And babies are all well and good but if you had seen the rockslide—it's nearly perpendicular. I mean straight up perpendicular for over a thousand feet. Hopping up from rock to rock like a demented toad with seven pounds of baby meat slung across your chest? No thanks. A second time and I'd chuck it in the river."

There was a stunned silence.

"But thank you for asking," Anna said.

Rhoades snorted.

Roland squashed her annoyance between thinning lips.

Rhoades and Roland.

Nancy and Manny.

Manny Rhoades. Many roads. Nancy Roland. Nancy Ronald. Ronald Reagan. Nancy Reagan. Aliases? Why Anna's thoughts ran down that rabbit hole, she wasn't sure. Neither name was unusual or uncommon but they rang a false note. Anna let it go. When every bell rang a false note one had to move on or cross from borderline to genuine paranoid.

Nancy managed a belated laugh. "You have a wonderful sense of humor, Anna. Of course I meant rescue . . . Helena . . . a second time in the sense of helping us to get her the care she so desperately needs."

"She can get that from you?" Anna asked.

"She can get that from me—from us—" Nancy included Manny.

Anna resisted the temptation to ask if either one of them was breastfeeding at the moment.

"Mrs. Martinez is having trouble letting go of the baby," Nancy confided. "It's perfectly understandable. She's recently given birth herself. The mothering instinct is strong right now. But it is best for the baby if it can have proper medical care and so forth."

"What's the mailing address of your office in Midland?" Anna asked Manny.

He looked at Nancy as if he could crib answers from her face.

Nancy started to speak, presumably to give the address for him.

Anna held up a hand to silence her. "What street is it on, Manny? What's the phone number there?"

"Manny hasn't been with us long," Nancy said sharply. "I don't see where you're going with this, Miss . . ."

Anna stood up. "Could I see some ID?"

An awkward silence descended on the sofa. The cat yawned audibly. Manny started to get up.

"Stay," Anna said. He sat back down but he didn't like it.

"You want to see our driver's licenses?" Nancy said carefully.

"Let's start with that," Anna said.

Nancy rearranged her face into sterner lines. "Really, I don't think you can demand ID of us. You're not a policewoman, are you?" This was said with sugary politeness, the kind women use to best other women in arguments, to show they, at least, have risen above vulgarity. It was not a weapon Anna ever chose because it was not sharp enough.

"And I'd like to see identification from your office."

"This is absurd," Nancy said. "Do you want me to call the police? I will if I have to and you could serve jail time. Interfering in the care of a child who is the ward of the state is a serious crime in Texas."

Before Anna could respond the piercing sound of a baby crying cut through the thick atmosphere.

Nancy went on point with the hunting instinct of a bird dog. Manny rose from the couch, looking not at all like a nerd and every inch an enforcer.

"The kid's here," he stated flatly, as if that was the end of the discussion of the proper care and feeding of a foundling.

"That's Edgar," Anna said with as much dismissal as she could dredge up through a voice box tight with fear. "Lisa and Freddy's youngest."

A second wailing joined the first.

"And that isn't," Nancy said.

Anna snatched up a heavy lamp from an end table, her hands choking its neck as if it was a Louisville Slugger. "Lisa! Run!" she shouted.

THIRTY

"Get the baby," Nancy ordered her associate.

"Don't," Anna said. Adrenaline and something very like exaltation were tingling in her veins. Fear was in the mix, but not for herself. At that moment Anna felt invulnerable; nothing short of kryptonite could take her down.

By the look on Manny's face Anna knew he figured a hard right to her jaw would do the trick.

Nancy had him cramped in the corner at the end of the sofa where it butted against the wall by the hive-shaped fireplace. She tried to scramble out of his way but didn't move quickly enough for his taste. He stepped over the coffee table, his long legs clearing it easily.

Manny wasn't agile and most of his strength was in his upper body, the part that showed in the mirror, but he was big and, superwoman or not, Anna knew when all else was equal, big won. Young won.

The point was to make sure all else was as unequal as possible. The moment Manny was astraddle the small table, Anna stepped in and swung hard, aiming for his knee. The lamp's plug caught in the socket for an instant before the force of her swing pulled it free and the main impact struck Manny on the thigh, the long quadriceps muscle absorbing the blow. He yelled as much in surprise as pain, Anna guessed, and slowed not at all.

From what seemed exceedingly far away, Anna heard pounding and hoped it was Lisa running out a back door with Edgar and Helena in her arms. Whoever the impostors were, they weren't after little Edgar Allan Martinez, but she didn't credit them with the sensitivity to distinguish one child from another.

Clear of the coffee table, Manny lost his balance for a second, his thigh feeling the hit when his weight came down on it. Anna swung the lamp again, again at his knee. Manny knew what was coming this time and got his hand down in time to protect the joint. The heavy pottery base smashed into his fingers, crushing them against the kneecap. This time his scream was not of surprise but pain and rage.

Jumping back, Anna cocked the lamp for another swing. Fractured crockery parted and the two halves clattered to the tile floor, leaving her holding nothing but a bit of wire and a turquoise shade.

Time stopped for a heartbeat and the three of them

glared at one another. The room soaked up the violence and returned silence. Into it came the pounding again. There was no back door; the hall dead-ended at the master bedroom. Lisa was trying to get a window open.

Freddy had been worried about "punks" in the neighborhood. Had he rigged the windows so they wouldn't open?

"The back of the house," Manny said to Nancy. "No door. I checked. Go get the damn kid."

To crab her way around the couch, Nancy had to pass near Anna. She opted for climbing over the back. The cat had disappeared at the first change in the atmosphere. Nancy Roland, aka Wretched Bitch, had to be the brains of the team; she was clearly not adept at the physical side, unaccustomed to using her body for anything but sitting and standing.

Moving fast, Anna swatted her hard in the face with the lamp shade and the woman fell backward onto the cushions in shock at the attack and the sting. It wouldn't hold her long. Soon the temper Anna had suspected of being close to the surface would burn through and demand action to feed on. Flinging the lamp shade at Manny's head as a distraction, Anna retreated to the kitchen, knocking over chairs and small tables in her wake. If Manny got ahold of her, she would be in trouble.

"Back room, God dammit!" Manny shouted, and he came after her. Nancy edged in behind, waiting for him to neutralize Anna before she committed herself to the room. On a good day, Anna would have put her money on Lisa against Nancy even though Lisa was older. Carrying two squirming and undoubtedly shrieking babies changed the odds.

Grabbing the coffeepot from the stove, she hurled it across the kitchen. The pot banged into the wall, spattering both of her assailants with hot liquid but not enough to do damage. With the half second this bought her, Anna pulled a knife from the block on the counter and a dish towel from the sink.

The knife was designed for cutting big pieces of animal flesh, the steel blade two and a half inches wide where it went into the haft and eight or nine inches from base to point. The black wooden handle felt good in her hand but, against Manny's superior height and weight, unless she got lucky with her first strike, he would take it from her and use it against her. Whipping the dish towel around her left arm for what little protection it could provide, Anna grasped the knife in her right hand. She didn't hold it low and to the side the way knife fighters are characteristically depicted in the movies but with the point toward the floor and the haft in her fist the way Norman Bates did in *Psycho*.

Uttering a shriek she hoped was horrible enough to terrify banshee children, she charged.

Manny was expecting it.

Nancy wasn't. Back against the kitchen wall, mouth in a horrified *O*, eyes about the same size and shape and just as empty, she froze. Anna smashed into her, knocking the breath out of her and rattling her brains with unaccustomed trauma. Before she could recover, Anna was behind her, the towel-wrapped arm around her throat, the butcher knife perpendicular to her jugular and touching the flesh of her neck.

Nancy recovered quickly and the temper Anna had seen simmering beneath her smiles blew up. She began to struggle, then the chokehold and the knife blade reminded her what a bad idea that was. She began to yell.

"You bitch, you fucking bitch. Kill her, Danny! If you think you're going to get away with this . . . You psycho cunt . . ."

Like most women, Anna was not fond of the "C" word. Unlike some of them, there was something she could do about it. The butcher knife moved fractionally and Nancy shut up with a squeak.

"Danny, Manny. Not very creative," Anna said to the man hovering in the doorway, unsure whether to let Anna kill the woman and get the job done or if his interests would be better served by keeping Nancy alive.

Nancy must have seen the decision wavering in his eyes, as well, because she said in a voice that rang of authority, "Don't even think about it, asshole."

"Little pitchers have big ears," Anna said, and moved the knife a teensy-weensy bit.

"You are fucking kidding me!"

Another wee twitch of the steel and Nancy desisted. Anna realized she was not kidding. Edgar and Helena might be preverbal but if their first word was to have four letters, she wanted it to be Mama.

Adrenaline strength would soon begin to dissipate

into shakes. Rather like the proverbial car-chasing hound, now that Anna had caught Nancy she didn't know what came next. The threat of the knife was empty. Not that she wouldn't use it to defend herself, or people she liked, but she wasn't going to slash Nancy's throat. There was no point in it. Nancy alive might prove a shield, a bargaining chip. Nancy dead was just a mess on Lisa's kitchen floor.

For what seemed too long, Anna said nothing, did nothing. She'd never expected to be the knife-wielding hostage taker. All her training had been the other way around. True, she had been spoiling for a fight, but now she wanted it over. Like sexual fantasies, vengeance fantasies were more enjoyable in thought than in deed.

"I want you to leave," she said evenly. "Is your boy Danny going to cooperate with me or is he going to make me slit your throat?" she asked the woman smashed against the front of her body.

"Yes, he is," Nancy choked out.

Tension had caused Anna to half strangle the woman. She took a bit of the pressure off Nancy's trachea.

"Is what? Going to make me slit your throat or going to cooperate?" Anna addressed the question to Nancy but she was only interested in what Danny intended to do. At home or the office or the rock these two had crawled out from under, Nancy might be the one in charge. Maybe Danny didn't like it that way. Maybe he didn't like Nancy. Maybe they didn't even know each other and had been brought together for this job. There were those who snatched babies for love—or the closest their crippled hearts could come to it—but Anna didn't think that was the case with these two. That left perversion and money with money far in the lead. Maybe Danny would get her pay as well as his if he was the last man standing.

In the back of the house one of the babies was still crying. Edgar, Anna knew, and was amazed that she could distinguish the different voices so soon. Edgar's cries sounded like a nonverbal person pleading for help. Helena's cries sounded like a nonverbal person imperiously demanding assistance.

Danny's gaze followed the sound.

"Don't you do this to me, you bastard," Nancy hissed. "You won't live long enough to savor it, you worthless prick."

Anna could feel her vibrating with fury, a thrum that gave off an almost imperceptible electrical current, or so it felt where Anna's skin touched her captive's.

Danny stared at the two of them. Behind the glasses, his eyes were unreadable. The electrical charge coming from Nancy amped up till Anna was vibrating with as much unvented emotion as she was.

"Let's be reasonable," Nancy said, and Anna had to admit she sounded pretty in control when she wasn't spouting obscenities, like it wasn't too late for them to be reasonable, to settle this amicably and all go home with a job well done.

"We all have the child's welfare at heart. Let's stop the fighting, sit down and work this through. I don't see why Helena can't stay where she is," she said as if she had not let it be known that Manny was Danny and did not have a knife at her throat. As if none of this had transpired and the clock was turned back to when they were passing as kindly social workers.

Anna marveled at the insanity, the same insanity that allowed politicians to stand on the national stage and tell the same lie again and again. If they found a lie people wanted to believe, it didn't matter that it wasn't true, that scholars and researchers and videographers were screaming that it wasn't true; nothing mattered but that they said the right words. The crowd's need to believe it was getting what it wanted did the rest.

Anna felt that pull now. She wanted to end this reasonably, to work things out rationally. She wanted to believe Nancy was going to give her what she wanted. The phenomenon was mind-boggling. The hatred that had goosed up her energy level on and off since returning to Terlingua flamed up.

Everything in life that she hated boiled out of the abyss. Cruelty and fear, greed and the wanton destruction of the world so people could keep their SUVs, animals tied up and left to starve, dogs beaten, trees cut down to make room for billboards, men preying on women and women preying on one another, lobbying to get hate made law. And lies. Lucifer was said to be the father of lies. Lies made the rest possible. People lying to themselves and one another, to their children and their bosses, to make themselves bigger and others smaller, to steal and cheat and take.

More than anything she hated lies.

No. More than anything she hated liars.

Her hand trembled on the handle of the knife as if the hatred had taken over wrist and fingers and arm till Anna didn't know whether or not she was going to end this one liar's life.

Danny's voice seemed to come from the devil in Anna's mind: "Go ahead and kill her if you want to," he said, and headed down the hallway toward Lisa and Edgar and Helena.

THIRTY-ONE

Anna didn't slit Nancy's throat, though she probably should have. Leaving a dangerous person behind and unfettered was seldom a good idea. The sound of wood splintering let Anna know Danny had kicked in the door to the bedroom where Lisa and the babies—if Lisa hadn't managed to open a window—had barricaded themselves. Flipping her wrist, she drove the haft of the knife into her hostage's temple and was gone before Nancy hit the floor.

The door to the master bedroom was open, fresh wood showed clean where it had splintered around the lock. Knife in hand, Anna ran down the hallway. She had little fear of ambush; Danny wanted to get Helena and get out as quickly as he could.

"I've called the cops!" Lisa yelled.

Anna didn't know if Terlingua boasted a police force, the town was so tiny, but she knew Lisa hadn't called. Her satellite phone was on the mantel in the living room.

"Where is it?" Danny demanded. He did not shout. Though there were no near neighbors to hear, in his line of work he would know the value of not calling attention to himself.

Anna was through the bedroom door. A king-sized bed with a head- and footboard made of twisted wood Freddy must have collected from the river took up most of the small room. Walls and floor were bright with Mexican rugs and pillows. Perforated tin shades covered the bedside lamps and created rustic sconces on the walls.

In this cheery sanctuary the man Nancy called Danny radiated a darkness Anna could almost see. His broad shoulders blocked the light from the single high window; his long arms were simian, covered in dark hair. He had his back to her, facing Lisa, who stood on the far side of the bed with a single door behind her. The closet, Anna guessed.

Quicker than he had been before, Danny turned, hearing Anna's arrival. He held up one hand like a cop stopping traffic. "You ladies don't have to get hurt," he said. "Just give me the baby and I'm out of here." There was nothing of promise or negotiation in his voice. Danny was making a statement of fact. He had no compunction about hurting them to get what he came for; he just didn't want the extra work.

Between him and the children stood Lisa, armed with nothing but courage. She had hidden Helena and Edgar and locked the door but hadn't found anything with which to fight. It came to Anna almost as a revelation that there were people who did not expect violence, who did not run through scenes in their heads at night, private rehearsals for disaster, true innocents.

"Give me the kid," Danny said. "We all go away happy."

Danny had not a clue what it meant to individuals cursed with hearts to give "the kid"—any kid—into the hands of the likes of him.

"Get out!" Lisa shrieked, and began throwing things: a lamp, paperback books, a bedside clock, a cactus plant in a ceramic sombrero.

Babies started to cry, wails leaking from the closet where she'd stashed them.

Crooking an arm over his face to protect it from flying objects, his eyes fixed on Anna and the knife, Danny caught up a green-and-white-striped cotton throw from the bed.

He was so damn big. In the living room, seated, in the soft light of the kitchen, Anna hadn't noticed how big he was. Huge. He seemed to fill the bedroom, his shoulders brushing the ceiling. Though on some level she knew she was suffering the same phenomenon people did when looking down the bore of a gun or, undoubtedly, into the gaping mouth of an alligator, the size of him was brought home to her in a visceral way.

The man would break her in two like a cheap chopstick.

Lowering the knife, she took a step back. "You know, Lisa, the guy is right," she said, and was relieved that her voice sounded fairly normal, aggrieved with a bit of whine Chrissie would have been proud of. "He doesn't want Edgar; he only wants the little Mexican girl. I don't see how it will help anybody if we get hurt over this."

Danny had that same wary squint she'd noticed when she'd first met him. As he listened to her it grew warier and squintier.

"You aren't going to hurt the baby, are you?" Anna asked. "I mean somebody just wants a kid of their own to raise and love, right?"

"Right. That's right." Confusion infiltrated the wariness. A positive sign, Anna thought. A better sign would be if his face was being infiltrated with blood but one had to take what one could get.

"Lisa, give the guy the river baby," she said.

"Anna! What are you doing?" Lisa wailed, and the betrayal in her voice singed Anna's insides.

"Don't be an idiot," Anna said harshly. "It's not your kid. God knows it's not mine. You want to die over this? Orphan your kids for some foundling? Some Mexican drug lord's by-blow?"

"Anna!" Lisa cried again. The shock of Anna's words was undoing her more than an unknown man kicking in her bedroom door.

"I'll get the damn thing," Anna said to Danny, who was standing in a pool of indecision holding the striped blanket. Stalking around the end of the bed to where Lisa stood between the children in the closet and the world, she threw her words back at the thug. "Get that other blanket," she ordered, and pointed vaguely in the direction of the headboard. "It's softer and smaller, easier to carry."

Danny turned. Perhaps to get the baby blanket that wasn't there, perhaps only because the cat fight had unsettled him to an extent he was obeying orders from Mom. Whatever the reason, for a second, his attention was not on Anna.

Sudden as a snake striking, she spun, brought the knife up from where she'd let it lie forgotten along her thigh, and drove the blade into his center mass with all her strength. He fell to the bed and Anna fell onto him.

"Get the babies out," she yelled to Lisa and saw her jerk the closet door open and grab a laundry basket full of dirty clothes. The man beneath Anna bucked and roared and tried to rise. Slippery with blood, her fingers lost their grip on the knife and she had no idea where she'd hit him, if the blow was fatal or glancing.

Danny had fallen with his legs twisted, his left side on the bed, feet on the floor. Anna was across his upper body; their heads too close for comfort. Before the waking giant could head butt or bite, Anna grabbed an ear and a handful of hair and shoved his face into the pillow. Ramming a knee in the small of his back, she scanned him desperately for the knife. Blood led her eyes to the haft, and the haft was all that was protruding. She'd stabbed through his forearm and buried the knife in his hip, pinning his arm to his side. She let go of his ear, grabbed the knife handle and yanked. It didn't budge. The blade was jammed into bone. Danny screamed and rolled, trapping her underneath him.

She wriggled and kicked and bit, clawed and pounded and shoved with not much more effect than Helena trying to resist a clean diaper. The pain in his arm and hip more intense than anything Anna could inflict with her feeble attacks, Danny didn't seem to notice she was battering him. Roaring, he threw a punch over his shoulder with his free arm. Knuckles smashed into the side of Anna's skull.

The impact stunned her. An off button was pushed in her head and strength ceased pouring from whatever conscious source it pours from. Muscles went slack, vision blurred, thought faded. It wasn't more than a second or two before she brought herself back but it was too long. Danny was off of her. He had a fistful of her hair before she could do more than note this disappointing turn of events. Lifting her by her hair, he flung her toward the far wall with the ease of a brat throwing his sister's doll.

The edge of the bed and Lisa's penchant for strewing surfaces with colorful pillows broke Anna's fall. In an instant she was on her feet. Raging like a wounded cougar, Danny moved between her and the door. Eyes crazy with pain and fury, he jerked the knife from his bone with a shriek and started toward her.

A crash of metal on metal reverberated through the house. Both of them froze. An engine screamed, followed by another grinding crunch louder than the first.

"What the hell is that?" Danny mumbled.

"Your ride," Anna said.

THIRTY-TWO

L ittle river otter, did you think I was going to throw you to the wolves to save my scaly old hide?" Helena, tucked in the crook of Anna's arm, squeezed her eyes shut and pursed her lips. "I've never seen a baby this new with such a beautiful face," Anna marveled. "Aren't they traditionally red and wrinkled and pugdoggish?"

Lisa laughed. "C-section," she said. "That little girl didn't have to fight to get squeezed into the world. You just went and got her."

"Did you hear that?" Anna said to the baby. "I'm the reason you're gorgeous." She was cooing and gurgling and generally making an ass of herself but she couldn't stop, didn't want to stop. Being a fool for life felt so good.

When Danny was made aware that the metallic crunching sounds were Nancy bashing her way through Anna's Honda with the rented Chevy Malibu with every intention of leaving him behind, he'd had a moment of reflection. Deciding being stranded in Terlingua with a bad knife wound and a kidnapped baby would be worse than returning to whoever had sent him with the mission unaccomplished, he'd limped from the bedroom as fast as he could and joined his compatriot in the rampaging rental car. Lisa had only made it a few hundred yards out into the sage, headed for their nearest neighbor. When she saw them leave she came back to see if Anna had been hurt or killed.

Terlingua and her sister city, Study Butte, had a permanent population of under three hundred souls. There was no police department. The county sheriff handled most complaints. Lisa called the park and the sheriff, and an all-points bulletin was issued for a smashed-up Malibu.

The Honda was totaled, Lisa's car scraped down the passenger side, and the house a wreck of blood and thrown and broken domestic items. Lisa and Anna and Edgar and Helena sat at the table in the kitchen full of joy because they were all there and healthy. Nothing irreplaceable had been damaged.

"Why would anybody want to steal a baby?" Lisa asked.

There were the usual reasons but Anna knew she meant this baby, Helena—who would want to steal her badly enough to send thugs to do it?

Anna had said something to Lisa when she was trying to distract their attacker. She'd said: "Some drug lord's by-blow." The words came back to her now. "It has to be because of who her mother was. If the mother was an important person, maybe the daughter of a member of a rich drug cartel, Helena could be wanted for ransom."

"Most bad guys kidnap good people's kids," Lisa said. "They're not scared of the police. A drug lord, that's something else."

"If Helena's mom was running from kidnappers—or maybe from her father or husband—and her death in the river was an accident of sorts, mightn't they want the child back? Maybe Helena's got an inheritance floating around that unsavory types want to collect for her."

It crossed Anna's mind that Freddy, who had a connection to the first woman drowned with her fetus, and an unusual interest in this case, Freddy, who was on the canyon rim where Anna and Paul had expected a shooter, had cavalierly ended his career with today's speech. A new baby, a boy in college—he would be in need of money. Freddy had been on both sides of the river his whole life. Everyone knew him. It was not only possible but probable that he knew drug dealers, smugglers and illegal aliens. Was it not also possible that he had engineered the kidnapping and it had gone sour, the woman and her unborn baby swept away by the river?

Freddy knew every inch of the river, better than anyone in the park. Better than anyone in the world, most likely. The location where Chrissie found Helena's mother troubled Anna. For her, at least, it negated the possibility that the woman was a Mexican national crossing to have her child on American soil. If Freddy had taken her and wanted to hide her where she wouldn't be found until he collected ransom, taking her deep into the canyon might not be a bad idea. In her condition she couldn't swim out. There was only the one place anyone could climb out and it was a hard climb. All Freddy would have to do would be to find a place she'd be neither heard nor stumbled upon by rafters and that was easy enough. She'd be where he, as the river ranger, had every excuse to be. Santa Elena and the Rio Grande would effectively hold her prisoner so there was no need to take the risk of bringing anyone else in on the deal.

Maybe it wasn't kindness that motivated Freddy to ask his wife to wet-nurse Helena, but a desire to keep the baby out of the hands of the authorities until he could figure out what to do next. Maybe he'd decided if thugs kidnapped the baby from his house, he'd be off the hook and have the baby to sell to whoever he was selling her to.

Anna didn't like the way that played out but, so far, it was the only plotline that made any sense.

"Ready for some lunch, little one?" Lisa's voice cut through Anna's thoughts. She'd finished feeding Edgar and was waiting to trade babies with Anna so she could feed Helena. Anna took Edgar and, using a towel the way Lisa had shown her so she wouldn't get baby spew down her back, she patted him and was startled at how well she'd learned to do it in such a short time. Not that patting a baby was such a complex task. Just weird.

Lisa tucked Helena comfortably in her arms and the baby took the nipple as if it was meant for her all along. "She's a good eater," Lisa said, and Anna felt absurdly proud of her tiny protégé.

Watching Lisa suckle the baby, Anna was as sure as she'd ever been about anything that, if Freddy was the one who started this mess, his wife knew nothing about it.

"If people wanted Helena's mother and, now, Helena, for ransom—drug lords or whatever like you were thinking—I can see why they would want to come over the border after they took Helena's mother," Lisa said, picking up where they had left off when Anna had mentally dragged her husband into the state penitentiary and given him a nice room on death row. "Not that those cartel people can't or won't kill Americans but they might have a harder time of it in the U.S."

"If that is what happened it explains a lot of things," Anna said. She stood and paced with Edgar. It felt like the right thing to do with a baby from whom one was trying to induce burping. She told Lisa of the bikini wax, the hands, wrinkled from so long in the water but free of calluses, the painted toenails. "She was wearing a cheap dress," Anna finished, "but everything else about her spoke of money."

Lisa thought about that for a while. Helena had had enough milk and Lisa put her on her shoulder and began patting her gently. Almost immediately she emitted a ladylike burp. Anna couldn't but note that Helena was a superior belcher to Edgar, who had not yet given up his stomach bubbles.

"She could have been made to put on a cheap dress," Lisa suggested. "To make her feel bad. You know, like breaking somebody down so they won't have the courage to fight back. The bad clothes could be part of something like that."

"Or maybe so the body wouldn't be so easily identified. If they intended for the mother to die after giving birth, they might have dressed her accordingly," Anna said.

"Why would they want to kill the mama and keep the baby?"

"An infant is a lot easier to hide and tote around than a grown woman."

"Yeah," Lisa admitted. "But you got to feed babies, and when they are so tiny sometimes they don't thrive on formula. I guess anybody evil enough to do the other things wouldn't care much about a baby, though."

"We'll get to the bottom of it," Anna said, and hoped the bottom wouldn't be where she'd find Freddy Martinez.

Giving up on Edgar's digestion, she gave him back to his mother and took the good baby, the Olympic-class belching child, from Lisa. "The chief ranger said Health and Human Services, the real Health and Human Services, is undermanned. They're still dealing with the refugees from Hurricane Katrina who stayed in Houston. Since Helena is being cared for in a family situation, they said they would come out at the end of the week to take custody of her. That's three days. Do you want Paul and me to take her somewhere else? Whoever is after her for whatever reason might decide it's not worth it and go back to where they came from, but we can't count on it."

Lisa didn't answer right away, and Anna appreciated that this was no little thing. Had she been a good person, she would have insisted they decamp immediately to protect Lisa and her family. Helena was the reason she let Lisa make the choice for her. The little girl was doing so well with the breast milk and the love and the company of another child that Anna didn't want to take her from this impromptu nest any sooner than she had to. Could she have removed the danger by removing herself and leaving Helena with Lisa, she would have done it. As it was, should Lisa be willing to keep Helena, she and Edgar would be safer with Anna and Paul around.

The great hairy fly in the domestic ointment was Freddy. The picture of him as kidnapper and probable murderer Anna had painted in her mind was not indelible, but neither could it be dismissed. Snuggling down with victim and suspect under one roof could have its awkward moments.

After this failed attempt, Freddy—if it was Freddy— might be less likely to have the baby taken from under his roof, afraid the connection would be too obvious. And, with Helena where he could control her disposition, he might be less desperate to take an action that might harm her.

These were the rational—or pseudo rational—reasons Anna listed to herself. The overweening reason was that, try as she might to avoid it, she trusted Freddy. She had trusted him nearly from the moment at the top of the rockslide when she and Paul tied him up and took his gun. Freddy was a very likable guy. Like Ted Bundy? Even evoking the notorious serial killer didn't put the fear of Freddy into her.

There was an aura around Freddy Martinez that was familiar and comforting. Mrs. Gonzales, Anna remembered, her best friend Sylvia's mother. Mrs. Gonzales worked as an operator for the phone company in the little town where Anna had grown up. Long after she and Sylvia had parted ways, Anna to a private Catholic boarding school and Sylvia to the local high school, whenever Anna called home the operator would say: "Anna? You haven't called your parents for a while. They'll be so happy to hear from you. Will you be home soon?" The sense of warmth and family she exuded always made Anna feel like she had someplace to go if ever she couldn't go home.

Anna's instincts wanted her to accept the kindness Freddy radiated. Long ago she had learned not to go with her instincts. They were as much a mess as the rest of her intrinsic workings. She would go with Paul's; if he thought they should go, they would go.

"I wish Paul would get back," Anna said, scarcely aware that she voiced her thought.

"I wish Freddy would come home. I wish Freddy had never left home today."

"Do you think they fired him?" Anna asked.

"No," Lisa said. "He got called out before he got to Chisos Basin. The park got a call that there were nearly fifty head of horses on the American side and they were heading into the park. Freddy is their best horseman. They jumped on the chance to keep him busy somewhere else all day."

"The park got a call? From whom?"

"She was anonymous," Lisa said with an impish smile.

Anna laughed.

"Freddy saves the world, I save Freddy—or at least his job. For now. Once Freddy gets the bit between his teeth about something, he goes all macho, Pancho Villa, man-of-the-house and makes me crazy."

Anna sat again and laid Helena on her lap. "Why would Freddy risk his job to talk against Judith Pierson?" she asked. "The closing of the border has been debated by everybody forever. Why make the big gesture now at what is, when you get right down to it, just a convention of academics?"

"It's not just academics. These people are big deals in Texas. They're teachers and university types but there's a lot of clout up here this week. But mostly it's because Freddy knows about Judith Pierson. If you listen to him, she's the anti-Christ. He says if she gets into the governor's house we're going to have to move out of Texas. That's a serious threat from Freddy. He's never lived anywhere but Texas—except Mexico, where it's so close it might as well be Texas. His mother brought him up in Texas. *The Alamo* was her favorite movie. He said she'd gather all the kids and grandkids and in-laws around every time it came on TV and she'd say the lines along with John Wayne."

"I thought his mother was Mexican," Anna said.

Lisa laughed. "She was. She said the movie was made up and she could like it if she wanted to and it was good about Texas. Freddy wanted to get her a VCR and a tape so she could watch it whenever she wanted, but then his sister died and his mom never got over it really. She didn't live all that long after. The doctors said it was a brain aneurism but Freddy and his dad think it was a broken heart."

"What happened to her?" Anna asked.

Lisa started as if the question had woken her out of a dream and she suddenly realized where she was. "Oh!" she said, and, "Oh. Gosh. It was a long time ago now. She died in a car accident, I think."

As a liar Lisa was positively embarrassing.

Anna let it go for the moment. "So Freddy thinks Mayor Pierson is the devil incarnate," she said.

Lisa was so grateful for the subject change she sprang panther-like upon the new topic. "We have relatives in Houston and Corpus Christi. My sister's nieces on her husband's side went to school with Judith. She was known as The Piranha in high school because she ate up everything that came near her: boyfriends, girlfriends, teachers. Anita—that's my sister—said her niece said Judith rigged the election so she could be voted student body president then made sure she was on all the scholarship stuff so she could suck up to the various civic organizations that gave out that kind of thing. Made out like a bandit, I guess, but didn't graduate with too many friends.

"My sister got to know her when she was on the city council and there was no love lost there. Judith was a climber. She'd grab on to any idea that was on the rise, not bother to do the work involved, take the credit if it worked and say she'd never been for it if it failed. She was quick to lay blame around too.

"Freddy and I met her just one time at a fundraiser. We rode my sister's coattails in for the free food and champagne, something to do while we were visiting Houston is all. Judith had recently been elected mayor and was in full blow at the party since it was all cronies of hers. She got on a roll about how she was making Texas a shining example of an impermeable border, that she was going to keep the Mexicans and their dirty drug wars from threatening the good citizens of Texas if she had to build the wall with her own hands.

"She wanted to get going building her persona, be the aggressive woman who wasn't too fancy to get her hands dirty. It was all hot air. Every waiter at the party was Mexican. The boy parking the fancy cars was Mexican. The caterer was Mexican and most of the hotel staff working the event were Mexican. If she closed even the borders of her own shindig her high-end contributors would have jumped ship. Those guys don't want to clean their own toilets. Shoot, if she closed down the borders that tight, who would she get to build her wall? A bunch of boys from A&M?"

"Freddy didn't take the hot air well?" Anna asked drily.

"Not so well," Lisa said. "Since his sister—" She stopped herself and got suddenly very busy with Edgar, who was sound asleep and didn't want to be tucked and jostled.

"'Since his sister died,' was that what you were going to say?" Anna asked gently.

"He still has bad feelings about that," Lisa mumbled.

"And after his sister died—in a motorcycle accident, you said?"

"I think so." Lisa was so busy with Edgar's blanket he was beginning to wake up and kick.

"After she died Freddy became politically active about the closing of the border between Big Bend and Mexico?"

Lisa gave up. Edgar was whimpering testily. She lifted him to her shoulder. "Why don't you talk to Freddy about this?" she said helplessly.

"Freddy's sister was named Gabriela, wasn't she?"

Lisa nodded.

"She tried to cross the Rio Grande after the World Trade Center was bombed and border patrol turned her back. She lost her footing and she and the baby drowned?"

"Freddy went a little crazy. He wouldn't stop looking until they found her body. After that, opening the border again kind of became a crusade with him."

"Why didn't he tell anyone she was his sister?" Anna asked.

Lisa sighed. For some, telling lies or evading the truth was easy. For Lisa it must have been a task that would have exhausted Sisyphus. In the short time she'd been trying to skirt around this truth she'd grown more drawn and haggard than the entire invasion of the baby snatchers had rendered her.

"Because she was a Mexican national," Lisa said. "She was crossing the border illegally to have her child in America."

"Freddy was ashamed of that?" Anna hadn't known Freddy then but it seemed so out of character it was hard to believe he had changed so much.

"No. It was a long time ago. Freddy was on with the park like he'd always wanted to be. His mom and I talked him into leaving it alone."

"Because if they looked too close . . ." Anna nudged.

"Freddy wasn't a citizen when he got on with the park. He didn't get citizenship until we got married. So he was a citizen when his sister died but Mama Martinez and I thought the park might fire him anyway, because he'd fooled them, fooled the authorities all his life."

Anna nodded without speaking.

Of the many things bureaucrats could forgive, being made to look the fool was not among them.

THIRTY-THREE

J udith was coming apart. The crying jag after Charles
made his announcement hadn't bothered Darden,
except that Judith was in a lot of pain. She was given to
outbursts of emotion, in private. High-strung, hard-
driving people needed a safe place to vent. Darden had
been the "safe" place for more than one big cheese.
Men raged. Women raged and wept.

What was gnawing at him was her secrecy. Judith was
keeping something from him.

He knew it the way wives know their husbands are
running around on them. Darden was an expert on secrets. He'd kept the secrets of presidents and first ladies,
ambassadors and their wives; once he even conspired
with a presidential child to keep secret the fact that his
presidential puppy had chewed the fringe of an historic

White House rug. Some secrets invested one with a sense of hidden powers, some with a private delight, but most were akin to the Spartan boy's fox; the closer they were held the more damage they did to the one holding them.

Judith's was eating her alive. During breakfast with Anna Pigeon he could sense the cracks widening. Though Judith did a masterful job of hiding it, he suspected Anna had noticed her brittleness and he was positive Gerry had. Gerry missed very little. He could almost see her nose twitching as she munched her toast and jelly and she watched Judith the way a cat watches a bird hopping closer and closer on the windowsill.

Judith had been on her satellite phone most of the night after the rafting party was brought in from Santa Elena Canyon; he could hear her through the wall—not the words but the intensity with which they were spoken.

Then there was Kevin. Not twenty-four hours after demanding his head on a platter they had apparently patched up whatever had put her in a firing mood

And the baby. Judith didn't have any interest in babies until they were old enough to vote. Was she trying to show Charles that she had a maternal side after all? The baby had become a bigger problem than Darden anticipated.

He realized he'd stopped in the middle of the parking lot between the lodge and the motel units, a target for any passing vehicle. He didn't know where he was going, didn't know what to do with himself: a soldier without an army, a bee without a hive.

"Talk about falling apart," he muttered, and forced himself to move. He didn't get far, but cleared the parking lot and sat on a bench without a view in a patch of desert that had been trampled to death on a strip of dirt between the cars and the downstairs units.

Twenty minutes later, when Gordon appeared in bright red jogging shorts and no shirt running smartly down the asphalt, he was still sitting there. Darden watched him coming around the bend from the cabins and remembered when daily fitness training had been a part of his life. He should get back to it. He should get up and out of the sun before his brain fried. As these thoughts petered out, he wondered if he'd had one of those tiny strokes doctors talked about, TIAs, transient ischemic attacks, they called them. That might account for the fact that his mind and body had short-circuited in a parking lot on top of the middle of nowhere.

Gordon saw him and veered, jogging over to the bench where Darden had come to rest.

"Hey, boss, you okay?"

Gordon was jogging in place, keeping up the pace. It annoyed Darden. "Sit down," he ordered.

Gordon sat. He pulled the threadbare hotel towel from around his neck and mopped his face and chest, then laughed. "In Houston I'd be wringing this thing out. Up here the sweat dries before I get to it."

"Yeah," Darden said absently.

Gordon waited patiently, his muscles growing cold, his workout disrupted. Finally Darden spoke. "What's with Judith and Kevin? I don't want the nitty-gritty, but if there's anything I need to know, tell me."

Gordon didn't answer right away and Darden wondered if he was worried about being a tattletale. "I'm not sure what you mean, boss," he said after a moment.

"Don't make me spell it out," Darden said wearily. "It's my job to protect Judith, even if that means protecting her from herself occasionally."

Gordon continued to look confused.

Darden sighed heavily. "Is Kevin sleeping with Judith?" he forced himself to ask since Gordon was intentionally or unintentionally not picking up on the hints.

"Boss, Kevin's gay. Didn't you know that? I'm not ratting him out or anything, he doesn't flaunt it but he doesn't go out of his way to keep it a secret either."

That penetrated Darden's fog. "Kevin's gay?" he said stupidly. "He doesn't look gay."

Gordon shot him a look.

"Right. Sorry," Darden said.

"Is this going to be a problem, boss?"

"No. I don't care who he sleeps with as long as it doesn't adversely affect the mayor's agenda." Firing Kevin was a bad idea but Darden had to get rid of him. Divided loyalties didn't work in his business.

Leaning forward, he rested his elbows on his knees and stared at the bit of dry dirt between his feet. A single ant was crossing the space in a straight line as if it had places to go and people to meet. He envied the bug. It had a sense of purpose.

"Have you got any idea what's going on with those two?" Sharing his ignorance with an underling—yet another sign it was time to retire.

Gordon mopped his dry body again, something to do while he thought. Darden hoped he wasn't thinking up lies or excuses. After a life of manufacturing them for various people, he had little patience with those who lied to him.

"Not really, boss," Gordon said. "He's pretty close-lipped. Not much of a conversationalist. He may be gay and all but he's not what you'd call sensitive. One of the big drawbacks to this job as he sees it is the lack of automatic weapons."

Darden laughed shortly. There wasn't enough air in the air up in the Chisos to laugh for any length of time. This mess was making him bone tired in a way it wouldn't have even two years ago. Untwisting the twists and wrinkles entangling those in power had once invigorated him. Maybe one had to be young to find the thrill in the seamier side of life. More and more he longed for his sunny kitchen, spices in pots on the deep window bay over the sink, the comforting hum of traffic coming through the tiny yard from the street.

Old man stuff. Sixty-three was too young to let the rocking chair get him but that's what he wanted. He'd do what he had to—whatever he had to—to straighten out this last kink in the tangle of dirty businesses, then he would retire to a good, clean, quiet life.

I'm as bad as a con getting Jesus, he thought wryly.

Darden sat with that for a while. The ant had made

it as far as his right shoe and was looking for a pass in this mighty mountain that had been dropped into its landscape. A shift of his weight and Darden could end its life. He'd killed before: spiders, mosquitoes, roaches, wasps, people. This was the first time it had occurred to him that these pests had lives. Not that he suffered guilt for ending them; he just realized how amazing they were. An ant, a creature so small he would have trouble seeing it without his glasses, and it could do all these amazing things. Military geniuses couldn't build anything as complicated and functional as a lousy ant and yet half the fools didn't believe in God and the other half thought they were smarter than Him.

"Finish your workout," he said to Gordon as he heaved himself up from the bench.

"What are you going to do, boss?" The concern in Gordon's voice both touched and annoyed Darden.

"I'm going to get a massage and a pedicure," he replied, and walked away, enjoying the look of consternation he'd left on the younger man's face.

THIRTY-FOUR

The sheriff's deputy had come and gone. A gas station owner in Study Butte reported he'd found the banged-up Malibu abandoned behind his grocery-cum-gas-station. Either the two would-be kidnappers had stolen another vehicle that was as yet unreported—not that unusual in a town where tourists routinely left cars unattended for days while they camped or rafted—or they had a compatriot come and pick them up. The car was impounded in the sheriff's barn. Anna doubted there was a Terlingua CSI. Trace evidence, even fingerprints, might not be collected.

Lisa had taken Edgar and gone to Study Butte to pick up a few groceries and, Anna suspected, to be free of the house where monsters had so recently been. Anna and Helena stayed behind with the intention, at least on the former's part, to straighten up the place before Lisa returned, to make it normal again. After the horrors her presence had brought down on the Martinez family, it was the least she could do.

She didn't even manage that.

She was still sitting in the kitchen, Helena clasped in tired arms, her left leg going to sleep, staring at the dregs of cold coffee in a festive mug with a handle fashioned in the image of a lariat, when she heard a car pull up in front of the house.

Feet crunched on gravel, then came a loud rapping on the screen door. A caller who knocked rather than kicking in the door. Still Anna stashed Helena in Edgar's crib. The carving knife that had served her so well with previous visitors had been taken by the deputy. She found a replacement before she answered the door.

"Darden," she said with surprise. The mayor of Houston's chief of security was the last person she'd expected.

"Mind if I come in?" he asked.

Anna stepped away, opening the screen door as she did.

Before he'd crossed the lintel he stopped. Alarms must have been clanging in his head. His shoulders straightened and readiness momentarily overruled the tired slump he'd arrived with. In that instant Anna realized how different he looked from the man with whom she'd breakfasted. Gone was the jauntiness; the age and slowness he pretended to were no longer pretense. Exhaustion dragged down the flesh beneath his eyes and the eyes themselves housed a fatigue so deep it was as if days of sleeplessness and worry had elapsed in the seven hours that passed for the rest of the world.

"This must have been quite a party," he said, taking in the shattered lamps and the overturned furniture.

"It had its moments," Anna conceded.

His vision narrowed to Anna standing quietly by his left shoulder, to the butcher knife in her hand, and she saw shock widen his eyes. He wasn't scared of her, she guessed; he was scared of himself. Mr. Security Guy hadn't noticed an edged weapon inches from his femoral artery.

"Chopping vegetables?" His dry wit was back, but there was a weariness to it.

"Come on into the kitchen," Anna said. "I can offer you reheated coffee and a straight-backed chair."

"That would be good," Darden said absently. His eyes were searching the small front room, looking for something.

"Through there." Not yet comfortable having anyone behind her, she used the butcher knife to point to the archway on the left.

Darden smiled at the knife but said nothing as he preceded her into the kitchen. While she poured a mug full of cold coffee and put it in the microwave, he gave the kitchen the same scrutiny as he had the living room, taking in the broken crockery and tumbled phone table.

"What happened here?" he asked as she set the nuked coffee in front of the chair he had finally settled in.

Anna told him.

If he was surprised that two impostors had come to take the river baby by guile or force, he didn't show it. "Ah" was all he said and: "Where is the baby?"

Anna didn't want to tell him. Suddenly she didn't trust him any more than she had trusted the two fake social workers. Before she could make up a convincing lie, Helena decided to make her location known and began to cry. Darden's exhaustion lifted momentarily, his interest pricking like that of a hound catching scent of its quarry.

"She's sleeping," Anna said.

"Pretty noisy sleeper," Darden replied, and took a sip of his coffee. A hint of a grimace flickered on his face but he managed to quell it.

Helena's crying went from whimpering on awakening to full-fledged shrieking for service. After scarcely thirty seconds, Anna could take no more.

"Excuse me," she said. Moving into the short hall of the West Wing, she took the butcher knife from where she'd laid it down by the coffeepot. Again there was a wisp of a smile on Darden's face.

He nodded at the knife. "That should teach her to be quiet."

Anna couldn't tell if he was joking. She was supposed to think he was joking. Black humor was her favorite kind but after a number of homicides and a violent interaction with Danny, she'd pretty much lost her sense of humor about knives and babies.

She backed into the hall then turned and walked quickly away. What might have been a chuckle followed her. She didn't care. It was better to make a fool of oneself than a corpse of oneself.

Helena stopped crying the moment Anna leaned over the crib. The honor was as great as that of having a cat choose her lap above all others, and Anna smiled down at the wriggling bit of humanity. "I guess cute is a survival tool for people too small and toothless to fight for their food," she said. Carrying both knife and baby wasn't practical and, like countless generations of women before her, Anna put down the weapon to pick up the child. Holding Helena, Anna was overcome with fear. She couldn't remember if she'd been afraid when she was facing Danny. Remembering how immense he had seemed, how it was as if he'd filled all the space in the room, she knew she must have been. In the bottom of Santa Elena, when the rifleman was shooting at them, she must have felt terror. That seemed so infinitely long ago now that she couldn't remember the fear, only the action.

The ability to do something to save oneself—or at least try to—was the only panacea for fear she'd found reliable. Standing unarmed with a baby she was responsible for and a large male person of unknown motivation sitting down the hall from her, Anna realized what a terrible disservice America was doing its women—all of its citizens—in teaching them never to do for themselves but to wait for the authorities to come and save them from whatever dilemma had arisen. No wonder people grew fat and lived in fear of going out at night or allowing their children to play in the front yard.

Taking a deep breath, she shoved the fear down with the intake of oxygen and slid Helena into the crook of her left arm. With her right hand free, she gathered up the knife and carried both back down the hall.

Darden didn't rise when she'd left and he didn't rise when she returned with the baby. By the twitching, Anna knew he wanted to, that he had been brought up to remain standing until women were seated and rise when they entered or left a room. That he didn't was a point in his favor as far as she was concerned. It indicated that he was sufficiently sensitive to know she would be more comfortable with him in a chair, that his size and strangeness and maleness needed to be cut down to size by sitting.

"So that's the girl, is it?" he asked as Anna leaned against the far counter, setting the knife on the tile ready to hand. He might have sought to reduce the ambient anxiety by remaining seated, but he was amping it up again with his narrow study of Helena. Leaning forward, his coffee forgotten, both hands flat on the tabletop, he stared fixedly at the baby. Instinctively, Anna held her closer, tucking Helena's face against her shoulder.

"May I see her?" Darden asked. Apparently unaware of Anna's discomfort with his single-minded interest, he held out his hands as if she would, in some alternate universe, actually put the child into them.

"Not a good idea," Anna said. "She bites. Vicious little thing, really. Birth trauma brings it out in girls."

"Babies don't have teeth at that age, do they?"

Darden asked seriously. Anna was pleased there was at least one individual in the world who knew less about infants than she.

"Pointy fangs," Anna said. "Real teeth grow in later."

Belatedly Darden realized that she was, if not precisely kidding, then relating false information. He dropped his arms and sat back. The beefy old security guy was doing the trick he was so good at; he was making himself look harmless and kindly, fat and slow.

"I wouldn't hurt a baby," he said. "Whatever you may think of me."

"I don't much think about you," Anna said honestly, wondering why he thought she would and would think badly of him.

"Fair enough," he said, and lifted his coffee cup to his mouth. Anna smiled. He wasn't drinking, he was pretending to drink, part of his kindly persona; don't insult the hostess's cooking.

"You don't have to drink that," Anna said, taking pity on him.

"Thank God." He pushed the cup away and smiled at her. The exhaustion in it did more to alleviate her fears than any of the tricks he'd learned over the years. "You can sit down. I'm not here to hurt you or the baby."

Anna didn't move. "Why are you here?"

"I wanted to ask you some questions about the woman you found in the river."

"You were there when Paul and I gave our report to the chief ranger."

"That was a report of the facts. I was hoping, if I asked you nicely, you'd tell me the rest: your impressions, those of your husband or any the college students might have shared with you. I'd like to know everything you know."

"Why? What is the woman in the river to you?"

Darden didn't answer right away and Anna was willing to bet he was thumbing through a well-used card file of lies for all occasions. He must have come up with a blank. "I don't know," he said. "I really don't know. Habit maybe. It happened while I was in the park. While I was on duty. Anything out of the ordinary that happens around Mayor Pierson, especially when she is in the process of lighting a fire under a lot of people, is of interest to me. That good enough for you?"

"I can't tell you much," Anna said. "We didn't spend what you would call quality time together."

"What did she look like?"

Anna leaned her hip against the counter, cradling Helena, not sleeping but quiescent, and thought back to the river gorge. "She was not young—at least not helplessly young, if you know what I mean. I'd say in her late twenties, maybe even early thirties. Tall. I don't have a good sense of it, she was never standing, but I believe she was five-foot-seven or -eight. Long black hair. If it had been straight and untangled it would have come down to the middle of her back. There was either a lot of natural wave in it or a very good perm. For a pregnant woman, she didn't weigh much. I doubt she'd gained more than fifteen pounds for a six-pound baby; her arms and legs were slender. She was wearing a cheap rayon dress and no jewelry that I noticed. White underpants, the kind with the stretch panel to accommodate a growing stomach.

"I think her skin was good, but it's hard to say after being in the water as long as she had been and undergoing a lot of physical trauma. She had a pedicure and a bikini wax. That's about it," Anna finished.

"What color were her eyes?" Darden asked.

"Brown, I think. Maybe light brown or even a touch of hazel. Mostly they were closed and I had other things on my mind."

Darden stared into the black depths of the coffee cup he'd pulled back toward himself during Anna's recitation. Tired of standing holding a baby that weighed more with each passing moment, Anna dragged a chair over to the counter and settled on it while the security man contemplated his coffee grounds.

After a while she was about to prod him; she'd promised to meet Chrissie, Cyril and Steve at a place called the Terlingua Porch around five. It was getting near that and she was looking forward to getting out of the house she'd not yet straightened and away from people she did not know but who refused to remain strangers. According to Lisa, the Porch was within easy walking distance and could not be missed. According to the sheriff's deputy and her own observations, that was a good thing. The Honda was totaled. The engine would start but the metal had been smashed back into the wheel wells until, if the tires could turn, they would be shredded.

"The Park Service is doing body recovery today, that right?" Darden asked without looking up.

"That's right," Anna said. "They'll be able to bring back the body of the outfitter who was shot but I'd be surprised if they find Helena's mother. She was down where the river-scour is powerful. The body would have been washed away. If they do find it, it will be down-stream a ways."

"That's okay, then," he murmured, and Anna didn't think he was talking to her. When she'd met him, Darden didn't strike her as the sort to talk to himself, at least not out loud, and most certainly not in the hearing of others.

"What's okay?" she asked sharply.

"Did I say something was okay?" Darden's gaze turned inward, then he started. "Getting old," he said, and seemed to mean it. "Okay that they'll find it downstream, I guess. My mind was on something else."

Anna didn't believe him. "You come all the way down here to get my take on things and your mind is some-place else?"

"Sorry," he said. Then, probably to deflect any more interest in what he had said and why, he said: "Tell me about the shootings."

Anna did. Why she was being so generous with infor-mation, she wasn't sure. Partly because it didn't really matter, most of what she told him was a matter of pub-lic record by now. Partly because she wanted to tell the story. Her sister, Molly, after a lifetime as a psychiatrist to the rich and twisted of New York City, had formed a theory that people had a need to water down the emotion in the stressful events in their lives by relating them a minimum of three times. Anna had told hers to the chief ranger, she'd related pieces of it to Gerry Schneider, and this was the magical number three. As she went through the tale again she had to admit her sister was a smart woman. With each telling she could feel a bit of the drama leak out.

"So," she finished. "Helena's mom died, Carmen died, Lori died and the rest of us lived happily ever after."

Again Darden was silent. It was wearing on her nerves. "What are you after?" she asked. "I've got a dinner date in about ten minutes. Maybe if you told me what it is you really want to know, we could get this over with."

The sharpness in her tone brought his gaze up from where it had retreated again into the cup of cold, vile-tasting coffee. "Dinner? Where is there to go to dinner around here other than the lodge?"

"The kids found a place called the Starlight Theatre. On a porch or something. I'm meeting them there and I should get going."

"Mind if I tag along?" He wasn't looking at Anna; he was staring at Helena.

"It's a private party."

"I understand," he said. "I'll leave you to it, then."

Anna stood behind the screen door and watched until his black SUV had backed out and driven away. Then she spent another thirty minutes feeding and changing Helena. She never did get around to cleaning up the house. Babies were incredibly time-consuming.

When enough time had elapsed that she was sure Darden White had left the neighborhood, she started out for the Terlingua Porch and the Starlight Theatre. Being out of doors brought a sudden freedom. Dry air smelling of dust and secret life filled Anna's lungs. Helena weighed less; the claustrophobic terrors of the house were gently blown away. Sere earth under her feet was solid, connecting her to the center of the planet. A sky of unfathomable size purified the world of men. Breathing deeply, she felt bands of steel she'd not known were bound round her rib cage falling away, and she was glad the wreck of the Honda had made her travel the half mile on foot.

She reached the T intersection where the narrow dirt lane leading to the Martinezes' house joined the main route through Terlingua Ghost Town. A few yards to her left the road forked and, beyond a sign showing the skeleton of a boy in a baseball cap riding a skateboard, she saw what had to be the Terlingua Porch. A long low building, raised four feet from the gravel of a wide parking lot, was fronted with a deep frontier-style porch. Benches lined up beneath the windows of a mercantile store, a museum and a façade sporting the sign "Starlight Theatre." Men who wouldn't have looked out of place in a sepia-toned photograph of the gold rush days in California sat smoking and drinking beer.

Anna turned to walk the last hundred yards toward this idiosyncratic outgrowth of civilization and saw

Darden White's SUV parked just off the road where he could see anyone coming or going down the road to the Martinezes'. He sat behind the steering wheel watching her as she hurried across the road, feeling her sense of freedom ripping away.

When she was close enough to the public eye to feel safe, Anna hazarded a glance back over her shoulder. The SUV was creeping slowly down the road. As she half-ran toward the sanctuary of the porch with its beer drinkers she heard the SUV rev up and crunch back toward the main highway.

THIRTY-FIVE

Images from books with titles long forgotten and movies she recalled only vaguely popped and fizzed in Anna's mind as, clutching an infant to her chest, she hurried across the gravel parking lot toward the Terlingua Porch: Liza on the ice, Tess on the heath, Little Nell on the streets of London, women helpless and fleeing. The visions and her present reality were alien to who she perceived herself to be and she felt an impostor, an overweening sense of having awoken in an alternate reality where this Anna was similar but not the same as the one she was accustomed to.

Helena was a newborn, maybe even premature, though her parts all seemed to be in good working order. She needed to be seen by a doctor. She needed to be in a safe environment. And Anna was carting her through the desert like a bundle of dirty laundry. She was probably killing her. Lisa shouldn't have left her alone with the child. She shouldn't have left the Martinezes' house. But the Martinezes' house no longer felt safe, nowhere felt safe.

This cascade of terror and misery washed away her aversion to turning Helena over to the authorities. By the time she reached the imagined sanctuary of the raised porch, Anna was ready to turn Helena over to the first kindly female and arrest herself for child endangerment.

Where the hell was Paul?

"Anna!"

She looked up to see Gerry Schneider staring at her from one of the benches, a beer in one hand and a cigarette in the other. Second-hand smoke; another thing that killed babies.

"What are you doing?" Gerry chided. She put out the cigarette and came down the wooden steps to meet Anna. Wordlessly Anna handed her Helena, took the beer from her hand and downed a long swig.

Gerry cradled Helena and led the way back to a bench a ways away from the smokers. "This baby is only a day old, Anna. She shouldn't be out breathing the germs of anybody who passes by. What were you thinking?"

Anna sat down, still holding Gerry's beer. The chiding served to deepen her helplessness. "A couple of thugs tried to kidnap her today," Anna said. "Then Darden White decided to drop by and act creepy. Gerry, we've got to get Helena somewhere safe, away from this place." Hysteria edged Anna's voice but there was nothing she could do about it. "Where are the people that do these things?"

Gerry was staring at her. Anna shut up.

"The chief ranger has been in touch with Health and Human Services," Gerry said. "They are sending someone down tomorrow to take custody. She'll be taken to El Paso, to the hospital there. What they do after that, I don't know. Bernard was trying to reach you today to let you know but no one was answering your cell phone."

Anna had forgotten who Bernard was. The chief ranger, it came back to her. She had forgotten she even had a cell phone, the thing had been so worthless in the Chisos Basin. It was packed away in the suitcases they'd brought down from the lodge and the suitcases were in the trunk of the totaled Honda.

"Oh," Anna said. Earlier she would have been upset at the news "they" were coming to take Helena and drop her in the machinery that devoured unwanted children. This evening the news was cause for celebration. She took another swig of Gerry's beer.

"I can buy you one of your own," the reporter said mildly.

"Sorry," Anna said, and put the beer down on the bench closer to Gerry than to herself. "Should we take Helena back to the Martinezes'?" Anna used the word *we* intentionally. She wanted nothing more at this moment than to abdicate all responsibility for the newborn. The fear that her incompetence would factor into death or long-term impairment of the baby was strong in her.

"Is there anybody there, besides thugs and creepy security guys?" Gerry asked.

"No."

"Why don't we wait, then."

Anna nodded and stared out at the range of mountains small with the immense distances of Texas. Low in the sky the sun painted the desert with soft hues of coming evening; the spiny, biting nature of her inhabitants was muted with pastels and a faint haze of dust.

They sat companionably without speaking. The weight of the baby was no more than six pounds, seven at the most, but the weight of responsibility was crushing and Anna reveled in having her arms empty, her lap unpopulated. To have a child was a form of incarceration, the acquisition of a tiny jailer who dictated the terms of imprisonment. Not having children was a decision Anna had made when she was a young woman. Those around her had told her, just wait, the biological clock will begin to tick at twenty-five, at thirty, at thirty-eight, and you'll change your mind. The milestones had passed and no ticking. She'd never regretted the decision, never looked back and wished, never envied other women their families. As attached as she'd become to Helena, Anna had not changed.

Gerry broke the silence. "Darden came by, you said?"

"Yes. Just now. He didn't do anything untoward. He wanted details about Helena's mother and he was fixated on Helena herself but he wanted something more—at least he sure seemed to. He was strung-out and tired. It looked like he'd been rode hard and put away wet since we had breakfast at the lodge this morning." Time had gotten skewed. Breakfast faded into a past so distant Anna could see it only through a fog of years instead of hours. Had she been younger then? At the moment she doubted she'd ever been young.

"I've known Darden a few years," Gerry said. "Never well, but the way people do when they move in the same circles. I liked him."

"Liked, past tense?" Anna asked.

"You know I smell something rotten about the mayor," Gerry said. "I was doing a bit of checking on the histories of people she's surrounded herself with, hoping to get a feel for what it might be. Darden has known Mayor Pierson since she was three years old. I don't know if there was anything perverted about it; he's twenty years older than she is and devoted to her. You always think of sexual abuse but, if that was the connection, it was never reported or hinted at and the mayor probably wouldn't have him on her personal security detail if that was the case."

"Stranger relationships between abused and abuser have happened," Anna said.

"True, but this doesn't feel like one—not that way. Before Darden was with the Houston mayor's office, he was Secret Service for thirty-five years. I couldn't tap into those years. I suppose a Woodward or a Bernstein might be able to dig that deep but not me, at least not in Timbuktu with an Internet connection that comes and goes as it sees fit. The last seven he's been with Judith during her first and second terms as mayor. That, I could dig into."

"Houston's Deep Throat?"

Gerry laughed and shifted Helena to her other shoulder so she could pick up her beer. "I do know a few people in town," she admitted.

"Did you find your tabloid bonanza?" Anna asked, remembering Gerry's self-deprecating humor at chasing scandal.

"Unfortunately, no. If Judith is being unfaithful or raiding the city's coffers or hiring her girlfriends or firing her in-laws à la Ms. Palin, I haven't been able to turn it up. She's sharky and ruthless and has a lot of enemies, but no smoking guns. I did turn up a bit of interesting material on Darden White."

"As it relates to creepy visits to orphans?"

"Maybe. During Darden's first years with the Secret Service he worked details with the CIA in Nicaragua, Paraguay, Pakistan and Serbia. As I said, that was as much detail as I could get. Only public record stuff. But those places were hot spots—some still are—and I don't think he was doing much running beside limos in parades or standing handsome and reassuring around White House parties. It is a good bet Darden White's hands are far from clean. The last fifteen years of his service, he was in the States working security for presidential and vice presidential nominees on the campaign trail, ex-presidents and their wives, high-profile politicians' kids—that sort of thing. I did get ahold of several of the people he'd worked with and the word they used most to describe him was loyal."

"Loyal's not a bad thing," Anna said. "Is it?"

"It depends, I guess," Gerry said slowly. "I got the impression from a couple of these contacts that 'loyal' meant loyal like an attack dog. Willing to do maybe questionable things to protect his clients."

"So. Darden is besotted with Mayor Pierson for whatever reason. He's also her head of security. A double dose of attack-dog loyalty there?"

"Once I got to asking around, it was pretty clear a lot of people were scared of Darden. People who decided to take the mayor down got bought off, scared off or left town. A photographer accidentally banged his camera into the mayor's jaw and Darden broke the man's arm before anybody knew he'd moved. A couple of years ago a college professor, of all people, was stalking the mayor. Darden got the police chief to throw him in jail on pretty flimsy grounds. The professor hung himself while in custody."

"Maybe the professor was crazy," Anna said.

"Probably," Gerry admitted. "But, taken with several more stories along those same lines, it's hard not to think Darden is happy to break bones and ruin lives to keep Judith in one piece and in whatever spotlight she sets her heart on."

"And while the Houston politician is in Big Bend a woman is thrown in the river, presumably to die in what appears to be a tragic illegal border crossing—"

"Neatly underscoring the mayor's big punch to get on the gubernatorial map," Gerry finished Anna's thought.

"Then the surviving baby is to be snatched . . . why? If the mayor was a man I'd think it was his illegitimate child. We've got the honorable John Edwards still holding the lead on that particular line of political suicide."

"Maybe it's her husband's, Charles's," Gerry said. "I talked with the clerk at the lodge and a very pregnant woman showed up there asking for Charles the day before this woman was found in the river."

Anna thought about that for a minute. If Helena was Charles Pierson's baby it would be the John Edwards thing all over again. Only this time, instead of merely losing respect for a husband, Judith would be losing respect for a husband and losing the respect of a lot of her constituency. The public had a love/hate relationship with the women who stood by their men on the evening news. The more strident wanted the women to disown the bastards and strike out on their own. Most felt pity for the injured wife. Infidelity was bad. Fathering a child with the infidel was worse. Ridiculous as it seemed, the fathering of a child bespoke a greater depth of relationship than mere fornication to many people, though in reality it suggested only a lack of responsibility by the parties concerned.

Or entrapment.

"Do you think Darden chose to murder the woman

and her fetus and make it look like an incident that would further Judith's aims? That seems a bit draconian."

"Politics, love and ambition are draconian," Gerry said, and drained the last of her beer. "And that would certainly clean the slate."

"Charles might have been behind it, covering up his indiscretion."

"Maybe," Gerry conceded. "But I don't think so. Charles Pierson is the antithesis of violent action, a gentle soul or a coward, depending on how you frame it. The Piersons are also loaded. Old Texas money that keeps on pumping out of the ground. If Charles wanted to get rid of an inconvenient liaison there aren't a lot of women he couldn't buy off with those kinds of resources."

"There are a few women who can't be bought," Anna said. "And there are those for whom the asking price is too high. Maybe she was blackmailing him for money even he couldn't afford or marriage and a place in society. Harvard for the child and Paris fashion week for herself. Things mere money might not be able to buy an unwed mother."

"True," Gerry said. She tipped the bottle again, realized she had emptied it and set it back on the bench between them. "You probably want to buy the next round," she said with a twinkle that penetrated through the heavily mascaraed lashes. "I don't think it's proper to take an innocent baby into a bar."

"My pleasure," Anna said. She stood and shook the kinks out of her legs. Until she took the time to sit still for a while, she'd been unaware of the bruising she'd experienced in the set-to with the beefy Danny. The parts of her that didn't ache had stiffened and the parts of her that had stiffened were beginning to ache.

"You seem a little off your feed today," Gerry said.

"Babysitting is a lot harder than high school girls make it look."

"Beer?" Gerry prodded when Anna remained shaking and stretching in front of the bench they shared.

"I forgot my wallet," Anna admitted.

"You are awfully pathetic for a heroine," Gerry said, but she dug a twenty out of her purse and handed it over. "I'm going to count the change," she hollered as Anna took the money down the long porch.

The inside of the bar carried through the rustic wood, old cowboy décor that the porch advertised. There weren't any false notes because, though the ambience was intentional and exploited, the building really was that old, the boards had weathered where they stood and the floor was worn by the application of thousands of booted feet rather than sander and awl. Beer could be purchased by the bottle or the pack. A cooler was provided so the regulars could buy a pack and keep it cold while they downed it at their leisure.

Anna got two Lone Stars, uncapped them and carried them back out to the porch. The parking lot was beginning to fill up. Half a dozen tourists had joined the locals on the benches or leaned against the six-by-six posts that held up the roof. Only the most unobservant would confuse the two groups. Native Terlinguans—at least those on the porch—both male and female looked as if they dressed out of dumpsters and didn't bother with dentists.

Old hippies, a lot of them. People who had dropped out in the sixties and seventies and drifted until they found a place that was, as Carmen had aspired to be, off the grid. As Anna walked, exchanging the occasional nod with someone who caught her eye, she remembered a scrap of information Cyril had shared when she'd visited their camp that morning. She'd only been half listening at the time but it came back to her now. The Starlight Theatre—now a restaurant—had been so named because when Terlingua's dreams were younger and its inhabitants had less gray in their long hair and beards, they used to gather in the old building, roofless then, and play music under the stars of Texas. The starlight theatre.

Anna liked it. She would have liked to have sat in on the music then, to listen, not to stay. The fringes of the world where dreamers and misfits eventually washed up held no allure for her.

"Ah, you're a dreamboat," Gerry said as she took the beer from Anna's outstretched hand. "Take the baby, will you?"

"Already?" Anna asked, and was annoyed at both the whine in her voice and the smile with which Gerry met it.

"You know what the Chinese say; you save somebody's life, you are then responsible for that somebody until one of you dies. Here's your somebody."

Feeling it was wrong on some level to be seen holding a beer and a baby simultaneously, Anna set the Lone Star between her feet under the bench where it wouldn't be so obvious.

"It would probably be a good idea to get her back where she can have a bed and a bottle of her own," Gerry said.

"I guess," Anna admitted reluctantly. She looked at her watch. It was well after six and neither Paul nor the kids had shown up. Anna was more annoyed than worried. Her worrying quotient had been used up by Helena.

"Would it be okay if I ate first?" she asked.

Gerry laughed. "You need my permission to eat?"

Anna felt a fool. In need of foisting responsibility off on another's shoulders had rendered her childish.

"We'll eat first," she said firmly.

Gerry didn't eat but kept her company and held Helena while Anna downed a most excellent chicken enchilada, refried beans, rice and enough guacamole and chips to keep a Super Bowl party going smoothly. Knowing she needed to keep her head but needing more to take the edge off one hell of a day, she washed it down with another beer.

At seven-thirty, she had run out of things to devour and she and Gerry had hashed over the Darden-dead-woman connection till they'd rendered it threadbare. It was time to go "home." Lisa might have returned and

Helena could have the comfort of breast milk and a real woman to hold her for a while.

Maybe Paul would be back as well. Anna craved his company and the strength of his personality the way she craved rest and food after a long, arduous hike.

"I guess we'd better go," she admitted as the waiter took the last of the dishes away.

"I've got a date," Gerry said. "And I believe mine has shown up."

Anna looked to the door of the restaurant to see the chief ranger, in civilian clothes, waving at Gerry. "You work quickly," she said.

"I have been called fast," Gerry replied with a smile. "One must catch them between divorces."

The chief ranger came to their table as Anna stood and took Helena, showing the world what a good quiet baby she was, from Gerry's arms. "Is the body recovery team back yet?" Anna asked.

"Only just. I heard them on the radio as I was driving down. They had some complications retrieving the victim and had to re-rig. I'd have called and let you know when Paul was coming back but you don't answer your phone. I've been trying to get in touch with you," Bernard said. "Health and Human Services out of El Paso—"

"Gerry told me." Anna saved him the trouble of repeating the news. "What time will they be coming for Helena?"

"Midafternoon is my guess. Everything in Texas is a long drive," Bernard said.

"She'll be ready." Relief at being relieved of responsibility, relief at the thought Helena would be safe and cared for, sudden startling pain at the thought of losing the little girl, fear of what sort of future awaited her smacked into Anna's emotional center all at once. Instead of taking her leave, she stood rooted beside the chair she had just vacated.

"Do you want us to give you a lift back to the Martinez place?" Gerry asked.

"No." Anna forced herself to come alive again. "It's not far and I need the air. Tomorrow," she said to Bernard.

"Turn your cell phone on," the chief ranger called after her as she left the table.

The long desert evening was doing a slow fade into night. Light was still clear and blue but colors had gone from the hills and into the sky. With the cooling air the bracing perfume of the sere tufted grasses and creosote bushes was lifted on the slight breeze coming down from the mountains to the east. Breathing deeply, Anna cleared her head of the beer and the talk and the close confines of the restaurant. Helena, too, was rejuvenated and began to squirm and make small but not unhappy sounds.

The eerie "Slow, Children at Play" sign with the skeleton child was not as amusing without the full light of the sun on it and, feeling superstitious and silly, Anna hurried past it to cross the main road. She was halfway down the dirt track to the Martinez house when headlights raked green from the desert ahead of her.

Paul was her first thought and she felt her spirits rise. Turning, she shielded her eyes from the glare of the oncoming lights.

It wasn't an NPS pickup truck or patrol car. The lights were on the front of an oversized, coal-black SUV.

THIRTY-SIX

Anna didn't hesitate. She turned and ran perpendicular to the road. A hundred yards or less from the dirt lane was a hill, long and low and as unglamorous as a berm pushed up by a John Deere caterpillar but steep enough she doubted the city-bred four-wheel drive could climb it. What was on the other side, she hadn't a clue.

Streaks of hard light slued across the rocky soil, igniting tufts of grass and sparking green and fuchsia from the barrel cacti. The beams aligned themselves with Anna and she could see her shadow running like ink in front of her nearly to the hill. The SUV was driving cross-country. This close to witnesses, Anna had hoped the driver wouldn't have the nerve to leave the road.

Holding Helena close to her chest and praying to

gods she hadn't believed in thirty seconds before that she wouldn't fall and crush the child before Darden got an opportunity to murder them both, Anna ran. Adrenaline and determination lifted her feet and she flew the first twenty yards. The second twenty, with the lights so hot behind her, she was blind to anything in her peripheral vision, and her thigh muscles began to liquefy, losing the ability to push as hard as they needed to. At fifty yards she had a cruel stitch in her side and could hear the smooth, unstoppable crunching of tires and engine murmur behind her. Darden wasn't going to bother with hands-on havoc; he was simply going to run them down. She turned abruptly right and fled into the relative darkness.

The ground grabbed at her feet and cacti snatched bits of flesh from her calves. Ahead she could see faint yellow lights from the Martinezes' kitchen window. Lisa would be home by now and, with her, Edgar. Maybe Freddy was back, as well, broad-shouldered, well-armed Freddy. Maybe he wasn't. Anna couldn't chance it. Turning once more she ran again toward the hill, now fifty yards and a million miles away.

White knives of light scraped across the desert, seeking her. In seconds they pinned onto her back and the engine roared as the driver pressed the accelerator pedal to the floorboards. There was no cover, no place to hide.

Anna stopped and turned to face the oncoming vehicle. Breath rasped so loud in her throat and ears she didn't know if Helena was crying or not. Any normal infant would have been screaming her head off. Any normal woman would have been screaming her head off. Anna screamed loud and long and hoped it would raise help from somewhere. Headlights bounced, lancing over her. She readied herself to jump whichever way the fates decreed when the SUV came within striking distance.

Thirty feet from her and the baby, the SUV skidded to a halt in a gout of dust and the driver's door flew open. "Anna, Anna, don't run, it's me, Mayor Pierson, Judith." The small blond woman appeared from behind the black metal door and walked toward her, hands up as if Anna held a gun instead of a baby.

"God you're fast," Judith said, panting as if she had been chasing Anna on foot. "You've got to come. I know everything Darden has done. He's coming for the baby."

"Stay where you are," Anna said, and Judith stopped. Moving out of the line of light until she could see the mayor but doubted the mayor had any kind of view of her, she asked: "What has Darden done?"

Judith Pierson didn't say anything. She turned her head and looked to the east where the Chisos were silhouetted against a sky of the faintest sea green. Headlights caught her hair and Anna could see it had been washed and set since breakfast. The side of her face that was lit up had tear streaks in black where she'd cried off her mascara.

"I think Darden killed somebody," Judith said quietly.

"Who?" Anna demanded. The woman caught in the river strainer was the expected answer but Anna had learned the expected isn't what necessarily happens.

"The baby's mother, the Mexican woman. At least I think he did—or had somebody do it." Judith didn't try to find Anna in the gloom outside the cone of light but kept her eyes on the distant horizon.

Having entered the place one came to in an investigation gone haywire where no one is to be trusted, Anna asked: "Why come here? Why not go to the rangers or your other two security guys?"

"Darden's coming for the baby, Anna. I think he means to kill it."

"All the better reason to call the rangers."

Breathing was becoming easier. No longer gasping like a landed fish, Anna could hear Helena's soft whimpering, the comfortable purr of the big car's engine.

"I couldn't," Judith said simply, and tears dragged more sooty tracks down the cheek Anna could see. "I was afraid they would kill him. You can call them but I was hoping you'd go someplace safe so there won't have to be any killing."

"Why didn't you just call me?"

"I did, damn you!" Judith yelled, anger breaking through. "You wouldn't answer your damn phone."

Anna couldn't fault her there. Persons of authority and consequence had already attested to the fact that Anna was not answering.

Another pair of headlights cut across the landscape in an arc moving from west to east, flashing off the shiny fenders of the black car. Hoping it was Freddy and he'd come out to see who was traveling off road in his neighborhood, hoping it was Paul and he would sense with that bond said to connect lovers that she needed him, Anna watched the lights.

Judith was watching them too.

The lights were high and wide apart with the cold blue-white glare of halogen bulbs instead of the warm yellows on older vehicles.

"It's him," Judith said flatly. "It's Darden. Get in!" She ran from the light and Anna heard the driver's-side door slam shut.

The second car was another SUV; Anna could see the black boxy shape against the lighter gray of the desert floor as it left the main road and turned down the lane toward the Martinezes'. Unsure what to do, she watched. There was no way she could outrun a four-wheel drive. In the dark she couldn't run far without doing herself and Helena serious damage. No cover but the hill fifty yards away and that would have to be climbed. Alone, able to grab and hold and crab on hands and knees, it wouldn't have been much of a challenge. With Helena and the night, she wouldn't make it up in the kind of time that was apparently left to her.

Running was out; standing and fighting was a bad idea. So she waited for a sign. When the gas hog turned from the road and began grinding across the sand and scrub toward her, she decided that was it.

"Wait!" She ran to the passenger side of Judith's

SUV, which was already rolling, wrenched open the door and hauled herself and the baby in by unauthorized usage of the seat belt.

Judith spun the wheel and gunned the engine. Had they been on pavement there would have been an impressive squealing of tires. The SUV had a big turning radius but Judith bettered the factory stats by a few yards. She nearly stood the behemoth on two wheels as she powered it around till the nose was pointed in the direction of the lane. Anna thought she would angle toward the main road or head the opposite way, toward Freddy and Lisa's, but she did neither. Aligning her headlights with those of the oncoming car, she floored it.

Anna had never liked the game of chicken and she yelled words she knew were permanently scarring Helena's tender psyche as they hurtled directly at the other car. Darden didn't swerve. Neither did Judith. Anna's cursing became one long moan of anticipation. Had she been on her own, or the car traveling more slowly, she would have opened the door and taken her chances diving into the nearest sotol bush.

Judith might have been yelling, as well, but in the clash of lights and the knowledge of certain death, Anna didn't hear her. Squeezing her eyes shut, she held tight to Helena, hoped Paul wouldn't be too handsome in his widower's weeds and prepared to die.

"Whooeee!" Judith was laughing. Anna opened her eyes. Darden was bumping out through the rough at an angle and they had reached the road in one piece. "He blinked!" Judith shouted as if this was a high school game of dare after several six-packs of beer and she had just won it.

"Don't do that again," Anna snarled.

"Sorry," Judith said, but laughter was bubbling beneath the word.

"Don't," Anna repeated, her anger at the danger to Helena and herself heating the word from the inside.

Judith looked over at her, her face limned with the faint illumination from the dashboard. "I am sorry," she said, and this time there was no laughter. "I wouldn't have done that with anyone but Darden. I knew he would break first. He always did."

Anna wasn't sure what that was supposed to mean and was too furious to pursue it. Nobody ever knew what anyone else would do, no matter what the existing pattern. Lives—especially hers—shouldn't be bet on the outcome.

They reached the paved road and Judith turned toward Study Butte.

"No," Anna said. "Left toward the Porch. The chief ranger is there. He has his radio with him. He can call in whoever he needs to."

"Is Bernie armed?"

The mayor was the first person Anna had heard refer to Bernard as "Bernie." Perhaps they had gotten close during the excitement of the past few days.

"No," Anna said. "He may have his weapon in his car."

"Then it's a bad idea. Look." Judith's eyes flashed

blue-green as she glanced in the rearview mirror. Two headlights jolted back onto the road and began bearing down on them. "Darden never goes anywhere unarmed. That car is fully loaded: automatic rifles, a couple of handguns that I know of. Bolted to the back of the seat is a piece that looks right out of Desert Storm."

Long guns that could pick off river rafters—or newborns—from a canyon rim a thousand feet above.

Terlingua looked too much like Okay Corral country for the image of public carnage not to take root in Anna's imagination. A wide brick porch loaded with people out to have a good time, a crazed ex-military man with automatic weapons, blood spattering the graying wood: though it was hard to think Darden was crazy enough to reenact *Rambo, the Evil Years*, it wasn't a chance Anna was willing to take.

Judith was proving a good driver. As the SUV pushed closer she picked up speed and moved the ungainly vehicle around curves with surprising skill. Better than Anna could have done, she admitted to herself as she fastened her seat belt tight across her hips. Without a car seat, the baby would be dead if Judith ran into anything. Afraid trying to buckle her into the backseat in some fashion would be more dangerous, Anna held her and hoped for the best.

Judith pulled onto Highway 170. She didn't turn east into the park but west toward the tiny town of Lajitas. Darden started blowing his horn and flashing his lights.

"Panther Junction," Anna yelled.

"Too far," Judith said calmly. Considering they were being chased at high speed by a man believed to be a homicidal maniac, Anna couldn't help being impressed by her control and alarmed by her detachment. "There's a high-end hotel there," Judith explained. "If we can reach it ahead of Darden, they can get their security to deal with him till the sheriff or posse or the cavalry arrives."

Lajitas was where Carmen and the merry band of rafters had put into the Rio Grande. That seemed so long ago, Anna wondered if Cyril and Chrissie and Steve had children of their own by now, if the river had changed course, if the rockslide had eroded down to a riffle of pebbles in a sedate stream.

A sidelong reading of the speedometer told Anna they were nearing a hundred miles per hour. Doable on the straight roads of Texas, where there was lots of visibility. "If we're lucky Darden's flashing and beeping will catch somebody's attention and we'll get pulled over."

"There's never a cop when you need one," Judith said. The relieved laughter that had followed the game of chicken was gone, but on a level Anna didn't want to dwell given her situation, the mayor seemed to be having a vicious kind of fun.

THIRTY-SEVEN

Darden's lights flared closer and he stood on the horn. Startled, Judith jerked the wheel and the SUV dropped two tires off the pavement onto the shoulder of the road. For a sickening instant Anna thought the ungainly vehicle was going to roll but Judith regained control. The close call seemed to have an effect on their pursuer. Darden stopped blowing his horn and dropped back until he was several car lengths behind.

Anna's pulse slowed slightly and she found she could think instead of merely react. "Why would Darden want to kill Helena?" she asked.

Judith sighed. "My husband has a habit of getting women into trouble," she said. "This time the woman showed up at the lodge nearly nine months pregnant and demanded to see Charles. She found me instead.

Her name was Eleanor Cheevers; she's the daughter of the ambassador from Argentina and an English engineer. Well-placed enough to know the damage her appearance would cause me. Ms. Cheevers wanted money; that's what they all want. I set her up in the Lajitas spa—at my expense, of course—and the woman agreed to refrain from contacting Charles until we could come up with the cash. I was buying time. At least I thought I was. Darden is a final-solution kind of guy. He thought killing her and the baby and making it look like the accidental drowning of a poor Mexican woman would solve the problem. Nobody puts a lot of time into investigating that situation.

"He had his goons take her down to the Rio Grande. They were supposed to kill her and let the body float downriver to give the elements a chance to destroy any forensic evidence and, if they were lucky, never be discovered at all.

"Evidently Ms. Cheevers proved a handful. She got loose and the river took her. Darden followed from the canyon rim to make sure she didn't get out of the water alive. When she got caught in the strainer and you saved her, he decided he had to kill her. She died on her own but the baby would be DNA evidence that could hook him to the murder. After that things got out of control.

"Darden was trying to help me. He is the most loyal person I've ever known. My success is more important to him, I sometimes think, than it is to me. He knew if I found out, I'd call the police, so he didn't tell me."

As they cruised down the highway at a slightly less alarming speed, Anna digested that bit of information.

"If all this mayhem was to cover up the fact he murdered several people, and wanted to murder Helena, going into a public place, guns blasting, would tend to be a little counterproductive," Anna said.

Judith pounded the steering wheel with such violence both Anna and Helena squeaked in alarm.

"He'd do it because he's gone crazy! You should have seen him up at the lodge after his two hired thugs failed to get the baby. They're dead, did you know that?" she demanded.

Anna didn't bother to answer.

"He told me. He said they'd called to get picked up because they had to ditch the car they'd rented. He had Kevin, his psycho protégé, go get them, take them to some deserted place west of Terlingua and shoot them.

"Oh God!" Judith shouted, and the car swerved dangerously. "I should have seen this coming. I might have been able to stop it, get him help. Darden's got post-traumatic stress syndrome from so many wars and skirmishes and dirty political assignments that he doesn't know if he is coming or going half the time.

"He worries about getting old, worries that he's losing it. His mom has Alzheimer's and he worries that he'll go that way too. Maybe this was his way of trying to prove he was the man he used to be, and when it got screwed up it pushed him over an edge in his mind. Maybe he's back in the jungles or deserts or villages or wherever he was for those years. I don't know. I do know that he's not thinking straight."

"Maybe a public bloodbath is his way of committing suicide by cop," Anna thought aloud.

"Maybe," Judith said, and there was nothing in her tone but sorrow.

They drove in silence for a while and Anna had trouble remembering they were in a high-speed chase. It felt more like O. J. Simpson's famous low-speed chase on the freeways of Los Angeles. Darden kept a safe but consistent distance behind them. Judith slowed down till the speedometer, at least as seen from the passenger seat, hovered around eighty miles per hour. The dusk that had been so lacerated by the slashing of headlights was settling into a deeper violet mood. Stars were coming out.

"I need to use your cell phone," Anna said into this new and unsubstantiated peace.

Judith's right hand darted away from the steering wheel as if on a mission of its own, then was snatched back into the ten-and-two position. "It's in my purse," she said. "And my purse is in the hotel room. Darden didn't leave me much time for the niceties."

An evil smell let Anna know Helena had run out of time for the niceties as well. She lowered her window a few inches. At eighty miles an hour the racket from the wind was considerable. Lajitas wasn't too far from Terlingua if she remembered right, between fifteen and thirty miles, probably closer to fifteen. At eighty they wouldn't have much longer on the road.

Breathing in the sweet smell of the desert—or as much as could penetrate the miasma Helena had instigated—Anna looked into the side mirror at the lights politely tailing them three car lengths back, the beams on low so they wouldn't blind the driver in the car ahead, and couldn't shake the dreamlike quality the night had taken on the moment Darden appeared at the door of the Martinez house wanting to know the gory details of the woman's—Eleanor Cheevers's—demise.

The hysteria with which she had left the house, the panic that she was harming a newborn by lugging it around like a satchel, was gone, worn out or dimmed by the events that came after. The fear and helplessness she'd suffered trying to outdistance Detroit's finest automobiles had run its course as well. Oddly empty of emotion, Anna let bits of internal film roll. Gerry outlined Darden's probably bloody history and proven violence where the good of his mayor was concerned. His mayor, and a woman he'd known since she was three years old, a woman he was in love with one way or another: sexual, filial, paternal or psychotic. At the breakfast the four of them had eaten together Anna had not been particularly attuned to the currents between Judith and her chief of security. In retrospect she watched Darden's glances at Judith wavering from anxious with unvoiced concern to irritated and, once, frightened. Maybe frightened, Anna corrected herself. Reading faces was informative as far as it went, but human beings over the age of two had learned to lie with all their faculties. She didn't think Darden had been guarding his expressions that morning but a lot of things factored into a twist of the lips or a raise of an eyebrow. Like babies, people might be smiling or they might just have gas.

As breakfast replayed in her head she remembered the reassuring tone Darden had used with Judith and her almost childlike reliance on him. It reminded her of the first time the three of them had met, in the chief ranger's conference room after they'd been brought back from the rim of Santa Elena Canyon, how Darden had intervened with the offer of soda or a careful word when Judith sounded as if she were stressed—or about to give away something better kept secret.

She watched Darden at the door of the Martinezes', unsurprised by the visit of the baby snatchers, how he'd asked for details about Helena's mom that she might not have shared with others, how he didn't show any interest in the brawl that had so recently taken place in the space they shared. Memory film fast-forwarded through Darden tracking her in his SUV when she and Helena walked to the Terlingua Porch, reappearing shortly after the mayor had come in an identical SUV, veering from the game of chicken because he "always" did, backing off when the chase became dangerous for Judith. She stopped the mind movie at the place where Judith gave every indication of having fun, of playing a game.

Readjusting Helena to her shoulder, Anna snuck a glance into the back. A leather strap snaked out from beneath the driver's-side seat, narrow tooled leather with a single gold link attaching it to whatever was beneath Judith's rump. Anna didn't doubt for a minute that it was the mayor's purse, the one she'd said held the cell phone, the one she'd said she'd left behind at the Chisos Lodge.

The SUV speeded up. From the corner of her eye Anna saw the sign for the Lajitas resort hotel flash by in a blink of halogen white.

"Oh shoot!" Judith said. "I overshot. There's a place to turn around at a park down by the river. It's not far; we'll make it and back before Darden figures out what we're doing."

Anna said nothing. Darden already knew what they were doing. He wasn't a lone psychopath, he was a member of a conspiracy, and Anna had obligingly hopped into the hands of the other member.

They were taking Anna and Helena to the river to kill them.

THIRTY-EIGHT

Anna had less than five minutes to curse herself for a fool and mentally apologize to the mothers of the world for any stray thoughts she'd had over the years that they weren't brave enough, or smart enough, or productive enough. Doing anything, *anything*, with an infant in arms was a near impossibility: thinking, fighting, moving, working, eating. Helplessness was how she'd seen it, but it wasn't that the women couldn't do for themselves. It was that they could not do for themselves unless they sacrificed their child. That women often chose to have more than one child was mindboggling; it must require the courage of several prides of lions.

Courage Anna had always lacked.

Left to her own devices, she would not have taken

Judith's offer of a ride; she would have run for the desert hills and trusted to her own abilities. A baby made that plan unworkable. Left to her own devices, she might have thrown herself from the moving vehicle as soon as it slowed rather than be taken to the place where the grim reaper was supposed to be waiting. With a baby, that couldn't be done. She daren't even grab the wheel and try to wreck the SUV. Held in her lap, Helena probably wouldn't survive the crash.

The actions left were the traditional actions of women with children: placating, lying, running and hiding. Anna chose lying; she played along so Judith would continue to believe all was going according to plan.

"Not much farther. There it is. Canoes put in here sometimes. Did you know that?" Judith chattered as they left the pavement and the SUV lumbered down a dirt and gravel path toward the water. "There's room to turn this thing around a ways down. I remember it from coming here once."

There was room to turn around on every side. This was the Chihuahuan desert, not the forested backwoods of Washington. Seven-forty-sevens could turn around pretty much anywhere one looked. Anna said nothing. She undid her seat belt and surreptitiously wormed her arm free.

Darden, creeping and black in his obese vehicle, didn't show lights behind them and Anna wondered if he'd missed the turn into the park on purpose or by accident, if he was circling around to join the party from another direction.

"Hey!" Judith said, sounding surprised. "We lost him. Good for us." The SUV rolled to a stop and she put on the parking brake.

Anna threw open the door, half fell out of the SUV and ran.

"Wait! What are you doing? Come back, damn you!" she heard Judith yelling after her. "Darden will be back and he'll kill you!" Judith shouted. Then the engine revved and screeched, Judith trying to pursue her but forgetting she'd set the brake. A ratcheting sound was followed by the crunch of tires on gravel and a banging that had to be the open passenger door flapping as Judith drove over uneven ground.

Already this night Anna had lost a footrace with an automobile. She had no intention of doing it a second time. They wanted her in the river and that's where she was headed. Headlights lashing her, she ran for the water and kept running till it was waist-deep and still she pushed on. The Rio Grande was low and she was grateful. Texas hadn't been handing out much in the way of breaks for the last few days and Anna deeply appreciated this one. At the put-in the river wasn't more than fifty feet across and tonight it ran slowly, almost languidly. The current pulled at her legs and feet but playfully, an invitation to swim rather than an invitation to drown.

The headlights of Judith's SUV slammed into her chest and face with the impact of a solid object and Anna turned away, Helena clutched to her shoulder.

The water was cool but not cold and they sank into

it until only their heads remained in the air. Tinier targets, she hoped, bits of oddly shaped driftwood lost in the darkness. The big engine roared with the anger of its driver and gravel rattled from beneath spinning tires. A tremendous splash followed and the headlights dimmed. Judith must have driven the vehicle into the river. Desperately wanting to look back, Anna kept her pale face away from the direction where Judith was still calling after them and let the river carry her gently downstream.

"Judith! Judy! Are you okay?"

Darden had arrived. Light as a bit of flotsam, Anna maneuvered herself and Helena toward the deep overhang of reeds. Helena's diaper was filling with river water. Anna unstuck the tape and let it float away. As she watched the white bobbing against the dark water she realized she had finally done it, she had hit bottom. She was littering.

There wasn't a reply to Darden's shout and, as Anna's spirits were rising at the thought of Mayor Pierson with a broken nose or her head bashed in by the windshield, she heard the woman shouting high and screechy: "Stay away, Darden. I told Anna what you did. She knows you're here to kill her. You get out of here."

"Judith, stop it!" Darden snapped, and there was silence.

They stopped talking; the night was too still and Anna too close for it to be otherwise. Even whispers would have carried over the water. As long as they kept each other busy, she and Helena were traveling. Reeds pushed out over the water two to ten feet, their stalks thick and yellow, leaves long, spiky and dark green. Uncut and without any creatures who liked to eat them, they'd taken over the banks and grown thick and tangled. Perfect for what Anna needed. Silt piled up nearer the bank and her feet touched bottom. Shrinking under the reeds, she was enveloped in total darkness.

Her invasion of these inky environs caused a stir. Around her she could hear the movements of those whose home she had invaded. A faint plop, a turtle sliding beneath the water, she thought. *Skritching*. Little birds awakened and scratched around for reasons held secret in their little bird brains. The unmistakable slithering rustle of a snake moving through dry grass.

Rattlesnakes were common in Big Bend, as were tarantulas, scorpions, black widow spiders and all manner of other animals who lived by tooth or claw or toxin. Lots of them came to drink at the river at night. Many would choose the cover the reeds provided as Anna had. Blinded and surrounded by them, Anna felt safer than she did with most of her own species—especially the two who had brought her here in dueling SUVs.

Resisting the temptation to put her hand over the baby's nose and mouth lest she cry and give them away, Anna listened. Car doors were opening and closing and heavy objects being dragged. It sounded as if Judith was trying to salvage items from the backseat of the half-submerged Chevy. A weapon?

"I don't need you, Darden, and Anna won't come

out if you're here. She knows what you are." Judith's voice cut abruptly through the sounds of rummaging and Anna realized how close she was. The reeds that had so kindly taken her and Helena in weren't very far downstream from where the SUV had charged into the water. Judith must have gotten whatever it was she wanted from the back of the car; Anna heard her splashing into the water.

Both Darden and Judith seemed to be playing that the other was the bad guy and they were the, if not good, then sane guy. Was it a game to keep Anna off balance? Were they both desirous of offing her and Helena but for different reasons? Even soaking wet, in the dark, hiding in the reeds with a baby in her arms, that seemed far-fetched. Had Darden been in on the killings right up to but not including the murder of an infant and, by the way, a federal law enforcement officer?

Feeling her way with her feet, one hand held loosely over Helena's face to ward off spiders and sticks and sharp-edged leaves, Anna moved slowly downriver. The more distance she put between herself and them the better her chances. If she could make it to a bend in the river or a dry wash that cut down through the reeds, she could get out of the water. On a warm night in a cool river, she'd probably last a long time before hypothermia started shutting down her body. She had no idea how long it would take for a person as small and new as Helena to succumb.

"I've come to help, Judy. You know that. When have I

ever not been there when you hollered?" Darden shouted. "This is more my line of work than yours, pumpkin. Why don't you go sit in the truck and dry off?"

If there'd been a falling-out among thieves it sounded as if it was all over now. Given the choice, Anna would have preferred Darden do as Judith asked and go away. This was, indeed, more his line of work, and even though he was over sixty and overweight, Anna would not underestimate him.

"You're here to help me? Scout's honor?" Judith sounded both the imperious mayor and the lonely little girl. The mix was eerie, as if a woman and a little girl were saying the same words at the same time but in two different voices.

The concept of multiple personalities blossomed in Anna's mind. There'd been a glut of stories about people housing between two and twenty differing personalities inside one body. Usually one or more of the personalities was homicidal, thus allowing the twist at the end of the plot. Judith sounded like a candidate but Anna was sure she'd heard that multiple personality disorder had been thoroughly debunked. Too bad, what with Mama Anna and Ranger Anna, she was thinking about signing on as soon as she got back to civilization.

Civilization. Anna longed for it and the unnaturalness of the emotion registered even as she crept through reeds in shoulder-deep water trying to keep herself and her charge alive. For most of her life she had felt more at home, safer, saner, stronger and more able in the wilderness than she had in towns and houses.

Babies changed that too. Since she'd taken over the care and feeding of one of the little buggers, Anna had wanted homes and diapers, stoves and sterilizers, warm, dry clothes and washer/dryers.

"You're a powerful little thing," she said in the merest wisp of a whisper near Helena's ear. "And you're a good quiet girl," she added, in case compliments would keep her quiet awhile longer.

Suddenly Anna's footing was gone. The current had scoured a deeper hole beneath the reeds where she walked. She and Helena were being carried farther into the bank. Anna fought to swim with one arm and keep the baby's face out of the water. Reeds scraped at their faces and leaves and stalks, borne down beneath the water by their own weight, wrapped slick fingers around her shoulders as if the plants were eaters of flesh and, having snared their prey, were trying to drag it under and drown it.

Shoving back panic, Anna struggled against the clutching fingers. Her feet hit bottom again and she nearly shouted with relief.

Helena began to wail.

THIRTY-NINE

S he's there!" Judith cried exultantly. Then the night was ripped apart by gunfire. A blow struck Anna's shoulder with such force she was slammed back and down. The black beneath the reeds flowed into her brain and she didn't know if she was above the water or below it, if she still held Helena or had dropped her into the ink of the Rio Grande.

Pain followed shock and Anna welcomed it; it brought her back to the world. Helena was still in her arms but quiet now. Either the noise had stunned her to silence or the bullet had passed through Anna's shoulder and killed the tiny person she was trying to keep alive.

Two more shots followed but both were wild. A flashlight beam raked through the reeds, clipping green from the darkness. Where it penetrated, Anna saw a natural nest; a creature of reeds and water had smashed down leaves so it might have a comfortable, safe place to rest.

"Don't die on me," Anna whispered as she laid the naked baby in the reeds.

"Don't shoot!" Anna yelled. "I'm coming out. Don't shoot." Leaving Helena, Anna swam rather than walked as far downriver as she dared before pushing free of the overhang of plants. "Here!" she shouted. "I'm over here. I'm coming out. Don't shoot."

Two more shots exploded the reeds next to her.

"Damn it, stop!" she yelled. "I'm coming." With that she waded through the waist-deep water into open air.

Judith had swum the deeper channel in the middle of the river and was close to the bank where Anna was, water curling around her upper thighs in a dark vee. Anna looked for Darden. From the sound of his voice she'd thought he was with Judith but he'd gone the other way and was forty yards upstream, close to where the SUV was nose-deep in the water. He walked toward them, staying close to the far bank where it was shallower. It didn't look as if he carried a gun, but in the surreal illumination of submerged headlights and faint desert glow, Anna couldn't be sure.

Judith did have a gun, a semiautomatic pistol. Anna hadn't counted the shots that had been fired but the days of six shots and reload were long past.

"Hands up!" Judith screamed, her voice at a shrieking pitch, the sound of an engine wound up so high the belts were carving into the metal.

Anna tried to comply. Her left arm refused to move but the effort pulled a moan from deep in her gut. The pain was hot and everywhere, scorching her bones and searing her muscles. "I can't. You shot me," Anna said, and was surprised at the weariness in her voice.

"Where's the baby?" Judith screamed. The skin of her face, partially lit by the light from the SUV, was translucent, the skull showing through in dark eye sockets and teeth and sunken cheeks. A form of insanity had changed her into a brittle beast that had left much of its humanity behind. There would be no reasoning with what was left.

"Where's the baby!" Judith hissed.

"I drowned it," Anna said. "It was a pain in the butt."

Momentarily, Judith's face blanked.

"Judy!" Darden called. "Let me take over from here, honey. Don't get your hands dirty with this."

Anna didn't take her eyes off Judith. The woman held a gun in her right hand like she knew how to use it. In her left was a six-cell flashlight, the kind that easily doubles as a club.

"Judith, I know how worried you are about Helena," Anna said gently. "I'm so glad you're looking after us. I don't think we would have gotten away if you hadn't picked us up. Shoot Darden, okay? That will make us safe, you and me. Then we can get Helena and go home."

Anna didn't worry that she wasn't making much sense; she doubted Judith's brain was still processing information in a logical manner. Carefully, slowly, Anna began closing the distance between herself and the mayor. Three yards, two. The gun wavered then steadied, aimed point-blank at Anna's chest. The flashlight beam shifted into her eyes. Anna held a hand up to block the glare.

"Shoot Darden," Anna whispered conspiratorially. "We don't need him."

"Shut up, Anna," Darden yelled. "Hang on, Judith, I'm coming."

The guy was keeping to the far side of the river and mincing around like he was afraid there were sharks in the shallows.

"Shoot him," Anna said gently. "Or, better yet, he's right. The mayor of Houston should not get her hands dirty. Give me the gun and I'll shoot him, then we—"

Judith turned and fired three shots into the reeds.

"No!" Anna yelled, and hurled herself at the other woman. Pain jammed her senses as she reached for Judith's gun arm, but she caught hold of a wrist or an elbow and held on. Her feet went out from under her and she couldn't get traction. Closing the fingers of her left hand brought down such a rapid-fire searing of nerves that Anna couldn't grip. Judith was twisting out of her right hand, flipping Anna in the river like a landed fish.

Water poured into Anna's mouth and nose, blinded her, but she didn't let go. Sinking her teeth into a part of the arm she clung to, she started working her hand down toward the gun. Judith shook her hard and Anna bit down harder. Liquid warmer than the Rio Grande flowed into her mouth and, absurdly, she wondered if one could suffer reverse rabies from biting a mad animal instead of being bitten by one.

Her hand closed on metal. She found her feet. Spitting Judith out, Anna pushed her head and shoulders out of the river, choking on the mixture of blood and muddy water. Darden was shouting. Judith was screaming. Anna was blind with wet hair streaming over her face. The flashlight smashed into her injured shoulder and Anna joined the screaming. Flesh rebelled; she felt her grip go slack, her knees give in to the pull of the current.

Judith tore free and began wading toward the dark fringe of reeds where Helena lay hidden.

Anna pulled herself back from the dark fringes of her mind where the pain had shoved her and dove after her. The river had turned viscous as lava and she seemed to make little headway. Judith had almost reached the reeds.

High, thin wailing stopped her for a heartbeat. Helena. Relief rushed into Anna that she was alive followed by the horror that she was found. Judith turned to the sound like a hound to the scent and began plowing through the thick curtain of leaves and stalks. In seconds the foliage closed around her and, but for the sporadic gleam of the flashlight, Anna would have lost her.

Narrowing her concentration on the light and on moving, Anna shut out everything else: the pain in her shoulder, the pull of the water, the fear for Helena, the fear for herself.

"Hello, baby."

The words cut cold into Anna and her breath stopped. Two more steps and she was in a claustrophobic cave of reeds and water. Judith had laid the flashlight down on the crushed leaves of the animal's bed and picked up Helena. The tiny naked scrap of life was held against her shoulder with one hand the way a little girl might clutch a doll, an indestructible doll that has life only as it is imagined by its owner. In Judith's other hand was the semiautomatic pistol, held against her chest, the barrel out of sight behind Helena's little body.

For what seemed a long time, neither woman moved. "You're bleeding," Judith said, sounding as if this revelation surprised and saddened her.

Anna glanced down at her left arm. In the glare of the flashlight it was startlingly red, the color vivid and beautiful against the backdrop of tans and greens. "It doesn't matter," Anna said. "Why don't you let me take the baby and we'll let bygones be bygones."

"This isn't your baby," Judith snapped savagely. "This is Charles's baby. This is my *husband's* baby. Another little Pierson to carry on the family name."

"Helena—"

"Shut up." Judith pulled the barrel of the gun out from under Helena, and for a moment Anna dared hope she was going to point it at her. In such close quarters she might have a chance of getting it away from her before she got shot again. The barrel did not swing out; Judith rested it on Helena's narrow shoulder, the bore of the pistol almost touching her ear, almost as big as her ear.

Revulsion joined with the terror in Anna's stomach and she was sick with it. Guns she'd lived with most of her adult life. Babies were new. Putting them together was a truth she'd never seen spelled out with such graphic clarity: innocence and evil, life and death, power and purity. Rage ran as red as the blood from her shoulder and there was no place to put it, no action to take. Judith held a gun to Helena's head.

"My in-laws put such importance on the carrying on of their sacred bloodline that Charles and I are only trust holders for the grandchild. This," and she looked at Helena with such loathing the child could have been a cockroach, "this spawn of Charles's and his whore would get it all. It wants my husband. Like its mother did."

Leaving the flashlight in the nest of leaves and twigs, Judith began backing out of the reeds.

Fighting to keep rage from blinding her, Anna followed, careful to make no sudden moves, to appear as docile as possible.

Several times she opened her mouth to speak but nothing came out. She was afraid words—the wrong words—would pull the trigger and Helena's head would explode into fragments. Should she beg or coax or threaten or cajole, should she reason or promise? Anna doubted there were any right words. Judith's face was set in the death mask that her hatred had made of it. Judith would destroy Helena. Any words of Anna's would only make it happen sooner.

They cleared the reeds. Darden was still on the far

side of the river but he'd waded in until the water reached mid-thigh. Held at his hip in an unconscious parody of Chuck Connors in *The Rifleman* was a long gun. Not the old wooden-stocked rifles Anna had grown up with, but a military weapon with its metal skeleton showing and a scope that took the sport out of hunting.

He raised it to his shoulder.

"Judy, honey, step away from Anna. You can relax, I've got it covered. Go ahead and lose the gun, Judy. Let me do this."

Judith Pierson half turned to look back at Darden. The death's head was still upon her, skin pulled tight across her cheekbones and away from her teeth. "If you want something done right . . ." she began, her finger tightening on the trigger.

Then half her throat disappeared in mist. In silence her body fell backward. Her arms opened and the gun fell from her hand. Anna snatched Helena as Judith went under the water.

"Catch her," Darden cried, but Anna did not give a damn about Judith.

Darden dropped the high-powered rifle and walked into the river until it was too deep for his feet to touch bottom. Anna watched him flounder, trying to keep his head above water, and realized why he'd stayed on the far bank. The man couldn't swim.

He had saved her life, he had saved Helena's life. Anna felt no compunction to save his. As he sputtered and gasped and flung his arms wildly, she supposed, had she two good arms and no baby to take care of, she'd probably fish him out just to keep her credit good. Things being what they were, she excused herself.

Sirens and flashing blue lights came down the incline from the direction of Lajitas. Darden must have called somebody. Anna wanted it to be rangers, not police, wanted it to be Paul. Three vehicles pulled up behind the SUVs and people grew up around them, seemingly woven from blue lights and darkness.

Oddly uninterested in the newcomers, Anna turned her attention back to Darden White. The water was over his head but not by much and grew shallower quickly. He did not drown but caught up with the body of his mayor and pulled her and himself onto a gravelly sandbar several feet from the riverbank. Legs splayed on the sand, Darden gathered the corpse of Judy Pierson onto his lap, supporting the nearly severed head the way a mother supports the head of a child too young to do it herself.

Judith's face was caught in the coming flashlight beams and Anna saw she was young again. The hatred had gone and she looked almost childlike, almost peaceful in Darden's arms. In that moment Anna knew what the love between them was. It was the love of a father for an only daughter and an orphan for the only father she'd ever known. Holding Helena, cried-out and hiccoughing in the crook of her good arm, Anna turned her back on the two figures on the sandbar. Whatever Judith was, whatever she had done or tried to do, however complicit Darden may or may not have been in it, the love and grief was real and Anna gave it the respect it deserved.

A man broke away from the cluster of lights she waded toward, skidded down the bank and ran splashing into the Rio Grande till it was deep enough he could swim.

Paul.

An old hymn Anna had heard in Mississippi played through her mind. *I'll be waiting on the far side banks of Jordan, I'll be sitting drawing pictures in the sand, and when I see you coming I will rise up with a shout and come running through the shallow water reaching for your hand.*

Anna began to run.

FORTY

The Rio Grande River, where it flowed between Mexico and Texas, had seen so much blood the addition of Anna's and Judith's didn't leave even a ghost of violence on the water. Leaning back against the center seat and pulling her legs up, Paul, Chrissie and the current doing the work for her, Anna tilted her face to the sun. The wild country didn't harbor memories the way manmade places did. Wind didn't retain stench or perfume from days past, water and sand and scrub shed their old skins and drew on new with each sunrise.

There were places that haunted Anna: the avenue in New York City where her first husband, Zach, had been killed, the nursing home where her mother had died, theaters where she'd seen plays, buildings that were no longer there and buildings still standing.

No place in the unpeopled lands haunted her. Though Isle Royale had been the background for an incident that had shaken her to her core, when she returned to the island, it would be new again.

So it was with the river. More than once in the last few days she had believed she was going to die there or be left with memories that would hound her back to the broken place where she'd been when she left Colorado. Yet the river could hold no ghosts; all of it was living and moving; there were no dusty attics or dank cellars in nature. Even caves were alive, growing, changing, renewing, becoming.

The gunshot she'd suffered had done amazingly little damage. Judith was shooting small-caliber bullets and the one that struck Anna passed through the flesh just under her armpit, missing bones and vital organs. The park's EMTs patched her up and she'd been driven eighty miles to Alpine in the ambulance. A doctor there cleaned and closed the wound. She had been spared even a moment in a hospital, a place she dreaded.

Helena had gone with them but she had not returned to Big Bend the following day. She was taken to the hospital. The baby was not injured but she had suffered rough treatment and the doctor felt she should be placed in the neonatal care unit for observation. When Anna and Paul went to the hospital the following morning to say their good-byes, Charles Pierson was there.

Gone was the debonair facade; he had lost weight and aged. Grief and the shock of the deaths, most especially of the woman he loved, the mother of his child, had carved lines in his face that would only deepen with time. Charles had been sitting by the bassinet where his daughter lay, holding one of her little hands with thumb and forefinger. There was no doubting that this little girl was the light of his life, at the moment the only light. Helena would be loved and cherished. Charles named her Eleanor Helena Pierson for her mother and for Anna, who had kept her alive.

Anna was satisfied.

Darden White was in a legal no-man's-land, and would be until the investigation was complete, but it looked as if he had no connection to the deaths of Carmen, Lori and Eleanor. It was he, not Judith, who had placed Eleanor at the Lajitas resort hotel. Judith had wanted him to kill her but, he said, he'd believed the mayor to be venting her rage, not plotting murder.

He'd been wrong.

Kevin, his subordinate, had been co-opted by Judith and convinced to dump Charles's girlfriend in the river. It was unclear whether or not Judith told him to follow the river and shoot the woman if she survived. Darden insisted she hadn't known and, when she'd found out, she'd demanded Kevin be fired. Kevin had been arrested and was waiting arraignment in El Paso.

The two impostors who tried to snatch Helena from the Martinezes' home had not been killed. They'd been tracked down through the car rental agency in Midland. They told police Judith hired them to kidnap the child but not to harm it. Whether that was true or whether at that point Judith had decided to kill Charles's child would never be known.

"Hard to believe this is the same river, isn't it?" Cyril asked from the other canoe. "This is like the Lazy River instead of the one we rafted with Carmen."

It pleased Anna to hear in her voice the simple joy of being out of doors, the easy way she could say the murdered river guide's name. The three surviving college students had recovered with the natural resilience of youth. There would be nightmares, but they would be able to tell their tale not a mere three times for medicinal purposes but hundreds of times throughout the length of their lives, which Anna hoped would be long and happy.

Since the killings the kids had spent their time scouring the banks of the river to the east of Santa Elena Canyon in the hope of finding Easter. The quest, though unfulfilled, had given them back their sense of control in the mysterious way being in nature blows the chaff off of humanity.

It had been Steve who suggested they rent canoes and finish the float trip that had been so violently aborted. For all of them it was the last day of their vacation. The word *closure* had been bandied about, but it wasn't closure they'd set out seeking, it was continuance. Life went on and they would go on as well.

The canoe trip through the canyon had been blissfully uneventful. They had floated and chattered like magpies, dreamed in silence and picnicked near Fern Canyon. The rockslide was an easy chute in low water, enough of a rush to be fun but without so much as a hint of the power it had shown during the flash flooding.

Anna was back in tune with the wild places but it wasn't that which had changed her. And she was changed; she could sense the abyss that she'd been running from was gone. There was a sorrow there, regret for her sins and the sins of others, for things done and undone that brought such pain into being, but the hopelessness had been banished. Helena had done that for her. That she had been instrumental in saving that spark of life and, to her awe, that Helena had been such a strong, determined little person that she hadn't allowed the poor treatment the world had greeted her with to kill her, had evened the scales. It was okay that people were monstrous. It was okay that people were godlike. Anna was content to have fallen ever so slightly on the side of the gods this time around.

She was half asleep when the shouting started.

"It's Easter! Look, there on the Mexican bank. It's Easter," Cyril was yelling.

"You've chased after so many Mexican cows that they won't come near the river," her brother said. "I bet you will be responsible for the whole of the agrarian economy collapsing because cows will thirst to death rather than come near the water."

"No, this time it is," Cyril insisted.

Chrissie laughed. "It always is. They all look like Easter. They're cows. They all look like cows."

"No they don't," Cyril said. "I'd know Easter. I'd know her in a herd."

"The last 'Easter' you knew had gonads the size of Staten Island," her brother said without rancor.

"We have to stop," Cyril stated.

Chrissie moaned. "We are a mile from the takeout. I'm tired. Can't you just order a steak for dinner and be done with the cow thing for this lifetime?"

"It's Easter." Cyril began paddling for shore and Steve, in the back of the canoe, sighed and steered toward the right bank. They'd floated free of the canyon and were on the flatlands where the park ended and Mexico began. Along the water, owners of livestock had built pens of sticks and wire that came into the river far enough that the animals could drink without escaping. It was to the latest of these ramshackle corrals that Cyril paddled with such fierce determination.

Anna pulled herself upright. The long day had brought the ache back to her injured shoulder, but she didn't mind. The easy pain of knitting flesh was reassuring in the way the desert and the mountains were.

Four scrofulous-looking cows stood dispiritedly beneath scrub trees no more prosperous than they.

Cyril and Steve beached their canoe in thick black mud liberally mixed with cow manure.

"I'm not getting out," Chrissie announced. This once, Anna was with Chrissie.

"Me neither," she said.

"That makes three on the neither end of things," Steve added. Paul laughed and remained uncommitted.

Cyril hopped into the muck. The first stride the stuff sucked her river sandal off her foot. Undeterred, she fished it out and slathered it back on a foot as vile and muddy as the shoe. "Be careful," Paul called as Cyril threaded through loose barbed wire so rusty and filthy it would inject lockjaw directly into the bloodstream if given the opportunity.

The cows scattered into the scrub.

"Nooo," Cyril cried. "Easter, it's me. Here, Easter, Easter, Easter."

"It's not a cat," Chrissie said. "I don't think that's how you're supposed to call cows. Come on. Let's go."

A bit of the old Chrissie whine was back and that, too, Anna was happy to hear. The natural orders reestablishing themselves. Maybe the physicists were wrong and the universe wasn't in a long downhill slide toward chaos.

Cyril's heartfelt coaxing resulted in a crashing as the cows fled deeper into the scrub.

"Come on," Steve said. "Easter's probably getting fat on somebody's spread in Louisiana by now."

Cyril crawled back through the wire and began pushing the canoe free of its muddy berth.

"Hey," Paul called. He was pointing to the shadows under the stubby trees. A cow had come back.

Cyril stopped what she was doing and turned slowly toward the wire enclosure. No one made a sound. After a moment's hesitation the cow stepped out of the shadows and lumbered to the middle of the pen several feet from the edge of the water.

"It's Easter," Cyril whispered.

"It's thirsty," her brother whispered back.

"She's come because I called her," Cyril returned.

Steve didn't say anything. The cow said it for him. Instead of coming toward Cyril's now-outstretched hand, it came warily down to the water and drank.

"Not Easter," Cyril said sadly.

"Look at the horns," Paul told her.

Blue threads, the color of the towel they had used to protect the raft from Easter's horns, were duct-taped to the base of one horn.

ACKNOWLEDGMENTS

My deepest thanks to Bill Wellman, Raymond Skiles, Mark Spier and David Ekowitz for their kindness, generosity and knowledge, but mostly for their love of and service to the national parks. For humor, inspiration, attitude and knowledge of the river, I will always be grateful to Marcos Peredes, Big Bend's river ranger. And, with great affection and fond memories, I thank our boatman, Carmen.

New York Times **Bestselling Author**

Nevada Barr

HARD TRUTH

Just days after marrying Sheriff Paul Davidson, Anna Pigeon moves to Colorado to assume her new post as district ranger at Rocky Mountain National Park. When two of three children who had gone missing from a religious retreat reappear, Anna's investigation brings her face-to-face with a paranoid sect—and with a villain more evil than she's ever encountered.

penguin.com

The
"STUNNING"
(*The Seattle Times*)

"EXCEPTIONAL"
(*The Denver Post*)

"SUPERB"
(*The New York Times Book Review*)

ANNA PIGEON SERIES
by Nevada Barr

Borderline
Winter Study
Hard Truth
High Country
Flashback
Hunting Season
Blood Lure
Deep South
Blind Descent
Endangered Species
Firestorm
Ill Wind
A Superior Death
Track of the Cat

penguin.com